THE DALÍ DIARIES

Stewart Ferris

BY THE SAME AUTHOR

THE BALLASHIELS MYSTERIES
The Sphinx Scrolls
The Sphinx Swindle (ebook short)
The Genesis Glitch (ebook short)
The Wodehouse Whispers (ebook short)
The Chaplin Conspiracy (2018)

STAND ALONES
The Reluctant Rescue
Oversleeper

THE DALI DIARIES

Published by Accent Press Ltd 2017

www.accentpress.co.uk

ISBN 9781786151865

Wednesday 1st May 2013

After decades in a shallow grave beneath the croquet lawn, the iron key felt underweight. The corroded shank had lost much of its circumference, but it only had to work one more time. He slid it into the lock: it went in easily, gliding over a lubricating layer of dust and grey webs. The rooms here on the second floor were originally the domain of servants. Many of them now resembled the shadowy interiors of a neglected brocante, smelling of musty leather and horsehair stuffing, but this one was different. It was different because it was locked, and had been in that state since before he was born – four walls, devoid of human contact for seventy-six years.

He thought about how the world had moved on. The room had missed a global war, Kennedy, the Berlin Wall, The Beatles. Science had progressed while society had, from his perspective, regressed. Was he about to enter a cocoon of 1930s England? Would it contain a slice of his ancestors' life, preserved and forgotten?

He recalled his grandmother's diary and the stern warnings she had written about this room. It seemed that the burial of the key in 1937 had been quite an occasion. There had been a procession with incense, Latin chants, a rendition of *Hark! A Herald Voice is Calling*, followed by the Lord's Prayer. The diary suggested that this little piece of metal had been accorded more pomp and respect at its untimely interment than he recalled seeing at his mother's sombre memorial service in the family chapel some forty years later. The one question the diary failed to answer was why the room was sealed. What could have been significant enough to justify such eccentric banishment? His mind flitted between various remote possibilities: an autobiographical manuscript exposing a murky family secret; stolen plans for an atomic bomb; a map pointing the way to illicit treasure; the body of a dead celebrity – Amelia Earhart had disappeared in somewhat odd circumstances that year, after all.

The idea that someone would one day find the key had apparently not occurred to those who were present at its burial. A future Earl with a passion for metal detecting was something they had failed to foresee. He hadn't even been looking for it. The hours he had spent in the grounds dressed in his ludicrous, tasselled leather jacket, with his detecting equipment draped over his shoulders, in search of a hoard of silver coins rumoured to have been buried by his wealthy and forgetful ancestors. No such hoard had yet been identified by the machine, and the key was his consolation.

Lord 'Ratty' Ballashiels coiled his freckly fingers around the key, ready to twist it, ready to enter the lost world of his forebears. A cold perspiration loosened his grip. He paused. To unlock this door would be to disobey a direct instruction from his late grandmother. To indulge his curiosity would be to commit the ultimate rebellion and would invite the sinister repercussions his grandmother had mentioned in frustratingly ambiguous terms in her diary.

But it was his house now. There was no one left to whom he had to answer for his actions. His grandmother's wishes were part of history, and, since the study of history was his greatest passion, he convinced himself that the unlocking of the room was an archaeological procedure. He was Howard Carter, about to step into the tomb of Tutankhamen. He was Hiram Bingham, striding through the clouds towards Machu Picchu.

He closed his eyes and turned the key. His face tightened in anticipation. Resistance gave way to clunks. The bolt eased into its housing. He put his other hand on the white porcelain handle and twisted it. The door swung free with a low groan. He opened his eyes, wiped the sweat from his dyed black hair, and looked into the forbidden room.

It was square, about fifteen feet along each side. The window was almost completely obscured by ill-fitting shutters, which allowed only a vertical slice of light to illuminate the dancing particles of airborne dust. There was a small fireplace to the right, a simple surround of glossed wood with a flat mantelpiece. The grate was piled high with a cocktail of fallen soot and nests. A lone bulb hung from a cloth-covered flex in the ceiling, refusing to be digested by the cobwebs that had engulfed it.

Ratty blinked in disbelief as he entered the stark room. Wide, bare floorboards held his weight in defiance of the labyrinthine perforations made over the centuries by microscopic chomping teeth. Each step he took was marked by a dull echo. He could hear himself breathing. He scratched his long nose in puzzlement that his grandmother could have been sufficiently potty to have locked up an empty chamber and prohibited entry for all eternity.

He folded the shutters into their recesses and the space overflowed with daylight. The walls were covered with a paper that Ratty recognised from other servants' rooms: an artless floral design that remained valiantly attached to

3

the lath and plaster despite its antiquity. He tapped the architrave around the door and stomped on the floorboards. Nothing gave way. No secret opening appeared.

The beginnings of a smile curled around the corner of his mouth, unveiling several crooked teeth, as he realised that a cheeky sense of humour did not belong exclusively to his generation. Seventy-six years ago, long before he had even been born, his grandmother had set up a wonderful practical joke. The tension and apprehension he had felt moments ago were gone. Now he simply had another space into which the detritus of a once-magnificent stately home could expand.

He forced the reluctant sash window open an inch, inviting a current of air to freshen the space. The draft caused a small rivulet of soot to slide from the fireplace onto the stone hearth. Poking out from near the top of the black pile was a tiny bone, part of a swallow that had once attempted to make its home high up in the chimney. Ratty crouched to look at the skeleton and noticed something else amongst the soot. It was a small, purple piece of paper. He pulled it slowly from the grate and shook the black dust away. 'Chocolat au lait' it read in a white, sans serif typeface. Below that it simply said, 'Lanvin'. There was also a mention of a competition to win a Kodak Instamatic camera. Closing date was 31st October 1975.

This was a sweet wrapper from the Seventies. Four decades after the room had been sealed, someone had eaten a chocolate bar containing a paltry thirty per cent cocoa. He became so deeply bewildered that anyone would want to taste such a vile and sickly culinary concoction that it was some moments before the deeper mystery became apparent to him.

***

4

'Hey, Ruby!' called a voice from the ruins of Château d'Opoul, on a hilltop close to the southern French village of Périllos. The accent was unfamiliar to Ruby: Manhattan crossed with Munich, lacking self-consciousness. 'Up here!' the voice crassly continued, tearing coarsely through a gentle Mediterranean soundscape in which it evidently did not belong.

She glanced up and sighed. This must be the notorious Rocco. Her earlier uncertainty at whether to agree to this unusual meeting was already morphing into regret. The man leaned precariously over a crumbling parapet, looking down at her from a position that Ruby knew would once have provided an unusual and revolting military advantage against marauding Visigoths: the castle's lavatories were positioned such that human waste would fall directly onto an attacking army. She swallowed hard and looked back the way she had come. Her uncommunicative taxi driver was already stirring up the dust with a hasty exit from the parking area at the base of the hill, swerving to avoid a Spanish-plated car creeping hesitantly along the dirt track. She couldn't slip away now. A full hour with Rocco was unavoidable.

As she entered the grid of tumbled stonework that was once part of a mighty fortress, she could see Rocco was not alone. A dozen or so people were gathered at this isolated spot, and most of them were staring up at the featureless sky. Others were squinting over laptop screens on picnic tables or taking video footage – seemingly of nothing – from little, handheld camcorders and smartphones.

Rocco Strauss strode purposefully towards some electronic monitoring equipment on a table, scanned the readouts and stared at the sky. He turned to face Ruby, revealing a shirt that was unbuttoned to a flat and hairy stomach beneath his cream linen suit. She grimaced as she approached him. Rocco flashed an enchanting smile and took her hand to a chivalric lip. With his rather ordinary features and centre-parted hairstyle he wasn't handsome in her opinion, but he had youth on his side. She guessed his age at about thirty and resented him even more for being younger than her.

'Ruby Towers, a pleasure to meet you at last. My name is Rocco. I've heard much about you. Mountebank talks about you all the time.'

'He certainly talks a lot, that's for sure,' she replied, wiping the back of her hand where he had kissed it and fully aware of her reluctance to return his generous welcome. 'You know me and Matt are not together any more, don't you?'

'You would hardly think so from what he says about you.'

The geographical and emotional separation from her former lover Matt Mountebank had lasted four months. Any feelings towards him were buried as deep as the ancient artefacts she routinely excavated in her day job.

'I heard nothing from him this year until he e-mailed me about you,' she said. 'Something about a new kind of archaeology. You were spearheading the research, Matt told me.'

'Did he say anything else?' asked Rocco.

'Only that I'd be mad not to see you while I'm working just the other side of the Pyrenees.'

'You are extending the site at Empúries, I understand? I read about it. Fascinating to think you could find a mixture of Greek and Roman archaeology on the Costa Brava.'

'Yes,' she confirmed. 'So here I am.'

'And clearly not mad.' Rocco smiled again. He

appeared to like her.

She brushed back her auburn, shoulder-length hair, revealing a neck that was newly tanned. He was studying her features, but not in an intimidating way. She knew she could benefit from losing a few pounds and ought to take more care of her appearance, but experience had proven that men frequently lusted after her raw, unembellished beauty and she had been around for long enough not to give a damn if they didn't. Her wardrobe had consisted of little more than jeans and cotton shirts for as long as she could remember, and Rocco showed no inclination to disapprove of her choices.

Ruby's defences were starting to soften. His charms were undeniable, but they were not yet sufficient to convince her that her efforts in coming here today would not be wasted. New ideas and techniques in her line of business were reported in academic journals. It seemed unlikely that Matt Mountebank, a writer of infamous fiction, would learn something new about archaeology before she did.

'How do you know Matt?' she asked.

'He came to one of my lectures. Actually, I don't think it was his idea. He was on a date and the young lady dragged him to the bar afterwards to meet me.'

'A date?' Ruby tried hard to hide her disgust, but sensed her facial muscles were not on her side.

'Personally I don't see how he could have eyes for anyone but yourself,' grinned Rocco.

'Hmm,' she growled softly, wishing Matt was with them so that she could slap his stubbly face for getting over her too quickly. 'Are all these people with you?'

'Watch this,' he whispered, stepping away from her. 'Hey, look, up there! That's the message!' screamed Rocco, thrusting his arm in the direction of a lone cloud.

Every head turned frantically towards where he was pointing. A clamour of whooping and hollering replaced any conversations. Cameras and detector devices recorded the sky across full spectrums of light, temperature and radiation. There were calls for hush, for calm, for control. Rocco waited patiently. Then he hit them with the punchline.

'Hey, guys, I was just kidding!' he shouted, scuttling away from the hisses and curses that were spitting in his direction. 'Come on, Ruby. I want to show you something.'

On a plastic table sat a pile of equipment that pinged and beeped with morose regularity. Ruby looked at the item at the top. It had a label attached which said 'ESA property. Not to be removed from Wachtberg'. A small screen displayed sine waves. A portable radar unit turned unhurriedly. Power came from a generator that droned softly in the background.

'How come everyone's so obsessed with the sky?' Ruby asked.

'The sky is a mere palette. A canvas that is currently blank. If it fills with words, we'll be ready.'

'Ready for what?'

'I'm a chrononaut,' explained Rocco, unhelpfully. 'Not an official one, of course. We're a sort of splinter group. The original chrononaut guys from Project Chronodrome are down there in a gazebo in the car park. Besides, it's not my real job. Just a hobby. I'm at the European Space Agency. ESA.'

'And what do you do there?' she asked mechanically, her mind drifting from a conversation that already bored her.

'Been there ever since I left university. They put me in charge of tracking stuff. Anything that gets close to our planet. Asteroids, comets, rogue satellites, aliens.'

'Aliens?' she echoed, plucked from her reverie by the unexpected word.

'OK, not yet. But one day, perhaps? Basically my job is to make sure the world doesn't end. I became quite high profile last year. I was the first to spot the approach of that thing predicted by those scrolls you found.'

That was a branch of conversation that she was not in the mood to explore. The mere mention of the scrolls she had discovered beneath the Sphinx in Cairo the previous year brought knots to her stomach. The events following their discovery still cast a shadow over her. She had barely escaped with her life.

'So what's a "chrononaut"?' she asked, returning to a subject about which she carried no baggage. 'You collect watches or something?'

'Just a minute,' he replied, adjusting the settings on a radiation detector. 'You heard of the Keo satellite?'

She shook her head.

Rocco was becoming increasingly agitated, glancing at Ruby, at his watch, at his equipment, at the sky, and back at the machines again.

'It's like the Sphinx scrolls you found,' he said without taking his eyes off one of the screens. He had unknowingly turned on a blender in her gut and failed to notice that she grabbed her belly. 'They were a message from the past, in a time capsule. The European Space Agency is doing the same thing. We're sending a capsule into the future. Not using time travel, of course, but by placing it in a high orbit that will take fifty thousand years to decay, at which point it will fall to earth. The capsule contains millions of pages of learning and culture, like a modern library of Alexandria. There is a diamond containing a drop of human blood and the DNA of the human genome. There are samples of air, sea water and soil. Fifty thousand years might seem a long way off, but it has a symbolic aspect. It was five hundred centuries ago that our ancestors began to experiment with cave paintings. So we are mid-way between those first artists and the people who will receive our capsule. And encoded in radiation-resistant glass DVDs – along with instructions on how to build a DVD reader – are personal messages from people all over the world. One of those messages is a simple request that the people of the future acknowledge receipt of the capsule. That's why we're here.'

She breathed deeply and calmed her inner turbulence.

'And when did you launch this time capsule?' she asked.

'Oh, not yet. There's been a few delays.'

She stared at him, looking for a sign that this was the second practical joke he'd pulled since her arrival. Nothing beyond wide-eyed enthusiasm was on display.

'So let me see if I understand this,' she sighed. 'You're here because you're looking for an indication that someone who hasn't yet been born has received something that hasn't yet been sent?' Rocco showed no reaction. 'Can you see one or two potential flaws in that ambition?'

'No, no, it's perfectly simple. Backwards time travel isn't really possible right now,' explained Rocco, 'but in fifty thousand years they'll have all kinds of new technology. Time travel could be feasible. We haven't asked for a person to be sent back in time. We're looking for light photons or a radioactive signature in the air. Something that's a bit easier to work with at a quantum level.'

'Matt said you were developing a new branch of

archaeology, though. Can we talk about that instead?'

'We are.'

'Looking for lights in the sky is not archaeology, Rocco.'

'I like to call it the archaeology of the future, instead of the past.'

'How is that supposed to make any sense?' she asked, barely hiding her frustration. 'This is pseudo-science. Fantasising. Daydreaming.'

To Ruby's surprise, Rocco nodded in agreement. The dreamy side of his nature often conflicted with the science that defined his usual work at the European Space Agency, but he never regarded it as an obstacle. If men hadn't dreamed about travelling to the moon, he would tell himself, they wouldn't have designed the technology and overcome the necessary scientific challenges to get there. Dreams dictate the future, he would say to critics who questioned the dedication with which he would follow peculiar conspiracies and outlandish theories. When accused of having a vivid or overworked imagination he would thank them. There was so much about the world, about humanity and about the universe that was yet to be discovered that he refused to close his mind to anything. All bets were on until proved otherwise. The impossible often turned out to be possible after a few years. He was proud to be a scientist, and equally proud to be a fantasist, and regarded himself as being at the cutting edge of the present, spearheading the way forward into tomorrow.

'Thank you, Ruby, but there is actually a more pressing question that you have yet to ask.'

If this was the archaeology she had travelled all this way to hear about, she had no desire to ask any more questions. Her instinct had been right. Matt was an idiot, screwing up her life even when he wasn't in it, sending her on a wild-goose chase to a meeting with a crazy German space scientist. If the taxi driver had waited she would have left that instant, but she knew he wouldn't be back until her hour was up. She glanced down the hillside at the car park below on the off-chance that he might have changed his mind, but there was only the gazebo containing the official chrononauts and a few cars, plus the driver of the Spanish-registered car she had seen earlier who seemed to be skulking around the other vehicles. Escape was still not an option. She might as well indulge her intellectual curiosity.

'Why?' she began, looking at the activity around her and trying to formulate the right question. 'Why here? Why now?'

'Correct. It was actually two questions. Well done.'

'Thank you.'

'You're welcome,' he replied, turning back to his monitoring gear and adjusting some dials.

Ruby looked in exasperation at the other people around her, but they were mostly staring into the heavens. She tapped Rocco on the shoulder.

'So, Rocco, are you going to elaborate?'

'Not yet. Too much to do. Very tight window.'

'Window?'

'A one hour slot. Right here. It's all in the time capsule.'

'Tell me,' she ordered.

'Otherwise we'll be up here for months,' said Rocco, still with his back to her. 'The message in the capsule asks the future people to send a signal to this spot between three and four in the afternoon, on any May first until 2050. So we come here for one afternoon a year.'

'How long have you been doing this?'

'Since 2000.'

'And there's been no message from the future in all that time?'

'Not yet. But the message will come,' stated Rocco.

'Unless you missed it.'

'Someone has been here every year. We can't have missed it.'

'What if it came before 2000?' asked Ruby. 'Perhaps this fictitious method of time-travelling e-mails isn't very accurate?'

'The earth spins and moves constantly,' explained Rocco. 'It never occupies the same patch of space twice. The solar system is drifting. The universe is expanding. If someone is able to send a message through time in any meaningful way, they have to pinpoint the precise spot in the universe where the earth used to be at the time they want the message to arrive. Otherwise it will get delivered into the vacuum of space. Therefore space and time calculations are inextricably linked and must be utterly precise. You can't have one without the other. When they send the message, it will be to the exact time and place that they intend to send it.'

'So why this spot?'

'Lots of reasons. We're precisely twenty kilometres due north of Perpignan train station. The air is clear and unpolluted. We have a panoramic view of the sky.'

'This is all crazy,' said Ruby. 'There's nothing in the sky and there isn't going to be.' She looked down at the car park instead. 'What's happening down there?'

A couple of people from the group of official chrononauts in the gazebo had broken away from their monitoring of the empty sky to chase someone away. They started throwing rocks at him. The man ran towards the Spanish car and jumped in, screeching away with wheels spinning and with his door still open. A plume of dust and grit enveloped the tent and the car park. People were coughing and wiping their eyes.

'Did you see that?' Ruby asked.

'See what?' asked Rocco.

'Down in the car park. It looked like those other chrononauts tried to stone someone.'

'Probably another splinter group,' said Rocco. 'We don't always get on particularly well.'

'Different groups of people fighting each other over a non-existent message in the sky. Remind you of anything?'

'This is science, Ruby. If the people of the distant future send us a message, we'll get it.'

Thursday 2nd May 2013

The Patient was seated in the heart of an ancient oak tree in the grounds of Stiperstones Manor. Secure on a low and wide branch, lit by the opaque light of dawn, he was devouring downloaded prose from his Kindle when Ratty knocked at the gnarled bark.

'Been searching for you all night, old chum,' gasped Ratty. 'Where have you been?'

'I have hitch-hiked across the Galaxy, and yet I have not moved from the branches of this oak,' replied the Patient, proudly showing Ratty a screen filled with the prose of Douglas Adams.

The Patient had displayed an obsession with trees in the months following his arrival in England. Ratty assumed it to be a rebound reaction from the unfortunate man's unnatural upbringing, incarcerated from birth by an abusive and twisted father deep under the volcanic soils of Guatemala City. Having spent his first forty-five years where even roots failed to reach, the Patient now appeared intent upon redressing the balance by passing his days in a woody embrace.

'Please come down from that branch, Patient chappy,' Ratty continued. He found it uncomfortable to say his friend's name in full. The words refused to trip lightly off his aristocratic tongue. Addressing the Guatemalan-born German as 'the Patient' to his face felt discourteous. And yet, having been conceived and cocooned as part of an unofficial – and utterly illegal – medical experiment there was only one label to which Ratty's friend would answer. He had grown up nameless, regarded as a collection of organs, a bank of spare parts for the high-flying twin he had never known. He had been a human being cultivated in laboratory conditions, denied the basic dignity of a name, referred to coldly by his father – a doctor – as 'it'. Nevertheless, 'the Patient' and even 'it' were distinct improvements upon the tarnished name he had inherited from his Teutonic family line: Mengele. And so the nickname of 'the Patient' had stuck. The Patient had no problem with it. The cruelty that defined his life could not be undone by changing his name, and so he simply accepted his identity. Ratty would have preferred something a touch more conventional, such as George, but if the British viewing public could follow the weekly science fictional exploits of someone called 'the Doctor' for five decades, Ratty was convinced he could eventually get used to calling his friend 'the Patient'. But, for now, he had to morph it into something that felt less impersonal.

The bond between the two men had been formed in an instant the previous year. Ratty, whilst on the trail of an archaeological prize in Guatemala, had encountered the Patient and his father, and had intervened to prevent the doctor assaulting his son. In so doing, he had helped to set the Patient free. Until that point, concepts of friendship and kindness were theoretical constructs that the Patient had merely encountered in books. In Ratty, he had seen those human faculties come alive for the first time.

At Ratty's invitation, the Patient had come to live in the dilapidated, gamekeeper's cottage at the periphery of the Stiperstones estate, finally free from the long shadow of his dysfunctional upbringing. The Patient adored this location. He could observe the wildlife and touch the textures of the mosses and ferns and weeds that grew around him, and he had the peace to read modern literature. Thousands of texts had been available to him in the Guatemalan basement in which he grew up. The collection of philosophical works in particular had made a deep impression on him, and it was from these books that his entire perspective of the world had been gleaned. But the private library contained little that was published post-1970, and he therefore had a certain amount of literary catching-up to do.

'This tree is most comfortable,' said the Patient. 'It is as if nature has grown an armchair for me.'

'Yes, but do tootle on down, old Kindle-worm. An urgent tête-à-tête is required.'

Ratty's peculiar take on the English language often perplexed the Patient. The aristocrat seemed to enjoy conveying his meaning within a package of beautifully wrapped prose. Sometimes it made no sense. Sometimes it made Ratty appear trite and trivial. But the Patient understood his friend, if not always his words, and he knew that the veneer of joviality hid a soul that was deeply troubled and hurting. A kind and warm soul, but one that struggled to make sense of the world.

'We are already engaging in discourse,' replied the Patient.

'Well yes, I know, but a topic other than trees would be preferable.'

'There is much to be learned from matters arboreal,' stated the Patient, climbing down and rubbing the moss stains from his blue jumpsuit. 'Publilius Syrus said you should go to a pear tree for pears, not to an elm.'

'Well quite. Glad that's cleared up. Listen, Patient chappy, I opened that room in the manor yesterday. The

17

one granny locked up before she buried the key.'

Ratty looked fervently around him, as if this act of defiance had surrounded him with a fog of guilt through which retribution would come charging at any moment.

'And did that particular metaphorical tree provide you with the fruit that you expected?' asked the Patient.

'I went to a pear tree and found a banana,' replied Ratty, not really confident that the analogy worked in any meaningful way.

'A banana?'

'Well, a curved piece of information. An unexpected twist. Hence "banana". Look, can we just talk in plain English, old persona grata?'

The Patient looked at him in a way that made clear his opinion that Ratty rarely spoke plain English.

'So the room was empty?' asked the Patient, shuffling sideways into a patch of shade, taking care to remain beneath the protection of the generous spread of leaves above him. His skin had lost little of its neoprene transparency and would not fare well in any battle with the rising sun.

'How could you possibly know that?'

'It has to be symbolic,' the Patient replied. 'The power of ceremony is in its symbolism, not its function. You have read to me your grandmother's diary and the theatrical energies she employed to celebrate the closure of the room. She was sealing away an idea, a piece of knowledge that frightened her, not an object. It is a reasonable deduction to make.'

'Golly. Well, yes. It was somewhat Spartan inside. A minimalist paradise. That's why I wanted to have this little chinwag. I dashed over to West Dean House in Sussex after I opened the room. Frightful place, West Dean. Flint turrets. Not a patch on the flaking limestone bartizans here at Stiperstones. Spoke to a lovely young receptionist filly about the history of the place –not a natural blonde, as far as I could tell, but a kindly face. Didn't pay much attention to what she was saying once I started imagining myself reading Homer to her on a firelit, winter's evening – but she did know about Granny Ballashiels. They have records that corroborate Granny's diary entries when she writes that she used to hang out at West Dean with Salvador Dalí and the Sitwells and wotnot. Sometimes even with the Mitford sisters when they weren't busy having tea with Adolf or supper with Winston. But Granny's diaries are peppered with vexatious lacunae. Her account of 1937 is particularly perfunctory.'

'That being the year she sealed that room?'

'How veracious you are. I had no record of her thoughts and movements leading up to that moment. But at West Dean House they have a visitor's book that shows she departed on the same day as Dalí, one month before the room here at Stiperstones was sealed.'

'Presumably Dalí was at West Dean as a guest of the owner of the house, the poet Edward James?' asked the Patient.

'I believe James was sponsoring Dalí to produce some pieces around that time. James was frightfully keen on helping the surrealist types, and he seemed to have a particular fondness for Dalí. There are still some Dalí creations in West Dean House. All locked away, lamentably, after that recent run of thefts of Dalí's paintings in New York and London.'

'I wasn't aware of those thefts. Is your art collection safe?'

'We have no Dalí doodles here. Unless, of course, the empty room thingummy was a Dalí surrealist wotsit. Now that would be rather splendid. If he left West Dean with Granny Ballashiels on the same day then it's possible that they came here.'

'It is entirely possible, as are many other destinations.'

'Quite, quite. So how are you getting on in the gamekeeper's cottage?'

'I found some books under the stairs,' said the Patient, as they strolled back to the half-derelict building. 'The previous inhabitant appears to have had a penchant for the works of an author called Timothy Lea. *Confessions of a Window Cleaner* was most beguiling.' His elastic face adopted a Mona Lisa smile. No wrinkles were apparent in his pale and supple skin, no matter what expression his features attempted to portray. Ratty often felt he was conversing with a teenager rather than with a man at the threshold of middle age.

'Ah, the gamekeeper. Huxtable, I think he was called. No one was better versed in bawdy fiction than he. Wonder what became of the fellow? Hey ho, Patient chappy, the reason I was looking for you was that I have formed a theory about Granny. Unlocking her forbidden room has started me off on a little historical quest. I think I know what might have happened in the weeks prior to locking the empty room. I think Granny Ballashiels might have gone to Spain with Salvador Dalí.'

'No she didn't,' the Patient replied.

The confidence with which the remark had been made caused more than a few of Ratty's hairs to stand to surprised attention.

'Why make such an impudent pronouncement, old acorn?' asked Ratty, smoothing down his hair. 'Have you dipped your nose in the Dalí canon?'

'Scarcely. Barely a dozen or so books, including his only novel and his autobiographical volumes. But it was enough to know that Dalí did not return to his homeland during the missing period of your grandmother's story. Probably because his friend, the poet Lorca, had been shot by a firing squad in the early days of the Spanish Civil War.'

'What rotten luck. Poor fellow. So Dalí had the good sense to keep away from well-armed philistine oiks? A policy I have always striven to endorse.'

They reached the cottage and stepped inside through the gap in the front wall where there should have been a door, carefully avoiding the gap in the floor where the boards should have been, and finally climbing onto rickety stools in the kitchen.

The full wrath of an English country garden had begun to undermine the building soon after the gamekeeper had left the service of the Ballashiels estate in the late Seventies. With no plans – or funds – to replace him, there had been no point in attempting to arrest the sinister encroachment of ivy and assorted delinquent weeds. The clean-up prior to the Patient's arrival had been superficial. Ratty assumed his chum would have continued the fight back against the allied forces of nature, but the Patient was simply too fascinated by everything to want to change it. Like a toddler, he would find wonder in the simplest mould, the oddest smell, the smallest insect. Within the cottage, these sources of fascination were to be found in abundance.

'Dashed peculiar business, don't you think, Patient chappy?'

The Patient said nothing, quietly waiting for Ratty to elucidate.

'First the key, then the room, then the chocolate,' Ratty continued. 'And so to this cottage. Somewhat unsuitable, I'm sure you'd agree. How would you like to move in to the main house?'

'Did you say chocolate?'

'Did I not mention it before? The room was devoid of chattels save for the wrapper of a chocolate bar in the fireplace. From the Seventies. Actually from the same year Mother went missing. And the chocolate was French, to boot. So what do you say? Come over to the manor.'

'And this is in a room that had been sealed since 1937?' asked the Patient.

'Supposedly, yes.'

'Could someone have eaten the bar upon the roof and dropped the wrapper down the chimney?'

'I dare say many is the time when my family took tiffin up on the roof for no apparent reason, but no one from my lineage would eat a vulgar, mass-produced bar of chemically enhanced cocoa. So what do you think? About moving out of this tumbledown ruin?'

'Someone entered the room when you were a child,' said the Patient. 'They left that wrapper behind. That is the only conclusion. May I see it?'

Ratty fumbled in the inside pocket of his leather jacket and produced an unimpressive wallet. In the slot that would have sheltered some of Her Majesty's promissory notes – had Ratty possessed any – sat the carefully folded confectionery wrapper. He passed it to the Patient, who gently opened it out.

'It is a message,' the Patient announced.

'A message? Well, yes, it's a message that says what kind of servant-grade chocolate is to be found within its inner lining.'

'The room was sealed immediately after your grandmother's involvement with Salvador Dalí in 1937. Correct?'

'Indeed. Shall I bring a trolley for your bags?'

'Therefore it is not unreasonable to assume a potential connection between your grandmother's experiences with Dalí and this forbidden room. Correct?'

'Well, yes. Exactly.'

'And yet this chocolate bar dates from the same year that your mother vanished? 1975?'

'Again, yes. But that has nothing to do with it.'

'On the contrary. I believe it has everything to do with it. It was your mother who entered the room. I cannot say what she found in there, but she left a message for you. She left you this chocolate wrapper.'

'Whilst one is disinclined to assume an antipodean position, Mother could not have entered that room. The key has remained buried since the Thirties. And she would not have eaten that chocolate bar. She had standards to maintain. This chocolate was French, don't forget. Now, we could just carry your things over to the manor.'

'No one is saying that she ate the chocolate, Ratty.'

'So, what did she do with it?'

'I mean that the fate of the chocolate itself is of no significance. Your mother chose that wrapper for a reason. And it appears that I was wrong.'

'Wrong?'

'When I said that Dalí didn't journey to Spain with your grandmother. Because now I have seen the chocolate wrapper.'

'Clear as mud, old boy.'

'The chocolate not only confirms your theory that your grandmother travelled to Spain with Dalí, but I believe it is also an indication of where your mother intended to go before she disappeared.'

'I say, I'm not following you at all, old sleuth. Don't you think you're reading rather too much into a random chocolate bar?' asked Ratty, sensing that his friend's mind lacked its usual guillotine sharpness. 'Perhaps we should forget about the chocolate. Now, as for your accommodation, there are twenty bedrooms that could be made serviceable with a little effort.'

'It is not a random chocolate bar. It is a carefully chosen chocolate bar. It is a Lanvin chocolate bar. And I am perfectly happy in this cottage, thank you.'

Ratty gazed at the squalid surroundings in which his friend felt completely at home, noticing only the degradation and the pungent odours and failing entirely to spot the human shadow that moved across the outside of the cracked window. The Patient did not share the same priorities as other people, and Ratty had to respect that. He plucked the wrapper from the Patient's fingers and folded it back into his wallet.

'And what is so special about Lanvin chocolate?' Ratty asked, standing up and preparing to negotiate the perilous exit route from the kitchen.

'At the time of your mother's disappearance, Lanvin had been using a well-known artist in its advertising. The brand and the artist became inextricably linked for some years. He was nothing less than the public face of Lanvin chocolate.'

'To whom are you referring, old croquembouche?'

'The artist was Salvador Dalí.'

The human shadow fell once more across the outside of the kitchen window.

The Graeco-Roman settlement of Empúries on the Catalan coast had awoken from its two thousand year slumber to a chorus of metal trowels and the grunts of perspiring archaeologists as they slowly revealed its forgotten secrets. And situated in a trench beneath a dusty street between the abandoned amphitheatre and the bone-white acropolis, a statue of the goddess Artemis threatened to crush Ruby Towers. One slip of the restraining strap, one unseen fault line in the snowy marble, and Ruby would be pinned beneath half a ton of stone. The health and safety protocols were strict and clear. She had lost count of the number of times she had drummed them into her students here at Empúries, but this morning her judgement was clouded by the exasperating arrival of a rotund young American called Charlie.

She adjusted her position and continued to scrape beneath the horizontal marble statue, patiently and respectfully detaching Artemis from the umbilical grip of roots and dry earth. The shattered arm of the goddess lay in too many pieces to be recognisable, and her head lay several feet away, and though her marble torso was intact it had, so far, refused to co-operate in any attempt to lift it.

'Artemis was the original female multi-tasker,' mumbled Ruby from the base of the trench, reluctantly making conversation with Charlie as he stood watching her from above. 'She was the Greek goddess of hunting, animals, childbirth, fertility and probably a few other things as well.'

'Shopping? Washing-up?' asked Charlie.

She ignored his attempt at wit.

'She's the best link we have around here to any antediluvian civilisations. As the goddess of fertility she's been revered for thirty thousand years.'

'At least the face looks nothing like you,' he yawned.

'Obviously.'

'Not so sure about her ass, though.'

'Are you going to stand there taking the piss all day?' she groaned.

'If I don't take the piss, who will?'

Charlie lowered his indelicate frame to the edge of the trench and squatted to get a closer look at the woman he idolised, triggering a cascade of dirt onto Ruby's legs.

'Hey, watch it!' she shouted. 'Don't get close to the statue. If it falls, it falls on my face. I'm already reaching too far underneath this thing. Don't put me off.'

'I can climb in and hold it for you,' offered Charlie.

'No. Stay.' Ruby shook her head determinedly and stretched beneath the statue to remove a stubborn root.

Suddenly Artemis moved. A fissure in the stone split wide open. The force of gravity took hold, slicing Artemis' torso in two across the chest. The safety strap held the lower torso in place, but the upper part and the surviving arm now dropped onto Ruby, pressing against her face and squeezing the back of her head hard against the stones beneath it. She couldn't speak. Charlie knew it required a considerable cataclysm to silence those English lips; if she couldn't talk, she was probably asphyxiating. He leapt into the trench and grabbed hold of the section of marble. His dramatic arrival sprayed dirt all around, and he half expected to be scolded for his carelessness, but her predicament made it impossible for her to complain. Grabbing it by the arm, he lifted the stone clear of her face. The limb snapped clean off. He threw it aside and picked up the remaining hunk of marble, thinking it was probably the heaviest thing he had ever lifted. It was more than he could throw out of the trench, so he dropped it at Ruby's side where it split into two large pieces and several chips, one of which he pocketed discreetly.

Ruby wriggled away from the remains of the goddess, holding her head in her hands.

'Ever thought of taking up a safer career?' asked Charlie, helping her to sit up and savouring every second of this unexpected physical contact with her. 'Like lion taming?'

He pulled away her hands and inspected the damage. Her nose was bleeding and there were sore-looking grazes on the back of her head, but the injuries seemed superficial. He produced a Dunkin' Donuts napkin from his pocket and offered it to her, steadying himself for the inevitable criticism that she would deliver either about his choice of diet or his rough handling of the statue. Or both. But the verbal abuse did not come.

'Thank you,' she whispered.

He looked at the shattered pieces of statue and wondered if the bang on the head had affected her more than he had realised.

'Coolsville. You're welcome, babe,' he replied, still bracing himself for admonishment. He decided to pre-empt it with an apology. 'Sorry for, you know, the statue stuff.'

She wiped the blood from her face, shook the dust from her hair and spat grit from her mouth. Charlie thought it was the most sensual thing he had ever witnessed. He had been obsessed with Ruby since he had watched a documentary about a dig she'd led in Cairo, broadcast during his recent student days. Ruby liked to think of him as her only fan, although he strayed frequently towards the boundary that divided fan from stalker and hence was not someone with whom she relished spending time. When she sensed a heavy, comforting arm making its way around her shoulders she wriggled out from beneath it and climbed out of the trench.

'Have you ever considered stalking an archaeologist your own age?' she asked.

He appeared to ponder the question intently, missing any irony or subtle criticism, before answering, 'Not really. Quite happy to follow you.'

'I'm almost old enough to be your mother, Charlie. Your obsession is unhealthy. Like your diet. And how did you find me this time?'

'Matt said you were here. I'll tell him you lost a fight with a goddess.'

Bloody Matt. Two days running he'd managed to interfere with her life even from the other side of the planet.

'You can go now, Charlie. I have work to do.'

'I want you to meet Van Gogh before I go.'

'Van Gogh?'

'The RV. Camper van.'

'I saw it when you showed up at Ratty's manor house last December.'

'Oh, that. No. This is different. Bought a new one.'

'Already?' asked Ruby.

'The old one had a fight with a tree. Tree won.'

Ruby rolled her eyes at the excruciating thought processes that flooded Charlie's mind where most people simply possessed a personality.

'So why is your new camper called "Van Gogh"? Because it's a work of art?'

'No. Didn't think of that. It's because I broke a wing mirror off. Come and see.'

She poured mineral water over her scratches. The pain and shock were receding, and a little walk to clear her head seemed fitting. She and Charlie strolled slowly back to the site exit along the remains of a street that had been constructed almost three thousand years ago, to the parking area where Charlie had left his camper van.

'Van Gogh' was easily distinguishable, forlornly lopsided. It was almost identical to the iconic Volkswagen buses of the Seventies, having been cast in South America just a year ago from the same moulds, tools and presses.

The sole concession to modernity was a water-cooled engine in place of the old, distinctive air-cooled lump, necessitating a radiator at the front of the van disguised as the familiar front-mounted spare wheel. Other than that, it was old school technology throughout: slow; clunky; and adorable.

'You're supposed to park under the trees, Charlie. You're partially blocking the road here.'

He shrugged. Rules were not his thing.

'Still stealing historic artefacts on your travels?' she continued.

'No, no. God no. Absolutely given that up. Won't be going there again. No, no. Anything but that. Oh, no.'

'Pockets?'

He produced from his trousers a slither of marble that once was part of Artemis.

'Sorry,' he grunted, handing back the piece of the statue. 'Not seen many artefacts on this mission.'

'Mission?' she echoed.

'To visit every branch of Dunkin' Donuts in Europe,' he replied, crouching down instinctively to pick up a piece of Roman amphora he'd spotted partially exposed in the soil at his feet. The curved clay fragment fell effortlessly into the capacious side pocket of his trousers. 'I'm on my way to Barcelona where there are two branches. Only they're not called Dunkin' Donuts there. It's Dunkin' Coffee. Weird, huh?'

'I'll let you keep that pottery fragment, Charlie, on the condition that you go now, and keep out of trouble.'

A spiral of dust announced the arrival of another vehicle at a velocity not normally associated with parking lots. A Renault Espace slid around the corner into view, picking up speed as the track started to fall downhill. But the car did not slow. On seeing Charlie and Ruby standing ahead of him, the driver swerved. The Espace sprayed their faces with dirt. Tyres ploughed sideways furrows in the grit. With a crunch of snapping fibreglass against steel, plastic and glass, the Espace slammed into the front of Van Gogh.

Charlie and Ruby pulled open the driver's door and extricated the man from the cocoon of airbags that had cushioned his impact, laying him carefully on the ground. Ruby did a double-take. It was impossible. How could her luck turn out to be so bad? This was the exasperating man with whom she had wasted an hour the previous day. This was Rocco Strauss. Charlie peeked inside the Renault. No part of Rocco's body had struck any solid surfaces within the car. That made it all the harder to explain the presence of so much blood all over his head and down to his unnecessarily exposed chest.

By the time the pair of damaged vehicles had been towed away to the nearest crash centre for repairs, the sun had almost fully set behind the distant mountains. Charlie and Rocco jointly expressed the need for a stiff drink to settle their nerves. Grudgingly, Ruby offered to drive them in her Volvo to the nearby marina town of Empuriabrava, where she was staying. Not wanting them to come anywhere close to her hotel, she chose to take them to The Britannia, a traditional English pub in the heart of a Mediterranean harbour, overlooking dozens of tall sailing yachts and imposing motor boats. Streaks of blood were still visible in Rocco's hair. He tried to rinse it away, but even with the assistance of the mirror in the tiny washroom of The Britannia his efforts achieved results that were inconsistent at best. Yet, despite his war-weary appearance, Rocco earned no sympathy from his companions. The complete absence of wounds on his body served only to confuse those who had attempted to assist him after the accident, and his uncharacteristic silence on the matter served only to irritate them further.

Ruby's intuition rang a klaxon in her head. Something was very wrong about Rocco's dramatic arrival. She couldn't place it, but she wanted nothing to do with it.

It took two glasses of the local *cerveza* to loosen Rocco's tongue sufficiently for him to make a confession.

'Stage blood,' he whispered.

Ruby almost choked on her rosé. Charlie's rounded cheeks glowed with fascination.

'Coolsville,' said Charlie. 'So you smashed into Van Gogh as a joke, huh?'

'There's a vial in the glove box. Had you fooled, didn't I?' Rocco gave a weak smile that was completely obscured by Ruby's frosty frown. 'I often use stage blood when I want to make a grand entrance. Life's too short to be conventional.'

Charlie was as enthralled by Rocco's attitude to life as Ruby was appalled by it.

'I want you to go,' she said. 'You and Charlie. I don't want either of you hanging around here. You're trouble. First thing tomorrow, I want you both to be on your way. Let me get on with my work here.'

'Is she always like this?' asked Rocco.

'Yeah. You kinda get used to it,' replied Charlie.

'I am still here,' Ruby interjected.

'Anyway, we can't go tomorrow,' said Charlie. 'Van Gogh and Rocco's Renault are being fixed up.'

Ruby glugged half a glass of wine in one go to numb the frustration, an action that went unnoticed by Rocco.

'In any case,' said Rocco, 'you haven't asked why I came to see you today.'

'Does it not occur to you that, perhaps, I don't care?' she asked.

'I think you will care when I tell you why. When we met at Opoul château at Périllos yesterday, you asked why we were scanning for a message from the future at that particular location.'

'I asked,' she replied, 'but that doesn't mean I really wanted to know.'

'Well, I have to confess that I only gave you half of an answer. The chrononauts chose that site for a far more interesting reason than its view. In the last entry of the last volume of his published diaries, Salvador Dalí wrote about the orgasm of inspiration he experienced at the train station in Perpignan. There was some kind of energy he sensed there, and his painting *The Railway Station at Perpignan* shows Dalí at the centre of an expanding universe of symbolism and light. Above him is a train, representing the station, and above that are some shapes in the clouds. These shapes match precisely the outline of the ruins of the château at Opoul. Dalí was hinting that there was something special about Opoul, and perhaps it was even more significant to him than Perpignan.'

'So you were led to Opoul by a picture of a cloud?' asked Ruby.

'It wasn't me who first discovered the similarity. I have to give that credit to the chrononaut guys. Out of curiosity I overlaid a photo of Opoul with a scan of Dalí's painting in Photoshop, and it was a perfect match. To them this was just a bit of fun, a way to put a thin layer of meaning onto their chosen location for receiving the sign from the future. I think the first part of the postcode of the village also helped –six, six, six – but it got me thinking. I started looking at other Dalí works and looking for patterns. I've found something, Ruby. It's not far from here. I want to share it with you. You know, in case something happens.'

'What do you mean?'

'In case something happens to me,' he continued. 'An insurance policy, you could say. A way to ensure that the thing I have found won't be lost to the world if I get assassinated. Besides, you're an archaeologist, so you're going to love it.'

Ruby was used to crazy types who tried to convince her they had found something amazing, and usually it turned out to be wishful thinking or an overactive imagination coupled with the discovery of something in the ground that was of no more significance than litter. Knowing Rocco as she did, her hopes were not high that his claim would be any more valid than those of previous pseudo-archaeologists and historians who had crossed her path.

'Why don't you just tell me?'

'I'm going to do a little more research first,' he answered, 'and when I'm convinced of the facts I will take you to see it.'

'I can't wait,' she lied.

'Can I come, too?' asked Charlie. 'I've done a bit of archaeology. Lasted two semesters of an archaeology degree at university before they threw me out.'

Rocco looked at Charlie, rolling his eyes across the considerable width of the young man's belly, and shook his head.

'I am sorry, Charlie, but for logistical reasons that is not going to be possible.'

'How come?'

'I could have used the accident today as a cover to start a new identity,' declared Rocco, quickly changing the subject. 'That would have been cool. Like Paul McCartney.'

'Huh?' asked Charlie as Ruby sank her head into her hands.

'He was killed in an accident in the Sixties. They replaced him with Billy Shears. Just took a bit of plastic surgery and some music lessons. The clues are all on the Abbey Road album cover and in the lyrics.'

'You can't compare yourself to that made-up story,' said Ruby. 'Your crash wasn't an accident, for a start.'

'It was!'

'You deliberately drove into Charlie's camper van.'

'I drove into it. But not deliberately.'

'Rubbish. You set the whole thing up with the fake blood and the accident.'

'Two separate events. Unconnected.'

'You expect us to believe that covering yourself in red paint and crashing your car was a coincidence?'

'When you put it like that,' said Rocco, suddenly adopting an expression of weighty concern, 'it does seem suspicious.'

'A confession. At last. Conversation over.'

'No. Not over. Just begun.' Concern appeared to slide into panic and terror. Rocco's eyes grew wide like a manga hero. His breath became shallow and fast. He put on his sunglasses despite the blatant lack of sunshine this late into the Spanish night and sank into his chair, as if to hide between the protective bodies of those close to him. His head twisted back and forth like a spectator at a tennis match.

'If you didn't crash into Charlie's van on purpose,' asked Ruby, attempting to extract from Rocco an explanation for his curious actions that might bear some semblance to rationality, 'why are you only now so freaked out by it?'

'Guess I was in shock. Couldn't think straight.'

'Nothing new there, then,' she mumbled over a sip of rosé.

Ruby looked the other way, gazing out across the marina. A yacht was making its way through the harbour towards the sea, its port side light undulating gently. From another direction, she could hear the excited screams of teenagers daring each other to skinny dip in the darkness. An English football match was showing on a giant screen inside the pub, watched keenly by a huddle of expats. Normal life abounded in this place, yet she felt cocooned in a bubble of delusion.

'Thought my foot might have slipped off the brake,' said Rocco, hiding his mouth behind his hands. 'But it's an automatic.' He announced it soberly, as if he had revealed the meaning of life itself, and waited for an acknowledgement of the profundity of his statement.

Ruby and Charlie said nothing.

'The blood was fake, but that's all,' Rocco eventually continued. 'A little wind-up gag.'

'And the fender bender stuff wasn't part of the plan, huh?' asked Charlie.

'No way. Why would I do that?'

'And the connection between the automatic gearbox and your current imitation of a paranoid lighthouse is what?' asked Ruby.

'Someone is out to get me. I can't believe I didn't realise before. Shock does terrible things to deductive capacities.'

Ruby gesticulated her request for elaboration with impatient hands.

'It can't have been an accident,' Rocco explained. 'It's an automatic. The brake pedal is huge. I couldn't have missed it. Therefore, someone wants me off this rock.'

Ruby resisted the temptation to point out that, from her

perspective, he appeared already to have left the planet.

He stood up, still thrusting his head from side to side in a manner that appeared more likely to result in a blur and a headache than a wide field of vision.

'They could be here in the marina. In those apartments. On those boats. Under the tables of this pub. I could be in their sights right now. There could be a spray of bullets coming my way. And you know the worst thing about it? I don't even know why.'

Again, Ruby found herself in a situation requiring a significant degree of willpower. It was not something in which she excelled, and the force exerting from her teeth down to her lower lip gave her cause for concern that she might draw blood. But she held on to her bite, and resisted the burning desire to point out the logical inconsistency in Rocco's comment that not knowing *why* someone wanted to kill him was worse than actually *being* murdered.

'Maybe it's those chrononauts, or whatever they're called,' suggested Ruby, relieving the pressure from her lip. 'You said there were conflicting groups of them.' She recalled the disturbance in the car park at Opoul castle. The troublemaker drove a Spanish registered car. She wondered if he had followed Rocco across the border back to Spain and was about to suggest this possibility when Rocco gave them both a tidy salute and edged away from their table, towards the marina. Once clear of the pub's terrace of chairs and tables, he sprinted towards the water, dived in and swam off.

Away from the lights of The Britannia his shape was soon subsumed by the night, and the sound of the splashes from his front crawl quickly merged with the background hum of yacht engines, yapping dogs and conversations in assorted European languages.

'I suppose I'll have to pay for his beers,' she groaned.

'And what are you grinning at, Charlie?'

'This is kinda romantic, don't you think? Just you, me, and these big yachts.'

'I still want you to get going, Charlie, as soon as your van is mended. And I don't want you hanging around the dig site while I'm working, all right?'

'What else is there to do around here?' asked Charlie.

'Look around you, Charlie. This area is a sporting paradise. There's sailing, snorkelling, hiking, kite surfing, skydiving.'

'Sports, huh?'

'There's even a wind tunnel where you can practise skydiving without jumping from an aeroplane. I've booked a training session in the wind tunnel for me and my students in a day or two. Can't wait.'

She looked at Charlie's bulbous shape seated in the chair, and realised she may have been on the wrong tack. He was evidently not sporting material, and as for the sky divers' wind tunnel, it was entirely possible that the huge electric turbo fans might lack sufficient strength to lift someone of Charlie's size even an inch from the ground.

'It's not all sports,' she added. 'What about cultural pursuits? You could start at the Dalí museum in Figueres.'

'Museum, huh?'

'This is the heart of Dalí country. He created his greatest works here. He was inspired by this coastline. The man was a genius.'

'Genius, huh?' Charlie leaned forward and scratched his backside.

Ruby tensed and braced herself for what she was about to say. It wasn't going to be easy, but a very small part of her felt sorry for her only fan and for a foolish moment she allowed her sympathy to take over.

'Charlie, I'm due to take some of my students to the

museum tomorrow morning. You can, you know, kind of tag along. If you want.'

She gulped. That had hurt.

'Like a date?'

'No, Charlie, not like a date,' she replied, her sympathy already waning. 'But if you want to join my group I'd be happy to show you around.'

'Like a private tour? That could be cool.'

A muffled tune began to play in Charlie's pocket. He produced his cellphone and answered it.

'Uhuh,' he said. 'Uhuh. Uhuh. Sure. Coolsville. Uhuh. OK.'

He hung up. Ruby crossed her arms in frustration at his unrevealing ineloquence.

'Message from the mechanic dude,' said Charlie. 'He says I can pick up Van Gogh first thing in the morning. Oh, and the brake lines have been tampered with on Rocco's Renault.'

FRIDAY 3RD MAY 2013

A figure slipped through the laurel bushes like an apparition in the morning mist. It glided into the nettles and brambles. Moments later, it disappeared beneath the tangle of trees that squatted upon gardens that decades ago ceased to be recognisable as the work of Capability Brown. Through the squinted sights of Ratty's blunderbuss, the figure flowed like a pheasant, scampering in and out of his firing line before he could pull the flintlock trigger.

The sightings of the shadowy poacher had come intermittently since he had left the Patient's cottage. At no point did he consider calling the police; they would have tiresome things to say about his desire to use antiquated firearms. Sometimes the intruder melted into the darkness on one side of the manor only to reappear on the other side impossibly quickly, as if somehow aware of the shortcuts between the outbuildings that only Ratty knew. Occasionally it seemed like there was more than one shadow out there, as if he were being circled by wolves. They would seem to lurk beneath his Land Rover then sprint to the coal shed. They would tiptoe to the dustbins and then crawl to the barn. He wasn't sure of anything he saw in the heavy gloom. Lack of sleep could have been making him see double.

As a frankly confusing and exhilarating night drew to a

close, he yearned for the chance to squeeze the trigger and bring this nocturnal hunt to a satisfactory conclusion. Rounding a corner by the stable block, the longed-for opportunity presented itself. He hugged his Barbour jacket tight and lifted the blunderbuss to eye level. The poacher was standing behind the tractor, facing away from Ratty, only a shoulder and the back of a head exposed to his unsteady aim. The cat-and-mouse game had gone on long enough. It was time for a resolution. He fired a spray of lead pellets. The figure fell forward, hit by the small quantity of shot that didn't ping harmlessly off the engine cowling. But within seconds the intruder was picked up by two other strangers and carried away. By the time Ratty had recovered from the recoil that had knocked him to the ground and left him breathlessly staring at the morning sky, the miscreants had vanished.

They won't be back in a hurry, he assured himself, dusting his waxed coat and heading to the vast kitchen at the rear of the manor for a well-earned fry-up. He was not displeased to discover upon his arrival that just such a repast was already waiting for him upon the kitchen table.

'If you want to eat well in England, eat three breakfasts,' suggested the Patient.

Ratty tucked immediately into a fried egg.

'Somerset Maugham, if I am not mistaken,' Ratty replied, between mouthfuls. 'Born in Paris. English by a mere technicality. I shall accept no culinary advice from one so poisoned by the base, uncivilised habits of our semi-evolved Gallic neighbours. Oh, and I shot the poacher.'

'No you did not.'

'It is an indisputable fact that I pulled the trigger, a barrage of shot was released in the general direction of our uninvited guest, and some of the aforementioned lead entered the rear of this fellow. Probably bagged the poacher in the shoulder.'

'Again, I assert that no such thing occurred.'

'Now look here, Patient chappy, I was up all night stalking this poacher and –'

'No you were not.'

'And, and I squeezed the trigger on this gun, which no longer contains shot because it was discharged towards the poacher. Proof incontrovertible.'

'Not.'

'I confess to finding your existential games a little tiresome at the wrong end of a night in which my bed played no part,' Ratty grumbled, immediately regretting the utterance of such harsh words to someone who had been warm-hearted enough to cook the kind of meal that he could no longer afford to pay anyone to prepare.

'I attempt only to point out to you the truth.'

'And what truth have I failed to spot in my recent heroic shooting of a poacher?'

'You have missed the fundamental reality. A significant detail in your account is based on an incorrect assumption, and it utterly undermines everything you have said to me this morning.'

The Patient made no sense without a cup of tea. Ratty placed his hand upon the teapot, delighted to feel its warmth. The tea wouldn't confound him with riddles. Tea was reliable. Comfortable. He poured a cup and held it close to his face. Already he felt stronger: Popeye with his spinach; Samson with his hair.

'I give in,' he said with a grin that was his admission that the Patient was bound to be right. 'Tell me.'

'You did not spend the night hunting a poacher. You did not shoot any poacher. I make that assertion due to one simple reason: on this estate there is no longer anything to poach. You have no pheasants, no trout, no boar, no deer, no –'

'That is a valid observation,' Ratty sighed, defeated.

'I also observed that some of the intruders were not dressed in the manner traditionally associated with the illegal capture of wild creatures on land that does not belong to them.'

'So the plurality of the intrusion did not escape your notice? A most bizarre situation.'

'The more significant point,' continued the Patient, 'is that if the visitors were not engaged in the relatively harmless pursuit of stealing wildlife, they must therefore be concerned with an enterprise of a different nature.'

Ratty finished his sausage while he absorbed the Patient's conclusion.

'Bad eggs, nevertheless. Bit of buckshot probably did them no end of good,' Ratty decided.

'The gun cannot answer questions. It can only eliminate the need for answers.'

'Quite, quite.'

'Had you enquired of them as to their desires, instead of stalking them behind your weapon, you might have learned something of value.'

The knife and fork clattered to the plate. Ratty slugged his tea and stood up, wiping his bleary eyes.

'To the village,' the aristocrat declared. 'Mrs Trundle may be about to sell a bandage. We may catch them there. Come.'

The Patient calmly followed his friend to the Land Rover, wiping his fingers across morning dew on the faded green paintwork as he climbed into the threadbare passenger seat. Ratty turned the engine over and waited for it to catch. After three attempts the vehicle came to life, merrily shaking its occupants and growling contentedly. A brief swish of the wipers cleared the moisture from the windscreen, and with a grind of gears they started to move.

'This is not a wise course of action,' suggested the Patient as he pulled the seatbelt tightly around him.

'Not now, old G and T. The time to judge this plan is after we intercept these interlopers.'

'It might be wise to consider my advice as a priority. As Cicero put it so eloquently, advice in old age is foolish, for what can be more absurd than to increase our provisions for the road the nearer we approach our journey's end?'

'So what do you advise?' asked Ratty, changing down a gear in preparation for a sharp turn in his driveway.

'I merely suggest that we continue our journey by other means.'

'But the Landy is a locomotive legend,' Ratty countered in defence of his dependable conveyance. 'This trusty mechanical steed has been in the service of my family since the days of that how-do-you-do over the Falklands. I hardly consider it appropriate to question the iron beast's loyalty after more than thirty –'

He abandoned his verbal protest in favour of a heart-sinking gasp when he felt the brake pedal travel to the floor with no resistance. Back-up options for bringing this old vehicle to a halt were few, and by the time Ratty had recalled that the handbrake never worked and realised there wasn't enough distance to slow down using engine braking, the crash had already begun. There was no dramatic squeal of tyres, no ear-splitting explosive roar, just the rustling of nettles and the tumbling of bodies as the car skated at a tangent from the road and pitched onto its side in the drainage ditch.

***

'Melting clocks.'

'Yes,' Ruby sighed, already regretting her decision to invite Charlie to the Dalí museum. He was plainly more suited to standing in a wind tunnel than indulging in any kind of cultural pursuits. 'Obviously. *The Persistence of Memory* is the painting that your lowest common denominator of a brain is referring to. But that's not all he's known for.'

'A dumb moustache?'

'Well yes, but I'm talking about his iconographic palette. There are recurrent themes in his works, like trademarks that brand his visual style. And do you have the faintest idea what I'm talking about?'

Charlie looked at the skirting boards and the fire exit signs. He stared at the cornicing, and marvelled at the flooring. He seemed determined to study everything in the gallery apart from the paintings on the walls.

'There a bar in this place?'

'This is a world class institution, not a drinking den, Charlie.'

'I bet all your students found a bar somewhere. They lost you pretty quick after you paid for everyone's tickets.'

'They'll be back. I'm teaching them thermoluminescence dating this afternoon,' said Ruby.

'Dating, huh? Always happy to help in that department,' said Charlie as Ruby shook her head in despair. 'Anyway, that Dalí dude can't have done all this sober. Look at this crazy shit. Windows in the sky. A chair with a light shining at the stars. Another dumb melting clock. People with flowers growing out of them. A doorway full of hair with a zipper down the middle. It's like he had Photoshop and went crazy with it. Dalí had to

44

be off his head. So why should we be forced to look at it without a beer or three? It's logical.'

'You sound like the Patient.'

'That pale-faced philosopher dude? Coolsville.'

'Only without any learning to back up your argument.'

Charlie stared blankly, as if knowledge was a disease he had yet to catch.

'You find a bar,' she told him. 'I'll come and look for you later. A few decades later.'

'Is that your English humour thing?'

'I just want to see the Mae West installation. Then we'll get lunch.'

'This Mae West chick. What's the deal?'

'It's an apartment designed to look like the face of Mae West. From a particular angle.'

'And you say the guy was sober?'

They walked across the central courtyard of the museum, an open space dominated by a 1940s car and dozens of Dalí's gold-painted mannequin sculptures. On arrival at the Mae West installation it resembled neither an apartment nor the actress after whom it was named. In fact, it looked like nothing in particular. There was a red sofa shaped like a pair of lips, some pictures on the wall, a staircase that led nowhere, brown floorboards, and drapes that didn't serve any recognisable light-control purpose. There was even a bathtub hanging from the ceiling, upside-down. Tourists took turns to reach the top of the stairs and take photos. Ruby joined the queue. Charlie shrugged at the apparent randomness of the objects in the room, climbed over a rope barrier and sat heavily upon the red sofa. It was his first opportunity to sit down all morning, and he closed his eyes in bliss, paying no attention to the shouts of frustration emanating from the top of the steps. They seemed to be aimed in his direction, but the languages involved were far too exotic for him to have any hope of comprehending them.

The shocked face and frantic arm gestures of a security guard in a canary yellow jacket left nothing to the imagination, however. Charlie stood up and strolled around the installation, noting that the camera flashes started up again as soon as he had put some distance between himself and the sofa.

Exiting the barrier with a yawn, and to the obvious relief of the guard, he waited at the rear of the room for Ruby to satisfy her curiosity about the view from the top of the steps. His ennui with the mind-mangling visual anarchy of Dalí's surrealism gave him a yearning to sit again, but other than the apparently out-of-bounds sofa there was nowhere suitable. In his peripheral vision, he sensed a dark table behind him in a far corner, an original Dalí work, out of sight of the security man. With a surreptitious wriggle, he reversed himself onto it, then jumped off immediately in a state of guilty panic. The table was bent down the centre, a shallow valley with its nadir precisely where he had sat. Convinced that he had cracked a priceless museum piece he sidled silently to the side, forced once again to stand in discomfort. It was as if the museum was determined to torture any visitor who lacked an appreciation of the works of this twentieth-century eccentric.

'It really does look like her,' called Ruby from the top of the steps, having waited patiently for her turn.

'Like who?'

'Oh for God's sake, Charlie, who do you think? I can see a perfect likeness of Mae West through the lens up here. There's her hair, lips, nose, eyes. It's amazing.'

Charlie was ready to climb the steps after Ruby to see what the fuss was all about, but was distracted from doing so by something clamping itself around his ankle. He looked down and saw a human hand. Was it part of the installation? Was he being seduced by another portion of this representation of Mae West? Perhaps this Dalí guy was cooler than he'd originally thought. Might even be worth delaying that drink for a few more minutes.

The hand pulled harder. Then a man's face appeared from behind a black door in a black wall. Charlie assumed the face and the hand were connected and concluded that this was not good. His attempt to kick the face with his free leg was thwarted by a second hand and the frustrated momentum of his defensive action almost toppled him.

'Don't move,' said the face.

'Rocco?' asked Charlie.

The door swished and in a moment Charlie found himself on the other side, blinking at a brightly lit, emerald paradise of plastic ivy and fake palms entwined around a double bed in which Rocco had plainly spent the night.

'Is anyone following you?' Rocco whispered, scrambling to his feet.

'You owe Ruby ten Euros, dude.'

'Huh?'

'She picked up your tab at the English pub last night. After you swam off in the marina.'

'I think I know who is after me,' Rocco rasped, signalling for Charlie to come closer while he produced some cash from his pocket.

'Don't worry about the tip.'

'I only have a twenty.'

'No problem. Anyone tell you your brakes were cut?'

Charlie pocketed the money.

The furrows in Rocco's usual paranoid expression stretched to valleys of dumbfounded horror.

'Don't look like that,' said Charlie. 'It's not that bad. I'm sure Ruby will give you change.'

'No, it is not the money. Someone has tried to kill me.'

'Yes, I know. I thought you knew that when you ran into the marina.'

'I believed it, but I didn't *know* it. They are different things. All my life I've believed in conspiracies, investigated mysteries, assumed everyone was out to get me. Most of it was fantasy. I guess I'm built that way. I need to feel there's a subtext to my life. I need to read between the lines, make two and two equal five.'

'Didn't think you could get a science doctorate with math like that, dude.'

'No, you're not understanding me. The conspiracy is real. There's a threat to my life. You think I swam off into the night for fun? I had to make sure no one knew where I was heading.'

'Which was where, dude?'

'Here. To the Dalí museum, of course, Charlie. I broke in and spent the night looking for answers.'

'Why here? There's not even a bar in this place.'

'I don't know yet, but somehow Salvador Dalí is connected to all this.'

'All this what?' asked Charlie.

'Project Keo. The Chronodrome experiment. I know it's impossible. Dalí died years before the project was even conceived. And yet there's something linking him. I looked all over the place last night. Didn't get the answers I needed. Just got more questions.'

'So you're saying you're scared of a dead painter?'

'I'm serious, Charlie. Someone is targeting me. And you and Ruby could be on the hit list too.'

'But I've got nothing to do with anything. Nor has Rubes.'

'I was there on the hill with Ruby at the Chronodrome experiment. Looking for the sign from the future. Waiting for the acknowledgement that the Keo time capsule was safely received and opened by our descendants. And you've been seen with us since. You're in it as deep as me. And it's going to get deeper.'

'How come?'

'Keo is the reason we're all at risk.'

'I still don't get it. Why are me and Rubes involved?'

'Trust me. You're both in this. Your lives are in danger.'

'Huh?'

The ensuing clarification triggered a bout of unsympathetic mirth that made Charlie's fat wobble uncontrollably.

'Don't you see, Charlie? Someone from the future is trying to kill us.'

The Regency teacup rattled on its saucer as if the library at Stiperstones Manor were experiencing a mild earthquake. Warm Darjeeling spilled down the cup's hand-painted sides. Rather than fulfilling its intended function as an alleviator of distress, the beverage played the unwelcome role of reminding its holder of just how shaken he was.

'I don't frighten easily,' lied Ratty. He put down the chattering cup and stretched his arms as if to banish the tremors from his soul. He wanted to recover, to show the Patient he possessed inner strength, to prove to them both that he was not beaten.

'Yes you do.'

Ratty grabbed the cup – this time with two hands – and took a slurp. The chemicals in the tea instantly soothed him. He was now slightly less annoyed with his friend.

'Tosh and splosh,' he said, showing the Patient a steadier hand than the one he had moments ago possessed. 'Perhaps we could move on from this discussion of the limitations of my anatomy and address the rather more exigent matter of the failure of the braking system of my poor upturned Land Rover?'

'I noticed a patch of oily fluid on the ground beneath the vehicle,' said the Patient.

'Amongst all those weeds in the ditch?'

'No. I mean the ground upon which it was parked outside the house.'

'You saw leaking brake fluid before we tootled off? And you didn't care to impart this factual nugget?' Ratty didn't do angry, but his mild displeasure was obvious.

'I told you the journey was unwise.'

'A two-thousand-year-old quotation from Marcus Tullius Cicero can hardly be regarded as a succinct warning of our impending catastrophe.'

'Again, I have to tell you that you are deviating from that which is significant,' said the Patient.

'I conject that your knowledge that we were going to crash was not entirely lacking in significance.'

'What mattered then matters not now. What matters now matters now.'

'Well I'm so relieved that you have cleared that up for me, Patient chappy.'

'What matters now is *why* the braking system failed. The Land Rover is of an age that puts into question its mechanical reliability, but the presence last night of uninvited guests in the estate is a coincidence that cannot be ignored.'

'You think someone performed an impromptu vasectomy on the old brake pipes?'

'It is a conclusion supported by the circumstantial

evidence, and a brief inspection of the chassis will be sufficient to confirm the hypothesis. I have already called for a mobile mechanic to assess the damage and repair the vehicle for you. He says it will be mended this morning. A clean cut of the pipes is quicker to fix than a hidden leak, he told me. Whether this vandalism is linked to the theft of the collection of Timothy Lea novels from the gamekeeper's cottage is, however, a matter of conjecture.'

'Timothy Lea?' asked Ratty. 'The Confessions of a wotnot and all that? You didn't mention that before.'

'They were absent this morning,' replied the Patient. 'That is all I know.'

Ratty picked up the teacup and saucer again, irritated to note that the two items appeared to be vibrating. He drank quickly, finishing the tea.

'Perhaps another cup?' he mumbled, placing the items back on the coffee table in embarrassment before unsteadily pouring a refill from the pot. 'I've done nothing,' he bemoaned. 'Nothing to trigger anyone's disquietude. Nothing to niggle the neighbours. Nothing to incommode the commoners.' He realised he was talking drivel, once again smothering his fears with a mouthful of poetic nonsense. He stopped talking and took a measured breath.

'No man is without sin,' said the Patient.

'Well quite,' replied Ratty, attempting to choose words that might be considered more or less normal. 'But all I've done recently is open grandmother's empty room.'

'Against her strict instructions.'

'More of a taboo, really. She did warn in rather stringent terms against anyone opening it, it has to be said, but the waffle and wotnot about the dark consequences of breaking the taboo was a mere theatrical flourish.' Ratty

51

sounded unconvinced by his own disregard for the warnings.

'No one besides you and I know about it,' said the Patient, 'apart from anyone with whom you may have communicated during your visit to the house of Edward James at West Dean. If there is a connection between your entry to the forbidden room, the intruders last night, the theft of those books and the failure of the Land Rover's brakes, it might logically emanate from your visit to West Dean. Your visit may have triggered a response from parties unknown.'

'Goodness.'

'And if we accept all the foregoing linked theories, then your quest to understand more about your grandmother's connections with Dalí could be more important than you realise.'

'Heavens.'

'And that brings me to the subject of the chocolate wrapper. Prior to the arrival of our uninvited guests last night we established that the item may have been left there as a deliberate message referring to Dalí, contemporaneous with your mother's vanishing. So we have two possible links with Dalí. What publications do you have in this library relating to Dalí? I'm only interested in those that have been here since before 1975.'

'That would be all of them,' Ratty answered, standing up and pointing to a section of shelf that featured books relating to artists of the twentieth century. The five volumes of Dalí materials sat together. 'I've read them all, over the years. There's nothing in them about my family.'

'Reading one book at a time cannot always give the full picture,' said the Patient, proceeding to remove all five. He placed them on Ratty's desk and returned to the shelf which now sported a noticeable gap. He looked closely at the space, and invited a confused Ratty to do likewise.

'I say, what's that?' Ratty asked.

'That,' replied the Patient, is what you miss when you only remove one book at a time. Take out the collection and a section of wall is revealed. In this case, there appears to be an envelope taped to it.'

Ratty ran his fingers across the yellowed Sellotape that held the envelope vertically to the wall. It peeled away easily. He extracted the envelope and was disgusted to notice that his hands had assumed an involuntary tremble once again. Looking into the Patient's eyes he expected to see a spark of enthusiasm willing him to open it, but there was nothing but calm indifference.

'If this is anything to do with Grandmother and her Dalínian sense of humour, it's probably a blank piece of paper inside,' Ratty said.

Still no sign of encouragement from his friend. It was as if he had served his purpose in making the deductive connections necessary to find the envelope and had since lost interest in the subject. Ratty sat at his desk and toyed with his discovery. The desire to open it pecked at him from within, restrained only by his dread of the information it might contain. If this was his grandmother's explanation for the empty room, then he would be fine with that, it might even help him understand the peculiar events of the past night. But if it were his mother's final goodbye to him, how would he react to that? His gut feeling told him that it was more likely to date from his mother's era than his grandmother's, owing to the relatively modern design of the envelope and the use of sticky tape. Plus, of course, the possibility that the chocolate wrapper was indeed a clue intended to point its discoverer to this spot. A lump lodged itself in his throat; his eyes filled with moisture, blurring his vision. He fumbled for his letter-opening knife and cut a neat slit across the top.

Inside was a single sheet of paper. He pulled it out and unfolded it. The page had been written by hand in an elegant, but hurried, calligraphy. He wiped his eyes in order to focus on the words. Reading the entire document took only a few seconds. He glanced at the Patient.

'Oh no,' he said. 'Not again.'

Charlie emerged from Rocco's hideout at the rear of the Mae West installation. Very little that Rocco had told him made any sense, and he instantly discarded the revelations from his mind. The German scientist refused to show his paranoid face in public, so Charlie left him behind and went in search of Ruby.

There was no sign of her in the vicinity. Charlie puffed his way through long, curving corridors lined with priceless paintings. He trudged up and down stairs between the different levels of the museum. Phoning her was not an option: she was sensible enough never to have given him her number. Such information in his possession, he knew, would be abused. The price he now had to pay for her wise caution was an exhausting search on foot.

Back at the vestibule that marked the museum entrance, Charlie nipped out to check if Ruby was hanging around in the plaza outside the museum. Hundreds of people were still waiting in line to get in, but Ruby was nowhere. He looked up at the geodesic cupola that capped the Dalí museum's roof – the grand architectural feature had gone unnoticed by him when he had arrived with Ruby; in her presence he only had eyes for her. He looked at the wall studded with representations of bread loaves and topped with giant eggs – equally new to him. This place was just as bizarre on the outside as within. He overheard an American tourist reading aloud from a leaflet that the building was the town's former theatre, originally constructed in the nineteenth century and destroyed during the Spanish Civil War. It had lain in ruins for decades until Dalí converted it into his personal museum and shrine in the Seventies. With a yawn, Charlie returned to the entrance.

The main door through which he had slipped outside was blocked by a lady official asking to see his ticket. He tapped his pockets and recalled that Ruby had paid to get him and her students inside. The tickets were somewhere inside her leather satchel, he realised, hanging from her kissable shoulder. The woman pointed at the line of people behind Charlie. It snaked across the square and out of sight around the corner. Hundreds of tourists were fanning themselves in the warmth of the morning and admiring – during the hour or more it had so far taken them to queue for tickets – a peculiar statue erected by Dalí for just such a purpose.

Charlie was morally opposed to queuing. He scouted for the main exit, which he found in a nearby side street.

Security at the museum's back door consisted of a bespectacled guard whose extremes of height and girth gave him a menacing aura. He wore a white shirt with badges and logos sewn on to its short sleeves. Around his waist was a sturdy belt that carried the weight not only of his black trousers but also a pistol, a walkie-talkie and a baton.

Behind this sole official was a set of glass doors which could only be opened from within. Hardly Fort Knox, Charlie told himself. He retreated to a doorway further along the street from which he could observe the exit.

Tourists walked out through the glass doors in an almost continuous trickle, carrying bags of souvenir books that would never be read. Some acknowledged the guard as they passed; most ignored him. Finally, a tired family laden with Dalí-branded carrier bags stopped and asked the guard to take a photo of them together. Charlie edged closer. The guard struggled to connect his bulbous fingers with the delicate controls of the camera. His distraction from his duty was total. Charlie strolled past, unnoticed, and approached the glass doors, inserting his arm as they opened to allow a pair of tourists to exit.

'Excuse me,' he said, 'left something inside.' He squeezed through and moments later stood in the museum's gift shop. Dalí trinkets and gifts of all varieties surrounded him in a surreal nightmare of complex juxtaposition. He felt like he had stepped into one of the weird paintings for which the museum was famous. But at least he had entered the building: no queuing; no paying. Exactly the way things ought to be.

Unlike the hand of authority he now felt upon his shoulder.

It was a weighty, bloated hand. Its tubular fingers were not unlike Charlie's own. With nowhere to run, not to mention a complete inability to propel himself at more than a waddle, Charlie turned round to face the consequences of his cheeky disdain for waiting in line.

The guard was taller, rounder, hairier, sweatier, and angrier than Charlie. The specifics of the guard's verbal torrent eluded the American, but the gist was clear: Charlie was in trouble. His offer of a stale donut to the arresting official was not taken in a manner that seemed likely to help his situation: the grim expression fixed upon the guard's curvaceous face did not crack. The humourless man shoved Charlie down a staircase and into a corridor beyond the reach of the public, where the walls were entirely devoid of Dalínian artistry. No one will hear me scream down here, though, Charlie.

The official unlocked an unmarked door and nudged his captive inside, confiscating his bag of donuts before swiftly securing the room once more from without. Charlie was alone in a small, windowless, basement meeting room. The floor and walls were tiled with white marble, creating a sense of cold sterility that made Charlie think of abattoirs and morgues. He shivered, and wondered if he was about to experience mind games and physical torture in a prison cell deep beneath the bowels of the building.

The rattle of a large collection of keys broke his reverie. The lock turned.

The man who entered the room was dressed immaculately in a fancy white suit, which, Charlie noted, was reassuringly free of bloodstains. Besides, he was an old man with pale skin and grey hair. As he sat down at the table, Charlie's torture worries evaporated. All he had done was to sneak into the gift shop, after all. They probably wanted to give him a boring lecture and then send him on his way. Piece of cake.

'So,' said the old man, his straight nose appearing to point accusingly at Charlie.

'Uhuh,' said Charlie.

'You have come fresh from New York and London?'

Charlie couldn't place the accent. It didn't seem to belong anywhere. There was nothing Spanish about it, nor was it American English or pure British English.

'Er, sure,' replied Charlie, sniffing his armpit. 'Not so sure about the fresh thing, though.'

'You think this is funny? You think this is a joke?' The old man's face was drained of expression, devoid of any hint of *joie de vivre*.

'If it helps get this over with, I'm real sorry. And it's not funny. Sir.'

'Nothing can help you now,' said the old man. 'Your illicit entry to our museum was spotted by several of our hidden video cameras. Ever since New York and London we have been expecting you.'

'You have?'

'Although I did not think you would be so incompetent. So blatant. So stupid this time.'

'That's kinda the way I roll, dude.'

'What happened to the last one that you stole?'

'That I stole?' Charlie tried to think back to when he had last outwitted an assistant in a branch of Dunkin' Donuts. 'Oh come on, man, that wasn't even in this country.'

'I know that. I just want to know what you did with it.'

'What do you think I did with it? Stuck it up my ass?'

'You did that?'

'No, of course not, dude. I ate it.'

The old man's skin turned even paler.

The texture of the door was a source of endless enthralment. The Patient ran his smooth hands across the cracked oak panels, sensing the embellished edges, tickling the exposed head of a nail, enjoying the looseness of the white porcelain handle. All of which was terribly off-putting for Ratty, who, currently on the other side of the door in question, was unable to convey his preference for privacy due to the unceasing flow of tears that drowned his face and choked his throat.

He had history here. This lavatory had been his frequent refuge in the difficult months he had endured after his mother's vanishing. He had lined its walls with photographs, water colours and oil portraits of her, and he had maintained this quirky shrine ever since. The servants had pretended not to know he was there, indulging his need to be alone with his misery, his confusion, and his books. He would focus diligently in his efforts to transport his soul to another world, to be absorbed into a fiction in which he could escape the torpor of Stiperstones in mourning. Sucked for hours at a time into stories by Dickens or Wodehouse in particular, he sidestepped the grieving and delayed coming to terms with his situation.

The sight of his mother's handwriting had triggered a disturbing regression to a state of mind that he had hoped never again to inhabit. The letter reconnected him to the past, a direct line to the moment his world flipped inside-out and ceased to make sense. He tried to zone out, recalling the mental tricks that he had developed as his childhood emergency exit from misery, but with the Patient's ceaseless fiddling with the door his efforts were fruitless. At length, he gave up, wiped his face, and released the sliding bolt.

'Come on, old pumpkin,' snivelled Ratty. 'Let's see if we can deduce what meaning Her Ladyship was attempting to impart. Right now, it makes no sense.' He had been presented with this kind of obscure communication before, and wondered what it was about women that made them want to use literary quotations instead of saying what they meant.

He blew his nose into a piece of toilet roll as he led the Patient along the dark and dusty corridors back to the library, where he laid the letter flat upon the desk and stared blurrily at it. When no meaning jumped off the page he cleared his throat and read the first line aloud.

'I wish either my father or my mother, or indeed both of

them, as they were in duty both equally bound to it, had minded what they were about when they begot me.'

'Indeed,' said the Patient. 'And what does it say on the letter?'

'I say, that wasn't … you're not … I mean, have you discovered a funny bone in that skeleton of yours?'

The Patient exhibited a flawless smile.

'It is a mirth-inducing formula which I have been meaning for some time to attempt. I hope it triggered within you a detectable degree of merriment.'

'Well I don't think Richard Gervais will be overly concerned,' said Ratty, secretly appreciating this wooden attempt to lift his mood. 'Now. The quotation. Sounds somewhat on the Sterne side to me; Larry, if I'm not barking up the wrong bird in the bush.'

'*The Life and Opinions of Tristram Shandy, Gentleman*. Laurence Sterne.'

'Agreed. But so what? Is it a code?'

'A code?'

'I think this room has an echo,' said Ratty, vainly attempting to distract himself from the ache in his heart with fake joviality. The Patient regarded him blankly. 'By a code,' he continued, 'I mean, perhaps, taking the first letter of each word and seeing if it says something rather jolly clever. In this case, you could spell L.O.T.S.'

'Lots?'

'Well, if you use some of the words and ignore the others. Hmm. Perhaps we should look at the second quotation?'

'It has turned out fortunate for me today that destiny appointed Braunau-on-the-Inn to be my birthplace.'

'Ah,' sighed the Patient, 'the opening line of a tome that is rather uncomfortably close to my own family history.'

'*Mein Kampf*, by a familiar fellow who only had one. No obvious clues there, as far as one can tell. Don't recall Mother ever mentioning a proclivity towards National Socialism. And she hated bratwurst. Let's try the next one. Appears to have been scribed by an author with many qualities similar to the previous fellow. Strong. Opinionated. Unlikely to win Moustache of the Year competition.

'Greer?'

Ratty nodded assent and read the quote:

'It is true that the sex of a person is attested by every cell in his body.'

'*The Female Eunuch*,' confirmed the Patient. 'An essential manual for comprehending the incomprehensible workings of the female.'

'Still not enlightening the mysterious matter at hand, however. The next one is clearly from Virginia Woolf.'

'"Yes of course, if it's fine tomorrow," said Mrs Ramsay. "But you'll have to be up with the lark," she added.'

'*To the Lighthouse*, of course,' said the Patient.

'But we don't have a lighthouse.'

'Was that a humorous construct?' enquired the Patient after a momentary silence.

The two friends stared at each other. Other than establishing the existence of a nascent sense of humour in the Guatemalan and confirming a shared knowledge of literature broad enough to shame a university lecturer, they had not arrived at even the most tenuous interpretation of the letter. Even the infinite wisdom of the Patient had yet to produce a theory. The sheet of paper contained two more quotes. Without optimism, Ratty read out the next lines from his mother's handwriting.

'When Farmer Oak smiled, the corners of his mouth spread till they were within an unimportant distance of his ears, his eyes were reduced to chinks, and diverging wrinkles appeared around them, extending upon his countenance like the rays in a rudimentary sketch of the rising sun.'

'Hardy,' said the Patient.
'*Mayor of Casterbridge?*'
'*Far From the Madding Crowd.*'
'Of course. Hardy's openings often put one in a discombobulatory state. Any clues therein, Patient chappy?'
'Sometimes it is necessary to look without in order to see within,' he replied, obtusely.
Ratty glanced at the window before settling his eyes upon the final quotation on the page.

'At an epoch a little later than the date of the letter cited in the preceding pages, he did a thing which, if the whole town was to be believed, was even more hazardous than his trip across the mountains infested with bandits.'

'A translation, I presume?'
'Gosh. Not sure. Doesn't read like an opening sentence.'

'Are you in possession of a conveniently situated computer?'

Ratty slid an unfashionably bulbous laptop from inside a drawer and placed it on the desk adjacent to the letter. He fussed with cables and sockets and began the lengthy process of booting the machine.

'Confounded contraption,' he moaned as he typed the full sentence in his browser's search box. An antiquated modem made a series of clicks and whirrs that formed a most agreeable tune to the unjaded ears of the Patient. A minute later a connection had been made and a page began slowly to form upon the screen. Pixel by pixel the screen morphed into recognisable words.

'And we have a match,' Ratty declared. 'You were right about the translation thing. Victor Hugo. *Les Mis*. And it's not the opening, but Chapter Ten of the first book.'

He closed the lid of the laptop and returned his attention to the letter with the six short quotations. The Patient was staring at the bookshelves, as if no longer interested in the mystery of the letter.

'So, we have six books,' said Ratty, starting at the only facts of which he was certain.

'We do not,' replied the Patient.

'I'm pretty sure it was six,' sighed Ratty. '*Tristram Shandy*, *Mein Kampf*, *The Female Eunuch*, *To the Lighthouse*, *Far from the Madding Crowd*, and *Les Mis*. Count them. We have six books.'

'We do not,' repeated his irritating friend. The Patient pulled selected volumes from the shelf, matching the list of titles Ratty had just recited, with the exception of one. 'Five of the six books are present in this library. One is missing. See? Where is *The Female Eunuch*?'

'But the clues are inherent in the words, are they not?'

asked Ratty. 'What use is the actual book anyway?'

'Until a search is complete a man cannot truly know what he had been searching for.'

Ratty picked up Hitler's hardback rantings and flicked through its demented pages. There were no markings inside it save for the letter 'W', which was inscribed in the margin beside the opening line in a type of calligraphy that matched his mother's writing style in the letter. His face lit up.

'Patient chappy, look.'

They flicked open the remaining books in rapid succession. Further inscriptions were located adjacent to the words quoted in Ratty's mother's list. They now had a series of letters: 'E', 'R', 'W' and two instances of 'L'. Without the sixth book, there was no way to know what the final letter would have been. When the Patient enquired as to its fate, Ratty looked sheepish.

'Jumble sale,' he mumbled. 'Church fête last year. A boy scout chap came asking for donations for the book stall. Dib-dib-dib and wotnot. *The Female Eunuch* was the only tome with which I could bear to part.'

'We have to find who bought it,' said the Patient.

'There are no official records of that sort of thing, don't you know? A jumble sale is a most unbureaucratic affair. But one does have an inkling of where to begin such a search.'

'Where?'

'The only spinster in the village.'

'Follow me,' warbled Rocco with a nervous vibrato in his voice. He grabbed a length of tattered tow rope from the boot and walked in impatient circles around Ruby's Volvo, shaking his arms as if limbering up for a sporting event. 'Hurry, before anyone sees us.'

64

'Hold on, Rocco. I need to check the handbrake is working. If the car rolls from here it goes straight over the cliffs into the sea.'

Satisfied that the car was secure, Ruby climbed out of the driving seat and looked around. Cap Creus was a barren outcrop, just a few miles from Dalí's birthplace at Cadaqués. It was the easternmost end of the Pyrenees mountain range, the point at which sea smashed against granite. No one lived here. This isolated promontory offered spectacular vistas across the Mediterranean, but the price for that clarity of view was the merciless *tramontana* wind that could blow for days at a time with the strength of a hurricane. It was only thirty minutes' drive from the Dalí Museum at Figueres, but to Ruby it felt like she had arrived on another world.

'Come on, Ruby. It's this way,' said Rocco, skidding down a steep incline towards what appeared to be a lethal drop onto the rocks of the bay. 'Be quick. I don't want to be seen.'

'Why not?'

'Because I don't want them to kill me, remember?'

'Oh yes, your conspiracy obsession. I almost forgot about that. Well, there's no one here.' She looked around at a landscape devoid of human life. 'In fact,' she continued as she tried to follow him, 'there's nothing here at all.'

'On the surface there is nothing. It is what lies beneath that I want to show you.'

'But this has never been an inhabited area. Conditions are too harsh to form settlements. Communities only form around places of shelter, usually with fresh water and fertile soils. It's not a good place to start looking for archaeological remains.'

'I agree. Come on.'

'I hope you're not thinking of tying me up with that rope.'

'Any more silly questions and I might be tempted!' he replied, with a mischievous grin.

Hiding from Charlie in the Mae West room at the museum had seemed like a good idea to Ruby an hour previously. As soon as she had lost sight of him she had ducked beneath the steps of the room's viewing platform and waited for him to leave. Her plan backfired immediately. As soon as Charlie left the installation in search of her, Rocco had emerged and lured her away with enticing tales of a buried treasure of such immeasurable value that it was worth abandoning her responsibility to her indifferent students.

As Rocco tied the rope around a lump of rock and started to lower himself over the edge she began to sense an imminent anticlimax.

'Why did I let you ruin my time at the Dalí museum for this?' she called.

'Believe me. It gets boring when you spend the whole night there.'

'I barely had an hour. And when are you going to tell me why you were hiding out in the museum, Rocco?'

'Forget the museum,' said Rocco. 'It is merely a front.'

'A front for what?'

'You'll see. When I reach that ledge, I want you to take this rope and climb down.'

'You must be kidding,' objected Ruby, looking down at the frayed rope from which Rocco was partly suspended. 'I'll go back to the car and wait for you.'

'You have to trust me, Ruby. This cave is important. Its contents will astound you. It could change everything.'

Within his words Ruby detected a suggestion of pride. What he could be proud of she had yet to ascertain. It plainly wasn't his ability to keep out of trouble. She glanced beneath her. Rocco was now on a ledge about twenty feet below her, and at least twice that distance above a grumbling sea. He released the rope and signalled for her to begin the short descent.

She sat on the edge and studied the terrain. There were hand and foot holds here and there. It looked feasible to make the climb without the rope, and Rocco had only intended to use it as a safety measure. She could do this, she told herself. Her Altberg walking boots could take the strain. Her hands were tough enough to cling to the rocks and the rope. Three points of contact at all times, she reminded herself. Stick to that rule and she would be fine.

Grabbing the rope with both hands she eased herself over the edge and utterly failed to find a foothold. She was left dangling in mid-air above a shoreline that threatened to break her into tiny pieces.

'To your right,' called Rocco. 'There's a place for your foot. And put your left hand in that cavity.'

She found the holds and caught her breath, suppressing the sense of embarrassment at her incompetence. Don't look down, she told herself. Just find somewhere for a foot or a hand, one inch at a time.

'That's good,' said Rocco. 'I know it's a little rough, but it will be worth it, I promise.'

He guided her down the final few feet to the ledge and gave her a moment to compose herself.

'That wasn't so bad,' she said.

'No,' he replied. 'The hard bit is getting back up again.'

She considered whether now might be an appropriate time to slap him, but given their precarious situation she chose to delay retribution. Rocco sidled past her to the inner recess of the ledge and pointed his arm into a vertical fissure in the rock. It scarcely seemed possible that this was the entrance to a cave; from the front it was almost entirely invisible. Turning himself side-on, he breathed in hard and squeezed through the fissure.

Ruby stood alone on the ledge wondering about health and safety. Her head was still sore from the incident with the stone goddess. Should they be wearing protective hardhats in the cave? Was this gap in the mountain stable? Could the sides close in behind them, trapping them for eternity beneath millions of tons of Pyrenean stone? Having to turn sideways to squeeze into a mountain triggered a sense of claustrophobia beyond that of digging in tight trenches –and she had more curves to cram into that space than Rocco – but she felt there was no viable alternative. Sometimes you just have to go for it, she decided, sliding uncomfortably through the fissure and into a cavern.

Rocco produced a transparent, waterproof bag from his pocket, slid it open and extracted a smartphone. With two finger swipes he switched on its flashlight app. Ruby could now see that the cave was about thirty feet wide and sufficiently high that if any stalactites came loose it would hurt. The air was stale and damp. Rocco's beam of torchlight swung carefully, lighting everything apart from one wall. Shadows danced eerily. He turned off the app and they were engulfed in pure darkness.

'Imagine, Ruby. Sense this place. Feel its history.'

'Get on with it. I don't trust you without the light on.'

'The year is 1937,' said Rocco.

'No it isn't.'

He sighed.

'Imagine it is 1937. Catalonia is in turmoil. The civil

war is raging all around. Salvador Dalí is at the peak of his fame. He has travelled and worked throughout Europe and America, and he wants to come home to his beloved Catalonia. But he is terrified for his life. He knows of the tragic fate that befell Lorca in the hands of the revolutionaries and he daren't show his face. He feels the urge to paint a great work close to home, but he knows it can never be publicly acknowledged. So he comes here. To this cave.'

'Are you saying you've found a painting Dalí left behind in a cave?' she asked, not knowing if she was facing her invisible companion.

'Sense his presence, Ruby. His slim body sliding through the fissure in the rock face, into a cave that only he knew about. Picture him with his paints, projecting his dreams onto the wall so that the image would remain here long after his life was over. You can feel him standing here, can you not?'

'There's no mention that Dalí did cave paintings in any of the books about him. This must be a fake.'

'No one knew, therefore no one wrote about it. That doesn't make it impossible,' replied Rocco.

'So how come you've found something that no one knew about?'

'I'm sure you're aware of the legends of portals in the Pyrenees,' Rocco began.

'Only in the sense that Dalí had a fascination with the idea and depicted portals in many of his paintings,' she replied. 'Are we going to stand here in the dark all day or are you going to show me this thing?'

'Some think that caves might be the entrances to such portals. Dalí also wrote about a sacred cave that he had found, and most people believe it to be the Devil's Cave, which is just a kilometre or two from here. But I studied his paintings of the era. I compared the shapes of objects and clouds with the coastline of this area. The clue was there for all to see. It's just that I was the first to see it.'

'So just turn on the bloody torch and let me see this painting,' groaned Ruby, attempting to cloak her childlike enthusiasm.

'Are you ready for this?' asked Rocco.

'If course I am. Get on with it.'

Rocco fiddled with his smartphone and produced a beam of light which illuminated their feet. He teased Ruby's eager eyes by shining it back and forth without actually showing her the wall. Finally, he relented and pointed the light directly at the spot that Dalí had worked on decades before.

The wall of the cave was blank.

'Where is it?' she asked.

'What? Shit! What happened? It was here!'

He shone his light around the rest of the chamber in the vain hope that he had lost his bearings and was looking in the wrong place. There was nothing.

'Really, Rocco, you've gone too far this time. I'm fed up with your stupid practical jokes. I could have been killed climbing down that cliff face. Once I've dropped you back at Figueres I never want to see you again.'

'No,' he protested, 'it was here. I saw a genuine Dalí right on this wall. I can't believe those maniacs destroyed it.'

He sounded earnest. He believed his little story, even if she thought it ridiculous.

'And what did this fictional painting depict?' she asked him.

It took him a few moments to compose himself before he could answer coherently.

'It incorporated many of the themes that appear in his works from that period,' he explained. 'There was a door representing a portal in the sky above the mountains, which you see in lots of his pictures. There was a crutch, a loaf of bread, some dismembered bits and pieces of I don't know what. Wait. What am I thinking? Look on my phone. I have the photos I took last time.'

He fumbled with the screen and produced a slightly blurry image of a painting that covered almost the entire wall of the cave. Its themes were surreal. Mind-bending.

'It is his style I suppose,' she said.

He flicked through a series of shots of the same picture, a mixture of close-ups and varying angles that resulted from his attempts to avoid a reflective glare from the flash.

'Interesting,' said Ruby.

'I accept your apology.'

'What apology?'

'Very gracious of you.'

'But Rocco, tell me why you think it dated from the Thirties? After all, you could have done this,' she said. 'Anyone could have come here and painted something in the Dalí style.'

He turned the flashlight app back on and searched around the floor of the cave.

'Ahah,' he said, bending down to pick up a small tin box from the floor. It was heavily calcified by its decades-long exposure to water rich in minerals. Ruby failed to recognise it as anything in particular. 'I found this, and several others. These boxes contained his paints. I have opened one. They are packaged in a way that was discontinued in 1940. And that correlates to the date Dalí has put in the bottom corner of the painting.' He switched from the flashlight to the photo of the painting and zoomed in on the appropriate part. 'Thirty-seven. See?'

Ruby had to admit that it resembled Dalí's hand, and

the photographs appeared to show a tinge of age and patchy calcification over the painting that meant it could not have been created in recent times. The idea that this had been a genuine, lost Dalí masterpiece started to plant itself in her sceptical mind.

'If you're right about this, Rocco, it would have been worth millions.'

'Millions? Absolutely. But no one could have taken it away in one piece.'

'They got a Banksy off a wall,' pointed out Ruby. 'It can be done.'

Rocco aimed the light at the base of the vandalised wall. He picked up some pieces of rubble and turned them around in his hand.

'Look. Paint. It's all still here. They smashed it but they didn't steal it.'

'Perhaps it can be put back? I've restored Roman murals that were in smaller pieces than this. We'll have to get this place officially protected.'

She had no need to question the reason for Rocco's sudden laughter. His distrust for authority was blatant in his expression.

'Who else knows about it, then?' asked Ruby.

'Obviously, someone with an interest in Dalí is aware of this place. And I'm fairly sure it's the same person who wants me dead.'

'You think someone connected with Dalí is after you?'

'It's not just me,' he replied. 'Other chrononauts had brake failures too. All of us associated with Project Keo have been targeted. While we were all looking up at the sky, someone was under our cars sabotaging them.'

Ruby recalled the Spanish car she had seen making a rapid exit from the car park at Périllos. That could have been the culprit. She was glad to have used trains and taxis that day.

'But the chrononaut message in the sky thing was over the border in France,' she said. 'It had nothing to do with Dalí.'

'It's Project Keo that's the problem. I know too much.'

'Could have fooled me,' she mumbled.

'Seriously. I think someone from the future is trying to change their past by eradicating me and the other chrononauts.'

Now it was Ruby's turn to laugh.

'I don't see why your knowledge of Keo is a problem to anyone,' said Ruby. 'The Keo satellite hasn't launched. The time capsule is still on the ground somewhere. What's the big deal about Keo?'

Rocco said nothing. He drew a deep breath for dramatic effect, then produced one of the photographs on his phone once again. He slid his fingers to magnify the part of the painting that featured an open door in the sky, signifying a portal to another dimension. It was a glass door, and there was writing depicted on its far side, readable in reverse.

'O. E. K,' said Ruby.

'Keo,' said Rocco. 'Don't you see? Keo worked. The time capsule will be received in the future. A message will be sent back in time.'

'You mean like the one you were looking for at Périllos?'

'Exactly. Only it came too soon. Maybe they had a reason to send it too early? Who knows? But what I know is this: a message was sent. And the person who received it is the same person who painted the picture in this cave.'

'So, when the chrononauts chose Opoul castle at Périllos as the site for the receipt of the message, they based their choice on a clue in Dalí's painting of the station at Perpignan, not realising that he had created that painting precisely because he had already seen the message they were looking for?'

'You are correct, Ruby.'

'So what do you think the message said?' she asked.

'If I can figure that out, perhaps I can find out why they want to kill me. And you.'

Charlie yawned. The reclining chair was too comfortable, accommodating his bulk with ease. As a form of imprisonment and torture, Charlie reckoned he could do worse. At times during the hours he had spent alone in this plain, subterranean room he had drifted off, dreaming of the busy museum above his head, then waking up and wondering why the old man was keeping him locked up for so long.

When the old man finally unlocked the door and entered the room, he appeared to have lost none of his earlier irritability.

'You're a busy guy,' said Charlie, standing up, 'so I won't keep you any longer. Thanks for the chance to use this chair and stuff.'

'I have a proposal for you,' the old man said, pulling a digital camera from his pocket. 'Sit down.'

Charlie sat back down in the chair. He didn't know what the old man meant by a proposal, but it sounded like it might involve work. This could be bad.

'You are in a great deal of trouble,' stated the old man, his unique accent laden with gravitas. 'But if you will do something for us, we will not prosecute you and we will not inform the authorities in London and New York that we have you in our custody.' As he spoke, he fiddled with the controls on the tiny camera, seemingly unfamiliar with its workings. When he eventually mastered it, he took a close-up snap of Charlie's face, and then returned the camera to his pocket.

Charlie's fears were confirmed. There was going to be work involved.

'I'm kinda booked up,' said the American, 'but I could probably fit you guys in next year sometime.'

'You will immediately embark on this task. Our museum has a fine collection, in spite of the efforts of crooks such as yourself. But there is a piece missing. A classic Dalí painting. It was stolen from us many years ago. We have tracked it down. It is not far from here. You will steal it back for us.'

'Can't you guys just ask them nicely to give it back?'

'The keeper of this painting is not someone to whom it would be appropriate to make such a request.'

'What is he? Gangster dude? Godfather?'

'I cannot tell you anything about the person from whom you will retrieve our property.'

'What about sending the cops to get it?'

The old man seemed to shudder.

'Police know nothing about art. We need a professional.'

'And he's coming with me, is he?'

'Who?'

'The professional dude.'

The old man failed to betray even a glimmer of a smile. This obese American art thief had a relentless sense of humour, and humour was something that the old man had never been able to comprehend. The earlier comment about eating a Dalí portrait, he now understood, was something known as a 'tongue-in-cheek' remark, but why anyone would make such a remark remained a mystery to him.

He didn't trust Charlie, but that didn't matter. The

75

mission was not important in itself. The artwork Charlie was going to steal for him wasn't even genuine and the person from whom he would steal it wouldn't even object. For the painting in question hung on his own wall, in his own home. He just wanted to know if this brazen thief would obey his instructions. If not, he was no great loss. The police would deal with him in their own way, probably deport him back to the United States or to London to face prosecution for the recent thefts of Dalí paintings. But, if he returned with the painting, he would be instructed on the true mission.

He handed Charlie an address and a postcard-sized print of the painting. There was a bed and a chair in the foreground, with depressions in the mattress and cushions suggesting the presence of invisible people. Adjacent to these items was a pedestal upon which sat a sparkling ruby.

'This it?'

'This is the portrait. *Surrealist Composition with Invisible Figures.*'

'Can't be worth much.'

'Why would you make such an observation?'

'Tiny.'

The old man again failed to smile. His inability to relate to the sense of humour of his new recruit caused an icy moment.

'You must cause no visible damage to the property or to the painting, which, I'm sure I do not need to point out, measures a metre in height with the frame.'

'No damage, huh?'

'None whatsoever. I want you to show me how professional you can be. The property is secured with five lever locking systems and a remote-monitored Yale alarm system, with movement sensors in every room and a magnetic sensor behind the painting.'

'Magnetic sensor, huh?'

'Yes.'

'Interesting.' Charlie knew nothing about magnetic sensors.

'You know how to deal with this challenge?'

'Piece of cake.'

Ratty pressed his nose against an opaque pane. The window rattled loosely on its sashes and the glass misted up. Through the condensation he could see two sofas, a coffee table and a bookcase. Bull's-eye. He stepped aside, crushing a chrysanthemum, and let the Patient stand next to him in the damp shrubbery.

'That's her book collection,' he said.

'How can an individual nurture their mind on such a meagre library?' asked the Patient.

'Precisely,' replied Ratty. 'Her attitude to the male sex may indeed indicate a paucity of learning. Greer has a great deal to answer for. Anyway, she's out. Come on.'

He led his friend to the rear of the cottage. They were dressed in the nearest Ratty could find to an all-black costume appropriate for housebreaking and burglary: dinner suits minus the bow ties. The Patient carried an old chisel with a wooden handle, and Ratty held a hammer in his hand. Constable Stuart, had he cycled past them on his daily beat, would have had trouble believing their pre-prepared excuse of doing a favour for a neighbour with a sticky door, thought Ratty. It was a risk he was comfortable taking. Retrieving his mother's copy of *The Female Eunuch* would give him the final letter in the series of clues she had left for him before her disappearance. He took the chisel, held it against the edge of the door, and whacked it with the hammer. When it was jammed in the gap between the frame and the lock mechanism he pushed it from side to side until the catch popped open. He pulled the door, nodded at the Patient, and the two men compounded their criminal damage with trespass by entering the home of their victim.

'Don't touch anything,' whispered Ratty. 'Finger dabs and wotnot.'

The Patient had already run his fingers along the textured wallpaper. Ratty turned round and saw him feeling the cold, steel bumps on the radiator. He shook his head and entered the living room. There was the bookcase. He scanned its resident tomes, cringing at some of the overtly intellectual and female-centric titles. And there, on the second shelf down, was the book he had come for.

'Did you bring something to replace it?'

The Patient nodded and produced a hardback book from inside his dinner jacket. Ratty swapped the books, noting with amusement that the Patient had selected a collection of the invectives of Jeremy Clarkson to exchange for *The Female Eunuch*. The theft would be mitigated by leaving a replacement volume, and that eased Ratty's conscience as he gripped his mother's book and led the Patient back to the rear door of the cottage.

He was feeling so satisfied with the execution of Operation Book that he barely noticed Constable Stuart standing in the garden, surveying the damage to the door frame. Ratty recognised the policeman and ducked behind the kitchen table before he had been spotted. The Patient, however, walked out the door and introduced himself.

'Pleased to meet you. I am a friend of Lord Ballashiels.'

'Justin? Is that you in there?'

Ratty stretched to his full height, but couldn't lift his

shamed head. He had been caught in the act. This was going to take some explaining. The officer had seen it all during his long career, and his path had crossed with Ratty's on many occasions, not all of them social. Most recently he had been involved in the repossession of Ratty's stately home following years of declining wealth and accumulating debt, and decades previously he had been there during the sad months when the whole village had searched for Ratty's mother. He appeared to have a soft spot for the aristocrat, and had expressed pleasure upon learning that a benefactor had bought the manor and returned it to its rightful owner.

'Obviously, I have an excellent explanation for my behaviour, constable,' said Ratty.

'Obviously.'

'And I intend fully to provide you with that explanation. No questions will remain unanswered, of course.'

'Of course.'

'And I understand that anything I say may be taken down and wotnot.'

'So, Justin, what are you doing in this property?'

'We are here to steal a book,' explained the Patient. '*The Female Eunuch*. Perhaps you have read it?'

'Indeed?'

Ratty sighed. His friend had his uses, but he could sometimes be a significant liability.

'Even though petty crime may seem an unlikely venture for those such as Lord Ballashiels and myself, our guilt in this enterprise is beyond question,' explained the Patient, digging an even deeper hole in which Ratty felt himself falling. 'However, statistically speaking, the presence in this garden of an officer of the law at the precise time of our criminal undertaking is beyond the likelihood of random chance. I therefore conclude that you had prior knowledge of our intentions. And since that is impossible, I must also conclude that something deeply disturbing is afoot that I have yet to comprehend.'

Constable Stuart looked at Ratty and raised his eyebrows.

'Your friend's a right one, isn't he? All that nonsense about you two committing crimes together. Never heard anything so funny in all my years. Come on, lads. Off you go. Don't mention any more about that feminist malarkey, and I won't mention anything about anything. Understood?'He winked at Ratty.

'Er, right ho,' Ratty replied. 'Gosh. Look at the time. Come along, Patient chappy.'

They scurried out of the cottage like scolded schoolboys, high on the buzz of the oddly successful mission. Parked on the street outside was a locksmith's van. Constable Stuart waved at the locksmith. He grabbed a bag of tools and trotted to the rear of the cottage, ready to make good the damage.

Ratty and the Patient looked at each other with eyes that registered disbelief and mutual suspicion. But neither could have leaked their plan. It had been a spur of the moment decision to walk to the village and raid the home of the local feminist, with only minutes of planning and preparation during which neither of them had been alone. No one else could possibly have known. The only other person at the manor was the mechanic fixing the Land Rover's brakes, and he hadn't even entered the house. And if someone had discovered their plan, how come they were acting as if to assist in their quest? The Patient's considerable capacity for logical deduction was on overdrive, and yet it had failed to reach a conclusion other than that something was very odd about this village, and that included the behaviour of two darkly dressed men across the street who ducked behind a telephone box and tried to remain incognito by pulling hats over their faces.

Back at the manor, the mechanic had completed his task and was wiping his oil-stained hands in preparation for handing Ratty a bill for his services.

'I will send you a cheque in due course,' lied the aristocrat, pocketing the invoice and politely shooing the overawed mechanic off his property.

Ratty and the Patient made directly for the library, where they placed the stolen book on a table next to the others. Ratty had resisted opening it until now. There was even a possibility that this wasn't his mother's copy. He opened it and searched for a sign of his mother's handwriting.

It was the letter 'O'.

'Rowell?' asked Ratty, combining it with the letters already extracted from the other books. 'What's a "Rowell"?'

The Patient considered the matter briefly, then announced an alternative.

'Orwell.'

'Orwell? Georgie Boy? Goodness! He was a queer sausage. Orwell. Gosh.'

'So your mother's final message to you concerned Salvador Dalí and George Orwell,' concluded the Patient. 'And are you aware of any connection between them?'

'Orwell thought him a rotten painter. Said so publicly.'

'There is something else that may be indicative of your mother's intention, however.'

'Golly. What else linked Orwell and Dalí, old potato?'

'Catalonia.'

'As in bullfighting and all that kind of how's your father?'

'As in Dalí lived and died there. Orwell chose to go there to fight in the Spanish Civil War. And did you notice, Ratty, that the quotes are all opening lines of books apart from the one from *Les Misérables*, which is from the middle?'

'Can't say I paid that nugget too much heed, old maraca.'

'Do you think it is possible that she intended *Les Misérables* to be the odd one out? Could it be that she wanted you to notice that one more than the others?' asked the Patient.

'I wouldn't have noticed any of them if it hadn't been for you, my friend.'

'Not having been acquainted with your mother I am reluctant to draw excessive inference from these things, but the quotation from *Les Misérables* talks about crossing the mountains. Do you see?'

'Clear as mud, old riddler.'

'If Catalonia is the message she is trying to send to you, the reference to traversing a mountain range might be relevant, since Catalonia can only be reached by crossing the Pyrenees between France and Spain.'

'That seems to be quite a deductive leap from a few literary lines and a jumble of letters. I think we may be over-reaching ourselves.'

'The message is simple because the means of communication must leave no room for ambiguity. The Dalí books point us to Catalonia. The Orwell reference is purely there to reinforce that conclusion. It is the control in a scientific experiment. It is the piece of corroborating evidence. And it is my belief that your mother went to Catalonia to see Dalí in person.'

Ratty walked to the window, so deep in reflection that he failed to notice two men approaching the house.

'I don't know, Patient chappy. Do you really think she went to Spain?'

'Does the evidence point to anywhere else?'

'But she never came back. No one saw her there or anywhere. Are you saying the Dalí fellow bumped her off?'

'No. I'm merely saying that it was your mother's intention to visit him. For reasons we have yet to deduce, either she never reached him or, having done so, she failed to return.'

The bell above his front door tolled. Ratty peered out of the window at the portico. Two figures stood there, hats tilted low to hide their identity, holding garden tools in a manner that did not suggest their intentions were horticultural. He invited the Patient to observe them.

'The same men were watching us in the village,' said the Patient. 'From behind a telephone booth.'

'Box, Patient chappy. We call them "boxes". And something about their ignoble posture reminds me of the intruders I chased away last night.'

'Then it is not impossible that we face a situation of some gravity.'

'How much time do you need to prepare for a trip to the continent, old teabag?' asked Ratty.

'None at all.'

'Passports. Toothbrushes. Back door. Quick. To the Land Rover.'

'What did you do with the rope, you idiot?' shouted Rocco from the ledge.

'I wish I'd tied it round your bloody neck, Rocco,' replied Ruby from within the cave, recoiling at his unanticipated aggression. 'I left it hanging. If it's not there, it's because you didn't tie it properly, which means you might have killed me. I think I know who the idiot really is.'

She emerged into the brightness and looked at their dire situation. The climb to the top appeared almost suicidal. The route down to the sea was certainly so. And there on the rocks far below, utterly out of their reach, lay the rope.

'This is bad,' said Rocco.

'Well I'm so glad you pointed that out,' said Ruby. 'What are we going to do about it?'

'Think of Dalí.'

'Dalí? Now is not the time, Rocco.'

'No, I mean Dalí had to come here on many occasions to work on this painting. He was no mountaineer. He didn't fall. If he can do it, so can we.'

'Perhaps he was better at tying knots than you?'

'Ruby, I was a Venture Scout. Back in Munich. I know a thing or two about knots. That was a bowline. They don't fail.'

'Venture Scout? Hah.'

'What's that supposed to mean?' asked Rocco.

'Scouts are supposed to be prepared. What are your contingency preparations?'

'Do you have another rope in the car? A luggage strap, maybe?'

'I don't think so. And I don't see how that's going to get us out of here. We're just going to have to phone for a humiliating rescue from the authorities.'

'No. Never. We can't risk alerting anyone to our presence here.'

'So we're just going to stay put, are we?' She crossed her arms defensively, then changed her mind and resumed holding on to the cliff wall.

'Wait here,' Rocco ordered.

She rolled her eyes at the stupidity of his instruction and watched as he began to climb the rock face. The narrowness of the ledge meant that she couldn't see more than the soles of his feet once he was above her, inching his way up the perilous cliff. At one point, he clung to his position for more than two minutes, as if stuck or too frightened to continue. Ruby considered asking if he was in difficulty, but since she didn't really care whether he was or not, she decided not to voice any concern.

The feet moved once more, swinging athletically from side to side before finding their next point of contact. Rocco continued his journey upwards. Minutes later he was able to grab the remains of his bowline. The knot had held fast. The rope had been cut.

Ruby watched him disappear from view, only for his face to return a few minutes later.

'Why did you lock the car?' he shouted.

'Why wouldn't I?'

'I was going to cut out a seatbelt and lower it down to you. Do you mind if I smash a window to get in?'

'Oh for God's sake,' she replied, taking a deep breath and beginning the hazardous ascent, determined to arrive before Rocco destroyed her Volvo. Three points of contact, she told herself again. Two feet and one hand, or two hands and one foot. She had to get it right this time. There was nothing to save her if she screwed up as she had on the way down.

The first handholds were within comfortable reach, and she gripped them both hard whilst inserting her right foot into a recess two feet above the ledge. She was committed. Don't look down, she told herself. Don't loosen a hand until the left foot is secure. With both feet implanted in the rock, she reached up with her left hand

and found a notch that felt solid. She eased her body higher, straightened her legs and released her right hand in search of the next level.

This wasn't so challenging, she decided. Stick to the very simple rules and nothing could go wrong. Only look up, and only release one limb at a time. She said it aloud before each movement. She conquered the sense of panic that frequently rose to the front of her mind by breathing steadily. Before long, she could see the stub of rope dangling a few feet above her head. Rocco was leaning over, watching helplessly.

'Nearly there,' he called down to her, extending his arm towards her approaching head.

She reached out her right leg in search of the next foothold. Nothing seemed to be in reach. She adjusted her weight and returned her right foot to its previous slot, then commenced searching for a new position for her left foot. Again, no protrusion or hole was within the circle described by her lower leg.

'You're at the tricky bit,' shouted Rocco. 'You need to swing sideways.'

'What do you mean, sideways? Which side?'

'Er, I think there's a foothold to your right. Or is it left? Hold tight and swing both legs and you'll find it.'

'No way, Rocco. That's too dangerous,' she replied.

'Or if you can take all of your weight in one hand, you can pull yourself straight up.'

This option was equally unappealing to Ruby. She shook her head and clung tightly, saving her energy. The rope was about three feet above her head. Almost within reach. She wondered if it was feasible to reach it with her left hand if she held her body higher with her right whilst abandoning the footholds that currently ensured her safety. Perhaps, but there was no way to test it, and the price of failure was too horrible to contemplate.

'Take your time,' added Rocco, knowing that she was doing precisely that.

Even in her stable position of two footholds and two handholds, there was a limit to how long she could remain there. Her muscles were tiring. Circulation was faltering. Her situation was beginning to look serious. She started to wonder if the longer she took to think about her next move, the less strength she would have with which to execute it. When the wave of panic washed over her once again, even her deep breaths could not control it.

She was going to have to commit to taking a risk that would determine her entire future. Upwards or sideways, that was the question. Her instinct wanted to go directly up, but she doubted that she had the capability to hold her weight in one hand. A sideways swing in search of a foothold was now her only chance. As she refreshed her grip on the two handholds above her head, ready for them to take the load of her body in motion, she felt something hit the top of her head. Thinking it might be a rockfall, she tucked her face tight against the cliff.

'Can you reach it now?' called Rocco.

She felt the top of her head. The rope was swaying there, within her grasp. She wrapped it around her wrist and pulled against it. There was resistance. She pulled harder and grabbed it with her other hand.

The rope dragged her up the rock face and onto horizontal ground.

'Quickly. Let's get moving,' said Rocco, glancing all around him. 'The line was cut. They left the bowline around the rock. I managed to untie it and lower it down to you.'

She lay panting, relieved to be out of danger but

conscious of a nagging frustration that she now owed Rocco a considerable debt of gratitude.

'Someone cut the rope?' she asked, getting up. 'How can you be sure?'

'We're in trouble. Come on.'

They walked briskly, unable to hide the urgency in their feet. The steep march back to Ruby's car rendered them vulnerable to anyone perched upon one of the numerous mountainous outcrops, or so Rocco thought. But Ruby was growing tired of his conspiracy paranoia.

'There must be a simple explanation for the rope breaking cleanly like that,' she said breathlessly as stones slipped beneath her shoes. 'Perhaps it was already damaged? It's an old one that came with the car. I never used it, but who knows what the previous owner towed with it?'

Rocco reached the car first.

'Open it. Quick,' he told her, throwing himself prostrate and sliding under the car.

'What are you doing?'

'Brake lines,' he replied. 'It's their usual trick. These mountain roads will kill us if they've cut your brakes too.'

Ruby sat in the driving seat and waited for Rocco to resolve his paranoia. When he was satisfied that no catastrophe was imminent, he took his seat.

'So Dalí painted the word "Keo",' said Ruby as they re-joined the single-track road, 'if indeed it really was painted by him, which I admit seems likely based on the calcification. But did you consider whether his use of the word Keo and the current satellite project could be a coincidence?'

'Everything in life is coincidence if you track it back far enough. Us meeting at Périllos. Us both being born in the same century. On the same planet.'

Ruby grinned, recalling that she had previously considered Rocco to be sufficiently weird to make him something other than indigenous to the planet Earth. And yet she had detected a change in him since his car accident. The practical jokes had ceased. He had become more intense, more serious, more annoying.

'But have you eliminated the possibility that Dalí was referencing another Keo? Something contemporaneous with his lifespan? Something completely unrelated to the time capsule?'

'The Cypriot beer brand Keo was around in the Thirties. Dalí never went to Cyprus. So he wouldn't have known about that beer.'

'Someone might have told him,' suggested Ruby. 'He might have read something.'

'Dalí did not subscribe to the Good Beer Guide or any such thing,' explained Rocco, beginning to sound frustrated at the wall of cynicism he always had to climb. 'And you are missing the most important point. You were there. At Périllos. We received no message from the future. Can you not see what that means?'

'Apart from it meaning that you're clearly bonkers for thinking it would arrive in the first place?' asked Ruby as she threaded the car down a twisty lane.

'If we send a message to the future and we get no reply, it means something serious.'

'Like what?'

'It means they sent the reply to someone else, to Dalí. And if they did that, it was because they had a good reason. Something has gone badly wrong somewhere.'

Ruby let out a snort of derision and amusement.

'Rocco, a lack of message at the requested time could mean a million different things,' said Ruby, beginning an attempt to return some sanity to the conversation. 'Maybe the Keo satellite never gets launched in the first place. Maybe the rocket blows up. Maybe the time capsule survives but is never found. Maybe it's found and ignored. Maybe it's found and read but it turns out they haven't conquered the art of sending messages back through time after all, which wouldn't surprise me since it's impossible anyway.'

'It doesn't point to that,' said Rocco. 'The capsule will arrive, I know it. A message will be sent ... has been sent ... you know what I mean, but they didn't send it to us. The plan has changed because something bad has happened. Well, I mean something bad is going to happen. It hasn't happened yet, but it will. Do you follow me? And that means it's not too late to stop it.'

'Why do we need to stop it?'

'We have to stop it because we need the future to go right. Something went wrong and that has changed the past. So the past has gone wrong, too. And that affects everyone.'

'You're making no sense, Rocco. Again,' said Ruby.

'The message didn't come to us at Périllos in this century like we asked. The message inside the Keo time capsule says to send the message to Périllos, on the first of May, between three and four in the afternoon, and in any year from 2000 to 2050.'

'So it might not be coming to us for a few years?' asked Ruby.

'Weren't you paying attention? That painting in the cave proves that they've already sent their message. They sent it almost a century too early. They sent it to Dalí. It's the only way he could have known about Keo.'

'Why would they send the message earlier than the capsule instructed?' asked Ruby.

'I have no idea, but I think I'm onto something huge.'

'If Dalí got a message from the future about Keo – which he didn't, because it's impossible – he probably couldn't understand it, which is irrelevant because he didn't receive any such message anyway, but I'm trying to see things from your skewed perspective. So you probably think in your little world of delusion that he painted all that crazy and surreal stuff, trying to interpret what he saw, becoming obsessed with immortality, and painting portals to other dimensions? Is that what you're getting at?'

The car had now reached a junction. Ruby took the right fork to Figueres.

'Where are you going?' asked Rocco.

'To the Dalí museum, of course.'

Rocco grabbed her leg, almost causing the kind of accident he had been so keen to avoid. She shook away his hand and steadied the wheel.

'We will not go back there,' he ordered.

'They need to be told about the painting in the cave. They'll have experts who can verify it better than me, and they can ensure that it's repaired and preserved. We can't just let it rot.'

'The museum already knows about the painting. Trust me, Ruby. I did some research while I was hiding in that place. I found files. I hacked computers. Something is going on. I don't know what it is, but I don't like it.'

'So where *should* we go? If you're in as much danger as you seem to think, should you consider leaving Spain altogether? I'd be happy to drop you off in France.'

She pulled into a side road and made a three-point turn, ready to head the other way.

'That won't be enough,' said Rocco in a sombre, resigned tone. 'It's both of us. They've been watching you too. We're in too deep. They won't rest until they have us.

We can't hide and we can't beat them.'

'So what are we going to do?' asked Ruby, now sensing a growing disquiet in her stomach that threatened to develop into outright fear in spite of the calming effect of the rational side of her mind.

'Back to your original plan. Go to the museum. Get them to think we're on their side.'

'Of course I'm on their side, for God's sake,' said Ruby. 'I'm an archaeologist. I'm on the side of any museum.'

'Not like this one, Ruby. This was set up by Dalí himself. He designed it. Built it in memorial to his own greatness. But someone there is rotten to the core. I don't know if this was Dalí's intention, but someone there is working to a higher agenda. Connected to Keo. Important enough to kill for. Driven by the future. We have to start working with them.'

The ridiculous situation was making her head spin. She was tempted to turn back to Figueres and drop her companion off at the railway station so he could get out of her life and allow her to return to normality.

'Fine. Just make your mind up,' she said.

'Our only chance to find out their motives and goals, and to remove ourselves from their most-wanted list, is to infiltrate their organisation at the highest level.'

'Just how exactly do you expect to be able to change someone's mind from wanting to assassinate you to being your best friend?' asked Ruby.

'Not me. Us, remember? And it's all part of my plan.'

'Which is what?'

'I'm working on it. Give me twenty-four hours to come up with something, then we'll go see them.'

'But since we're going there anyway,' said Ruby, 'I'm going to let them know about the possible Dalí painting we found vandalised in that cave.'

'That will not be necessary.'

'Why not?'

'Because I'm convinced it was someone from the museum who destroyed it.'

'In this so-called country,' explained Ratty as he swerved to correct his instincts after driving off the train at the Gallic end of the Channel Tunnel, 'the locals drive on the wrong side of the road.'

'One man's wrong is also another man's wrong,' replied the Patient.

'And the French eat anything that moves. Frogs. Snails. Worms.'

The Patient was no longer paying attention to Ratty's sardonic mutterings. He was studying the other cars snaking their way out of the terminal. He suspected one of them, a black Ford Focus, had followed them from Shropshire to Folkestone, maintaining a respectful distance all the way.

'We must not drive in the direction of Spain,' decided the Patient.

'Isn't that going to make it somewhat tricky to get to Spain?'

'We are being pursued. We must not let them know our true intentions.'

'So what do you suggest?'

'Drive to Belgium.'

'Home of real chocolate. None of that Lanvin nonsense. Which way's Belgium?'

The Patient pointed left just as Ratty turned right. They drove on in a vaguely southerly direction, quickly forgetting the Belgium plan, sticking to the *Déparmentale* roads which better suited the leisurely pace of the Land

Rover. The sinister Ford Focus was no longer behind them. The continent opened out ahead. Beneath the patchy shadows of trees, all seemed right with the world to Ratty.

A sign indicated an imminent side turning. The rule of *Priorité à Droite* applied: give way to the right, slowing down to allow a waiting vehicle to join the road. A black car sat at the junction. Ratty squeezed his recently repaired brakes.

'Curse de Gaulle and his insane proclamations of priority,' groaned Ratty as he slowed almost to a halt. The car at the junction began to move forward.

'Keep going,' said the Patient. 'It is that car again. Don't stop.'

It was too late to accelerate, however. The engine responded to the heavy right foot with plenty of noise and very little action. The Ford now blocked their way completely. Ratty jabbed the brakes again, with equally minimal effect. The lumbering beast of the Land Rover collided with the rear of the Ford. There was no visible damage to the already battered Land Rover, but the Ford was severely dented. One of its light clusters had shattered, the bumper was cracked and hanging off, and the hatchback door was crumpled. In spite of the Patient's suggestion that they drive off, Ratty felt it would be inappropriate not to swap insurance details. Besides, for better or worse, it would answer the question regarding the identity and intention of the driver. He turned off the engine and climbed out.

The Ford Focus driver came towards him.

'Fancy bumping into you in France, Justin,' said Constable Stuart.

'Er, yes, sorry about that, officer. Bit of trouble with de Gaulle's rules. Seems my old Landy has redesigned the rear of your runabout.'

Stuart looked at the damage to his car and shook his head.

'I don't know what you're talking about, Justin. I can't see any damage.'

'What about the lights, and the bumper, and the dent?'

'Nonsense. It was probably already like that.'

'But there is a piece of your indicator lens stuck to my front bumper, constable.'

Stuart picked the plastic fragment from Ratty's bumper and threw it onto the road.

'No there isn't. Now run along, and let's not hear any more of this.'

The Patient joined them at the roadside.

'I don't have the capacity to work out the odds against our meeting like this on foreign soil on the same day as our encounter at that cottage this morning, but I suspect we have gone far beyond the believable realms of coincidence,' said the Patient.

'Can't a village bobby take a holiday?'

'In uniform?' asked the Patient.

'Without your lady wife?' asked Ratty. 'And where are you going to, anyway?'

'Don't you concern yourself with minor details like that. I'll keep well out of your way. You'll hardly know I'm here. By the way, the best route to Spain is via Rouen if you want to avoid the Paris *Périphérique*.'

'But nobody knows we're going to Spain,' protested Ratty before he realised he might have walked into a verbal trap.

'That's right,' said Stuart. 'Nobody knows. And let's make sure we keep it that way, shall we?'

'Gosh, right-ho,' said Ratty.

'Good. Well I'll be off then. Looking forward to my holiday immensely.'

Constable Stuart returned to his car and drove slowly away, part of his plastic bumper dragging along the road behind him. Before the road turned out of sight of Ratty and the Patient, the Ford Focus stopped. Stuart remained in the car, calmly looking in his rear-view mirror, waiting.

'Does anything about this incident strike you as queer, Patient chappy?'

The Patient was distracted by a snail he had found close to the road. He picked it up and held it in front of his mouth.

'This is the staple diet of a Frenchman?' he asked.

'No, not like that. Even Johnny Frenchman wouldn't eat it raw.'

The Patient returned it to the ground.

'Do you not see, Ratty? The concept of eating a gastropod mollusc is, as you say, queer, but it happens, and there is a reason for it. I can only assume that the reason is related to being in a state of imminent starvation should the snail be omitted from the dinner plate, but that isn't important. Do you follow me?'

Ratty nodded, relieved not to have been subjected to the sight of his friend attempting to eat uncooked *escargots*.

'And if culinary queerness can be explained away to a state of rationality, of normality,' the Patient continued, 'then surely the oddity of a Shropshire village policeman following us to France and, presumably, all the way to Spain, must have a reason too. Behind the strangeness is that hidden rationality that makes everything seem normal.'

They returned to the Land Rover and drove off. As they passed Constable Stuart, still waiting in his car, he pulled away and followed them at the same polite distance that he had maintained all the way from England.

Ratty and the Patient exchanged glances and pushed on, unsure what to think of their police escort.

'Since we're on the trail of Dalí and Orwell, what do you know of Orwell, old encyclopaedia?'

'He went to Spain to fight in the civil war and was shot in the throat,' replied the Patient with uncharacteristic brevity.

'Right. Too tall for the trenches, I heard. Head and shoulders above his comrades. Bad show. Not good for the old G and T consumption. I shouldn't wonder. Pour it down your throat and it leaks out all over your neck. Bally waste.'

'The question we must ask,' said the Patient, 'is why an Englishman should feel motivated to fight in the war of another country.'

'I see your point. Peculiar thing to do, but there must be a reason. And if Orwell had good cause to go to Spain and get shot in the neck, Mother must have had her reasons too. Orwell is her way of showing that abandoning me and father and dashing off to Catalonia was done for a jolly good purpose.'

Ratty paused to dislodge the lump that had just materialised in his throat. He took a couple of slow breaths before continuing.

'She wanted me to follow her trail when I was old enough. She wanted me to find her.'

Once again, the contrary plans of his body forced him to stop speaking. There were tears to form, cold sweats to develop, and knots to tie in his stomach. It was as much as he could do to keep driving under such an emotional onslaught. The Patient waited in silence while Ratty struggled against his sentiments. A considerable while later, and with a sense that the Land

Rover was being pushed to its admittedly modest upper limits of speed, Ratty managed to say, 'Golly, I do rather hope I haven't left it too late.'

Charlie looked once again at the address he had been given, but the words on the card bore no relation to the street signs, which in turn appeared completely unrelated to the roads currently showing on the satnav unit. His evening was starting to suck. Art theft was boring. He abandoned the task he had been set and drove towards Empuriabrava, hoping he could stalk Ruby for a few hours.

Seconds later he glimpsed it: the road sign indicating the address he had been sent to burgle. He pulled up outside the house and stared at it. The property was modern, minimalist, its design principles dominated by Le Corbusier but with an unsettling hint of Speer. There were large windows with no curtains, and from over the garden wall he could see immense paintings hanging in the living room, lit by a single lamp. He exited Van Gogh and crept closer to the main gates. The level of security became obvious: sensors; cameras; wires. He walked up to the iron gates and pressed the button set into one of the adjacent pillars.

A woman's voice crackled through the intercom.

'Hi. Speak English?' Charlie asked.

'*Sí*. I mean, yes,' replied the woman. 'The owner of the house is out. I am his housekeeper. Can I help you?'

'I've come for the painting,' said Charlie. 'Am I at the right house?'

'Yes, of course. Is this something to do with my boss?'

'Boss? Dunno. Some old guy wants it for the museum. The Dalí dude museum.'

'Ah, no problem. He said someone might try to take

the picture for the museum tonight.'

With a buzz and a click, the gates swung majestically open. Charlie strolled up the driveway to the front door where the housekeeper was waiting. She was a few years younger than the man at the museum who had set this task for him. Her complexion was dark; her deep, shadowy features owed far more to the region's gene pool than those of the old man. And she certainly didn't look like the kind of person who had stolen a priceless work of art.

He showed her the postcard size print. She nodded in recognition.

'I'll give you a hand with it,' she said. 'It's rather heavy.'

She turned off the alarm system and, with Charlie's help, lifted the portrait from the wall and carried it to Van Gogh where it fitted comfortably upon the rear bed. Without a scratch, the artwork was ready to be returned to the museum, and nothing had been damaged at the house. Charlie had managed to do something right.

He drove back to Figueres with his proud booty and phoned the old man to come and meet him on the street beside the museum. When the old man stepped outside and inspected Charlie's booty he showed no evidence of pleasure or gratitude, but Charlie was grateful nevertheless for the absence of anger.

Charlie followed the old man back inside. This time he was led upstairs to an office. On the door was a modest aluminium sign that read 'Director'. The old man ushered Charlie into the room. It was furnished with a large desk, a leather swivel chair, a filing cabinet and a meeting table. There was no hint of any association with Dalí. No artwork, sculptures or books that would connect this 'director' to the museum below. It was as if the old man had a different agenda from the stewardship of surrealist paintings.

Another man was present in the room, sitting at the meeting table and holding an envelope. His chubby middle-aged figure was squeezed into an expensive suit that must have been made for someone else and the stubble atop his shaven head glistened with an oily hue. Charlie felt a sickening sense that this was how he might end up looking in later life if he didn't start taking care of himself. The portly stranger nodded a greeting, squeezing his double chin out to the sides like a balloon as he did so. Charlie reached out to shake his hand, but found instead that the envelope was forced into his palm.

'This is Grant,' said the old man. 'He is one of my people. He has been preparing everything you will need.'

Again, Charlie succumbed to a fascination with the old man's accent. It was as if he was not the product of any country. The voice belonged nowhere. The old man spoke with an undertone of tragedy, like a lost soul, abandoned by the world.

'Everything I need, huh?' asked Charlie. 'Need for what?'

'Everything you need for your mission, sir,' said Grant in a clipped and elegant voice that surprised Charlie because it seemed to carry an undertone of menace just beneath surface of the rounded English vowels. Charlie eyed Grant cautiously and squeezed the envelope. It felt bulky.

'My mission?' He wondered how these guys could have known about his plan to visit every European branch of Dunkin' Donuts.

'Take a seat, sir,' said Grant, pulling out a chair for Charlie.

'Grant has left nothing to chance,' said the old man. 'He has done well to assemble these things at such short notice. Open it.'

100

Charlie made himself comfortable on the chair before ripping open the envelope and sprinkling the contents onto the table.

'First class travel documents. False passport. American money. It's all there, sir,' said Grant.

'First class, huh?'

'Yes. You will feel more refreshed upon arrival, sir.'

'They do donuts in first?'

Grant ignored the question and fanned through the banknotes.

'Sixty thousand dollars, sir. We can drop off more if you need it.'

Charlie's face lit up. He began spending the cash in his head immediately and became so engrossed in his fantasies that he scarcely noticed when the old man dismissed his assistant. Grant nodded, left the room, and closed the door behind him When Charlie's mind had filled to overflowing with the fabulous consumer goods he was going to buy with the money, he smiled with satisfaction and asked his next question.

'Where am I supposed to go?'

'New York,' came the old man's reply. 'You fly this evening.'

'To do what?'

'Listen very carefully. This is important.'

'Important, huh?'

'Yes, and you are not listening.'

'I am so.'

'Then why do you keep interrupting?' the old man shouted, before calming himself with deep breaths. 'Listen. In 1939 the New York World's Fair took place at Flushing Meadows. Salvador Dalí designed one of the exhibits. Next to his exhibit they buried a time capsule containing items that represented society in the Thirties and ten million words on microfilm. It was intended to remain buried for five thousand years.'

'Coolsville.'

He handed Charlie a slim book. In slightly wonky print the cover read simply "THE TIME CAPSULE". He flicked through its yellowing pages and read the full version of the title inside: "The Book of Record of The Time Capsule of Cupaloy deemed capable of resisting the effects of time for five thousand years – preserving an account of universal achievements – embedded in the grounds of the New York World's Fair 1939."

'This book contains all you need to know. Location. Contents. How to find it.'

'Why do I need to find it? It's not been a hundred years, yet alone five thousand.'

'You will locate it. You will dig it up. And you will return it to me.'

Charlie looked at the photo of the capsule. It was the size of a missile. Not the kind of thing that would be easy to hide from customs officials.

'It looks big,' he said.

'It is about two metres in length. How you reach it is not my concern. How you get it back to Spain is not my concern. Just ensure that you succeed, because I do not tolerate failure.'

'Sure. Failure sucks,' agreed Charlie, as if he hadn't spent his entire life magnetically repelled from success.

'You have experience in smuggling across international borders, I assume?'

Charlie could not deny this. He had brought Mayan pottery across several Central American borders, although his one attempt at smuggling something as big as this capsule – a human cargo – had been an utter disaster.

'Sure. Borders, schmorders,' he replied, looking more

closely at the book. There was a section describing the contents of the capsule, plus a key to the English language and even a message from Albert Einstein. The people who had prepared this time capsule had taken it all very seriously, but they didn't seem to have buried anything of great value. It was mostly everyday items – a hat, cigarettes, a toothbrush, a Mickey Mouse plastic cup, a light bulb, and loads of other junk. Nothing seemed worth the trouble of stealing the whole thing.

'I can tell that you are questioning my motivation for sending you on this mission,' said the old man. 'The answer is simple and, as an expert on Dalí, it should be obvious to you.'

'Pretty obvious. Sure. So, why?'

'As well as the objects and the microfilm books, the capsule contained copies of great artworks including *The Persistence of Memory.*'

'*The Persistence of Memory?*' echoed Charlie, suddenly remembering Ruby's eloquent insults when he had mentioned Dalí's melting clocks. 'That lowest common denominator shit? Hah.'

The old man nodded. Charlie's summary of Dalí's most famous work coincided with his own opinion of that over-commercialised painting. Charlie was definitely the man for this job.

'Dalí was represented in the collection of objects in the time capsule in an official capacity,' said the old man. 'But we have reason to believe that Dalí may have interfered with the contents of the capsule before it was sealed. He had access to it over a period of many weeks. He may have placed something inside it. Something that was not recorded in this book or in any official records. Something which will be of interest to my organisation.'

'Your organisation? The museum?'

'Of course not, Charlie. The museum is a tourist attraction, a frivolous enterprise. The people running it are doing an excellent job of protecting and promoting the works of Dalí, but there is something more important to me than the museum. I need this capsule, Charlie. You must not let me down.'

'And if I don't do it?'

'You will go to jail, young man. For a very long time.'

'And why was this Grant guy here earlier?'

'I wanted him to meet you,' whispered the old man. 'As a precaution.'

'Against what?'

'I considered it wise for him to be acquainted with your face so that he doesn't kill you by mistake.'

The mighty medieval cathedral of Chartres rose high above the windswept plain, its twin spires lit against the stars by floodlights that gave the appearance of a radioactive glow. The Land Rover moved as part of a steady stream of traffic, Constable Stuart never dropping too far behind in his Focus, easily keeping up with the Land Rover's distinctively austere rear lights. Ratty chose to drive through the heart of the city rather than taking the bypass, hoping that the small and congested streets would set them free from their uninvited escort. He threaded his way through random roads, ignoring the direction he was supposed to be taking, sometimes doubling back on himself and even taking a couple of laps around a one-way system close to the cathedral.

The process did not shake the policeman off his tail. On the contrary, it highlighted to the Patient, who had the opportunity to study such matters in more detail from his position in the passenger seat, that other vehicles were also tagging along. Sometimes they would be separated by traffic lights or by Ratty's last minute decision to turn into a side street, but it was never long before the procession re-formed.

'We seem to have quite a fan club,' said Ratty, looking at the cars in the rear-view mirror.

'Curious in its own right,' observed the Patient. 'Yet it has told us something valuable. Something that may be to our advantage.'

Ratty couldn't be bothered to play word games. He waited for his friend to elucidate.

'For the various vehicles to locate us so easily, they must have planted a tracking device in our car.'

The Patient climbed into the back seats. He didn't know precisely what he was looking for, but logic suggested that anything that wasn't dented and rusty was a likely candidate for the piece of technology in question. He lifted seat cushions, reached into door pockets and felt his way through a bag of old hammers and wrenches. Nothing. The utilitarian vehicle could not hide a tracking device easily. The interior was mostly bare metal, every functional element visible and obvious. The Patient wasn't certain, but he guessed the tracker would need to fix on a satellite, and that meant it was more likely to be near the windows or the roof than on, or beneath, the floor. He felt the window frames and the roof. Still nothing. He climbed back through to the front seat.

'Anything beeping away back there?' asked Ratty.

'I think I may have been looking in the wrong direction,' the Patient replied. 'What do you see in front of you?'

'France, mostly.'

'I see a spare wheel on the front of this car. A tracker placed there would have an unobstructed view of the sky.'

'I'll stop this jalopy so you can dash out and check,' said Ratty.

'No, that would make it obvious to those on our tail. We must keep moving.'

'The ventilation flappy thing. Open it. See if you can get your arm through.'

The Patient opened the rectangular flap beneath the windscreen and felt the rush of cool air entering the cab. A layer of gauze to keep out flies was easy to dislodge, and the Patient was able to put his entire left arm through the gap, provided he held himself at an angle that resulted in his face pressing against the gear stick. His arm groped blindly. It found the spare wheel. His fingers made their way over the rubber and into the steel hub. He was at the limit of his reach.

It was sufficient. Something was taped to the inside of the wheel. He ripped it off the hub and brought the little Garmin satellite tracker inside.

'Lose them again,' said the Patient, 'and I'll lose their tracker when they can't see us.'

'Righty-ho.'

Ratty zig-zagged through the narrow streets until they had earned a few seconds of privacy. The Patient opened his window and tossed the tracker into the half-open rear of a passing sheep lorry.

'Let's make indirectly for Spain,' said the Patient. 'No one can follow us, and no one will find us if we drive west for a few hours before we turn south.'

'Who were those other people?' asked Ratty. 'Did you count how many cars there were?'

'I think there were two, besides the police officer.'

'Two? How flattering to warrant such attention.'

'There is another oddity,' added the Patient. 'Constable Stuart implied that he knew of our destination.

If he knows where we are going, why does he need to follow us so closely? Why not just meet us there?'

'I rather fancy the idea that he has taken it upon himself to protect us.'

'He certainly shows no ill-feeling. But from whom do we need to be protected?' asked the Patient. 'One can only assume the intruders from the other night were the same ill-intentioned visitors at the door of the manor today. If Constable Stuart's job is to protect us from the men in those other cars, I fear he may have taken on more than a man of his years can manage.'

'He should be on the verge of retiring,' said Ratty. 'The fellow looks old enough to have stuck two fingers up at the Frenchies at Agincourt.'

'And he holds the rank of constable?' asked the Patient.

'Constable Stuart. No idea if he has any other name. That's what he's been throughout my life.'

'My understanding of careers is that people generally progress and get promoted during their working lifetime. The rank of constable is the lowest rung of the ladder. It is where young men begin their policing, but Constable Stuart appears to have been in this job for over forty years. Doesn't that strike you as unusual?'

'Golly. Never thought about it before. He's always been the village constable, for as long as I can remember. Some chaps are born deficient in the ambition department.'

'Forty years of loyal service. Always there, in the background, ensuring you never came to any true harm. Almost as if he is more than a village police bobby, as you call him.'

'But the fellow isn't my private bodyguard. He's not on the family payroll. No one has been able to live off us

Ballashiels types for years.'

'And if a trust fund had been set up by, say, your late father, perhaps?'

'Not entirely impossible but utterly bonkers. And where was he when I got into a bit of a pickle in Guatemala last year?'

'Could it be that his contract of protection is similar to the breakdown cover that you have for this car? It covers you for the United Kingdom and Europe. If your metaphorical engine needs repair in Guatemala, they won't want to know.'

'Poor Stuart. Outnumbered. Outgunned,' said Ratty.

'Are you thinking what I'm thinking?'

'I'm thinking about having a banana when we stop.'

'No, my friend,' replied the Patient. 'Perhaps we need to go back. He might not know what he's up against.'

Ratty pulled over into a lay-by and turned to face the Patient squarely.

'Are you seriously proposing that we should go back and guard my bodyguard?'

'Tell me, Ratty. If the constable is indeed attempting to act in your interests, to overlook your misdemeanours – as he clearly has already done – and perhaps even to defend you physically, how does that make you feel?'

'Golly, well, obviously one feels rather whizzo about the whole shebang. The chap is plainly one fish-knife short of a cutlery set if he's doing so off his own back, but there's a large slice of my gratitude heading his way with a hefty dollop of appreciation on the side.'

'And did not Henri Frédéric Amiel say that thankfulness may consist merely of words, but that gratitude is shown in acts?'

'Yes, but he probably meant a bunch of flowers or a box of choccies, not putting yourself in the way of angry strangers armed with lethal gardening implements.'

'And did Cicero not say that gratitude is not only the greatest of virtues, but the parent of all the others?'

'Agreed, Patient chappy, but I don't think he had our peculiar situation in mind when he said that.'

'It is my view, and the view of many philosophers, that you should live by your feelings of gratitude. You should return to him. If only to ensure that he does not need our help, or to advise of the threat that may be posed by those men in the other vehicles. And if we let him continue to follow us directly, we may find he is there for us when we truly need him.'

Ratty took a deep breath and performed a begrudging U-turn. He hadn't asked to be followed through France, either by the forces of good or evil, let alone both at once, but the Patient's reasoning was, as ever, indisputable. The prospect of heading back into Chartres and encountering the menacing vehicles made him squirm with nerves. If they had discovered the Patient's ruse with the tracking device in the sheep lorry they would have even more reason to be angry with him. If he was going to search for the constable he wanted to get it done before the shakes made it tricky to drive.

The futility of the search made itself quickly apparent. Two pairs of tired eyes, dazzled by headlights, unfamiliar with the geography, could never hope realistically to locate the constable that night. Ratty turned into the grounds of an old monastery behind the cathedral. According to the sign, the monastery was now a hotel. The car park was hidden from the main road. They would be safe for the night.

It wasn't until his second gin and tonic that Ratty's nerves began to settle. The Patient had begun his usual thing of touching stonework, caressing ancient structural timbers and sniffing unfamiliar scents: his first encounter with French medieval construction enthralled him. He was so engrossed in marvelling at the hotel's vaulted arches that he didn't notice Constable Stuart walking along the opposite side of the cloister towards the bar.

'*Pression, s'il vous plait,*' the policeman said to the barman.

Ratty looked up from his comforting glass, alerted by the sound of French being spoken with a broad Shropshire accent. The barman pulled half a litre of lager into a glass. The customer at the bar had his back to Ratty, but the uniform made his identity obvious.

'Good evening, Constable,' said Ratty. 'It seems the coincidences continue. Would you care to join me?'

'Very kind of you, Justin.' Stuart pulled up a weighty armchair and settled into it, facing Ratty directly. 'Good to get the weight off me feet. Been a long day.'

'Well it hasn't exactly flown by from my perspective,' said Ratty. 'The old noodle is positively spinning. Having trouble making sense of it all, quite frankly. My private research seems inadvertently to have stirred up a hornet's nest.'

'And boy can those hornets sting. You were lucky I followed you today.'

'I was?'

'Those other cars. Did you notice them?'

'Rather.'

'Is that why you came all the way back into the centre of Chartres?' asked Stuart.

'Wanted to warn you about them. Patient chappy didn't like the cut of their jib.'

'He was quite right,' the policeman replied. 'They had a tracker in your car. You sent them off to a farm.'

110

'How do you know?' asked Ratty.

'Because I had trackers in their cars.'

'Golly. But how the deuce did you keep up with me all this time? Tracker in my car, too, I suppose?'

'Goodness, no. The sluggish nature of your unroadworthy and highly illegal vehicle was enough for me most of the time. Really wasn't hard.'

'But we came back into Chartres at night in order to find you and warn you. So how did you find us again?'

'I didn't have a tracker in your vehicle, but the radio voice transmitter let me know where to expect you.'

'And is that kind of surveillance legal, constable?'

'Legal? Wouldn't have a clue, to be honest. Not really my area.'

The Patient returned from his exploration of their surroundings and sat with them.

'Patient chappy, look who has joined us again.'

Constable Stuart slurped his lager aggressively until the glass was empty and stained with white froth. He thumped it down on the table.

'I really ought to be turning in, now,' he told his companions. 'We have a long drive ahead of us tomorrow.'

'Before you retire to bed, may I enquire as to your reason for intersecting the paths of our lives so often in one day?' asked the Patient.

Constable Stuart looked at Ratty, indecision showing in his eyes.

'Perhaps another beer,' he said.

Ratty took the constable's glass to the bar and obtained a refill. Stuart settled even further into his seat, looking outwardly relaxed whilst turmoil raged within.

'Can you tell us what is going on?' asked Ratty. 'All this surveillance and wotnot, it's like we're suspects in a whopping great criminal thingummy. But apart from stealing that feminist book and driving into the back of your car we've remained on the less sticky side of the law all day.'

'Apart from when you went the wrong way down a one-way street,' corrected the Patient. Ratty kicked him beneath the table. 'And that kick might be construed as assault.'

'You boys have done nothing wrong, trust me,' said Stuart. 'It's just that you've got yourselves mixed up in something that I hoped would never come to fruition.'

'Who were those people following you following us, or whatever it was?' asked Ratty.

'They have been dealt with, that is all you need to know.'

'So they were gentlemen of ill-intention?' asked the Patient.

'They were no gentlemen. I followed them to the farm and resolved the situation.'

Ratty pictured the bobby giving the drivers and their passengers a stern ticking off and making a note of their names and addresses as a deterrent from future wrongdoing. Somehow it didn't seem adequate.

'And why is Her Majesty's Police Force paying for one of its finest officers to accompany us on our journey?' asked Ratty.

'Police? This has nothing whatsoever to do with the police. I'll probably be fired when I get back. Absent without you know what, and all that. It doesn't matter. This is far more important.'

'So the connection between us is not the usual state contract of police service protecting the citizens?' Ratty asked.

Stuart shook his head.

'A hidden connection is stronger than an obvious one,' stated the Patient.

'Clearly,' said Ratty. 'So you are with us in a private capacity?'

Stuart leaned forward and gestured with his finger for the others to lean in close to him.

'I am not alone in this. Perhaps you would like to follow me to the car. There's something I'd like to show you. It may make things a little clearer for you both.'

The three men put down their glasses and walked along a cloister lined with the graves of medieval monks, soon reaching the parking area within the walled grounds of the hotel. The Ford Focus was parked in one corner, its rear bumper now absent entirely. Stuart opened the boot and rummaged amongst his bags. In one holdall was an arsenal of weaponry, and Ratty and the Patient caught a glimpse of it as the policeman fumbled for the item he was looking for. They instinctively stood back from the car, their trust in this man suddenly gone.

'Actually, it doesn't matter,' said Ratty. 'Ought to be going now.'

Stuart looked at them over his shoulder and realised what had happened.

'The guns? Don't be alarmed. They are for your benefit. Without them we wouldn't be here. Ah, this is the thing I was looking for.'

He produced a scrapbook and flicked through its pages. It was full of news cuttings, mostly from minor regional papers, concerning court cases. Each one had resulted in lengthy custodial sentences. Ratty looked at the yellowing photos in the dimly illuminated car boot. Things started to click. That was the family cook from his childhood, a Frenchman named Clement. There was the butler, Grant. And the gamekeeper, Huxtable. All had ended up serving time soon after leaving his family's employment. Their crimes seemed utterly unrelated to his memories of those individuals and their personalities. Almost as if they couldn't really have been guilty. Almost as if it were a stitch-up.

'All the servants went to prison?'

'All of them.'

'But they weren't a bad bunch of eggs. I couldn't imagine any of them suddenly turning rotten.'

'Men acquire a particular quality by constantly acting in a particular way. You become just by performing just actions: temperate by performing temperate actions, brave by performing brave actions,' said the Patient.

'Is he always like that?' asked Stuart.

Ratty nodded.

'What I mean is, their characters were formed long before they left your service,' explained the Patient. 'If they were wrongdoers after they left Stiperstones, they were wrongdoers before.'

'So all the Ballashiels staff are doing porridge?'

'Were, Justin. Were.'

'Fascinating, but what exactly has it to do with our rather odd current predicament?'

'One of them died in jail. Your old chef. Dropped dead from food poisoning. Quite funny, really, when you think about it, I suppose. Probably couldn't handle thirty years of English prison food. Can you imagine what that does to a French chef with taste buds tuned to perfection? But then something went wrong. The others got out. Released on the same day. Last week. Should never have happened. We tried to fix things so they would never come out. Big cock-up through and through.'

'Grant and Huxtable are free?' asked Ratty, trying not to sound as pleased as he genuinely was for them.

'Not just free,' warned Stuart. 'They are on a mission of vengeance. They are coming for you.'

'Coming for me? What do the servants have against me? I was just a whippersnapper when they were around.'

'Something big is happening, Justin. Events are unfolding fast. I'm not at liberty to reveal why, but I will do my level best to protect you.'

SATURDAY 4TH MAY 2013

Tired hinges groaned. A door clicked. Ratty opened his eyes, instantly alert to the possibility of an intruder. He fumbled in the unfamiliar darkness for the switch on the bedside lamp. He guessed it was between the side table and the mattress. He began to twist his body to a position that would allow his arm to locate the switch, but stretched too far off the edge of the bed and found himself in a coil of duvet and electric cable on the floor.

'Anyone there?' he whispered to the silent hotel room. 'Well, if you are there, would you mind awfully helping me up?' Somewhere in the back of his mind he was toying with the option of using the lamp in hand-to-hand combat the moment the intruder initiated physical contact. He reached back over his shoulder and grabbed the stem in readiness. Another door creaked open and banged shut. Voices erupted and ebbed in the corridor. Ratty finally turned on the lamp and was embarrassed to discover himself alone in his room.

But he had slept well that night, fortified by the concept of a well-armed personal bodyguard in the adjacent room. This morning, despite his contretemps with the duvet, he was invigorated, powered by the kind of *joie de vivre* that he hadn't felt in many years. If they set off early enough, it was possible that he and the Patient would, with the protection of their bodyguard, reach Spain today. The quest for his mother would continue.

The Patient had already finished his continental breakfast when Ratty sauntered into the foyer to check out.

'I'll skip *petit déjeuner* this morning, Patient chappy. Want to get on the old *rue* as soon as the constable is ready.'

'I fear we will not benefit from his company today, Ratty.'

'*Pourquoi* not?'

'I observed that a maid has already begun to clean his room and that his key has been handed in.'

'So he's checked out ahead of us. Keen fellow. Marvellous. Perhaps he's waiting in his car?'

'His car is no longer here.'

'I'm sure he'll catch up with us *en route* later on. Let's bash off anyway.'

The receptionist called Ratty back to the desk.

'*Monsieur*, I nearly forgot. Someone left a letter for you.'

Ratty took the envelope. It was sealed. He held out his hand in anticipation of being handed a letter-opening knife, but his expectations remained unfulfilled, forcing him to enter the unfamiliar and faintly distasteful territory of having to rip the envelope open with his fingers. The note inside was handwritten, and appeared to have been scribbled in haste. It took him a few seconds before he was confident that he understood its message. He thanked the receptionist and ushered the Patient to the Land Rover, saying nothing until they were inside and the doors were shut.

'Change of plan,' he told his friend. 'This has thrown something of a Spaniard in the works.'

'What does it say?'

'It tells us to abandon our journey to Spain in the hunt for my mother. Only by returning immediately to Blighty will Constable Stuart's life be spared.'

Having slept on the events of the previous day, Ruby felt calmer. She didn't share Rocco's conspiracy fears. The vandalism of cars and caves could have been random incidents, unconnected and without motive or agenda. The idea that museum officials would destroy the very thing that their institution existed to preserve was preposterous. The museum was the appropriate body to inform of the discovery in the cave, she was convinced of that. Rocco's motives for attempting to befriend the museum staff were highly questionable, but the result would be the same: the painting would be painstakingly restored, protected and studied and would add to Dalí's body of work.

She found Rocco waiting for her outside the museum, studying the seemingly endless line of tourists queuing for entry. In the morning shade of the city square the air was cool, causing the more optimistically dressed visitors to huddle and rub their bare arms.

'I'm not happy about doing this,' announced Rocco directly into Ruby's ear so that no passing strangers would hear, 'but we're in too deep already.'

'Stop saying stuff like that, Rocco. Not everything in the world is a conspiracy, you know. Most people are honest and hardworking, and very few people can keep anything secret. Human nature is to share information. It's why conspiracy theories spread like wildfire when there's no substance.'

He looked at her as if she was crazy and said, 'Follow me.'

Rocco knocked on an unmarked door at the side of the building. A few seconds later it opened and they were invited in by a brawny museum official who led them to a windowless office in the basement. Rocco and Ruby were left alone in the plain room for several minutes. They said nothing. Ruby relaxed while her companion tensed.

Finally, the door clunked open and an old man with pale skin and a straight nose entered. He was dressed in a white suit that looked expensively tailored, and there was not a speck of dust on his glistening Barker shoes. Upon seeing Rocco's face he seemed to do a double take, an expression of horror spreading from his mouth like an earthquake. Rocco gulped hard, stood up and offered his hand.

'Doctor Rocco Strauss,' he said, in what he hoped was a confident tone. 'Pleased to meet you.' The old man said nothing, allowing his facial muscles to return to a position of neutrality. 'And this is Doctor Ruby Towers. Archaeologist,' Rocco continued.

Ruby offered her hand to shake, but the old man remained aloof from her, still standing, as if preparing to spring from the room at a moment's notice.

'I cannot decide,' began the old man after an uncomfortable pause, 'if you are depressingly stupid or incredibly brave.'

His lack of civility unnerved Ruby. Museums the world over had always welcomed her. The possibility that there might be some substance to Rocco's paranoia began to enter her head.

'Hear me out,' said Rocco. 'I know you guys have a problem with my interest in Keo, but that's cool. All in the past. I want to start again. I want to join you. We both do, right?'

Ruby nodded, already regretting it.

'Out of the question,' stated the old man, flatly.

'Why?' asked Rocco.

'You don't know what you are dealing with. Your request is entirely unrealistic. And your arrival here presents me with a problem.'

119

'What kind of problem?' Rocco's assertive façade was crumbling.

The old man leaned against the door and sighed, his spirit suffering the same rate of decline as Rocco's confidence.

'Why do you have to meddle so much?' asked the old man. 'You complicate my life. I do not need this when there is so little time.'

'You had time to destroy Dalí's cave painting,' said Rocco.

'Rocco, you can't just accuse people of that with no evidence,' admonished Ruby. 'I apologise for his directness, but we did find what appeared to be the remains of a painting in a cave at Cap Creus. There are signs that might link this painting to Dalí, so I think it would be a good idea if you sent someone to take a look at the remains and subjected it to a more rigorous inspection than I –'

'You really think I do not already know about Dalí's cave painting?' interrupted the old man.

'Of course he knows, Ruby,' said Rocco. 'He's the one who ordered its destruction.'

Ruby looked to the old man for a denial of the accusation, but his face remained blank.

'Your interest in cave paintings does not bother me,' said the old man. 'It is your preoccupation with Keo that I find disturbing. It has made you too much of a threat to everything we are working towards. You will wait here while I decide what will be done with you.'

'Screw this,' said Ruby, standing up and making for the door. The old man stood aside and let her rattle the handle in frustration. 'I'm not playing games!' she shouted. 'Let me out!'

The old man knocked twice on the door and it opened

for him. The bulky security guard forced Ruby to remain in the room with Rocco while the old man exited. The door shut. She could hear the key turning again.

'That went well,' Rocco whispered, winking at her. 'He reacted exactly as I wanted him to. He doesn't know that he has walked right into my trap by refusing to let us join their organisation.'

Ruby was about to contradict Rocco's unlikely statements when he held a finger to his mouth and pushed a note to her. 'Bugged room,' it said. 'Play along.'

'Yes,' said Ruby, sighing. 'They've walked right into your clever trap. You're clearly too smart for them.'

If their English was good enough to detect her heavy irony she would have blown his plan aside, but even Rocco appeared to think she was sincere.

'Logic doesn't solve our conundrum,' complained Ratty, still sitting in the driving seat of the motionless Land Rover. 'There is no way to make our decision logically. It has to come from the heart.'

'Decisions of the heart are invariably inferior to decisions of the head,' said the Patient.

'Right now my head is throbbing. It isn't fit to choose our course of action.'

'If we do not return to Stiperstones, Constable Stuart will be killed. The logic is simple and unavoidable.'

'There are too many ifs, buts and wotnots, old fellow. These ne'er-do-wells could be bluffing. The constable might be in danger anyway, and if we continue to Spain, we may again cross paths with these ruffians and have a chance to help him. What if they have no means of knowing where we are? What if we drove home then jumped on the next flight to Girona? Would that count?'

'We must do that which causes the most good and the

least harm,' said the Patient.

'One does one's best.'

'Do you agree that attempting to save the constable is a good thing?'

'Of course,' agreed Ratty.

'And that by rescuing him we would reduce the risk of harm coming to his person?'

'Indeedy.'

'And yet by attempting to do good we increase the risk of harm by not following the instructions of his kidnappers. Is that correct?'

'Yes,' Ratty sighed.

They had been sitting in the hotel car park at Chartres for over an hour. While the Patient's ability to argue about probability, ethics, law, and morality seemed boundless, Ratty was growing weary of their inaction.

'So can we say,' continued the Patient, 'that an attempt to find and save the constable is neither a good nor a bad thing, because its nature depends upon its outcome?'

'I suppose it is morally neutral, yes.'

'And what are our chances of a successful rescue? Do we feel confident about our abilities or are we concerned about our lack of fighting skills, our lack of weapons and our inexperience in this field?'

'Er, when you put it that way, we're up against it somewhat, yes.'

'Therefore we know, when beginning such a rescue attempt, that the chances of failure run at more than fifty per cent. Would you agree?'

'Absolutely.'

'Therefore,' droned the Patient, 'by attempting to be heroic we are tilting the balance in favour of harm to the constable, and probably to ourselves, and therefore –'

Ratty put his hand over the Patient's mouth.

'Follow me,' Ratty whispered. The two men climbed out and walked to the other end of the car park. 'I have a solution, but I couldn't tell you in there. Remember Stuart said he had bugged our jalopy? If the kidnappers have his car, they could be listening on the same bug. And they might have put another tracker in there somewhere. How else would they know if we were heading back home? But I know what we should do.'

'And your solution is what?'

Ratty returned to the Land Rover and opened the rear door, selected the wrench from the canvas tool bag, then walked round to the front and opened the bonnet. The engine was dirty. Its coolant pipes were beginning to perish. The wires were blackened with oil.

'This is my solution,' said Ratty. He looked over his shoulder, then began to hit the various engine components with the wrench. 'Rather jolly good fun, actually. Care to try?'

The Patient shook his head. Ratty checked that the car would no longer start, then closed the bonnet and took out his mobile phone. He called the breakdown insurance company and demanded that his car be returned to England for repair and that they provide him with a rental car so that he could continue his journey. When the call was finished, he smiled at the Patient, who expressed a look that suggested Ratty's actions had been entirely logical.

The absence of natural light in the museum basement served only to fuel Ruby's contempt at her incarceration. Two hours without daylight, without food and water, and without a reprieve from Rocco's incessant paranoiac babbling was driving her to the edge of sanity. He seemed to have forgotten his earlier concern about the room being bugged, and had been jabbering about every conspiracy theory he had ever encountered.

'How is your plan coming along?' she asked him in a tone that was loaded with sarcasm.

'I've calculated that they won't shoot us in here,' replied Rocco. 'Too much risk of a bullet ricocheting from those walls.'

'Reassuring.'

'But something's not right,' he continued.

'I know. I just assumed you were born that way.'

'I mean, why hasn't the old man come back yet?'

'Maybe he hasn't decided which conspiracy he's part of, and he's trying to make up his mind?'

Rocco glared at Ruby for mocking him at a time of crisis.

'No. It's something else. Something deeper. I think this is a test, Ruby. He is testing us.'

'A test?' she asked, trying not to roll her eyes in irritation.

'He is testing our loyalty. We said we wanted to join them. I have a hunch that this door is not actually locked.'

'But we heard them locking it two hours ago,' protested Ruby.

'And have we tried the handle since then?'

'Of course not. We'd have heard if it was being unlocked.'

'What if the door was not locked in the first place?' he suggested. 'A twist of the key back and forth can sound like the lock is turning whilst leaving the door open.' Rocco approached the door and gripped the handle. 'I believe,' said Rocco, 'that we are not waiting for him. He is waiting for us.'

'Rubbish.'

'If we go and look for his office, I bet we'll find him

sitting in there playing cards with the security guard, waiting for us to prove we are worthy of membership of whatever their organisation actually is.'

This sounded profoundly unlikely to Ruby, who thought it more probable that the security guard was about to return to this room and offer them a drink. Rocco looked at her all-too-familiar cynical expression.

'It's a leap of faith,' he continued. 'I'm going to prove to that old man that I'm worthy. I'm going to find him.'

He pushed the handle and the door snapped open. Ruby's eyes dilated in surprise. He pulled it wide to demonstrate that no one was waiting on the other side. She followed him out into the gloomy corridor, but walked directly towards the stairs that led to the exit.

'I don't trust him,' said Ruby. 'We should leave while we have the chance.'

'If we go now, we'll never find out what his agenda is. But I won't force you into anything, Ruby. Go if you want to. I'm going to find him.'

He watched her disappear up the steps and took a deep breath. He was now more deeply immersed in his own conspiracy than he had ever dreamed possible. He felt the force of destiny carry him forward, step by step, until he arrived at a door that was labelled 'Director'. This had to be the old man's office. Rocco opened the door and poked his head inside.

'So, did I pass?'

The old man regarded him quizzically from behind his desk.

'Pass?'

'I mean, this is all a setup, right?' continued Rocco, fighting to mask his nerves. 'An initiation test.'

'I have no such thing in my organisation.'

'So what does a guy have to do to get in?'

'There is no way in.'

'None at all?' challenged Rocco. 'There's always a way in.'

'If there was, you would need to have desire.'

'Desire? Like a passion for art?'

'Art has its place,' said the old man, 'but history is of greater concern for me. Without art we are poorer, of course, but without history we are destitute.'

'Right,' said Rocco. 'History, not art. Got it. So why do you run an art gallery?'

'Our organisation exists for something bigger than art. Nothing is more important than our core values and beliefs.'

'And your values are what?'

'To change the world,' said the old man. 'To make a better future.'

That didn't seem too conspiratorial or sinister to Rocco. He wondered if he had overestimated the motives of these people.

'A better future? Sure. I'm all for that kind of thing. So that matters even more than history, does it?'

'You do not understand. A better future will result in a better past. And a better past will result in a better present. Everything is connected.'

'Better past, present, and future. Yes. That's my philosophy.'

'No, you still do not understand. It cannot happen in that order. We are in the centre, the present. We cannot change the past unless we change the future. The future must come first.'

'So why is Keo such a thorn in your side?'

'Keo is a bridge to another world. It connects us to our descendants in a way that is unnatural and unwise. Keo changes our future in a bad way because it will cause something to happen that changes the past.'

'That's cool.'

'There is nothing cool about it. The Keo threat is very serious. People have no idea of the impact a time capsule can have upon a civilisation. They are foolish to send these things forward in time.'

'So you guys don't want Keo to launch? I get that. Just don't see why you tried to kill me when I started searching for a reply from the future to confirm Keo was received.'

'No one has tried to kill you. We have merely attempted to divert you from your path. It was an attempt to scare you away. Clearly it didn't work, as you seem to be more involved than ever, but I think you might be of some use to us. You have shown initiative. Hiding in our museum was a clever move. Of course, we knew all about it and watched you every minute. It has been interesting to study you. And your motives will not matter in the long run. As long as we achieve our goals, the future will become better, and so will the past.'

Rocco appeared enraptured, as if suddenly in love. To receive confirmation that his conspiracy theory was built upon sound foundations was a joyous moment for him.

'So how does Dalí fit in?' he asked, excitedly. 'How did he know about Keo?'

'He is the problem that we must fix. The Keo recipients sent a message, but they sent it decades too early. Dalí and his companion witnessed it in 1937. It changed everything. That is why we must alter the future.'

'What did it change?'

'I am afraid that is a secret I will never be prepared to divulge.'

'Cool. I like a challenge. So, what now?'

'See me tomorrow,' said the old man, pointing at the

door. 'I may have a project for you.'

'I can't tell you how much I appreciate this opportunity,' Rocco said. 'By the way, I didn't catch your name. It just says "Director" on your door and when I googled the museum I couldn't find anyone in the organisation who matched your description.'

'A name can be a curse,' the old man replied. 'A name engenders pre-judgement. It changes attitudes. For that reason, I rarely use it.'

'Excellent. Whatever you prefer.'

'It is not "excellent",' sighed the old man. '*Nothing* is excellent. Do not exaggerate your significance to me. It has been your choice to make yourself available. You are now in. That means there is no way out. Do not underestimate the risks of failure. You have no idea who you are dealing with. And you have no conception of the consequences of triggering my displeasure.'

The three-dimensional representation of the planet Earth cast confusing shadows in the morning light. The outline of countries depicted on the twelve-storey-high Unisphere globe at Flushing Meadows appeared reversed and elongated where the weak sun shone through the hollow structure. Charlie wiped his tired eyes and hoisted his shovel up over his shoulder. The Unisphere was his first attempt to get his bearings within the grounds of the park. Charlie recognised the iconic monument from the movie *Men in Black* and enjoyed a private fantasy about shooting aliens as he walked past it.

He pulled the book out of his bag and read the three words on the cover. *The Time Capsule*. He had intended to read the entire book during the transatlantic flight from Barcelona to JFK, but the selection of movies available on board had been too good to resist and he hadn't dipped into the book at all. A park official had told him where to find the time capsule: it was located behind the New York State Pavilion, a decaying and abandoned relic of 1960s optimism for the future. He could see the distinctive towers of the pavilion directly ahead. The short walk left him puffing for air, and he found a circular granite bench on which to sit, surrounded by a ring of trees. The rear of the New York State Pavilion was now in front of him. The time capsule couldn't be far away. Without moving from his cold seat, he scanned the trees looking for a marker. Nothing stood out. The granite began to make him uncomfortable, in spite of his generously padded behind. He stood up and walked around the hunk of stone. He noticed words carved into the side of it:

"THE TIME CAPSULES DEPOSITED SEPTEMBER 23, 1938 AND OCTOBER 16, 1965 BY THE WESTINGHOUSE ELECTRIC CORPORATION AS A RECORD OF TWENTIETH-CENTURY CIVILIZATION TO ENDURE FOR 5,000 YEARS"

The old man with the weird accent at the museum hadn't said anything about two capsules. He hoped it would be obvious which was which when he found them. And he hadn't said anything about the site being capped with a ton of rock. It would take a bulldozer to shift that. He looked at his puny shovel and sighed. Charlie wasn't prone to philosophising, but the morality of his task also concerned him. Sure, he had skipped the line by entering through the rear door of the Dalí museum, and his conscience was fine with that level of wrongdoing, but to dig up a time capsule that belonged to the people of the future seemed to be in a different level of wrongness altogether.

129

His mind explored ways to justify the crime he was about to attempt. The old man had contacts everywhere. There was no one close to him in the park other than a few joggers, but he had been threatened with spies and heavies who would be watching his actions and monitoring his progress, determined not to let him just slip away into the night. So it wasn't as if he had a choice. Presumably, if he didn't do it, someone else would get blackmailed into doing it instead. And sure, the people of the future wouldn't get their 1930s hats and light bulbs and Mickey Mouse cups, but did that really matter?

He walked around the spot in ever-increasing circles. It was isolated, but not sufficiently devoid of life that he would be able to dig a hole without someone questioning his right to be there. The roar of the Grand Central Parkway's eight lanes of traffic just behind the trees would mask his noises, but any attempt to dig right on the spot was doomed to failure, even if he could move the enormous granite block that capped the hole. And how deep was he expected to go? He looked in the book for the answer. It took him a few minutes to locate the information, and when he read it, he didn't believe it.

Fifty feet below ground. This was insane. There was no way he could dig that far, even if he wasn't obese and didn't have to do the job in secrecy. Was this a practical joke on the part of the old man? He didn't seem the type. He thrust his shovel into the soil out of curiosity. It went in easily. The ground was soft and marshy: easy to dig, but difficult to prop up into a secure tunnel. That ruled out digging by hand. And then Charlie had an altogether different idea.

People dug tunnels all the time, he told himself, and they used machines to do it. He googled tunnelling machines on his iPhone and found a bewildering selection of second-hand junk that seemed to resemble elongated lawnmowers.

Next he walked around the abandoned pavilion in front of him, researching facts about it on his iPhone as he went. Built as part of the 1964/65 World's Fair, he learned, on the same site as the 1939 one, it had been abandoned and left to decay for over four decades. The colourful glass that had once covered its distinctive bicycle wheel-shaped roof had been smashed, destroying much of the unique floor laid out in the style of a vast map. Like the Eiffel Tower almost a century earlier, it had been intended as a temporary structure, due for demolition after the fair had ended. Due to its planned obsolescence, untreated wood was used for the pavilion's foundation piles. Surveyors inspected the condition of those foundations every couple of years.

Charlie had found his cover story. If he could convince park officials that he was there to survey those foundations, he could get away with bringing in digging equipment, and would be left alone to do his shameful deed. From within the boundary of the pavilion, he could dig down just a few yards from the granite marker point above the capsule, at an angle of about forty-five degrees, and, provided he did his sums right, intersect with the time capsule at precisely fifty feet below ground.

He returned to the capstone above the time capsules and sat down again. Could he really go through with a plan as audacious as this? The likelihood of success was slim, but he realised audacity was his only hope. The sheer scale of the project was beyond anything achievable on a clandestine basis. His only chance was to be brazen and confident. Genuine surveyors and builders were able to work within the park. There was always something happening – this morning he had passed a small

131

construction site on the other end of the park, close to the tennis courts. All they needed to gain access was a hardhat, high-visibility jacket and a piece of paper giving them authorisation. The hat and the jacket he could buy. Paperwork he could forge. He just needed to know what it should look like. He looked at the wad of cash in his wallet. The old man had been extremely generous in his expenses. Charlie wasn't thinking of bribery, however. His next stop would be a clothing store.

'A thought has just lodged itself within my noodle,' announced Ratty. He was driving the hybrid Lexus provided by his insurance company as a replacement for the Land Rover, and found it so relaxing to operate, despite the controls being on the wrong side of the car, that his mind had begun to analyse recent events.

'I do hope it doesn't die of loneliness,' quipped the Patient.

'What's that, old boy?'

'The thought inside your head.'

'That's the spirit, Patient chappy. Best effort yet. Jolly well done.'

'Yes, I thought so.'

'So, I was thinking about this, that, and what-do-you-call-it, and it occurred to me that if all of the staff at Stiperstones in the Seventies were rum fellows, they might have been connected to Mother's predicament. The way she coded and hid her message must have been to ensure those barbarian servants didn't find it.'

'I thought that connection was sufficiently obvious to negate the need for discussion.'

'Quite, quite. And I also am beginning to wonder if she thought her life was in danger if she remained at home.'

132

'Do you think she discovered something to their disadvantage?'

'Presumably. And I think it was connected to whatever Granny had squirreled away in that room.'

'So we have an object, or a piece of information, originally discovered by your grandmother, possibly whilst travelling to Catalonia with Dali in 1937, and locked in a spare room. This, in turn, attracts members of staff who all belong to a group of people with a profound interest in the contents of that room. Would you agree, Ratty?'

'Golly, yes. Seems so.'

'We don't understand the motives of the servants, but your mother must have stirred things up in 1975. She went into that room and took its contents with her, leaving clues that pointed towards Catalonia in Spain, and hoping the servants wouldn't pick up the trail.'

'Perhaps the servants saw themselves as guardians of the locked room?' suggested Ratty. 'So, when Mother found a way to gain access to it, she rather put the feline amongst the flying rodents.'

'I have only a vague understanding of your meaning, but I think I would concur.'

'Meanwhile Constable Stuart had been watching the servants and ensured they were all imprisoned after leaving my family's service. What do you make of that, Patient chappy?'

'Absolutely nothing at all. The sense of that history is too remote for our eyes to focus upon it. We must connect with it. We must immerse ourselves within it. For only then will the truth emerge from where it has been hiding for so many years.'

The efficient and quiet Roman road network led them gently down into the Loire valley. Opulent châteaux appeared with pleasing regularity. The delay caused by arranging the replacement car with the insurance company meant that reaching Spain was out of the question for yet another day, especially when avoiding the motorways and the many traffic cameras that might be used to track their progress.

'Granny made this same journey with Dalí. Mother made it alone, thirty-eight years later. How many years further on are we, Patient chappy?'

'If your mother made the trip in 1975, that was thirty-eight years ago.'

'A pattern?'

'If there is symbolism in the numbers, the meaning will become clear when we investigate Dalí's home territory, I am sure.'

'Do you have an inkling already?'

'Well, of course the number thirty-eight appears in the Bible five times.'

'Golly, you did spend a long time alone underground, didn't you?'

'And Frederico García Lorca was thirty-eight when he was shot, shortly before your grandmother made this journey.'

'And 1975 was the year that Franco popped his Spanish clogs,' added Ratty.

'Whatever that means, I'm sure you are correct.'

Ratty grinned. Then he remembered Constable Stuart's plight.

'I don't suppose there's any point in keeping an eye out for the constable, is there?'

'None whatsoever,' replied the Patient. 'If we ever see him again, it will be at our destination, not on the journey.'

'You think they'll be waiting for us?' Ratty asked.

'As soon as they realise you sent the Land Rover home

without us inside it, they will wait for us in Catalonia. And if the constable is alive, we may find him there.'

'And he's more likely to be alive if we can find him before they realise we're not back in Blighty.'

'Correct,' said the Patient.

'In that case we must share the driving and keep going through the night. How do you feel about taking the wheel?' asked Ratty.

'You are aware that my ability to drive is like my surgery?'

'Liable to leave lots of scars, you mean?'

'I mean it stems entirely from theory learned from books, that is all,' replied the Patient, missing Ratty's wordplay.

'You'll have no trouble – just keep pointing in the right direction and wake me up if you need to do anything complicated like stopping. But I want to find a hardware shop first. I think it would be prudent for us to "tool up", to use the vulgar vernacular.'

'What kind of tools did you have in mind?'

'I have one or two ideas that should iron the odds a little flatter should we find ourselves immersed in an unsavoury encounter.'

The Patient located the nearest branch of Castorama on Ratty's smartphone, and they drove directly there. From the industrial and hobby clothing aisle, Ratty selected a hunting jacket with pockets all over it. He then led the Patient to the tiling section where Ratty picked up a box of small stainless steel wall tiles. His intentions were beginning to become plain, but Ratty demonstrated anyway.

'See this tile, Patient chappy? Fits into a pocket thusly. Stuff them into all of the pockets and, hey sesame, a bulletproof jacket. The tile also makes a handy drinks

135

coaster for when the dangerous stuff is finished.'

'So far all we have is defensive. Are you considering the purchase of items that could be used in offensive tactics?'

'Not really my style, to be frank. Never was much of a fighting sort.'

Ratty squeezed the new jacket over his leathers and stuffed its pockets with the shiny steel tiles. The combined weight caused him to stoop more than usual and made it difficult to move his arms.

'Go on, hit me.'

The Patient shook his head.

'It's fine. Go on. I need to test my theory. Pretend you're one of my former ruffian servants and hit me.'

'I do not think you are protected, Ratty.'

'Nonsense. Go ahead.'

'Very well,' sighed the Patient, throwing an effeminate punch at Ratty's unprotected face.

'Ah, very good,' he said, rubbing his sore cheek. 'Thinking dirty, just like they would do. I like your style.'

'I fear our enemies may find amusement in your style.'

'Pretend inferiority and encourage his arrogance, as some fellow in a sunny zoo once said.'

'Well,' said the Patient, 'I don't suppose a façade of military inferiority will test our skills at pretence very hard.'

'Can I see your permits?'

The site manager looked up from his desk in the temporary office building. The portly visitor standing in his doorway was dressed in a black suit with a thin black tie and a white shirt, and was wearing dark sunglasses even though the afternoon was cloudy.

'I said permits,' repeated Charlie, now folding his

arms and trying to look like Tommy Lee Jones. The site manager seemed nervous at this intrusion by what appeared to be an oversized extra from the film *Men in Black*. He scrabbled amongst the floor plans and piles of receipts on his desk.

'I had everything cleared with the authorities before we started work,' jabbered the site manager.

Charlie looked around him at the grubby contents of the office: a kettle and dirty coffee mugs, hard hats and raincoats, and health and safety notices plastered across the walls.

'Well guess what, dude? I am the authorities. And I need to see your permits,' said Charlie. 'Now!' he added, purely for effect.

'It's here somewhere. I wasn't expecting to need it today. We don't normally get inspected at weekends.'

'Are you trying to hide something from me?'

'No, of course not. Here. This is it.' He thrust a folder in Charlie's direction. 'It's all there. It's all in order.'

Without opening the folder, Charlie turned away and walked to the door.

'It had better be,' he said. 'It had better.'

'Wait, you can't take that with you. I'm supposed to keep it on site in this office until we're done.'

Charlie began walking away briskly. It had all been too easy up to this point. Now he sensed the spell was starting to break.

'If it's all in order you'll get it back tomorrow,' called Charlie, breaking into a lolloping half-run from the site.'

'Tomorrow's Sunday,' called the site manager. 'We don't work Sundays.'

'Whatever,' replied Charlie. This would work in his favour. It gave him an extra day to forge his own version of the permits and to source the tunnelling equipment he was going to need.

He looked over his shoulder. The manager was following him out of the construction site. Two muscle-clad workers joined him. Charlie had no prospect of escape. The options of fight or flight were both closed to him. He gulped hard, turned around, and marched boldly back towards them.

Something about his imposing disposition had an effect. The men stopped dead. Before he reached them, Charlie also stopped and held out his arm, pointing at their building site.

'I strongly advise you guys to go back to work,' he shouted. 'Harassment of an official doing his duty is an offence. Even if your paperwork is in order, I will close you down for having a bad attitude. Do I make myself understood?'

The ensuing seconds crawled slowly by. Charlie's underwear filled with the sweat running down from his back. His legs shook. Either he would win, or he would be found out and beaten to a pulp.

The three builders conversed quietly amongst themselves. Behind his dark glasses, Charlie closed his eyes, shutting out the terrifying reality.

Sunday 5th May 2013

The old man stared at the packet he had found. A hangover from the old days. An envelope of hope from the era when he had none. He opened the envelope and shook its contents onto the desk in the white walled office at the rear of his modernist home.

A single pill rolled onto the glass worktop. It clattered and span in a wide arc before settling at arm's length. The pill was unmarked and came with no instructions, but the old man knew precisely what it was. He knew its ingredients. He knew its chemical make-up, the history of its development, the effects and the side-effects. In the Sixties, he had invested millions into the creation of this drug, sponsoring a laboratory and a team of doctors and chemists who dedicated themselves to perfecting a pill that would offer permanent relief from the pain that he felt within his heart.

The research had not been successful. Memories of those experiments returned to him. He wished he had not found this pill. He wished he had used it or disposed of it years ago. But he was now cruising fast towards the conclusion of his life. All the people he needed were in place. More people than necessary, in fact. His plans contained layers of redundancy. If his plan worked, this Sunday morning would be the last that he would experience. For that uncharacteristically sentimental reason, the old man had decided to use this final opportunity to go through his files and to reflect on his life. To prepare for his annihilation, he would embrace the memories of all that had happened to him, both good and bad.

There was very little good.

He opened another drawer and extracted a cardboard file. Inside was another envelope, much older than the one containing the pill. It was addressed to him in faded calligraphy, and carried an Argentine postmark.

This envelope had arrived on his eighteenth birthday, an occasion he remembered more vividly than most due to the realisation that it marked the granting of his inheritance. For inside the envelope was a piece of paper containing the name and address of a bank in Switzerland, and a series of numbers.

On that day, he had inherited wealth beyond his imaginings. The funds were secure in an unnamed account, untraceable, accessible with no questions asked. There was an almost limitless supply of cash available to him.

To possess it gave him no pleasure. Spending it was equally joyless. For the money was poisoned with the blood of millions.

Charlie had no idea what he was looking at. The eBay advert had shown some kind of machine on a pallet which was supposedly capable of digging a tunnel wide enough to accommodate the time capsule, and the vendor was desperate enough to be rid of it that he was happy to meet up on a Sunday. But the rusty wreck in front of Charlie in this New Jersey construction yard in the shadow of an oil refinery could have been anything. He couldn't even see where the driver was supposed to sit.

He had been lucky the previous day –the builders had

backed down – but would his luck continue today, or had he just bought some worthless junk?

'Sit?' replied the vendor when Charlie enquired on the subject. 'This ain't *Journey to the Centre of the Earth*, son.' He laughed.

Charlie chuckled too, already regretting having won this auction.

'How do I dig, then?'

'Just crawl behind it. Shore it up as you go. Conveyor to take the spoil to the surface. This baby can make ten yards a day with the wind behind it.' He laughed again.

Charlie sighed and handed over some of the cash he had been allocated for his mission. It was becoming steadily more complex. He wished he was back in Europe, driving Van Gogh to donut stores and generally wasting his life.

'Can you deliver?'

'Sure. What's the address?'

Ah. That would be a problem, thought Charlie. He couldn't give his hotel address. The machine had to be delivered directly to Flushing Meadows. He was going to have to forge his permits by the next morning.

'I've been commissioned to survey some foundations on one of the old World's Fair buildings,' he explained. 'As soon as I have the permits in place I'll be able to accept delivery of this beast.'

'No problem. Do you need anything else while you're here? I have skips, portable office units, signage, fences, you name it. All for rent if you prefer.'

'Why not? I'll take the lot.'

'How long for?'

'Ten yards a day, huh? Well, just a week then.'

The man laughed again.

The remote mountain track across the Pyrenees into Spain was lined with scorched trees from a recent forest fire. It seemed an ominous welcome to Ratty, who had taken to wearing his home-made bulletproof vest for the final miles through southern France and into Spain, and it was starting to make his neck ache. The Patient had driven his shifts with basic competence, managing to avoid the motorway and its heavily monitored toll booths, arriving in Catalonia just as the sun began to rise above the Mediterranean

'Where shall we begin our search?' asked the Patient.

'I think Mother wanted to visit Dalí. He was connected to whatever she found in the locked room. We should start at the house he lived in during the Seventies.'

Ratty programmed the satnav for Port Lligat, and the Patient took the next turning towards the coast. More evidence of the forest fire gave a bleak backdrop to the view. Eventually they reached the remote coastal village and followed the signs to Dalí's former home, now open to the public by appointment.

The whitewashed house clung to the rocks of the serene bay, a jumble of original fisherman's cottages and sympathetic extensions created by Dalí over the course of many decades. Its outbuildings were capped with giant eggs, similar in style to the roof of his museum in Figueres. After the Patient had managed to park the car with only minimal scraping against a neighbouring vehicle, Ratty stood on the beach and stared in silent reverence at the house.

He wondered if his mother had made it far enough to enjoy the same view. Had she stood on this same beach, thirty-eight years ago, with tears in her eyes at the thought that she could never see her son again? Ratty began to choke with emotion, but the Patient's new fascination with the texture of the stones that littered the foreshore brought him back to his present reality and the awareness that he was sweating profusely beneath the leather coat and the jacket full of metal tiles.

'The trail is cold,' said the Patient eventually.

'I don't know what I expected to find here,' said Ratty, deciding to remain inside his heavy jacket despite his fear of passing out in the heat.

'We pass through life, we visit places, and very rarely do we leave a mark.'

'Quite, Patient chappy, but Mother left a mark at Stiperstones. She left the message for me. Could she have created something at this end of the trail?'

'Catalonia is not just this village,' explained the Patient. 'It is twelve thousand square miles. Seven million inhabitants. If she did not visit Dalí, how do we know where the trail ends?'

'She must have come here. If the thing Granny locked away was connected to Dalí, Mother had to confront him about it.'

'So we must venture inside the house.'

'The website says "entry by appointment in advance only". We can hardly book a visit in our own names if those pesky servants are still waiting to bump me off.'

'Then our only course of action is to lie low until after dark and explore the house on our own.'

'Golly. Sounds rather naughty. What about alarms and wotnot?'

'Leave that to me.'

'Ought we to scout around for the constable while we wait?'

'I fear such a random search would be fruitless. We need to know more about the people against whom we

143

appear inadvertently to be pitted. If we don't find clues in the house tonight, the next step is to invite them to come to us.'

Ratty patted his metal tiles for comfort.

'*Paella*?' he asked, looking at the beach café behind them.

'I can think of no finer breakfast under the circumstances.'

They sat on bench seats and studied the menu.

'Dalí published two volumes of diaries, but he doesn't mention your mother or your grandmother,' said the Patient.

'Nothing personal, I'm sure. Those diaries were partly fictitious. They build on the surrealist mythology, blending fact with wotnot and whatever.'

'He may have kept private diaries which were never published, and which contain only facts,' suggested the Patient.

'If so, he left everything to the institute that he founded. *Paella por favor.*'

'*Dos*,' added the Patient, handing his menu back to the waiter.

'But the institute kept it all on display in that house. This could be a jolly interesting night.'

The last visitors left Dalí's house shortly after six in the evening just as two elderly women arrived, one carrying a bucket crammed with bottles of cleaning fluids, the other carrying a small vacuum cleaner. The old women entered the building unhurriedly and without vigour. Ticket office staff shook hands and closed the doors. Guides bade each other farewell and set off for home. A lone security guard took up a position in front of the building and started reading a magazine. Ratty led the Patient to a section of whitewashed garden wall, out of sight of the guard, where he considered entry might be more easily attained.

'This has gone too smoothly,' observed the Patient. 'We have spent an entire day in this village, and no one has treated us oddly or displayed any suspicion towards us despite the fact that your armoured clothing makes you look as if gravity weighs twice as heavily upon you as it does for others.'

'You really think they know we're here?'

'I consider it probable. Expect the unexpected whenever you least expect to need to expect it.'

'A pithy motto indeed.'

When the cleaners finally departed, exiting the house with the same lack of urgency with which they had entered it, the Patient attempted to lift Ratty over the garden wall but the additional weight of his armour plating made the manoeuvre impossible. Ratty took off the jacket and dropped it over the wall where it landed with an attention-grabbing clatter upon a flagstone path. Ratty followed it and put his armour back on before helping to lift his friend high enough to join him.

The rear gardens of the property were screened with trees, and the men were able to move without fear of being seen. Dalí's phallic-shaped swimming pool lay still, its pumps turned off, its pop art sculptures and decorations oddly sinister in the silence.

The Patient led the way to the rear of the house. He tried the first door they encountered: locked. Round the corner was another entrance. The handle on this one turned easily.

'Probably the guard's route from the house to the gardens when he does his rounds,' suggested the Patient.

'Which room shall we try first?'

'Easy,' said the Patient, who had spent much of the

145

day reading online about the contents and features of the house, 'his dressing room. Full of private photos of him with celebrities and friends.'

The dressing room seemed overloaded with vanity. Each wardrobe door – and there were many wardrobes – was plastered with photos from Dalí's life. There he was, pictured with the stars of the Thirties, Forties, Fifties, Sixties and Seventies. Ratty scanned the pictures carefully, looking for his mother or his grandmother. Nothing.

They tried to force open one of the locked cupboards, but after the door had creaked open it turned out to be empty. In other rooms, there was a smattering of books, but no personal papers. They returned to the dressing room. Ratty stood for a moment to imagine his mother's presence in the building, to sense a connection with her, but the way the house had been sanitised and prepared for public viewings left it without its soul.

'This obviously isn't the place where his personal documents are kept,' said the Patient.

'So where are they?'

The Patient searched online and found the answer.

'It would appear that there is such a thing as "The Centre for Dalínian Studies",' he announced. 'It's in Figueres, at the main Dalí museum.'

'So we're in the wrong place?'

'This website says there are thousands of Dalí's documents, photographs and books at the other place, but it's been closed to researchers for the past year.'

'Well let us make haste to Figueres,' said Ratty, full of a new-found bravado. 'If we can infiltrate one museum, we can infiltrate two.'

The clomp of footsteps elsewhere in the house silenced them. The Patient began to retrace his steps out of the room.

'Keep still,' whispered Ratty. 'Perhaps he won't come in here.'

'It would be more prudent to split up. One man cannot apprehend two if we are not in the same room.'

Before Ratty could attempt to dissuade his friend from abandoning him at this sticky moment, the Patient had smoothly made his exit the way they had come in. Ratty looked around him at the wardrobes, wondering if he could squeeze inside the one they had opened, but remembered the noise made by its ancient hinges.

And now it was too late. The security guard entered the room and appeared to be surprised at Ratty's presence.

'Fair cop,' said Ratty. 'Go on, old chap, shoot me here.' He tapped at his protected chest. 'Or punch me, just here.' He slapped his metal-encrusted stomach.

The guard sighed. He was in his fifties, and appeared to Ratty to have been doing this lonely job for long enough to lack the enthusiasm that the apprehension of an intruder should have sparked. He smoothly produced a pair of handcuffs, which he applied to the errant Lord without resistance before radioing news of his catch to his superiors.

The Patient waited silently in Dalí's garden until the commotion of Ratty's capture and removal from the house was complete. It was odd to watch his friend being subjected to less than civilised treatment and he felt guilty about not attempting to intervene, especially since it was such an intervention from Ratty that had initiated their friendship and ended his enslavement in Guatemala. But the Patient had thought everything through carefully. It was clear that he would be captured too if he tried to free Ratty, and it made sense for at least one of them to remain on the outside. In the darkness, it would be impossible for him to follow the vehicle in which Ratty was driven away, for a lone pair of headlights behind them on quiet country roads would make his presence too obvious. He noted, instead, the type and registration mark of the car, the number of people in it, and its direction – although with only one road out of the village, that didn't tell him much. He considered it incumbent upon him to attempt the next stage of their plan alone, and prepared to visit the closed Centre for Dalínian Studies the next day.

'I refuse to say anything without my lawyer.'

The old man stared at him.

'I am not a police officer, Lord Ballashiels. Therefore, a lawyer would not be of any help to you.'

'Therefore I refuse to say anything without a gin and tonic.'

The old man left the room, returning a couple of minutes later with the requested drink.

'Awfully kind. I don't think we've been formally introduced. Justin Ballashiels, Eighth Earl of wotnot. My friends call me Ratty on account of the conk. And you are?'

Ratty tried to hold out his hand, but as it was shackled to the one holding the glass, it created a mild agitation of the liquid.

'It goes without saying that I have been expecting you, Your Lordship.'

'For how long? You can't have been waiting more than a day or two, since we sent the Land Rover back home.'

'A day or two?' The old man gave a world-weary sigh. 'I have been preparing for your visit for rather longer than that. I have been expecting you here since 1975.'

'Golly. Sorry I'm late, old fellow. Been a tad busy

with this and that, don't you know? The Eighties were particularly chocka.'

'We didn't anticipate that you would visit Dalí's house before the museum, however, otherwise we would have picked you up sooner.'

'Jolly decent of you to go to all that trouble, but I think I'll bash off now,' said Ratty, slurping the gin quickly.

'You will remain here.'

'And where is here, exactly?'

'We are in the Centre for Dalínian Studies. We have a room reserved for you.'

'With a bath?'

'I don't understand,' said the old man.

'Not awfully keen on those continental shower thingies.'

'It's very late, Your Lordship. We will continue our discussions in the morning. Someone will show you to your room shortly.'

'Do you happen to know a fellow called Constable Stuart? Police chappy. Penchant for stashing rifles in the boot of his car.'

The old man ignored the question and stood at the doorway.

'You know, it really is appalling that you have left it so long to visit me,' he told a surprised Ratty.

'Visit you?'

'In fact, you are very nearly too late,' the old man added. 'Very nearly.' He left Ratty alone to consider his curious words.

MONDAY 6TH MAY 2013

The office smelled stuffy, as if someone had slept there. Rocco sat down across the desk from the old man, and noticed he looked weary and unshaven. The old man yawned. Rocco thought this was rather rude, but chose not to mention it.

'Reporting for duty,' said Rocco, wondering if he ought to offer to come back later. 'You said you had something you wanted me to do.'

'There is much I want you to do. My dreams are beyond the scope of one man. But I need to know a little more about you.'

'Rocco Strauss. Ph.D. German national.' The old man reacted to the news of Rocco's nationality with a facial twitch. Rocco paused for a second, unsure if the reaction had any significance, then continued, 'Rocket scientist at ESA. Taking extended leave to research the enigma that is Project Keo. Kind of a hobby, I suppose. As Keo appears to have some resonance with you, I thought we could work together rather than in competition.'

'A hobby? You are not part of a larger organisation?'

'Hey, it's me that's usually the conspiracy theorist. I'm the lone investigator. You're the one who seems to be the bigwig head of an organisation. And my theory, if you don't mind me saying so, is that you report to the ultimate secret society.'

'Ultimate secret society? Why ultimate?'

'Because I think you're reporting to the people who are going to receive the Keo time capsule in fifty thousand years. I think they are directing you. And I want you to know that I think that's pretty cool.'

'Well, Doctor Strauss, I am afraid you couldn't possibly be more mistaken in your assumptions. I report to no one. And I certainly do not have any direct contact with our unborn descendants.'

'So you're not agents of the world of the future?'

The old man shook his head. Rocco's mouth dropped.

'I am a man of the present. The present world, the world as it should be. That is my concern, my passion, my obsession. And I need to know why you wish to be a part of my plans.'

It was clear from the expression on Rocco's face that any burning desire to join this club was down to its last embers.

'It sounds like I've got you all wrong. You're not studying the future after all.'

'There is much you do not yet know or comprehend. If you perform the tasks I set for you, then you shall be rewarded with knowledge. Your curiosity will be satisfied.'

'So how can I help?'

The old man stood up and walked around the room. Rocco sat calmly, observing him.

'When were your parents born?' the old man asked suddenly.

Rocco was confused by the apparent irrelevance of the question, but answered it honestly.

'1947.'

The date seemed to satisfy the old man. Quite why he was pleased to discover that Rocco owed his existence to the post-war baby boom was unclear.

'You are very fortunate to have experienced the life you have known.'

'It's been cool at times.'

'It must have been hard for your grandparents. The war must have changed their life plans.'

'I guess so. Never knew much about them. My family never liked to ask too many questions about that period. You never know what it might have dug up, and it's usually the kind of stuff you'd prefer not to know anyway.'

'You are lucky to have had the opportunity to walk upon this earth. It should not have been this way.'

'How do you mean?'

'I mean that were it not for the war you would not have been born because your parents would not have been born. Instead of being apart during the war years, your grandparents would have procreated sooner, and different babies would have been born instead of your parents. They wouldn't have needed to wait until the war was over before having children. So, without the war, your parents would not have existed. And, therefore, you would not have been conceived.'

'Well, I suppose so. Puts rather a different slant on things. But what does that have to do with me helping you guys?'

'Oh nothing, nothing at all. Just how my mind annexes one thought after another. Now, let's move on. I don't have much time. I need to decide if you can be useful to me. Before I make up my mind, tell me about your work at the European Space Agency ...'

Ratty heard a familiar voice. A servant. Offering him a cup of tea. It was normality personified. It was how things used to be and therefore how things should always be. It was blissful, like a morning from his lost childhood.

He opened his eyes and blinked at the bright lights. The room was windowless. He had been sleeping on an inflatable mattress on the cold, tiled floor of what appeared to be a basement. As he craned his neck to see the source of the voice, the airbed wobbled unpredictably and rolled him onto the floor.

'Would you care for a cup of tea, Your Lordship?'

He sat up and looked squarely at the servant. The voice fitted, but the features did not belong exactly to the face he remembered. Gone were the side whiskers and generous, brown hair, replaced by a shaved head with a few stubbly patches of grey. The eyes looked tired, ringed by bags instead of sparkles, and the chin had multiplied a couple of times.

'Grant?' asked Ratty, hoping he hadn't insulted the fellow by getting his name wrong after all those years. If this was the man he was thinking of, it was the family's former butler, superficially a thoroughly decent type who'd always seemed to have time for Ratty back in the day, but with a distant look in his eye that could sometimes leave the young aristocrat ill at ease. 'It is you, isn't it?'

'Indeed, sir. I trust you still take it without sugar.'

'Yes, of course. Crumbs, how have you been since –'

'Since 1979?'

'Is that when you left? *Tempus fugit* and wotnot. Been busy?'

'Busy, sir?'

'Work, I mean. The buttling. Did you carry on as a servant?'

'In a manner of speaking, yes. I was serving at Her Majesty's pleasure.'

Grant held the chipped mug while he waited for Ratty

to find a comfortable seating position on the floor.

'Ah, yes, the old constable chappy mentioned that. Must have been rather horrid for you.' Ratty took the tea and sniffed its aroma.

'It was not easy.'

'Still, all water under the whatsit now, eh? Reformed character, I'm sure. Done your porridge, as they say. So what brings you to these parts?'

'The same thing that brought me to Stiperstones in the first place, sir.'

'Clear as mud, old boy.'

'I came to Stiperstones, as you are now doubtless aware, for the same reason that all of the other members of staff did.'

'Yes, well perhaps if you could elucidate somewhat it might jog the old synapses.'

'It was for the same reason that I am here, now. Salvador Dalí.'

'He does seem a popular chap round these parts.'

'I came to Stiperstones because of the link between the painter and your grandmother.'

'I know he painted her, but I'm only just starting to find out a little more about their relationship. What else is there?'

'In 1937 they shared an experience that changed the world. A few miles north of here, near Perpignan, they both witnessed the reason for all that has happened since. The most important event in human history. Only they didn't understand it. We didn't understand either. It is only recently that the jigsaw started to fit together.'

'Could never get the hang of jigsaws.'

'Your Lordship, none of this is your fault, and I hold no personal malice towards you, but you were born by accident into the centre of something rather larger than you could possibly imagine.'

'Probably best if I finish this before you tell me more,' Ratty said, sipping the tea repeatedly.

'I won't be telling you anything else,' said Grant. 'The boss needs to see you as soon as he is free.'

'Done his porridge, too?'

'As soon as he's finished his current meeting, Your Lordship. Wait here, please.'

He left the room. Ratty tidied himself up as best he could under the circumstances and tried to make sense of all of the odd things people had been telling him. He had journeyed to Spain in order to answer the major questions of his life, but had succeeded only in learning that there were far greater questions still to be asked.

The key turned in the lock. He steadied himself, ready for more bizarre discussions with the old man he had met the previous night. But the face that peered into the room was a far more welcome sight.

'Ratty. Quick. Follow me,' said the Patient.

Ratty did as he was told, grabbing his bulletproof jacket and resisting the urge to verbalise his admiration for the Patient's apparent cunning and courage. They walked to an internal fire escape, a concrete staircase that led up to the other floors. At ground level, Ratty expected them to make their escape onto the street, but the Patient kept climbing until they reached a door which he opened using what appeared to be a home-made key.

'The Dalínian library,' whispered the Patient.

The door opened out into a vast room lined with book cases, filing cabinets and study tables. Some building work was ongoing in the corner of the room, and all of the furniture was covered with dust sheets.

'How did you get into this building, Patient chappy?'

'No building is secure. All are designed to permit the

entry and exit of the human animal with minimal disruption. In my former life, the first skill I ever developed was the construction of keys from visual memories. Those keys unlocked a world of knowledge for me when I was able to break into my father's library every night. Locating you within the building was then just a process of logical deduction and trying many rooms until I found you.'

'This is where we should have come in the first place, isn't it?'

'It is.'

'I say, good show, but don't you think we ought to get away from these odd fellows? I just met my old butler. Queer experience.'

'We are safe in this room. It is closed to researchers until further notice. If builders find us they won't be concerned at our presence. We can look for evidence of your family's links with Dalí.'

Ratty was glad to have had the opportunity to drink a cup of tea before commencing such an undertaking. He rubbed his tired eyes and opened a filing cabinet. It contained thousands of photographs, sorted and catalogued according to the year in which they were taken. He grabbed a bundle from the section dated 1937. The Patient, meanwhile, had located a stack of handwritten pages and spread them across a desk.

'These are the original drafts of his diaries,' the Patient explained. 'He doesn't mention your grandmother in the published diaries, but that doesn't exclude the possibility that she may feature in an unpublished draft.'

Ratty was too engrossed in the collection of photographs to pay attention to his friend. He flicked rapidly through the black and white shots, squinting to ascertain whether a blurry female may or may not have been his ancestor. For some reason girls in the Thirties all seemed to look alike, bedecked in generic and unflattering fashions that masked their individuality.

Something other than his grandmother caught his attention. A photograph of a flint turret. Just like he had seen at West Dean House. He flicked through further. There were shots of the interiors, and, finally, a group of young women smiling and waving at the camera on the lawn in front of the stately home. He looked at them closely. There were one or two Mitfords, several individuals that he couldn't name, and right at the edge, almost out of shot, was someone familiar. He moved the photograph further away from his nose and then back towards him again. Could it be his grandmother? Ratty stared at the woman in the picture. She seemed slightly detached from the rest of the group. The others all appeared utterly carefree, but she was different. It was as if her relationship with the photographer, which he presumed to be Dalí himself, was something deeper. He knew that was too much to read into the snapshot of a single moment, though. Besides, if it truly was his grandmother, she might simply have been consumed with planning the big prank of locking the empty bedroom. Might have been the highlight of her year.

Ratty looked at the back of the photo for any documentation that might enlighten him further. Dalí had scribbled 'West Dean' on the reverse, and a sticker gave the photograph its catalogue number within the collection. There were other West Dean shots, including several of the house's owner, Edward James, but Ratty's grandmother didn't appear again. He returned to the filing cabinet and picked up another batch from the same year. Dalí had photographed some of the sights from his journey through France that year, and amongst these Ratty found the evidence he had been looking for: a portrait of his grandmother set against a backdrop that was unmistakeably a village in southern France. He now had clear evidence that she had travelled with Dalí in the months prior to the sealing of the room and the ceremonial burial of the key. He looked for anything else of note in this section: they were all landscape views and occasional quirky close-ups of objects and plants. One photo seemed to be missing, however. There was a place card with its reference number and a very brief description.

'Keo,' said Ratty.

'Yes?' asked the Patient.

'There's a photograph missing from Dalí's journey to Spain with granny. The placeholder card just says Keo. How's your search going?'

'I'm trying to pinpoint the section of his diary that relates to the same journey. I have a stack of pages, but they are too many to read here. It would be wise to make good our escape and study them at our leisure.'

'Well I must say this little jaunt has worked out rather jolly well, Patient chappy. Well played.'

The echo of footsteps on the stairwell caught their attention.

'Whilst it is true that to run away from trouble is a form of cowardice, the wise man does not expose himself needlessly to danger,' said the Patient, stuffing the unpublished diary pages into his pockets. 'Therefore perhaps we should consider prioritising an exit via the other door.'

'Wait. I want to search the photos from 1975. Perhaps there is evidence of Mother's visit.'

Ratty started rifling through the filing cabinet in search of potential photos. There were hundreds more from this era than from the Thirties, mostly in colour, and too many to scan through with sufficient rapidity to avoid detection.

'Leave them. We must go.'

'I can't leave these. I might not get another chance to search here.'

'Someone is coming. We have to go now.'

The footsteps stopped. They could hear a jangling key behind the door. Ratty removed the tiles from his jacket and piled them neatly on a table, filling his pockets instead with bundles of 1975 photographs. Any that didn't fit he attempted to stuff into his other pockets or just to hold in his hands. He ran out of the room, following the Patient, and closed the door behind him just as the other door creaked open.

'Where now?' asked Ratty, loving the adventure and yet aware that his enjoyment was somehow morally wrong.

'We find the police constable. He might be here.'

'Constable Stuart? I'd nearly forgotten about the fellow. But this place is getting busy. People are arriving for work already.'

'So let us move with the utmost efficiency. You were being held in the basement level. I saw no other locked rooms down there, so I suggest we look instead to the other extreme.'

'The jolly old attic?'

They located another staircase and sprinted to the top where they found a small landing and a single door. Ratty turned the handle and it opened easily.

'Can't be here,' he said, briefly looking into the unlit room. 'Not secure.'

'Perhaps it doesn't need to be secure?'

'Meaning?'

'Perhaps the constable is restrained by another

method? Or perhaps he does not need to be restrained at all?'

Ratty sighed and marched into the attic room, tapping his hands on the wall in search of a light switch, but it was the Patient who found the switch and revealed to them the sight of piles of personal possessions stacked in neat boxes. There was no one waiting for rescue.

'Why would you question whether the constable needed to be restrained at all?' asked Ratty.

'Now that, young men,' said a voice behind them, 'is an excellent question.'

Ratty and the Patient spun around to see Constable Stuart standing at the doorway.

'Constable,' spluttered Ratty, 'I can, of course, provide an entirely reasonable explanation for our presence in this attic.'

'Of course.'

'We were endeavouring to locate you with a view to precipitating your rescue,' said the Patient.

'Precipitating?' asked the constable. 'Sounds like it's going to rain!'

'Why are you already free to roam around the building?' asked Ratty.

Before the policeman could answer, the Patient gave Ratty a nudge and started edging towards the stairs.

'Actually, constable, we have to be somewhere,' said the Patient. 'Perhaps we can continue this chat another time?'

'Where are you lads off to at this time of the morning?'

'Lots to do,' said Ratty. 'Starting with a pre-breakfast perambulation in the general direction of thingummy.'

The police constable stepped in front of them, blocking their way to the stairs.

160

'I don't think so, boys.'

'You don't?' asked Ratty.

'I think you ought to remain here for now. We'll look after you.'

'We?' asked the Patient. 'To whom are you referring?'

'Now that's another excellent question. My, you two are coming up with some right corkers this morning.'

He placed his hand on his hip, as if adjusting a hidden weapon beneath his trousers.

'Now look here, old fellow,' said Ratty, surprising himself with the courage his indignation had created, 'back at Chartres you made it abundantly clear that you were on our side. You took care of the other cars that were following me and said everything would be fine if we stuck close to you, but I can only assume from your attitude and the fact that you seem to be at home in this giant egg box of a building that your affinities lie with Dalí, not with the Ballashiels clan.'

'I am a police officer, young Justin. My affinities lie with truth and law and order.'

'Not with Dalí, then?'

'Emphatically not. Through no fault of his own, Dalí is the cause of more disorder in the world than you can possibly imagine.'

'Well, some of his paintings didn't quite hit the spot, but I think it's going a bit far to say that he was some kind of force of destabilisation, constable.'

'With respect, young man, you are not an initiate, and therefore you cannot understand the truth about history.'

'Surely first class dibs in the subject from Gonville and Caius counts for something?'

'I am afraid not. And whilst I am not a worshipper of Dalí, neither am I a fan of the Ballashiels line, despite past appearances to the contrary.'

161

'Why ever not, old chap? We've always done our bit. Provided a goat or two for slaughter at Harvest Festival. Let the commoners on the land once in a blue moon for village fêtes and wotnot. What is there to dislike?'

'I am sorry to inform you, young Justin, that your grandmother is as guilty as Mister Dalí. What they did has changed the world, and not for the better.'

This made no sense to Ratty. His quest for information about his grandmother was turning into a series of unsettling revelations.

'So let's get this straight, officer. When you caught us stealing a book from the village feminist, you were already waiting for us with a locksmith in tow, ready to cover up all traces of our crime. No arrest, no verbal warning, no yellow card.'

'Correct, Justin.'

'Then I crashed into your car in France, and you denied that there was any damage to your vehicle.'

'Also correct.'

'Then you follow us and when we threw our tracker device into a sheep lorry you followed the other cars who were also following us, ending up with you shooting them dead at a remote farm.'

'I don't know where you got that impression from, young man, but you are mistaken.'

'Did you just injure them? Scare them off? Have a word with them? What was it?'

'None of the above. I merely had a beer with them.'

'A beer?'

'Well, not a proper pint, you understand. Rather hard to come by on the continent, as I'm sure you're aware. And it wasn't as if I was officially on duty.'

Ratty appeared even more confused.

'What about all the guns we saw in your boot?'

162

'My guns, yes. A fine collection.'

'But you didn't use them?'

'On my very good friends? That would be a little unsporting.'

'So what was going on?'

'Rather amusing, really. We were all tasked with tailing you on the roads, but as time went on I realised it was not the wisest thing to be doing. I recommended to the others that we take a different approach: gain your trust, make it seem that I was putting myself at risk for you, make you happy to have me follow you. Ultimately, get you to follow me, rather than vice versa. In the end I knew where you were headed and didn't feel it necessary to stick around. Far more useful for you to think you might be able to rescue me from this building.'

'Well don't go expecting a contribution to the Police Benevolent Fund this year, constable. I think your behaviour is unbecoming and devious.'

'May I remind Your Lordship that you were driving an unroadworthy motor car, without due care and attention, and that you were caught attempting to rob the home of Salvador Dalí. Don't throw stones unless you are without sin.'

'A necessary evil is not evil if it is necessary,' said the Patient. 'And by necessary, of course, I mean in the context of achieving a greater good. Ratty and myself are embarked upon a mission to discover what happened to his grandmother before she locked up a room in Stiperstones, and we also desire to find out where his mother went after she apparently discovered whatever that room contained. The pursuit of that knowledge is, in our opinion, a greater good than any minor offences that may have been committed along the way.'

'Well that's a fine summing up speech. You'd make a

handsome barrister, no doubt. But you fail to appreciate that my own evil is for a necessary cause that extends far beyond personal interest and selfish motives. What I do is in the interest of many millions of people. It truly renders insignificant any rules that I have to bend along the way.'

'Well it's been marvellous, as usual,' said Ratty. 'We should do as you say, retire to some room or other.'

'Not with those,' said the constable.

'Not with what?' asked Ratty.

'Those photos sticking out of your pockets and those documents that your friend has stolen. Hand them over, boys.'

The forgeries were complete. Charlie held them adjacent to the real documents in the bright morning light that blazed into his hotel room. The job of scanning, typesetting, editing, and testing with the high resolution inkjet printer had kept him awake overnight, aided by the stomach-churning awareness that if his construction permits were discovered to be false he could be looking at a substantial prison sentence. But he was satisfied that he had done his best, and he couldn't envisage a minimum wage security worker having the skills to spot his forgery. The previous day he had sent an e-mail to the supplier of the drilling machine and construction accessories saying he was ready to receive the equipment on site. Now he had to prepare physically and psychologically for the task of carrying out this brazen deception. There was no second chance. If he screwed this up his world would fall apart very fast.

He showered and pulled on his *Men in Black* outfit. The disguise gave him confidence. He looked one more time at the faked permits from City Hall and rehearsed his spiel, testing one or two memorised anecdotes about previous foundation excavations he had carried out. After breakfast he checked his e-mail and received confirmation that the machinery would arrive at noon. The heist was on.

He took a cab all the way to Flushing Meadows, hoping to arrive in advance of the machinery so that he could facilitate their entrance to the park, and rehearsing his cover story over and over. Minutes from the park he looked up from his permits and notes and paused for a moment. A thought struck him: he was actually taking something seriously, possibly for the first time in his life. He was taking a complex task and seeing it through instead of walking away from anything to do with effort and commitment. And another realisation reached him: he hadn't eaten a donut since he'd arrived in the States. Was he changing? Was this what it was like to mature? The idea didn't repulse him, so some maturity must have been going on there. His confidence grew another notch.

At the park gates he paid the cab driver and waited out of sight of the security guard's hut, jumping out only as the convoy carrying his equipment arrived. A guard approached the lead truck. Charlie marched boldly towards him and intervened.

'New York State Pavilion. Foundation inspection,' said Charlie.

'Again?' asked the guard.

'Gotta be regular. But this one is more thorough than the last. We're going deeper and further. We think those piles are suffering real bad down there. The whole place could be facing imminent collapse.'

The guard looked at the forged permits. He read them in excruciating detail. He looked up at Charlie, standing there in his ridiculous outfit. He looked at the line of trucks waiting for his approval to permit them entry to the park. The blue collar drivers looked rough and unforgiving, impatient and judgemental. The guard was not easily intimidated, however.

'Come with me, sir.'

Charlie followed him into his hut. The room was formal, devoid of personality. This was not a guy who would respond with good humour to anything that wasn't precisely by the book. The guard sat behind his desk and invited Charlie to sit, too. Charlie read the guard's name tag. Dick English. He clamped his lips tight together and studied his foe. English was older than Charlie, but not much. He had a nice, clean uniform and his own desk. He had a role in life, a groove into which he fitted. It was everything Charlie had spent his adulthood trying to avoid.

'What the hell's going on here?' asked English.

'I've been asked to dig down to look at the foundations of the –'

'Don't give me that crap. I didn't wanna make a scene in front of the drivers, but I know this is bull. What are you really planning?'

'The trustees have ordered another survey, that's all.'

'The trustees of the New York State Pavilion have done no such thing. Now you can come clean with me and let me know what your game is, or I can call for back-up and we can have you guys thrown in the cells.'

'But I have the paperwork from City Hall. It shows the trustees have approved my survey.'

'The trustees did not approve any survey for today.'

'How would you know if they did or didn't, anyway?' asked Charlie, losing his cool amid rising panic.

'Because my father is one of the trustees.'

Charlie gulped. The old man's threats echoed in his head. This could be a turning point. Glory or disaster. He

166

was in so deep there was nothing left to lose.

'Listen, soldier,' he whispered, crossing his arms and wondering why he'd used the word 'soldier' when the guard was clearly nothing of the sort – it just sounded right – 'or can I call you Dick?'

When there was no reaction he continued regardless. 'This City Hall paperwork. You're right. Total bull. And I'm proud of you for being on the ball. You should be proud. Your bosses should be proud. You're a good worker, my friend. No, a great worker. You'll go far.'

'Go on,' said English, trying to resist the temptation to soften his attitude in the face of so much flattery.

'So the piling thing is bull, obviously, but the kind of hardware and people you see out there, they don't come together for no reason. Something big is going down, but I'm sure an intelligent guy like you understands why information is on a need to know basis.'

'So you're not a surveyor?'

'With respect, do I look like a surveyor? Of course not. I report very high up. Between you and me, this goes all the way to the White House.'

'It does?'

'Sure does.'

'So level with me. If this isn't more bullshit, what is it?'

'It's the time capsule.'

'The Westinghouse capsule?'

'That's it.'

'Which one? There are two of them.'

'The Thirties capsule. Look, I know I said this was need to know stuff, but you're someone I think I can trust with the truth and I think you do need to know because I want you to feel comfortable about what is going to happen.'

'Which is what?'

'We're going to dig the time capsule out of the ground.'

'Uhuh.'

Charlie was resorting to his usual idiotic honesty in order to get him out of this hole, and into the hole he hoped soon to be digging. He toyed with the idea of introducing the catch-all ace of the threat of terrorism, but couldn't think of a way to connect a 1930s capsule with a modern threat to the safety of New York. So he stuck with a story that was as close to honest as he felt able to go.

'In 1936, Salvador Dalí was working on an exhibit for the World's Fair, right next to where the time capsule was being prepared. Information has come to light at the highest levels that Dalí tampered with the capsule before it was sealed and buried.'

'Dalí? Melting clocks guy, huh?'

'Right. For reasons of national pride and national security, I've been charged with the job of inspecting the capsule to make sure there is nothing that will cause embarrassment to our nation or that will harm the people of the future. That Spaniard was a practical joker. We think he may at that time have also been a communist or even a Nazi sympathiser. We need to know what he did to that time capsule, and the only way to check is to dig the damn thing up.'

'Dig it up, huh?'

'That's right. Now you and I both know that it's going to be hell on earth right here if word gets out about this. That's why we're going in under the foundations of the New York State Pavilion. Tunnelling at forty-five degrees will get us to the capsule in less than a week, and no one will be any the wiser. The City Hall paperwork is legit, the works will be screened and out of anyone's way, we'll check the capsule, put it back, seal it up, and move the hell out of here.'

The guard actually appeared satisfied by this explanation.

'You know the two capsules are not in the same hole?' he asked.

'Er, kinda,' said Charlie.

'They buried the Sixties capsule ten feet due north of the Thirties one. The capstone is actually between them. From the New York State Pavilion aim five feet to the left of the capstone.'

'Got it,' replied Charlie, aghast that this man was being so helpful.

The guard reached across his desk for a box of security passes.

'Give one to each of your guys. They have to wear them at all times when entering and leaving the park. Keep the noise down. Keep the mess down. Keep outta trouble.'

Charlie shook his hand.

'Your co-operation is appreciated,' said Charlie. 'We had a lot of guys on stand-by ready to roll right over you if you gave us any shit. I'll order them all to stand down. Well done. You made a good call today.'

As he walked outside he could feel the jelly-like wobble in his legs, and the aftermath of the adrenal rush that had pumped his brain with the necessary sharpness to maintain the illusion of authority. The dig was on. The hard talking was over. The hard labour would now begin.

'It has been a long time in coming,' said the old man. Ratty fidgeted in his seat and the Patient sat calmly. The old man shuffled the photographs in his hands like a deck of cards. With the slick hand movements of a magician he

169

suddenly fanned them out and flicked a single photo towards Ratty. 'Is this perhaps the one you were hoping to see?'

Ratty grabbed it and held it close to his face. This was the photo he had dreamed of finding. He checked the date on the back. 1975. The colour picture showed Dalí and his mother standing arm in arm on a beach that appeared to be Port Lligat, just outside Dalí's house. He thought of all the police and inhabitants of Stiperstones village who had searched the hedgerows and fields after his mother's disappearance. A five mile radius around Stiperstones Manor had been examined with a fine toothcomb. Key spots in the wider county had also been searched. Hundreds had been interviewed. No one had thought it necessary to knock on the door of an elderly painter living a thousand miles away. No one had found any hint of a trail leading to Spain.

The photo made Ratty well up. To his enormous embarrassment, he sensed a tear beginning to leak onto his face. Emotions were breaking out of the secure part of his brain where they were normally locked away, and now their force was something to which he could offer no resistance. The single tear was followed by a full scale blubbing and a brief wailing. The old man and the Patient sat uncomfortably while Ratty tried to regain some composure.

'Frightfully sorry,' he managed to say between sobs. 'Takes me back to a somewhat rum part of my life.'

'May I take it that you knew about Lady Ballashiel's visit to Dalí's house in 1975?' asked the Patient, doing his best to move things forward during Ratty's temporary incapacity.

'Knew about it?' asked the old man. 'Of course I knew about it. I instigated it.'

'So why didn't she come home?' asked Ratty in a broken, high-pitched voice that made him sound like a lost child.

'Life is far more complex than you realise,' said the old man. 'Fate throws curved balls. Shit happens. You can't always get what you want.'

'Are you in a position to advise Lord Ballashiels as to the fate of his mother after this photograph was taken?' asked the Patient.

The old man shook his head. Ratty pulled himself together.

'Goodness me, what a performance,' said Ratty. 'What must you think of me?'

'I think you are foolish to come here,' the old man replied.

'I say – you've just admitted to being the reason for Mother's visit to Dalí, and now you insult me for wanting to know what became of her.'

'I think you should leave immediately,' the old man said, emotionlessly. 'There is nothing for you to learn here. Only bad can come of your involvement in our affairs.'

'I must say, your attitude seems a little harsh, old fellow.'

'I am giving you a lifeline that you are fortunate to be able to exploit. You will have the chance to return home where you will spend the rest of your days at Stiperstones.'

'Bit of a rotten opportunity if you ask me. Look, I'm frightfully sorry for the break-in and wotnot. Obviously you're a tad miffed but I'll happily pay for any damages. Do you want proper money or do you prefer those funny little Euros?'

'There is no need for money to change hands, Your

Lordship. Enjoy whatever money you have while you still have a life with which to enjoy it.'

'To the uninitiated, your words have a tendency to sound as if they are loaded with threats,' observed the Patient.

'Not threats,' replied the old man. 'Advice. His Lordship is fortunate to have lived any life at all, and I am advising him to enjoy whatever may be left of it.'

'Still sounds like something of an undercurrent to me,' said Ratty. 'It's the sort of advice one might give to someone whose days are numbered. And not a particularly big number, to boot.'

'All our days are numbered,' said the old man. 'We must simply do our best for the planet with the days that we have. I can't let you obstruct what I am doing to improve the world, which is why I can't let you remain here. Your village police constable will escort you both home where I expect you to remain out of trouble. Otherwise your safety cannot be guaranteed and the number of days you have left may be seriously curtailed.'

'Well now, this has gone far enough,' blurted Ratty, thoroughly miffed at the attitude of the old man and the hindrances placed in his way when all he wanted to do was to find out what happened to his mother. 'We mean no ill to anyone, and we are on an honest quest for information about a missing woman. Your attitude is not only unhelpful, it's positively beastly.'

There was a knock at the door. Constable Stuart let himself in and whispered something into the old man's ear.

'What? Why would he do that?' asked the old man.

'No one knows, but this time he was caught in the act. The police are holding him in the cells right now.'

'But Florida? How could he have got there? My men

are watching him in New York.'

'All I know is that he was caught stealing a painting from the Dalí museum in St. Petersburg, Florida.'

'Which painting?'

'I believe it is called something like *Daddy Longlegs of the Evening.*'

'That's a small one. I wouldn't have thought he would struggle with that. But anyway, he can't be in Florida because I know he's started digging at Flushing Meadows. My men in New York confirmed this just minutes ago.'

'If I may interject,' said the Patient.

'You may not,' replied the old man. 'This is not your business.'

'Nevertheless, you appear to have hit a philosophical conundrum that is solvable only by making a sideways step,' the Patient continued.

'Go on, young man,' said the policeman before the old man could contradict him.

'You appear to be of the opinion that someone you are observing in New York has attempted to steal a work of art in Florida at the same time. Therefore you must step sideways and entertain the possibility that they are not the same person.'

'But the man in Florida has confessed to the New York and London art thefts,' said Stuart. 'That means it's the same man we sent to Flushing Meadows.'

'How can you be sure that the man you sent to Flushing Meadows is guilty of those previous thefts?' asked the Patient.

The old man held up his hand to cease the conversation. He appeared to be deep in thought. 'I may have sent to Flushing Meadows someone who is not a professional art thief? An interesting situation. A loose cannon, working hard, getting the job done, even though he isn't who I thought he was. Very interesting indeed.'

'If he's not who you think he is,' said Stuart, you don't have any hold over him. His only crime was skipping the queue at the museum. If you can't threaten him with the consequences of those art thefts you have no control at all.'

'Do you really think my preparations would be so sparse as to rely on the efforts of one man? Of course not. I don't need him. If he delivers, fine. If not, I have other people to put in his place.'

'We could send someone else to watch over him,' said the constable. 'Just to be safe. And I think I have just the person in mind.'

'We could observe this character on your behalf,' said the Patient.

'Could we?' asked Ratty.

'A ridiculous idea,' said the old man. 'I happen to have someone far more suited to the task. Constable Stuart will escort you both home.'

'Is that wise, sir?' asked Stuart.

'Explain your thinking.'

'We have them both here. There isn't long to go, now. Perhaps it would be better for them to remain here under our watch, than to give them any kind of freedom.'

'Very well. Soon their presence will cease to matter anyway.'

'Have you enquired as to his friend's parentage?' asked the constable.

'What is your name?' asked the old man.

'The Patient,' replied the Patient.

The old man looked at him quizzically, but did not pursue the matter of the odd name.

'And when were your parents born?'

'That is a subject that is best avoided.'

'Were they post-war baby boomers?'

'In what sense?'

'Did the end of the war influence the date of your conception in some way?'

'I think it's fair to say the war was a relevant factor, yes.'

Ratty regarded the Patient carefully, sensing that the line of questions was creeping close to subject areas that were disagreeable for his friend. The Patient was normally unflappable, but it was hard to be reminded of his family's connection to the worst atrocities of the Second World War.

'Good. In that case we have nothing to fear from either of you. You have both been very fortunate to have been born. I will keep you within arm's reach for your remaining days on this planet. I trust you will make the most of the time you have left.'

Rocco was convinced he was being followed. He spent much of his life under such an apprehension, but today it felt more real than ever. Since his meeting at the Dalí museum he had remained in central Figueres, waiting for the call that would confirm whether or not the old man had found a use for him. He had wandered through the shopping areas, he had stopped for coffee in more than one café, but since he began strolling aimlessly through picturesque ancient streets in the medieval quarter he sensed a set of footsteps had been mirroring his own for too long. Without looking back he darted down a side road off a central square and into the open vestibule of an apartment building.

A smartly dressed man stepped into the vestibule and stopped before him. He had a shaved head with patches of grey stubble, and a portly frame that squeezed out two chins where there should have been only one.

'Please don't be alarmed,' said the man.

'Bit late for that,' replied Rocco.

'Allow me to introduce myself. My name is Grant. I was sent by my boss to request your company at the museum at your earliest convenience.'

'Your boss?' asked Rocco.

'The Director at the museum.'

'Ah, that old man. Doesn't he have a telephone?'

'He likes to work on a personal level, where possible,' replied Grant.

'What are you, some kind of butler?' Rocco looked at the man's inappropriately stuffy suit and tie, and wondered how his leather shoes could retain such a dazzling shine amid these dusty Spanish sidewalks.

'I have been employed as such earlier in my career,' replied Grant. 'I work in a more varied role these days.'

'So, the old man wants to see me?' asked Rocco.

'Now.'

This was the news he had been waiting for. He was about to enter the conspiracy. The Keo mystery would be solved.

Down in her trench, scraping the soil a millimetre at a time, Ruby felt at peace. She wanted nothing to do with Rocco and his desire to involve himself in a bizarre and incomprehensible conspiracy. The dig at Empúries was progressing well. Soon after the imperfect extraction of the statue of the goddess Artemis, fragments of another marble deity had been located, and the search was on to find enough sections to be able to identify it. Always in the back of her mind was the possibility that she might discover more evidence that tendrils of culture had

176

crossed the Atlantic in ancient times, linking Europe and the Middle East with Central America, sharing the technologies and ideas that were destined to become lost for so many millennia.

When a shadow fell across her, she knew better than to look up. She continued scraping, and merely whispered,

'What do you want?'

'I have news,' said Rocco.

'Not so close. You'll collapse the sides of the trench,' said Ruby.

Rocco ignored her lack of enthusiasm for his presence and jumped into the trench next to her.

'Careful, Rocco! There are priceless artefacts just beneath the soil.'

'Ruby, have you been wondering what happened to your friend Charlie?' asked Rocco.

'He's not my friend. He's my stalker.'

'Well he's not stalking you now. The old man from the museum has sent him to New York to do something that I'm not allowed to know yet. But he wants me to go to New York this evening and oversee whatever it is that Charlie's doing out there.'

'So you're not going to be getting up my nose anymore?'

'I came to say goodbye.'

Ruby's mood lightened visibly. She looked up from her scraping and smiled.

'That's wonderful news.'

'You sure you'll be able to cope without me?'

Ruby glared at him. Rocco climbed out of the trench.

'Wait,' she said, standing up. 'Do you think Charlie's going to be OK?'

'What do you mean?'

'Charlie's not the sort to work for anyone. He has no

ideals, no work ethic. Why would he give up his tour of Europe for a job he doesn't need?'

'You're worried about him, aren't you, Ruby?'

'No. Of course not. It's just, he's, well, I just wouldn't want any harm to come to him. I know he's a bit obsessive about me, but his heart is in the right place.'

'I understand,' said Rocco. 'I'll try to take care of him over there.'

'I just don't get why he would do this in the first place. First the old man at the museum tries to kill you. Then he recruits Charlie. Then he recruits you too. It doesn't add up.'

'You know as much as I do,' replied Rocco. 'Charlie and I seem to be working for something or someone that is hiding behind the shadows. Eventually they'll tell me. He promised me information if I do what they want.'

'Have you tried just asking that old man what he's up to directly?' Ruby asked.

'Of course. He's not going to give me all the facts off the cuff. Look, I have to catch a taxi to the airport. I'm being flown out to New York tonight. He's bought me a first class ticket. Movies and a massage all in the same seat, several cocktails, a good sleep and I wake up in America. Investigating conspiracies has never been so much fun. It's been good knowing you, Ruby.'

She looked away, deep in thought. Rocco could barely take care of himself, let alone Charlie. They had no idea what they were getting themselves involved in. No sane person accepted people off the street and sent them first class across the world to do important work. She wanted answers. She needed to know what risks Charlie was really facing. She resolved to face the old man one more time. The idea of going back into that building and confronting him in his office gave her butterflies in her stomach, but the rational side of her soothed that feeling. After all, she had dealt with museum officials all over the world. They could be cantankerous, moody, intimidating and secretive, but they were never dangerous. The old man wouldn't harm her. As soon as she finished her section of dig today, she was going back to Figueres.

Ratty and the Patient found themselves once again in the attic storey of the building, locked in a secure room used for the storage of works of art when they were not on display. The room had been cleared of valuables before their incarceration, but some of the paraphernalia of a busy museum remained behind: steel frames on trolley wheels for moving artworks around; specialist cleaning equipment; piles of dust sheets.

'How are you enjoying your first visit to Spain?' asked Ratty, making small talk to mask the guilt he felt at having instigated the journey that had led to their imprisonment.

'I find the local people most accommodating,' replied the Patient.

'I don't know what to do now. Can't go home. Don't want to give in to whatever this old fellow wants. And yet I don't know how I can further my research in this area now that they've locked us up.'

'Perhaps you are forgetting one thing, my friend?'

'Is it something to do with philosophy?' Ratty sighed.

'It is my ability to fabricate a key from sight. It may require several visits from our captors, but I am confident that I can fashion a functional device from the items we have around us.'

'I do hope so, otherwise we could spend the rest of our days here, unknown to the world, soon forgotten by all. Rather like Mother, in fact. Oh my goodness, that's it,

179

Patient chappy! The potty old fellow must have treated her the same way he has treated us.'

'You think he locked her away back in 1975?'

'It's possible. He does seem rather keen on the habit.'

'What could his motive have been?' asked the patient. 'It wasn't blackmail or kidnap. It wasn't terrorism. She had committed no crime against him. Illegal imprisonment is not something a man undertakes lightly. I have had enough experience of that myself to know that there is always a powerful reasoning behind it, however twisted or evil that reason may be.'

'Mother was a baby boomer, I believe. He does seem to have a bit of a thingy about them. Perhaps his goal in life is to round them all up?'

'Unlikely. Why maintain a front as the curator of an art museum? There has to be a connection between Dalí and his unfathomable motives.'

'I wonder if there is any evidence that Mother was once held in this building? What do you think, Patient chappy?'

'Dalí restored this building in the early Seventies and it opened in 1974. Therefore the arrival of your mother a year later makes it conceivable that she was held within these walls.'

'Golly. Make that key, Patient fellow. I sense a nocturnal maternal hunt coming on.'

'Have you considered, my friend, the possibility that we may not only be looking for traces of past incarceration, but of the present also?'

'Are you trying to say she could still be here?'

'It is mathematically possible. She arrived as a relatively young woman. Statistically speaking, the chances of her still being alive, with appropriate exceptions for accident and murder, of course, are quite high.'

Ratty appeared to wobble. In his mind, she had been dead since the memorial service and the legal documents that had made it so official in his early teens. He had considered this journey mainly as an investigation into the mysterious circumstances of her death. The possibility that she might actually be alive had always seemed beyond probability, but once he allowed a chink of hope to shine into his mind, he was drawn inexorably towards it.

'Hurry, Patient chappy. There isn't a moment to lose,' said Ratty, gathering an armful of cleaning materials and handing the bundle to the Patient. 'Start making a key now. You can refine it when we next receive a visitor.'

The Patient looked at the items in his hands. He spread them on the floor, then went to the door to study the keyhole more closely. It was an old door, contemporaneous with Dalí's renovation of the original building in the Seventies. He could see the dimly lit hallway through the keyhole and was able to gauge the depth and likely width of the key.

'Please hurry,' repeated Ratty, jigging around and being generally restless and irritating.

'Mathematical theory is no guarantee of reality,' explained the Patient. 'Please do not set your expectations so high. The fall will hurt you when it comes.'

'Pain matters not a jot to me, old boy. After all I've been through I don't think there's anything that could hurt me now.'

'If no one comes until morning there's no way that I can progress my duplication of the key.'

'I can't wait that long, old chap. What other options do we have?'

'From the shape of this room I would guess that we're in the square turret. It has no windows. No apparent roof access. This is a very secure space. Our options are limited to our ability to penetrate the brick structure or to force the door open. With only a collection of cleaning items both procedures are unlikely to succeed.'

'But I've seen the old films. We could build a glider. Dig three tunnels. Dress up as local peasants. Tie bedsheets together.'

'Be patient,' said the Patient. 'I will make that key at the first opportunity. Now I think we should rest.'

'No, I thought of something else,' said Ratty. 'We could send a message asking for help.'

'Our phone was confiscated.'

'What did people do before telephones? Simple. Message in a bottle.'

'I don't think messages in bottles were the primary means of communication in pre-telephonic times,' said the Patient.

'It doesn't matter. If we can just get a written message out to the people on the street below, our problems will be over.'

'I fear that any such missive will merely be mistaken for litter or for a joke and will be disposed of summarily.'

'Must you obstruct every great idea that springs forth from my lips, Patient chappy?'

'I was merely guilty of suggesting obstructions in the wrong order. I should have pointed out the impossibility of getting a piece of paper from here to the streets through solid walls, and even if the paper floated to the ground no one would pay it any attention.'

'Patient chappy, you need to think in a more surrealist manner. What would Dalí have done in this situation?'

'Nothing. He locked himself willingly into this place in the final years of his life.'

'I mean he would release the message with a flourish.

Those giant eggs on the roof. Punch a hole in one of those. Stick the message inside. Then push the egg off the roof so it smashes onto the pavement. That's the surrealist way. That would get us the attention we need.'

'That would still require roof access, however.'

'Help me climb onto that metal picture transporter. I'm going to see what this ceiling is made of.'

With the site at Flushing Meadows screened from public view, Charlie had a spacious area in which to carry out his theft. He had paid for the vehicle operators to do the works for the first few days, and his plan was to relieve them of their duties on the final day. No one but himself would be permitted to witness the great discovery of the time capsule.

The quantity of soil brought to the surface by the tunnelling machine was staggering. It wasn't enough just to let it pile up at the mouth of the hole: the space would soon have become overwhelmed with dirt if he'd done that. An annoyingly cheerful man in a mini-digger carried heaps at a time to the furthest corner of their screened zone and deposited the soil before driving back and forth over it, minimising the height of the hill. Another man, far less jolly than the first and therefore much more palatable to Charlie, clicked pre-fabricated tunnel walls into place, securing the passage as it progressed.

Charlie let the professionals do their thing while he wandered around the ruined pavilion, looking at the remains of the road map of America that had once graced the floor. He left the site a few times to buy coffee and donuts for the men, and tried to maintain his image as a knowledgeable surveyor, even though he had no knowledge of the subject whatsoever.

'Hey, bud!' called a voice from the site entrance.

Charlie waddled over to it. Dick English was standing there with a steaming coffee mug in his hand.

'How's it goin', Dick?' Charlie asked.

'I've been thinking about this time capsule shit,' said English. 'All this need to know crap. It seems the higher you are in the food chain the more interesting stuff you're allowed to know. There's a whole lot of crap no one's telling me because I'm at the bottom of the heap.'

Charlie looked at him blankly.

'What I'm saying,' continued the guard, 'is I want to be like you. I'm sick of being told I'm not important enough to know what's going down. I want to work at your level.'

'My level?'

'Do me a favour. Tell me how you got there.'

At first Charlie sensed a cunning ploy to wean information out of him that would prove his credentials false, but the guy seemed genuinely interested in working for whatever fictitious government agency Charlie had pretended to be from. And Charlie hadn't researched or rehearsed anywhere near enough back story to be able to tell a convincing tale. He simply lacked the fundamental knowledge even to be able to try.

'I'm sorry. I'd love to help, but what you're asking me for is classified information.'

'I'm asking about career paths. Qualifications. That kind of stuff isn't classified.'

'It is today. I mean it's too long to tell right now. Let's meet tomorrow and I'll tell you what you need to do.'

English seemed satisfied, and Charlie had some breathing space. If he spent the whole night on the Internet researching how to become what he had pretended to be, he could probably pull off this next level of the deception.

'Hey, Charlie!' called the irritating man in the digging machine. For the first time, the mindless grin was absent from his face. 'Big problem. We've hit water.'

'Do you have any thoughts as to why the old chap has a bit of a beef about the baby boom generation?' asked Ratty as he clung precariously to the ceiling, held up by the metal picture trolley and a broom.

'There are those who say the boom generation benefited from a prosperity that has been denied to their children,' replied the Patient. 'When a population bubble retires, all expecting their pension payouts at the same time and ceasing to contribute to the economy, it falls upon the shoulders of the young to pay their way. That is the fundamental cause of the recent recession, according to the writings of some economists. Those still in work may work longer for a smaller pension than their parents enjoyed. But that doesn't explain the position of the old man, since he is clearly of the generation for which prosperity blossomed.'

'Indeed. Pass me a paintbrush, old boy.'

The Patient handed a brush up to Ratty.

'Are you sure you're safe up there?'

Ratty turned the brush back to front, so that he gripped its wooden handle in his palm like a knife. He stabbed it at the ceiling repeatedly. Chunks of white plaster rained down upon his hair and shoulders. He blinked as the dust gathered in his eyes.

'The fellow clearly has issues. Says he wants to change the world for the better but won't explain why that should require our incarceration, nor will he reveal his knowledge as to the fate of my mother.'

He dropped the brush and braced himself so that he could use the broom handle to continue chipping away at

185

the small hole he had already made with the brush.

'It is the custom in these parts to construct ceilings from concrete beams and brick infills,' said the Patient. 'Unfortunately plasterboard is rarely used, and therefore I suspect you will have difficulty in making a significant impression.'

'The rotters,' said Ratty. 'Perhaps a substantial hammer of some sort would be more effective?'

'The only item in this room capable of providing the leverage and momentum required is the steelwork in the trolley, but the metal sections of the trolley are bolted together and we would need spanners to separate them.'

'Perhaps the old fellow has a psychological disorder, something that makes him hate everyone of a certain age and their progeny. We're not baby boomers ourselves, so I can't see why he has it in for us.'

'It is possible, though such a psychosis has never been recorded in any scientific papers.'

Ratty climbed down and examined the metal framework of the trolley. He picked up a bottle of brass polish and studied its metallic cap.

'What do you say, Patient chappy? Think we could mould this little wotsit to fit those nuts?'

'It's conceivable, though whether it would survive the newtons needed to make a nut turn remains to be seen.'

'Do your best, my friend. I'm getting out of here today. I'm going to find what that old man did to my mother.'

'Have you considered the possibility that you do not need to get out of here in order to discover more about your mother's fate?'

'Of course not, old potato.'

'Are we of the opinion that the person responsible for our current predicament is the same one who somehow prevented your mother from returning home in 1975?'

'The old man, yes.'

'And what did he choose to do with us?'

'Locked us up in this turret above the museum.'

'Do you have any reason to believe that he would have done anything different with your mother?'

'Not particularly. Gosh, you're not saying that she might have been kept in this room, are you? How frightfully rotten for her.'

'I am saying precisely that. We must entertain the theory, at the very least. And what do we also know about your mother's behaviour when in a sticky situation?'

'Hansel and Gretel,' said Ratty.

'The fairy tale?'

'She tended to leave a trail behind her. Hoping to be rescued and wotnot.'

'So perhaps instead of attempting to leave this room by means that are at best optimistic and at worst dangerous, we should give it closer examination?'

The two men slowly spun around, conducting a quick survey of their surroundings, no longer looking for the means of escape but for the kind of clue that Lady Ballashiels had cleverly left at Stiperstones. The room didn't have much to offer, but Ratty knew from his experience with the empty room at Stiperstones that his mother could be most ingenious.

'No fireplace. And no books. So where do we start, Patient chappy?'

'We should look for marks on the walls. Signs that an area has been painted over. And if there is no fireplace, we must tap the walls to deduce if there ever was one here.'

Ratty tapped the walls at the level of his knees, hoping for the hollow thump that might indicate a boarded up fireplace. All of the walls were as solid as the floor and the ceiling.

'It's no use, old sleuth, this place is a sealed box.'

'Then we must examine the items within it,' said the Patient, tipping up the trolley to look beneath it for signs of tampering or writing. Ratty did likewise with all of the smaller items in the room, but there was nothing to indicate the former presence of his mother.

'What is there in this room that hasn't changed in the past few decades?' asked the Patient.

'Only my haircut,' confessed Ratty. 'And the floor.' He looked down at the tiles beneath his feet. Dark terracotta squares with wide grout lines blackened by ingrained dirt. 'These tiles look as if they've been here for a few decades.'

'It would be hard to inscribe a message in the surface of the tiles themselves, but grout lines are softer,' said the Patient.

'And completely obscured by filth,' added Ratty. 'You're not seriously suggesting that we clean all the grout on the floor?'

'It is a long shot, but we need to eliminate the possibility of a message in the floor.'

'You know I'm not really an expert in the cleaning department,' whispered Ratty, shamefully.

'We have everything we need in this room. Abrasive pads and cleaning solutions. They are most likely for the maintenance of picture frames, and may even be for the restoration of paintings. I think they will be perfect for our endeavours, being gentle enough to remove only the top layer without harming any possible carved lettering or printed writing on the grout beneath.'

Ratty picked up a selection of bottles and sponges. He gazed at the Patient with the look of one who was lost. The Patient sighed and took the items from his friend's hand, sprayed a sponge with detergent and began scrubbing the grout lines on the floor. Ratty clumsily copied, starting on the opposite side of the room, and soon the black lines began to turn pale grey.

'Anything to report, Patient chappy?' Ratty asked, as he paused for breath having cleaned ten tiles.

'Nothing here. We must scrub every centimetre of these lines.'

'Inches, please,' puffed Ratty. 'No need for that continental nonsense.'

The cleaning continued, both men on their hands and knees, following an ever-shrinking circumference. The room became noticeably brighter, but remained devoid of hidden messages. Ratty and the Patient reached the last tile together. It marked the centre point of the room. Ratty stood up to let his friend have the honour of cleaning the final section of grout. He didn't even bother to watch. It seemed to be just a floor. A very clean floor.

'O,' said the Patient.

'Oh what?' asked Ratty.

'There is an "O",' explained the Patient. 'Carved into the grout at the corner of this tile.'

'Could be anything,' said Ratty. 'Tiler probably dropped a coin on the wet grout. Hardly sufficient to constitute a coherent message.'

The Patient skipped a section and went to the next corner.

'R,' he said, wiping the damp dirt away. 'It's been scraped by hand using a simple tool such as a piece of cutlery.'

Ratty's face lit brightly. This was familiar territory.

'Orwell?' he suggested. 'Do you think she's marked Georgie's name again to prove she was here?' He placed his face next to the floor and scanned the areas already cleaned in case the other letters had been missed.

The Patient went to the next corner of the centre tile and scrubbed it free of grime.

'D,' he said.

'Are you sure?' asked Ratty as he scanned the grout lines. 'You can't spell Orwell with a "D".'

The final corner had already been revealed before Ratty had finished speaking.

'O,' the Patient stated, plainly.

'ORDO? What kind of a clue is that? Or is it RODO? Or DORO? Or ROOD, perhaps?'

'I think the letters spell DOOR,' explained the Patient.

'Door? You think this tile in the middle is a trap door? Doesn't look big enough to squeeze through.'

Ratty stamped on the tile in question. He danced a jig, then bent down to grab its edges with his fingers. It was stuck down as solidly as all the others.

'There is another door, Ratty.'

The Patient put down his cleaning materials and walked to the only entrance to the room. Ratty abandoned the floor tile and followed him.

'The door looks original,' Ratty admitted, tapping it lightly to determine if it was hollow. 'Sounds solid, too.'

'How would you inscribe a message on a door in such a way that it would remain undetected?' asked the Patient.

'Tough one. Along the top edge, I suppose. The only place no one ever looks, and rarely gets repainted up there. But she would have needed the door to be open to write a message up there, and we can't get it open to read it.'

'Equally, she would not have had the opportunity to open the door sufficiently to write directly upon its top edge. But even with the door closed it would be possible to write on a strip of paper, apply some glue from the picture repair

190

materials stored here and slide it into the tight gap at the top. It would remain out of sight and attached to the door indefinitely. Why don't you take a look?'

Ratty hopped in an effort to see the top edge of the door, but couldn't discern anything in particular.

'Try scraping it with something,' the Patient suggested. 'Do you possess any of those plastic cards?'

'Credit cards? Hardly. Not exactly credit-worthy, am I? I'll try the membership card of my London club.'

He pulled out the card from his wallet and ran it slowly along the top of the door. Halfway along it met with some slight resistance.

'I think I've hit something.'

'Careful. It will be fragile.'

With a hand that shook with excitement, Ratty dislodged a piece of paper from the top of the door. It fluttered to the ground. Less than half the size of a credit card, it appeared to be folded once along an edge that was brittle with age. When he unfolded it the seam split, but the two separate pieces were clearly legible and the implied message was unambiguous.

Charlie's first entry into his own tunnel felt like a one-way journey to the mouth of Hell. Claustrophobia began to overwhelm him. The walls were sturdy, but they were so close to his stomach and his face that he doubted whether he would have the dexterity to turn around and get out again. His safety back-up was a rope tethered to his waist, the other end of which was held by one of the burlier workers up at ground level. The torch in his hand bounced reflections off the water that sat below him, at a depth of about fifteen feet.

The water table was higher than it was supposed to be at this time of year. He was going to have to bring in the pumping equipment sooner than planned.

'We won't be able to make it all the way down to fifty feet,' said the voice behind him.

'Why not?'

'Pump won't hold enough water back. It'll fill faster than you can get the damn stuff out.'

'What if we have two pumps?' suggested Charlie, trying to stay focussed despite the paralysing sense that he was going to die in there.

'You don't understand. You can pump the ground water out for a few feet, but if you keep digging below that line you're back in the ground water again and the whole damn thing's gonna flood.'

'So how did they bury that thing all those years ago if they had the same problems?'

'They didn't use a tunnelling machine. It's the wrong tool for the job. This far down the mechanics will soak and drown. Your machine's designed for horizontal tunnelling. It's gone beyond its depth and moisture limits.'

Charlie sighed and dropped his torch down into the water.

'Beam me up,' he said, preparing to brace his arms to prevent him slipping back down as he was dragged up to the surface. It took two men to pull him clear of the tunnel.

'So how did they dig a hole deep enough for the time capsule in the first place?' he asked

'Not with a tunnelling machine,' replied his worker. 'They drilled. You can drill through anything because the engine stays at the surface.'

'Shit.'

'Yes. Shit.'

＊

192

'Where did she get all this chocolate?' asked Ratty, looking at the faded and fragile Lanvin wrapper in his hands.

'The Hansel and Gretel analogy seems ever more apt. Your mother has again communicated with you via the medium of chocolate. She had no need of words. The Lanvin wrapper is sufficient evidence of her incarceration here. So now we can be confident that she was present in this room in 1975. With no indication as to where the trail heads from here, we are now in a position where only one course of action will secure the information that we need to progress.'

'Back to putting our little message in an egg on the roof and smashing it to the ground?'

'No,' said the Patient. 'I have an altogether different plan in mind. First I need that cleaning cloth and the bottle of varnish.'

Ratty handed him the items, and the Patient soaked the rag with the varnish. He then laid the rag flat so that he could slide it under the door, with a small section exposed in their room and the majority sticking out into the hallway. He poured the remainder of the varnish onto the door.

'That stuff gives off quite a pen and ink,' said Ratty.

'The flammability of the fumes is crucial. Pass me that paintbrush.'

The Patient began plucking the hairs from the brush, a slow and challenging task using bare hands. Eventually he was left with a wooden handle and a square steel casing, empty of bristles.

'Finally, please pass me the sheet of sandpaper.'

The Patient placed the sandpaper on the floor next to the varnish-soaked rag and began scraping the steel of the paintbrush against it, back and forth, trying to get it to spark.

'It is a plan with two possibilities,' he explained. 'When I achieve combustion, the rag and the door will burn. Either the smoke will trigger an alarm and someone will come to free us, or the door will catch fire and burn down, allowing us to escape.'

'Spiffing plan, Patient chappy. Any sign of a spark, yet?'

'That is the hardest part of the plan. The materials are not ideal for the purpose.'

'Would you care to borrow my lighter?'

The Patient looked up, astonished.

'You're carrying a lighter? You don't even smoke.'

'But I don't like to be caught out if ever there's a lady in need of a light.'

The Patient smiled and took the lighter from him. It produced a level flame at the first attempt, and he lit the rag with ease.

'Let's throw a few more rags and cotton wool buds onto the flames, but keep everything else clear,' said the Patient. 'We don't want this to spread.'

The fire quickly licked its way up the door, and they could hear it doing likewise on the other side. Ratty listened for a smoke alarm to ring, but there was no sound other than the crackle of the flames. He stood back from the fire, coughing as the smoke started to spread across the room.

'I wonder if Mother came up with anything as ingenious as this,' he shouted.

'Stay low to the floor. The air will be clearer there. If there's no alarm system up here, I just hope we're not dealing with a fire door.'

'What difference does it make?' Ratty asked.

'A fire door is filled with concrete. It doesn't burn all the way through. We will find out in due course, I'm sure.'

'It's a fine blaze you've made there. Looks like the whole surface of the door is alight. The ceiling is turning black. The old man's going to be ever so cross when he sees the damage.'

The fire raged for a few minutes before dying back, leaving a blackened hulk of a door, steaming across its surface, glowing red hot in places. The Patient took hold of the picture transportation trolley and pushed it as hard as he could against the door. The charred and weakened wood splintered and cracked all the way through. He pulled the trolley back for a second attempt. This time it crashed through to the other side, leaving a hole wide enough for them to squeeze through, covering themselves in hot charcoal as they did so.

'Straight to the exit this time, dear fellow,' said Ratty.

'Follow me.' The Patient led him the opposite way from the exit.

'Where does this lead? It's not the way out.'

'Do you want to find your mother or not?'

They were outside the old man's office. The Patient opened the door marked 'Director' and stormed in, with Ratty reluctantly following. The old man was seated behind his desk studying a map of South America. He immediately folded it up and sat back in surprise.

'What have you done with his mother,' demanded the Patient. He pulled the de-bristled paintbrush from his pocket and held the sharp steel stub against the old man's throat. The movement was too quick for him to tell that it was not a knife, and the old man held his hands up in supplication.

'And don't bring the constable into this,' added Ratty. 'There's something fishy about that fellow.'

'What do you want to know?' the old man asked Ratty, wearily.

195

'I want to know where she is.'

'I don't know the answer to that question.'

'If you don't start being more helpful,' said Ratty in as gruff and deep a voice as he was able to generate, 'we are going to start being rather ruddy frightful.'

The Patient looked at him, unimpressed with his ability to be threatening, and pushed the stub of the paintbrush with renewed vigour against the old man's skin.

'All I can tell you is that she came here in 1975 to investigate her mother-in-law's relationship with Dalí. She remained here for a time. Then she disappeared.'

'Remained here of her own free will, or kidnapped by you?' asked Ratty.

'Does it make any difference after all this time?' croaked the old man, his skin chafing against steel.

'I think we can assume the latter,' said the Patient. 'And when you said she remained here for a time, what length of time are you implying?'

'Look, remove that thing from my neck. Please.'

The Patient glanced up. Ratty nodded. The paintbrush was withdrawn.

'"Kidnapping" is not the appropriate word,' said the old man. 'She remained here by choice. Because she felt that she had no real choice. And she stayed for many years.'

'How many years?'

'I believe it came to about thirty-eight in total.'

Ratty and the Patient looked at each other.

'So she is alive?' asked Ratty.

'Apparently, in spite of your best efforts to the contrary, she is still breathing,' announced the old man.

'My efforts?' asked Ratty. 'What on earth are you implying?'

'It really doesn't matter. Your lives are a mistake.

Anything you do within those lives is a mistake. You're both on a wasted trajectory. Your lives are leading nowhere. That's why you mustn't concern yourselves with minutiae.'

'Mother's fate hardly counts as minutiae, old Rottweiler.'

'But it is. Because her entire existence is irrelevant. And therefore your entire existence is irrelevant. You are part of the big mistake that has affected so much and any efforts you make to find her, or to punish me, or whatever you instinctively feel you must do, will be a waste of time.'

Ratty was dispirited. The old man's riddles had thrown his thought processes off-course and dragged a fog of confusion over the situation. His enthusiasm for his quest was receding. He tilted his head towards the door, inviting the Patient to leave with him.

The Patient pushed the stub of the paintbrush firmly against the old man's throat once more and shook his head.

'We have come a long way. This man still holds the information we need. I suggest a different line of questioning.'

'But we're taking too long, old wotnot. Someone might come and we'll be right back where we started.'

'In what year were you born?' asked the Patient.

The old man looked up in surprise at this question, but had no reservations about answering it.

'I was born in 1940,' he said.

'Which country were you born in?'

'England,' sighed the man, without any apparent fondness for the place.

'And where were you conceived?' the Patient continued.

'Please, life has been hard enough. Do not make things

worse than they already are. My offer still stands; let Constable Stuart escort you home and you will have no more contact from me or my people.'

'Tell us when Lady Ballashiels departed and where she now is and we will do as you request,' the Patient said firmly.

'She left just a week ago. My people found her soon after, but she escaped again. She is now on the run and could be anywhere on the planet. That is why I can't help you.'

'Goodness, I've had a thought,' shrieked Ratty. 'If she's out there right now, she must be looking for me. All the time I've been looking for her, I've just made it harder for her. We must return to Stiperstones immediately. Let him go, Patient chappy. Oh, and sorry about the fire.'

'What fire?' asked the old man.

'We instigated a small conflagration,' explained the Patient. 'There was damage primarily to the ceiling of the square turret and to its door. But such damage is, according to your world view, an irrelevance.'

'Get out! Live the rest of your meaningless lives and keep away from me!'

There was a knock at the door. Ratty had feared this. He had no desire to fall back under the control of the constable. As the door began to open, he ran to the opposite wall next to the Patient, his mind completely devoid of any plan that might improve the situation. But when he saw the face of his closest friend from Cambridge University days, the woman for whom he had for so long carried an unrealistic and optimistic romantic flame, he relaxed. He had played a small part in the rescue of this woman, after her discovery of the Sphinx scrolls had resulted in her ending up in something of a predicament last year. She had even stayed as his guest at

Stiperstones for the first weeks following the Patient's arrival there. Her face was a welcome and unexpected sight.

'Ruby! What a pleasant wotsit!'

Ratty rushed over to her and gave Ruby Towers a hug. She shook him off, coughing at the charcoal dust that now stained her hair and face. The Patient nodded respectfully at her.

'Don't tell me he's got you two signed up to his organisation, too?' she said, unable to hide the accusatory tone in her voice. 'I should have guessed you'd be mixed up in this nonsense,' she went on. 'Remember Charlie? He's part of it. Whatever it is. But I suppose you knew that, since you're already at the heart of the operation.'

'No, nothing of the sort. We just popped in on an unrelated matter,' said Ratty.

'Popped in? You both look like a bomb's gone off in your faces. You look like Victorian chimney sweeps.'

'If I may explain, Doctor Towers,' said the Patient, 'Ratty has reason to believe his mother came to this place after she disappeared when he was a child. We are trying to trace what became of her.'

'You are? And that has nothing to do with Charlie?'

'We have no idea where Charlie is or what he is doing,' said the Patient. 'And why this gentleman appears to be hiring people he knows nothing about and who cannot be expected to show much loyalty is yet another mystery.'

'People, be quiet!' shouted the old man. 'None of your trivial conversations are of any significance. I hire people who are disposable. If they betray me, I will dispose of them sooner. If they fail in their tasks and fall foul of the police, I can wash my hands of them. Charlie is disposable and matters not. Lady Ballashiels, even less.'

'Well, dash it!' Ratty retorted, offended that his family should be belittled in such a way.

'I think we should all take a deep breath and calm down,' said Ruby. 'We're not going to get anywhere by shouting.'

'Frightfully sorry and all that rot,' whispered Ratty, even though Ruby's glare was fixed upon the old man.

'That's better,' she continued. 'Now, I have to admit that I don't like the way you talk about Charlie,' she told the museum director. 'He's not exactly my friend, but I still care for his wellbeing, and I think it is not unreasonable for me to ask you a few simple questions. What exactly is your organisation?'

'It is the Dalí museum,' the old man replied.

'Thank you for your answer,' she said, forcing a tone of civility that didn't come naturally to her in moments of stress, 'but I don't mean that one, and you know I don't mean that one. The Dalí stuff is something that you are using as a cover. So would you mind telling us what you are really trying to do?'

Suddenly the old man's character shifted despite Ruby's palliative tones. He stood up, stuck out his straight nose, bellowed at full volume and waved his hand maniacally as he shouted,

'You fools are mired in a reality that will change. Soon no one will remember any of you. No one will even remember me. Seventy years of pain will be undone. The great mistake will be corrected and the course of history will run smoothly.'

'Proper little Hitler, aren't you?' mocked Ruby, unimpressed by his passionate rant.

'Get out!'

After they had shuffled out of his office, the old man

grabbed the telephone on his desk and pressed a stored number.

'Grant? They are all exiting my room now. I want you and Stuart to follow them off the premises and see to it that they all are kept permanently away from me. I have an inroad to Keo and I think the day is closer than we expected, so I don't want them interfering any more. Make it look like an accident if you can.'

In an inconspicuous café on the other side of town from the museum, they felt secure. Figueres was bustling with local people going about their business and life seemed, once again, normal. Ratty, Ruby and the Patient sat in a corner table with a clear view of the street from where Constable Stuart's surveillance of them continued unnoticed. Ruby ordered coffees and croissants for everyone.

'Crikey, what a to-do,' said Ratty. 'First this, then that, and now the other.'

'I think it's all bluster,' whispered Ruby. 'We should just keep away from that awful man and forget all about this. No one is really going to hurt us.'

'So why are you whispering?' asked the Patient.

She thought about it for a moment. Clearly there was more apprehension in her system than she had appreciated. She had been shouted at by museum officials in the past, but never quite like that. The tone of the old man's voice had shaken her to the core and she had to remind herself that he was just an old man who worked in a museum and who seemed to be running some kind of private research project on the side. The chances of there being a sinister conspiracy were so small as to be laughable. She would move on, get on with her life, and not get sucked in any more. Charlie would be fine. Rocco likewise.

'Tonight I shall be sticking to my original plans,' she stated at normal volume. 'I'm taking my students to the wind tunnel to have some fun. They've worked hard in the trenches at Empúries. They need to let off steam, and so do I.'

'Wind tunnel?' asked the Patient.

'It's a training tool for sky divers, over at Empuriabrava,' she explained. 'The tunnel is vertical, and you float on the jet of air. Sounds like a laugh.'

'And I'll bash off back to Blighty,' decided Ratty. 'The old man said Mother's still alive. She left Figueres just a few days ago.'

'That's wonderful, Ratty. I'm so pleased for you.'

'Thank you, old chum. Mother must be looking for me. I have to go home where she can find me.'

'Then you definitely don't want to stay for the wind tunnel flying!'

'Doesn't sound entirely like my cup of tea,' admitted Ratty. 'Prefer to read a book, generally. Probably a tad awkward so to do whilst floating in a tube in hurricane-force winds.'

'Typical Ratty,' giggled Ruby. 'Hides behind a book at the first sign of danger.'

'Precisely,' he agreed. 'Sounds a somewhat unnecessarily risk-filled venture to me. What if there's a power cut whilst you're up at the ceiling? What if you burst through the roof and into the sky?'

'Oh, Ratty,' she laughed. 'Always the silliest notions. They have multiple generators for power. They won't all fail at once. And you can't go through the roof.'

'Nevertheless, I must go straight home. Not sure if Mother has the key to the place, and don't want her having to camp in the stables until I get back.'

'I really hope you find her, Ratty,' said Ruby. 'It

would be lovely to resolve that hole in your heart after all those years. Judging by the way you turned out, if she's still alive I'll bet she has a wonderful personality.'

'Beautifully benevolent of you to say so. And what about you, Patient chappy?'

'Perhaps I will catch up with you at Stiperstones in a day or two, Ratty,' he replied. 'I am intrigued by this wind tunnel. I think I would like to experience the feeling of raw flight.'

'Always room for one more,' offered Ruby. 'And Ratty, be careful on your way home.'

'Why?' he asked.

'It's nothing. It's just something that Rocco said.'

'Rocco?' asked the Patient.

'Rocco Strauss. He's a scientist from the European Space Agency. Though quite why a space agency would employ someone like him for a serious job is anyone's guess. The man's one pepper pot short of a picnic. A complete basket case. Last week Rocco crashed his car into Charlie's van. Apparently, the brakes had been cut on Rocco's car, and he couldn't stop in time. He seems to think the old man at the museum is behind it. So be careful, that's all I'm saying.'

'Gosh. Someone cut the brakes on my Land Rover, too,' said Ratty.

'Oh no, really? That's terrible, Ratty,' she said, suddenly losing her former bravado.

'I'm sensing a pattern,' the aristocrat continued. 'But why would the old fellow commit such dastardly beastliness?'

'Because Rocco was researching the effects of Project Keo,' Ruby replied. 'Looking for a message from the future saying that a time capsule had arrived, or will arrive, safely. All total nonsense, of course, but the old man seems to have some kind of obsession with Keo.'

'Keo?' asked the Patient.

'Yes. It's the name of the satellite that's about to be launched,' Ruby explained. 'It contains a time capsule destined to fall to earth in fifty thousand years. And inside the capsule there's apparently a message asking for a confirmation to be sent back in time to show that it has been safely received.'

'What was written on the placeholder of the missing photograph from 1937, Ratty?' asked the Patient.

'Keo,' Ratty replied.

'Really?' asked Ruby. 'So there was a photo from all those years ago labelled "Keo", but we don't know what the picture was? Well you may wish to know that Rocco found a painting in a cave which appears to be the work of Dalí. It dates from around 1937 and also features the word "Keo".'

'How can a twenty-first-century satellite have been known about in the Thirties?' asked Ratty.

'It is possible,' said the Patient, 'that the satellite was named after something from that time, but it is also possible,' he continued in a softer tone that caused the others to lean in towards him, 'that the message from the future confirming receipt of the Keo time capsule was received after all. However, it was sent to the wrong era and was seen by Dalí and your grandmother, instead of by Rocco and his friends in the following century.'

'That's what Rocco thought,' said Ruby. 'There's circumstantial evidence to back it up, but nothing solid enough to build a coherent argument. So, personally, I find it extremely doubtful, and even if it did happen, I can't see what effect it would have on anything.'

'Dalí didn't write about any such incident in his published diaries, but we found unpublished sections of the manuscript which may shed light on the matter,' explained the Patient. 'Regrettably the pages were taken from us before we could study them.'

'All I know is that Granny went a little potty after travelling with Dalí that year. Cancelled her trip to Germany and went straight home to do that locked room thingy.'

'What trip to Germany?' asked the Patient.

'Oh, it was nothing significant. Just something she blabbered on about in her diary. She'd been corresponding with her friend in Germany, one of the Mitford sisters. Unity, was it? The girl was infatuated with Hitler, though Unity's initial motivation appears to have been an attempt to get one up over her sister who married that blighter Sir Oswald.'

'Mosley?' asked the Patient. 'Leader of the British Union of Fascists?'

'Indeed,' replied Ratty. 'Anyway, Hitler had started seeing Eva Braun, and Unity was getting rather miffed about the whole affair. Eva was similarly frustrated at the Führer's divided attention, and won him back by attempting to pop her cork. Unity then saw that as the necessary step to winning the oily fellow back again, and wrote to Granny about her plans. Needless to say, Granny was horrified. Never a fan of chaps with insipid moustaches anyway, Granny wanted to persuade Unity to end the relationship with Hitler and get out of Germany, but she couldn't put that kind of message in writing so she planned to visit Unity in person. Then something happened when she was with Dalí and she was never the same again. And, of course, that event also had some effect on Mother and might have had something to do with her disappearance.'

'We could try to get those Dalí diaries out of the

museum,' suggested Ruby. 'Perhaps they will tell us what this old guy is trying to do? He spoke very strangely about life. He really gives me the creeps. And, if I'm honest, I'm even a bit worried about Charlie being under his spell. But we have to find a legitimate way to obtain them. I won't consider breaking in to that place.'

'It is not necessary to break in,' said the Patient. 'It is sufficient to enter legitimately and to remain there until others have left. I will accompany you, if you will permit me. I know where the documents are kept. If they have been returned to their proper place it will be a simple enough task to retrieve them.'

'Rocco found a place to hide in the museum,' said Ruby. 'He hid behind the Mae West installation. Maybe we could conceal ourselves there, too?'

'I think it is you who must be careful,' said Ratty, standing up to go.

'We'll keep you posted if we find anything,' said Ruby.

Ratty bade them farewell and stepped outside. The narrow streets were smoky with the exhausts of diesel cars. He glanced around for a taxi to take him to the high-speed rail terminal. Paris by morning. London by tomorrow lunchtime. Home for tea with Mother. His recent *joie de vivre* returned, and the light-headed effect almost got him run over. The hoot of a car horn brought him to his senses and he walked quickly in the direction of the nearest taxi rank on the opposite side of the road where a single cab was waiting with its engine running. He squeezed his long frame into the back seat and closed the door, wondering if his knowledge of classical Spanish would be sufficient for a Catalan taxi driver to understand where he wanted to go, hoping he would manage to avoid having to make a noise like a train.

The central locking clicked shut as he fiddled with his seat belt. Before he could attempt to direct the driver to the station, the car pulled away sharply and an unwelcome face turned to him from the front seat.

'Well, well, young man.'

Ratty's dreams evaporated. 'Are you familiar with the expression that relates to a bad penny, constable?'

'Indeed I am, Justin. And in many respects it could be applied in the opposite direction. From my point of view you're causing me more trouble than you're worth.'

'I don't suppose I could ask you to drop me at the station, old chap?'

'I don't suppose you could, no.'

'Look,' said Ratty, 'whatever that old man is paying you, I'll halve it.'

'Not a question of money, young man. Some things in life are more important than a bunch of readies in your hand.'

'I just don't understand why you have it in for me, constable.'

'When I said it was nothing personal, I meant it. But you are uniquely placed to threaten the goals of our organisation. Your family has always been at the centre of it, and when your curiosity finally got the better of you and you opened that forbidden room in your house, that's when we all had to spring into action.'

'But that room was sealed in 1937. What does it have to do with you?'

'You ignored the warnings that your grandmother wrote, Justin. She said there would be dire consequences if anyone had the temerity to break in to it. And dire consequences there were indeed, as soon as your mother found a duplicate key in the servants' kitchen and indulged her own curiosity in 1975. Just look at what a poor choice she made that day. Having to give up everything she loved, including her only son, all because she ignored your grandmother's warnings. We all sprang into action at that moment, just as we did when you followed in her footsteps. Of course, it took a little more effort to regroup this time, what with the core team either being in jail on those trumped-up charges or dead, but the old man has connections everywhere and pulled strings at the highest level.'

'So it wasn't you who put the servants in jail?'

'Of course not. What influence does a village bobby have over the criminal justice system? Not a lot, that's what. It took your father's old school network to achieve their incarceration on the basis of his gut feeling that something was wrong. Couldn't happen today, of course. The old boy networks just aren't strong enough. Too many busybodies poking their noses in looking for trifling details like evidence. But back in the Seventies it was easy to manipulate the system when you'd been at school with the right people. Worked a treat for Lord Lucan, didn't it?'

'Father never mentioned this to me.'

'You were young. He didn't want to concern you with it. If only you had kept your nose clean, boy. There was no need for you to get involved in this. If you'd left that room sealed, as your grandmother intended, you would be safe now. Ditto your mother, of course.'

'What are you planning to do with me this time?'

'The boss has had enough of your meddling, young man. He's looking for a permanent solution to the Ballashiels problem.'

'That doesn't sound particularly agreeable.'

'It isn't, Justin. It isn't.'

Ratty sat despondently in the back of the car while the

constable drove him out of the city centre. He considered whether he might be able to grab Stuart's neck from behind and throttle him before he could reach for his gun, but such an attack seemed excessively unsportsmanlike for his tastes and would have brought with it the possibility of injuring third parties as the car lost control.

'Where are you taking me?' Ratty asked.

'Won't be long now. Just heading for the coast. Should be there in twenty minutes or thereabouts.'

'Any chance you could drop me off before we get there?'

'Don't you like the beach, young man?'

'Tend to feel seasick just from looking at the sand. Prefer not to go near the wet stuff, if at all possible.'

'Well now, that is a shame, isn't it?'

'I do hope you're not expecting me to get my feet wet.'

Constable Stuart said nothing and continued to drive in an unhurried manner towards the coast. Ratty tried to recall the basic martial arts moves he had learned the previous year, and hoped they would be sufficient to extricate him from the sticky situation in which he expected to be mired as soon as they stopped. If only he hadn't removed the bulletproof tiles from his jacket.

Stuart turned onto a bumpy track between two fields, and pulled up in a sandy car park behind the dunes. There were no other cars present.

'This ought to be far enough.'

'Jolly good. Now, look old fellow, perhaps we can discuss the rather delicate matter of your motivation?'

'Please step out of the car, young man.'

'Of course. But –'

'No time for buts, Justin. Come along.'

Stuart opened Ratty's door for him and the aristocrat

climbed out, watching the constable closely.

'This is it, then? You're going to do me in amongst the sand dunes?'

Stuart closed the door and invited Ratty away from the vehicle.

'Do you in? That sounds rather melodramatic in my opinion. I'm not going to harm you. Please relax your fists.'

Ratty looked at his hands and realised he had subconsciously screwed them up into tight balls ready to hurl at the constable's face the moment any sign of trouble kicked off. He flexed his fingers and stepped back from the man, eyeing him suspiciously.

'The car is bugged, Justin, and there are operatives around Figueres. I had to make sure we got away before coming clean to you.'

'Coming clean?'

'There's something I haven't yet told you, young man. Many years ago, your father set up a trust fund.'

'Father had some money left? Blimey. He kept that quiet. How much have I got?'

'The fund wasn't set up for you. It was for your protection. It pays my wages and expenses and nothing else.'

'So we were right.'

'We?'

'Patient chappy and myself speculated this exact possibility. Well, it was mostly Patient chappy who came up with the theory.'

'Anyway, your father employed me to look after you for as long as I am physically able to do so. I am a man of my word, and I gave your father my word and now I am honouring it. I must admit I failed in my duty last year when you went off into Central America without a word to anyone, and I was mightily relieved when you made it home safely after your adventures.'

'So why did you take those photos and diary manuscripts off us at the museum and then lock us in the turret?'

'Ever heard of a double agent, Justin?'

'Crikey. How exciting.'

'I had to act as if I was working on behalf of the old man while I was in his building. Truth is, he's up to no good, but for the life of me I can't put my finger on what it is he wants to achieve or why he seems to think you're such a thorn in his side. I know he has some kind of resentment for you and your mother, but he's positively vicious when he speaks of your grandmother. To him she's the Antichrist. Oddly enough, he seems to hold Dalí himself in an equally contemptuous regard. I was hoping you'd be able to get to the bottom of it, to be frank.'

Ratty was overcome with relief, and only just managed to prevent himself from giving the constable a hug, which he knew would have been hugely inappropriate from a social perspective. He settled instead for a modest shake of the hand, signifying their shared values.

'What did you do with those photos and diaries you took from us, constable?'

'Unfortunately I had to return them to the Centre for Dalínian Studies. Now that he knows precisely what you're after, the boss had them secured in a safe.'

'Golly, how inconvenient '

'But not before I was able to make copies.'

Ratty threw his arms around the policeman and squeezed him tightly, before stepping back and coughing with embarrassment.

'Terribly sorry, old chestnut. Don't know what came over me.'

'Not to worry, Justin. I understand. The stress and uncertainty you've been through are enough to give anyone a queer turn.'

'Where are the copies, constable?'

'Well, now. That's the thing. You see, I had no choice but to keep them in the museum. Couldn't risk walking out with them.'

'Can we pop in and get them?'

'We? The old man thinks I've bumped you off. You have to remain hidden otherwise I'll have some explaining to do.'

'Of course. And did I point out that I'm rather grateful to you for not having bumped me off?'

'I think such gratitude is implicit in your demeanour, young man.'

'Is it? Jolly good. Just wanted to be sure.'

'I'll retrieve the copies this evening. Where will you be staying?'

'I wasn't planning to stay, actually. Since all that stuff about Mother came to the fore, I thought I should return to Stiperstones in case she's trying to find me. You could give the copies to Ruby and the Patient, perhaps?'

'Your friends? Ah, now that might be a challenge.'

'A challenge?'

'Do you remember Grant, the butler?'

'Grant? Of course. Made me a spot-on cuppa this morning.'

'Yes, well now that he's out of prison the old man has been using him for various unsavoury tasks. He has sent him to take care of your friends in the same way that he sent me to deal with you. I rather fear it might be too late for them.'

'But couldn't you have done something, constable?'

'I was charged by your father with your protection

212

above all others. My duty to your safety had to come first.'

'Hang my safety, man! Ruby and the Patient are all I have! They're the only things that matter in the world to me. I couldn't bear the thought of being saved at their expense.'

Ratty clenched his head in his hands and walked in tight circles of distress.

'I am sorry. It is a cruel and imperfect world. We can only play our small part and try to make the best of it.'

'But we must do something for them, constable. That sweaty butler always had a shifty look in his eye. I don't trust him further than I can throw him, and that isn't very far.'

'I will go and find them, but I have to go alone. If you speak inside the car, the old man will know I have double-crossed him. If you're seen alive in Figueres, the same problem will apply. You must wait here.'

'On this ghastly beach? It's a nature reserve. There's not even a bar. Where's a chap supposed to get a gin and tonic?'

'Keep out of trouble, young Justin. I'll see what I can do about your friends, but don't get your hopes up. I can't be responsible for whatever Grant may already have done.'

Ratty waved the constable off, and walked across the baking dunes to the beach. It was deserted save for a few naked sunbathers, and he struggled to find somewhere to look as he sashayed across the sand towards the buildings he could see in the distance.

After half an hour walking he sauntered into a beach bar and ordered a gin and tonic. Just a few sips were adequate to settle his nerves after the shocking experiences he had been through. After all, he told

213

himself, trying to blot out the horrors from his mind with a little solitary humour, it wasn't every day that he had to walk past brazen naturists.

He felt a powerful desire to return home. A chance to be reunited with his mother after so many years was not something to be delayed, but he was also concerned about Ruby and the Patient. He had no way of knowing if the constable would be successful in freeing them from the devious butler. Having been forced – by the absence of gin at the precise spot where the policeman had dropped him off – to walk to civilisation, Stuart would have no way to locate him either. In spite of the constable's instructions to the contrary, and even though the thought of his mother travelling to Stiperstones and finding him absent made his stomach tie itself in knots, Ratty felt a far deeper duty in his heart. He had no option but to return to Figueres and do whatever he could to help his friends.

Close to the beach was a colourful parade of shops. An overflowing bazaar stocked nearly everything Ratty felt he would need for his disguise: wig; moustache; fake scar. At a nearby gentleman's clothing store he bought a suit that was reminiscent of the effete finery that defined his youth. The old leather jacket went in the bin on the way to a bookshop where he purchased a dozen copies of a small, square and chunky volume about the life and works of Salvador Dalí, which he squeezed into the dozens of pockets of his utility jacket which he put on beneath his shirt. His oddly lumpy appearance would be explained away, he decided, by the cover story that he was a tourist from the United States, and, in order to make that story more convincing, he bought a rather vulgar baseball cap and put it on his head at a most unsightly angle. A half-hour taxi ride took him to the centre of Figueres and he walked through the narrow streets to the Dalí museum and surveyed the scene.

All seemed normal: the line of tourists waiting to get their museum tickets; street entertainers making some kind of music for their captive queuing audience; waiters hurrying between tightly packed tables in the square. He thought about Grant, and wondered if he had managed to get his unctuous hands on Ruby and the Patient, or whether they were sticking to their original plan of entering the museum with the other tourists and hiding out in the Mae West installation until the place closed for the night. He walked along the line of visitors to make sure his friends were not still outside. No sign of them. Either Grant had done his dirty work, or they were in the museum somewhere. Ratty joined the end of the line and began the long, slow process of shuffling towards the entrance to buy a ticket.

Once inside, he fought his way through the throng to the Mae West room and peeked through the spyhole Ruby had told him about, to peer into the hidden chamber at the back of the room. No one was inside. He spent an hour checking all of the rooms and corridors of the museum. Now came the decision he had hoped to avoid making: should he try to bluff his way into the administrative offices of the museum where he and the Patient had been locked up and where the Dalí papers were kept? Security cameras pointed at him from every corner in the public parts of the museum, but he knew that the environment was slightly more relaxed away from the works of art and the tourists with their chocolate-covered fingers and tendency to sneeze.

Did he really possess the courage to go through with this? Parts of him were screaming advice in his inner ear, and that advice was to retreat. Get to a safe place. Do anything but show his face in the museum. He shook the voices from his head and breathed in a lungful of courage. His friends were in trouble. He was going in.

There was a guard at the door to the administrative offices of the Dalí museum. He was armed with a gun in a holster on his right hip. Ratty knew that cunning and intellect were the only advantages on his side. He walked around the corner, out of sight of the guard, then sprinted back to the entrance and tugged at the guard's sleeve urgently.

'Something's happened!' he shouted, conscious that his script was diabolical. 'Round the corner! You have to go and help!'

The guard lolloped towards the direction in which Ratty was pointing. Ratty slipped into the administrative offices and ran up the stairs. There was no sign anywhere that Ruby and the Patient were here. He peeked into rooms, opened cupboard doors, and even made it as far as the still-smouldering turret room. As he ran back down the stairs he smacked into someone coming the other way, both bodies spinning and falling onto the steps. Ratty instinctively offered the other person assistance in standing and found himself face to face with the old man. A suitcase and one of Dalí's mannequin sculptures lay on the stairs next to him, and Ratty bent to pick the items up and hand them back.

'Off somewhere nice?' he asked.

'I am finding things have become rather out of control around here of late,' said the old man. 'Your appalling disguise can fool no one but a fool. The Ballashiels curse upon the world has become too much for me. Your grandmother, your mother and now you, all blundering your way across this planet with no regard for the consequences, no understanding of the devastation that your family has triggered. I have waited. I have been

216

patient. I have endured sorrows and agonies beyond anything you could imagine. Do you have any idea what seventy-two years of pain feels like?'

'Have you tried aspirin, old chap?'

'I'm talking about the pain that lodges in my soul. The pain I was born with. The weight of the world that bears upon my shoulders. It is guilt. It is a yearning for a world that never was. It is a passion to find a way to create the world that should have been.'

'I'm awfully sorry, I don't think we were ever formally introduced. Who exactly are you?'

'That is a subject best avoided,' replied the old man.

'No one seems to know your name, old chap, but it would be appropriate under the circs if you could tell me. You know, given what you appear to have done to Mater for all those years.'

The old man stood still and silent. He looked Ratty in the eye.

'You really want to know?'

'If it's not too much of a kerfuffle for you.'

'My name is Mitford.'

'Mitford, eh? Any relation to *the* Mitfords?'

'Obviously.'

'Of course. The name is the clue. Silly me. Granny was very close to the Mitfords back in the day. Perhaps she knew your father?'

'I am named after my mother. I never met my father.'

'Gosh, what rotten luck. Do you have a Christian name?'

'I was not baptised, but my first name is Alois.'

The name connected with nothing in Ratty's mind.

'If you're a Mitford, and the Mitfords and Granny were pals, is this whole mystery a family feud?'

'In a sense, but it is far deeper than that. I really don't

have time to discuss it.'

Mitford started to walk away, heaving the suitcase and the mannequin with him.

'Slow down, old boy, you'll do your back in if you lug them like that,' said Ratty, chasing after him.

'With so little time remaining, the state of my spine has absolutely no relevance. Leave me alone.'

'So Granny did something that peeved you?'

Mitford stopped and faced Ratty once again.

'Look, your grandmother made the greatest mistake in the history of mankind, and I am one of millions who must bear the burden that she created.'

'And this mistake was something that happened when she came to Catalonia with Dalí in 1937?'

'It is.'

'And it is something to do with the Keo time capsule?'

'It is.'

'And it is also connected to the room that she locked up at Stiperstones?'

'Most certainly.'

'And whatever she locked away was the thing that Mother found in 1975 and caused her to come here and never return?'

'Correct.'

'And why are you admitting all this, old boy?'

'Because nothing matters any more. Keo finally has a launch date. The pain of my life and that of the world of the past seventy years will shortly be healed. There is nothing any Ballashiels family member can do to screw things up this time.'

'I wouldn't be so sure about that, old fellow. I happen to be quite adept in the screwing up department, don't you know!'

'No, Your Lordship. Even at your most incompetent

you will not be able to destroy the world that I am about to restore to its health.'

Ratty was unsure whether that was intended as a compliment or not, so he let it pass.

'I came here for my friends,' he said. 'What have you done to them?'

'Your former butler is taking care of them. There is nothing you or I can do for them, and soon it will not matter anyway. Perhaps he has failed, just as Constable Stuart appears to have done, but it really is of no importance. Look for them if you want. Kill Grant if you prefer. It makes no difference to me or to this world.'

'Right-o. Before I bash off to find them, just tell me this. Which Mitford was your mother?'

'The most tragic one. The saddest of all the Mitford stories. The one whose life was blighted due to your grandmother's decision. My poor mother was Unity.'

'Unity? Didn't she –'

'Yes, she did.'

'And doesn't that mean you could be the son of –'

'Yes, it does.'

The old man looked to the floor, as if shamed.

'Goodness me,' whispered Ratty, after a suitably lengthy and sympathetic pause.

'Go look for your friends. Go to England. Go anywhere. Nothing you ever do or have ever done is important. Now just leave me.'

The old man's Mitford ancestry intrigued and horrified Ratty. It sent shivers through him and gave him all the incentive he needed to do as the man wished and get away. No wonder his mother had been imprisoned for so long, he realised, as he scampered along a hollow corridor. A man with genes inherited from such a tainted paternal source was not going to be sympathetic to the needs of any individual. But he had to overlook that; he had to forget his mother and the copies of the Dalí diaries that the constable had stashed somewhere in the building. The only thing that was of immediate concern was the safety of Ruby and the Patient. Grant was clearly a bad egg, a rotten apple. He might be subjecting his friends to all kinds of ghastliness. But where? What was it Ruby had said about getting on with her life? Something about going flying in a tunnel. Back in Empuriabrava. He cursed silently in Latin. By coming to Figueres he had wasted time. Now it could be too late to save them. He ran outside, looking for a taxi that wasn't being driven by any current, or former, employees of his family.

'*Volamos*?' asked the sign above her head. 'Shall we fly?' Ruby gritted her teeth, determined to fly, adamant that normality would return to her life and her schedule. Figueres, the Dalí museum and all the odd and unsettling things related to it were ten miles away now. It felt sufficiently far to provide a buffer of safety. She led the Patient up the steps to the main level of the wind tunnel building at Empuriabrava. The cavernous room housed a vertical tube in its centre, made of thick, reinforced glass, surrounded by an amphitheatre of café tables from where viewers could enjoy watching people floating, flying and performing acrobatics in the wind. The tube disappeared below the floor level where it curved back towards the immense fans that provided the wind. It also disappeared above the ceiling level, seeming to rise to a dark and forbidding infinity.

'You look good in your flight suit,' said the Patient. 'I think it suits you.'

'And you look exactly the same as you always do,'

Ruby replied. 'This blue flying gear is just like your normal outfit.'

'When will your students arrive?' he asked.

'They're flying in the slot after us. They'll be here shortly.'

A flight instructor tapped her on the shoulder.

'Ready to fly?' he asked. Ruby looked round to see a handsome young Spaniard, dressed in an instructor's flight suit, smiling at her. 'My name is Fred. I'll be giving you a short training session downstairs in a moment. Come and join me in the briefing room in five minutes.'

Fred went to talk to someone else, leaving Ruby and the Patient with little to do but sit and watch the entertainment in the glass tube. A young girl was experiencing her first flying lesson, learning to balance on the jet of air before the instructor took her spiralling to the top of the wind tunnel, out of sight of those in the café. There were gasps of shock from the viewers as she vanished from sight, followed by audible collective relief when the girl returned safely with a huge smile on her wind-blown face.

'Excuse me, terribly sorry to interrupt. My name is Grant. I wonder if I could trouble you both to come with me?'

The hushed voice was scarcely audible above the hubbub of the busy café and the muffled noise of the wind tunnel. Ruby glanced up to see a rounded face leaning down from a position that was rather too close to her own, his piggy eyes staring at her and yet focussed on an undefined point in the distance, almost as if he were peering through to another time than the present.

'Can I help you?' she asked, leaning back from him defensively.

'There is a matter of the gravest significance that we

need to discuss,' he replied. 'Time is short, I am afraid. So if you would be awfully kind and follow me?'

'Take a seat, then. Talk,' said Ruby.

'Not in this establishment, madam.'

'Why not?' challenged Ruby. His excessive politeness provoked discomfort and suspicion within her.

'Please,' whispered Grant, leaning closer to her in order to maintain his intrusion of her personal space, 'you must come with me. Now.'

'When were you born?' asked the Patient.

'I'm sorry?' Grant stood up straight again, tripped by the unexpected tangent of the question.

'What year was it?' continued the Patient.

'What has that to do with anything, sir?'

'Are you working for the old man at the museum?'

'He is not my employer in any strictly contractual sense, no.'

'But you are part of his organisation?'

'Just come with me, if you would be so kind.'

'I fear,' said the Patient, 'that your answers to my questions have failed to give me the confidence I need in order to commit to embarking on any kind of journey with you.'

'Then perhaps this will provide the answers you need?' Grant pulled out a small handgun from his inner pocket, just far enough for them to see without attracting attention in the café.

'What the hell are you playing at?' shrieked Ruby.

'Quiet, madam, please. Just follow me out of the building and everything will be fine. You have my word as a gentleman's gentleman.'

Ruby and the Patient exchanged glances, trying to read each other's intentions without speaking. Ruby drew strength from the calm serenity exhibited by the Patient.

She felt safe in his presence.

'We're not going anywhere,' she told Grant.

'In that case you must listen very carefully,' he replied. 'In the late Seventies I was removed from my post at Stiperstones Manor and served thirty years in a British jail for my beliefs. So I am asking you both very nicely to come with me and do not allow me to utilise the burning rage that three decades of incarceration has produced.'

'Three decades?' echoed the Patient. 'I was falsely imprisoned for more than four decades. I used my time constructively. I studied philosophy, medicine, history, languages. I emerged smiling and content with myself and the world. You could have done likewise. Your anger will serve no purpose, for you cannot change the past.'

'I don't need to be a goody two-shoes like you, sir. For you are wrong. Things can be undone. My past *can* be changed.'

Ruby and the Patient locked at each other again to confirm their mutual feelings that Grant was crazy. The former butler released the safety catch on his pistol and pressed the weapon into Ruby's back. The Patient nodded at her and stood up. Without further hesitation Ruby stood also, accepting defeat.

Grant nudged them towards the staircase. No one in the café paid any attention to them, such was the complete distraction of the spectacle of human flight within the wind tunnel. The arrival of a group of young people temporarily obstructed the staircase. Ruby recognised her archaeology students, about ten of them, full of excitement and bravado for their upcoming flights. When they recognised Ruby they ran to her and attempted to kiss her in greeting, not noticing the gun held against her back.

Finding himself in the midst of a crowd, Grant slipped

the gun into his pocket and stepped away from his would-be captives. He was woefully outnumbered. The current flyers in the wind tunnel finished their session and exited. The Patient saw an opportunity. He grabbed Ruby's hand and led her to the entrance to the wind tunnel. It wasn't yet their turn, and they had skipped the instructor's briefing, but the Patient felt strongly that the public exposure provided by the glass tube would make it impossible for Grant to continue his attack upon them. Grant needed them to be secluded, shielded from view, to be able to use his weapon. There was nowhere more public than the tunnel. It even carried a video feed to a plasma screen on the outside of the building.

Ruby attempted to protest at being thrown into the vortex, but the noise and the wind made impossible any kind of verbal communication. She felt herself being lifted high into the rushing air, and watched as the Patient attempted to orient himself to a position that afforded him a view of an exasperated-looking Grant. Balancing on the column of air was harder than it looked. She drifted towards the glass and had to put out her hands to arrest her forward momentum, which created more lift and sent her rocketing up to the roof where she panicked and placed her hands on her head, which reduced her lift and sent her plummeting towards the wire mesh that separated flyers from the source of the wind. She landed uncomfortably, bounced high as if in reduced gravity, and tried to achieve the kind of equilibrium that seemed to come so naturally to the Patient who was floating serenely beneath her.

Grant burst into the control booth and started to struggle with the operator. An instructor dived into the wind tunnel and glided up to help stabilise Ruby. She looked into his eyes and recognised Fred. He winked at her, as if to say everything would be OK. She smiled at him, which was challenging given that her top lip was trying to wrap itself around her nose. Fred gave her a hand signal which meant nothing to her, then took hold of her wrists to bring her down to a safer level. She looked out through the giant glass tube on the way down: there was no sign of Grant in the cafe area. She guessed the Patient's ploy of making them too visible to shoot had worked. Fred indicated that he was going to take her to the door. She nodded approval. Just as they approached the exit, however, the wind speed increased dramatically and the three bodies were catapulted to the ceiling. Fred attempted to reduce the drag on his body by lowering his legs to a standing position, but the blast was too strong and he remained stuck at a dizzying height.

Down in the control booth an unconscious operator lay in a pool of crimson blood. Grant wedged the power lever to keep it at full strength and exited the booth, locking it and taking the key with him. While all eyes were staring at the commotion within the tunnel, Grant slipped outside to the rear of the building. Here were the generators that powered the fans, four diesel machines, providing redundant electrical power in case of failure. If one generator failed, another would kick in without missing a beat. Or another. Or another. He had to take them all offline, and he had to do so before anyone could break into the control booth and reduce the fan speed sufficiently to bring the three people down from the ceiling where they were currently pinned. A sudden and total loss of power might not be enough to kill them, but the sixty foot drop onto a tight grid of wires could cause the necessary damage that Mitford had requested. Broken bones, especially if they landed on each other. Possibly broken necks, too, if they landed headfirst. It wasn't as dependable as a shooting, but it was the best he could manage under these improvised circumstances, and it avoided the risk of detection if he had stayed in the control booth and tried to cut the power from there.

Grant opened the panel on the side of the first generator and found the emergency stop button. He punched it and the machine died.

Now for the next one. He glanced up at the plasma screen several storeys above him on the outer wall of the wind tunnel building. It showed an empty tube, but he knew that was because the camera didn't capture the very top of the tunnel. His victims were still there. He opened the panel and hit the button. Another generator died.

An alarm triggered within the building. He correctly guessed it signified that only two generators remained online. He rushed to the next one, opened it up and pressed the button.

Only one left.

'I say! Servant chappy!' called a voice that was as familiar to Grant as it was irksome. Grant looked round to see Ratty standing in front of the final generator. His former master was dripping with sweat, dressed in clothes that were peculiarly lumpy and ill-fitting. 'I recognised your bulbous neck from the taxi. I don't know what you are doing,' Ratty continued, 'but I have an inkling that a ne'er-do-well such as yourself is more than likely up to mischief and I want you to know that I shan't stand for it.'

Grant took a long breath of frustration and produced the pistol that he had earlier hidden from the crowds inside the wind tunnel café.

'You're an arse, Ballashiels. There. I've said it. I've wanted to say it for years. Stand aside from the generator before you get hurt.'

'I am not afraid,' lied Ratty.

'Don't be an idiot,' shouted Grant. 'I have a gun and I have no qualms about using it. Things are different now. The old social norms and niceties don't matter. The planet is about to change for the better and since you will never be part of that future it will mean nothing to me if I have to shoot you, and I will do so without hesitation if you don't get out of my way.'

Ratty patted the latest incarnation of his home-made, bulletproof vest for reassurance, and continued his defiant stance.

'Go ahead, butler. Engender my diurnal thingummy.'

'What the hell does that mean?'

'Make my day, punk chappy.'

Grant's hand was visibly shaking as he trained the gun on Ratty's chest. For all his warring words, Grant struggled to see Ratty as anything other than the grieving child he had served decades before. He shouldn't be in this situation. Stuart was supposed to have finished Ratty off. Even thirty years of prison life hadn't hardened him to this extent. He pointed the gun at the gravel and fired a warning shot. Ratty flinched and wobbled as the muscles in his legs lost their strength, but he stood his ground.

'Right now, your friends are trapped against the ceiling of this building by a jet of air,' said Grant, deciding on a change of approach. 'They are probably suffocating, or they may be hyperventilating. Either way, they are suffering. If I don't turn off this generator they can't get down.'

The old servant had to be lying, thought Ratty. If Ruby and the Patient really were pinned against the roof by the air blast, turning off the generator could be fatal for them. He would defend this machine until his dying breath. Or until help arrived. Preferably the latter.

'Oh, for God's sake!' shouted Grant, throwing the

pistol to the ground and charging at Ratty, head-butting him in the stomach and knocking him backwards to the ground. Ratty found, to his immense surprise and relief, that his martial arts reflexes kicked in seamlessly. As he fell onto his back he grabbed his opponent's sleeves and held them low whilst using his legs to accelerate Grant's upward momentum, sending him in a spinning arc that resulted in a heavy landing. Grant was winded and shocked, giving Ratty enough time to return to his feet just as Ruby and the Patient rushed over to him.

'Ratty, what on earth are you wearing now?' asked Ruby.

She was standing alongside the Patient, and seemed to be dressed far more eccentrically than Ratty. A bundle of flight instructors, fresh from smashing the door to the control room to save their injured colleague and lower the air speed in the wind tunnel gently, charged at Grant and dragged him away from the generator.

'I'm supposed to look like an American,' Ratty replied. 'Didn't fool anyone.'

'Promise me one thing, Ratty. Never go to a clothes shop unaccompanied again.'

'I know it looks a trifle queer, but I have beneath my shirt an extra layer for reasons that Patient chappy will understand. Given that my former butler has developed a fascination with pistols and the like, it seems a not unwise stylistic choice to have made. Sorry you weren't blown away by it.'

'Why does everyone who was ever connected to your family want to kill you, Ratty?' asked Ruby, ignoring his inappropriate pun and failing to notice that Grant had wriggled free of his captors and run off.

'Jolly good question. The old man at the museum has good reason to kill everyone, actually. Drew a pretty rum short straw in life, born to Unity Mitford and her German lover.'

'German lover?' asked Ruby. 'Who would that have been?'

'There is but one possibility.' said the Patient. 'Unity had an affair with Adolf Hitler. When he turned his attentions to Eva Braun, Unity shot herself with the small pistol Hitler had given her as a present. She returned to England and was rumoured to have given birth. Therefore the old man could be the son of the Führer.'

TUESDAY 7TH MAY 2013

Flushing Meadows appeared drab and ordinary to Rocco, just a slab of parkland sandwiched between the highways and hardly a suitable site for a time capsule that was supposed to benefit the people of the future. His disappointment didn't result from jet-lag or any other form of tiredness, for he had been pampered throughout his flight and had arrived refreshed and inquisitive. Rather, the almost childlike obsession and enthusiasm with which he approached matters of conspiracy and mystery – coupled with a variety of free cocktails – had served to elevate this unusual mission to a fantasy, a fairy tale quest, and now, facing the cold reality of something rather ordinary, he was temporarily deflated, returned to the corporeal state of rational scientist.

He strolled to the tatty wall of plywood panels that screened the New York State Pavilion, located the site entrance and rattled the lock. No one was operating the tunnelling equipment he could see through the gap in the gates.

Rocco felt a hand tapping him on the shoulder.

'Coolsville Catalonia! What are you doing here?' asked Charlie.

Rocco turned round to see someone very different from the young, rotund man he had been expecting. The bulk was still there, but it was wrapped stylishly in a dark suit, capped with a menacing black tie and sunglasses.

'Charlie? What happened to you? You look like some kind of government agent!'

'That's what everyone thinks. Managed to get permission to dig here. Except I used the wrong machines and now I'm waiting for a drill.'

'Did the old man say why he wants you to dig up that time capsule?' asked Rocco.

'Kinda. Something to do with that Dalí dude. The old man thinks Dalí put something into the capsule that wasn't recorded in the official list of stuff.'

'What kind of thing, Charlie? Did he say what it was?'

'No. Just said that Dalí was working on another exhibit for the World's Fair and would have had access to the capsule. If there's something inside it that Dalí put there, the old man needs it.'

'Why?'

Charlie shrugged.

'There's a connection,' said Rocco. 'Dalí painted the word Keo in the cave, and Keo is another time capsule. Dalí interfered with this time capsule too. This is as close to proving my theory as you can get.'

'What theory?' asked Charlie.

'The Keo satellite gets launched. It's been delayed for years, but it's due for blast-off in a few days from Guiana Space Centre. The people of the future receive the time capsule inside it. They respond to the request to send a message back in time confirming receipt. Only the message arrives early and Dalí sees it. If Dalí wanted to reply to that message, what options does he have?'

'His paintings?' suggested Charlie.

'Maybe. But a more secure method is to infiltrate another time capsule. The Westinghouse capsule is Dalí's opportunity to send his own message to the people who were on the receiving end of Keo. Does that make sense?'

231

Charlie shook his head before asking, 'Why bother?'

'Dalí appreciated the sense of wonder in conversing with the unborn generations of a future world,' suggested Rocco. 'Perhaps he wanted to get a second message from the future? Dalí was also obsessed with immortality. Given the likely increase in life spans and medicine in the future, perhaps he was asking them for the secret of eternal life?'

'Obviously didn't get it, did he?' pointed out Charlie. 'The guy's buried in a slab next to the female washrooms in his museum.'

'Anyhow, we'll find out as soon as you finish the extraction of the capsule.'

'I'm supposed to bring it to the old man in Spain. Intact.'

'Charlie, I'm working for the old man as well. He wants me to check up on your work. I'm kind of your boss,' said Rocco. 'And I'm telling you now that as soon as that baby is out of the ground, we're taking it with us and going into hiding. That capsule is going to be red hot, and we need to prepare a place to take it apart.'

'Hey, dude, that's not cool. The old man has me by the balls. If I don't deliver I'll be going to jail. I'm only doing this stuff because he blackmailed me.'

'What can he do to you while he's in Spain?' asked Rocco.

'He said he'd turn me in to the cops.'

'What have you done?'

'Nothing! Just tried to get into his dumb museum without a ticket and a few donuts here and there that I forgot to pay for.'

'Why would the cops over here care about that?' asked Rocco.

'The old man at the Dalí museum sounded pretty

pissed about it. Said I'd go to jail if I didn't do this thing for him. A guy like that has gotta have contacts. I don't want him making that call and turning me in.'

'Turning you in for what?'

'Stealing stuff, I suppose,' replied Charlie. 'And breaking into the boring museum.'

'Charlie, I'm no lawyer, but I shared a house with a couple of law students while I was studying for my doctorate, and have a sense of what's right and what's wrong from listening to their endless debates over legal cases.'

'Law students, huh?'

'Listen to me. I'm pretty sure that a misdemeanour or two committed in Europe means nothing in the States. Without an extradition warrant to take you back to Spain there's nothing they can do anyway.'

'Couldn't they lock me up here while they wait for one?'

'The old man must be bluffing. He hasn't told the police about you and he isn't going to. He has no evidence. He's manipulating you, Charlie. It's just another piece of this conspiracy that he's running.'

'You're saying he doesn't really have the hold over me that I thought he had?'

'The guy has nothing on you,' said Rocco. 'Relax.'

'Oh man, I'm outta here. This is great!'

Charlie ripped off his tie and threw it onto the grass. He took off his dark sunglasses and blinked as he marched in the direction of the exit.

'No, Charlie, wait!' called Rocco. 'What are you doing?'

'I'm done here. Going back to Europe. Back to Van Gogh and eating donuts and fantasising about Ruby's ass.'

'Don't you care about the time capsule?'

'Huh? Why would I give two shits about it?'

'Don't you see, Charlie, this is the ultimate conspiracy? A communication between Salvador Dalí and unknown people of the future! They might not even be people then. Maybe dolphins have evolved and taken over? Who knows what they might have been plotting with Dalí? Aren't you in the least curious?'

'Dolphins? Now that would make me curious. But I've been risking my ass every day out here for nothing. I've been watching over my shoulder expecting a raid at any time. I can't live like that any longer.'

'But I'll watch your back.'

'You sure?'

'Sure.'

'Coolsville. Listen up. There's a new drilling rig coming tomorrow. The guy in the security hut is gonna ask questions. He knows my permits are false, but I got him convinced this is a top level government operation. You're gonna have to dress in black like me.'

'Really?' asked Rocco. He beamed. His fantasy had returned for a split second until it was shattered by the phone ringing in his pocket. He pulled it out and looked at the unfamiliar number.

'Hello?'

Charlie watched his face as a wave of recognition washed over it. Rocco held the phone away from his head and whispered urgently,

'It's the old man. Say nothing.' He pulled the phone back to his face. 'How's it going? Charlie? He's working hard. Should have the capsule out in a day or two.' Rocco fell silent as the old man spoke to him at length. Finally, he ended the call.

'What's the deal?' asked Charlie.

'I don't get it. He's pulled me off your case already.'

'How come?'

'He needs me for something more important. He's accelerating his plans. Apparently, Lord Ballashiels has been causing problems and he just wants to complete his mission and get everything over with.'

'Complete what mission?'

'That's what I want to find out. That's why I signed up to this.'

'What does the dude want you to do?' asked Charlie.

'He's sending me to South America. To the European Space Agency launch site at Guiana. He knows I have access to the site from my real job. He needs some kind of favour when I'm there, but he won't tell me what it is until I arrive.'

'What about the capsule?' asked Charlie. 'Does he still want it?'

'Guess so. I just don't get him. And I'm not going to South America until I've seen what Dalí put into the time capsule, so I'll be sticking with you for now, Charlie.'

The purchase of a dark suit and glasses seemed pointless with hindsight. Rocco was covered in thick mud, his new outfit ruined beyond recognition and repair. It looked as if he had been wrestling on the wet ground. But Charlie remained clean, relishing his directorial role which involved getting Rocco to do everything for him. Once he had been instructed on the workings of the computer-guided drilling equipment, and after the rental guy had sent the machine down almost as far as they needed to go, Charlie had sent all other workers home. Only his trusted colleague would be there to witness his triumph.

Charlie sat at a makeshift table watching the monitor. The scoping camera was sent down into the waterlogged hole after every few feet of progress. He wasn't confident of being able to distinguish anything in the murky darkness, where visibility was no more than a couple of inches even with the powerful light attached to the camera. But when the lens bumped into the copper alloy side of a missile-shaped structure, he knew he had found it. Even with the blurry picture on the monitor he could tell that the capsule had been damaged by the massive drill bit. If water penetrated the seal, the contents could be ruined and Dalí's private message to the future could be lost.

He looked at the book the old man had given him about the capsule. There was a ring at the top of the casing, which was how it was lowered into the ground, but they had reached it at forty-five degrees, and had hit the capsule halfway up its side.

'Hey, Rocco, we got it. But we can't get it.'

Rocco scrambled over to Charlie's table, chunks of dirt falling off him as he leaned over.

'Is that it?' asked Rocco.

'It has to be,' replied Charlie. 'But we have to drill again. There's no way to retrieve it from here. We went too deep by a couple of feet. There's a ring on the top of it. If we can drill directly there and get a cable hooked to it, we can drag it out of there with the winch.'

'Drill again?' asked Rocco. 'You mean from scratch?'

'It'll only take a few minutes. You know what you're doing.'

The locked gate of their compound rattled suddenly.

'Hey!' called a voice from behind the fence. 'Open up. You're busted. The police are coming.'

The voice at the fence belonged to Dick English, the security guard who had seen through Charlie's forged permits from day one. Charlie reluctantly opened the gate and let the man in. There was a sense of inevitability about this moment. Rocco threw down his tools in disappointment. They were less than thirty minutes from getting that capsule out of the ground. Now their efforts would all be for nothing.

'You've been busted,' repeated the guard.

Charlie considered making a run for it, but he knew he wouldn't get far. So he held out his hands and waited for the guard to click the cuffs onto him.

'What are you doing?' English asked.

'You're taking me down,' sighed Charlie.

'Huh? No, I came to warn you. The fake permits have filtered through the system and City Hall is on to you. They're sending the cops round. They'll be here in thirty minutes. We have to move fast.'

'Huh?'

'Let's get this sucker out of the ground before they get here. We can do this. How can I help?'

'Er, right,' said Charlie. 'You heard the man. Let's get that time capsule out of there!'

The drilling process was manic this time. Once they had conquered the initial challenge of preventing the new hole from sliding into the old one, the procedure was fast and accurate. The scoping camera confirmed their success, showing the ring at the top of the capsule to which a hook could be attached.

The time capsule glugged out of the ground and flopped onto the mud. The high-fives were an indulgence that had to be rushed, however. The three of them were able to carry the time capsule to the rear of the guard's truck, parked just outside the gate. As they placed it inside and closed the doors, Charlie could see the flashing lights of approaching police cars passing by on the highway. If the cops took the turning into Flushing Meadows Park, they would be here in less than five minutes.

'Close up the site behind me,' shouted English. 'I'll get this thing out of here.'

Rocco and Charlie scrambled to collect any personal items that might identify them. They slammed the plywood gates closed and quickly thrust a padlock through it, before running into the shelter of the trees that surrounded the site. From there they watched English's truck with the hidden time capsule as it rounded a corner and disappeared from view, replaced almost immediately by the arrival of several police cars.

'Good work,' said Charlie, watching the police investigation from a safe and discreet distance.

'What now?' asked Rocco. 'Where's the rendezvous?'

'Rendezvous?'

'Where do we meet this guy and open up the time capsule?'

Charlie took off his dark glasses.

'Meet?'

Rocco sighed at the realisation that they had been duped. Under pressure, exhausted and frightened, they had naïvely placed their trust in a stranger.

'Come on!' shouted Rocco. 'We have to follow him in my car!'

While police officers massed around the muddy crime scene within the remains of the New York State Pavilion, Rocco and Charlie sped out of the park in Rocco's rented SUV in pursuit of the thief who had stolen their stolen capsule.

'He's turned onto Grand Central Parkway!' shouted Charlie. 'He's heading for LaGuardia.'

'No, look – he's turned onto the Van Wyck Expressway.'

'He's taking the exit. Quick, Rocco, get into that lane.'

They swerved into the exit lane and followed the security guard as he negotiated several sets of traffic lights and back streets until he passed back underneath the Van Wyck Expressway and turned into the parking lot of a branch of Home Depot. They parked up at the far corner of the car park and watched as he ran into the store, emerging minutes later with a trolley laden with power tools.

'Keep your head down, Charlie. Don't let him see us while he's loading.'

'Why don't we rush him now?' asked Charlie.

'In a public parking lot with video cameras everywhere?' asked Rocco. 'Not a good plan. We have to tail him until he's ready to unload it.'

English left the trolley standing as he drove away from the store. They followed again, ever more nervous that their continued presence would become noticeable to him, but he drove slowly and cautiously, respectful of the precious load he was carrying, and Rocco was able to keep up with ease. After twenty minutes of uneventful driving they arrived at a residential street in the district of Whitestone. The truck stopped outside a beachfront house and the security guard ran inside.

'This is our opportunity,' said Rocco. 'Let's get it.'

The two men rushed over to the truck and began yanking at its rear doors. English emerged from his house with a trolley and immediately reached for his gun.

'Good work, soldier,' said Charlie. 'We sure outsmarted those cops. Well done.'

English shook his head.

'I thought you were on our side,' groaned Charlie.

'Why did you think I let you go through with your farcical charade of forged permits and pretending to be part of some government agency, Charlie?'

'You didn't believe all that?'

'I didn't have to. I knew exactly who you were and what you were doing. My boss told me to expect you. The one thing he didn't expect was that you would do such a great job, and for that I'm grateful. But the time capsule stays with me, now.'

'Your boss?' asked Rocco, intrigued. 'Who are you working for?'

'His name is Alois Mitford. I am to deliver the relevant contents of this capsule to him.'

'In Spain?' asked Rocco.

'Spain? No, things have moved far beyond that. Mitford's almost ready to fulfil his life's ambition. It's gonna shake things up, apparently. Any day now he's gonna change the world. Not that I believe a word of it. Nor do I give a damn. He's got his agenda. I've got mine.' English waved his gun intimidatingly. 'Enough of that. Put the capsule on this trolley and wheel it to the dock for me.'

They did as instructed, and were surprised to find a flybridge motor yacht moored at the private dock to the rear of the house.

'Nice!' said Charlie. 'Must be a bit of a strain on a security guard's wages?'

'Mitford is paying me well for my services.'

They carried the time capsule into a cabin and placed it on a mattress. It fitted at an angle, and English strapped it down and covered it with blankets.

'Bring me the power tools from my truck,' he added. 'It's going to be a long voyage. I might open this thing up before I get there.'

'Long voyage?' asked Rocco, letting Charlie fetch the boxes from the truck. 'I thought you said you weren't going to Spain with this?'

'I'm not. Mitford is meeting me in Guiana.'

'Any chance of a ride, then?' asked Rocco. 'You and I are colleagues. I work for him, same as you. He wants me down in Guiana too. You don't need to work against me. We can work together.'

'Sorry bud, but this is between me and him.'

'What do you mean?'

'You don't think I'm just gonna hand this thing over to him when I get there? The guy is worth billions. I'm gonna take him for every cent before I give him what he wants.'

Alois Mitford felt a weight rise from his shoulders. The burden he had carried for most of his seventy-two years was lifting. Nothing in his life had made him happy. No pill could be synthesized powerful enough to negate his melancholy. No amount of inherited Nazi gold could compensate for the tristesse that gnawed at his bones. In his youth, before he commissioned his own medical team to research suitable pharmaceuticals for his condition, he had briefly turned to pre-existing mind-altering drugs to escape his reality, but he found his re-emergence from narcotic fantasyland into his true self to be more unbearable with each attempt. Eventually he had to suffer the excruciating ordeal of giving up opiates and other drugs altogether.

Suicide was a topic he had read about more than any other. He possessed a small library at his home on the subject. He was an expert on every imaginable technique of self-slaughter: fast, slow, painless, agonising, messy, clean –all had occupied his mind over many years. And yet, even in his darkest hours, he would always reject the option of termination. Something deep within him told him it was his duty to experience the living hell that he inhabited, and so the suffering continued, day after day, week after week, year after year.

He despised his cells. Hated his DNA. Loathed his entire being. He was fifty per cent Adolf Hitler. It was an impossible legacy to live with, yet somehow he had found the inner strength to do just that, and today that torment had begun to ease. The long and dark tunnel of his life finally had a point of light, and he was heading towards it.

He gazed out of the window of the private jet, looking down at the patchwork of dusty fincas, lush vineyards and huddled towns. From this elevation Spain appeared insignificant, the complex lives of its inhabitants meaningless. He thought about the pilots he had hired to take him to French Guiana. Both reasonably young men, probably had wives, maybe kids too. Would they shortly cease to exist? It was highly likely. Their children too. Would this plane vanish from the sky on its return flight? Would the leather on the seat that supported him so comfortably return to the cow from which it was taken?

In the opposite seat was the Dalí mannequin, liberated from the museum and given the honour of its own seat on the jet. Would that cease to have been manufactured? Mitford looked out again and saw a motorway stretching across an arid landscape. Would the cars on that road look substantially different soon? Would they evolve along alternative stylistic and mechanical principles? The motorway reached the outskirts of a town. Would the buildings over which he was flying shortly be eradicated from the soil, replaced by trees or fields or other structures, perhaps? Even the weather might be different. Global warming might be delayed ... or accelerated.

He wondered if those given the chance of life would be more worthy than those whose lives he would soon erase. It didn't matter. It was the right thing to do. The planet was populated by the wrong people. It was time to do something about it. Whatever the result would be, he would never know it. The world would change, he was sure of that, and his own life would be undone, his decades of pain deleted. Just a couple more days, now. There would be no heaven waiting for him, just the erasure he longed for, preceded by a few moments of glorious satisfaction that he had succeeded in his mission.

He felt the unfamiliar shape of a smile forming across his face.

Wednesday 8th May 2013

Stiperstones Manor glowed in the pale morning light, a dim beacon amid the mists that clung to the fields. Ruby put her hand on Ratty's shoulder as they stood before the quiet house. He gulped and handed his key to the Patient, who opened the heavy front door.

'I really thought she would be waiting here,' Ratty yawned, wiping a tired tear from his eye. 'Frightfully sorry if I've wasted your time.'

'We're your friends, Ratty. We couldn't let you go through this alone. Whether or not you find her, we're still here for you,' said Ruby. 'Right, Patient?'

'True friendship can exist only between equals,' said the Patient. 'We are friends. We are equal. We will share equally any joy or pain you are about to experience.'

Ratty acknowledged his gratitude with a nod. The three of them had already shared the tedium of the long drive from Spain to England. Ratty had not slept. He had been too fired up by the desperate hope of finding Lady Ballashiels waiting at Stiperstones and by the nagging concern that she might not hang around there for long. The Patient had repeatedly made clear his unhelpful view that returning to locate one person was statistically insignificant and irrelevant given that Alois Mitford appeared to have hinted at some kind of scheme that would threaten far more people and that, logically, it would make more sense to solve that mystery first.

Now they had arrived, however, and Ratty's positivity was beginning to wilt. The grand hallway betrayed no indication of his mother's presence. There were no scratchy glam rock sounds leaking from the record player in the music room –Ratty had been convinced his mother would want to play the Abba and Mud records she used to love. There was no female attire hanging from the coat hooks. No sign of a woman's touch in mitigating the filth that defined the interior of the house.

Sensing his friend's diminishing attachment to the optimistic energy that had recently fuelled him, the Patient said, 'Ratty, I propose that you head straight to the kitchen and make us all tea while Ruby and I search the rooms for any signs that Lady Ballashiels may have been here.'

Ratty noticed that the Patient's choice of words reinforced the sense of defeat that he was feeling. He walked slowly to the kitchen and robotically made tea while his friends searched the rooms. He had been blinded by his hopes, he realised. He had trusted the word of a crazy old man who claimed to be the product of the most repugnant romantic fusion in history, and who blamed the Ballashiels clan for starting a war. Pot, kettle, black, he thought to himself. There was no hard evidence that his mother was alive, or that she was free of Mitford's clutches, or that she had returned to England.

He began to regret that he had ever defiled his grandmother's memory by opening her forbidden room and embarking on this doomed journey. Fate had teased him with its characteristic indifferent cruelty. He had almost sensed his mother's former presence, almost felt the gentle warmth of her fading aura. Nothing would ever be the same again. He quietly sobbed over his tea.

He felt a hand upon his shoulder and a shiver of

comfort rattled through him. He wiped his eyes and looked up into Ruby's face. She kissed his cheek.

'Checked the bedrooms?'

She nodded.

'First and second floor?'

Another nod.

'Both wings?'

'Ratty, we've checked all of the upstairs room, even the turret.'

'Anything?'

She shook her head.

'Basement?'

'The Patient's down there now. I'd have thought he'd have a phobia about being underground but he said he feels at home there.'

'What am I to do, Ruby? I can't go back to Spain, but I can't rest here knowing Mother might be alive somewhere.'

'If she wants to find you, she will. And you can make that easy for her by waiting here.'

'I've waited here for over thirty years already. She didn't come for me then.'

Ruby felt a lump in her throat. There was nothing she could say to that. When the Patient returned she felt relief that he was there to share the awkwardness.

'The subterranean level displays no sign of current or recent occupancy,' declared the Patient.

'Outbuildings,' whispered Ratty. 'Would you mind checking the outbuildings?'

'No problem,' said Ruby, wrapping an arm over the Patient's shoulder. 'Come on.'

They exited by the rear door from the kitchen into the gardens. The door closed with a click. Ratty was now convinced his mother was not going to return. Mitford must have lied. Sending Ruby and the Patient to check the outbuildings would be a waste of time, but it gave him a few minutes of privacy to let decades of pent-up emotion spill out in a most un-British manner. It took almost half a roll of kitchen towel to extinguish the flow of tears.

The back door swung open. Ratty didn't look up. He sensed a woman's hand once more upon his shoulder.

'I wanted to see you one last time, boy,' said a soft voice.

Ratty rubbed his eyes. That didn't sound like Ruby. He looked at the hand on his shoulder. It was wrinkled, liver spotted, unfamiliar and yet familiar. There was perfume in the air, a scent he hadn't recalled since boyhood. And there was a sense of completeness in his soul. He looked up and gazed into the sad, penitent eyes of the mother who had abandoned him when he had needed her the most.

'Mater?' he squeaked.

'Oh, Justin,' she said, and stroked his forehead like she had last done when he was seven. He stood up and tried to hug her with arms that trembled wildly, but she backed away, wincing in pain. 'No, boy. The British only hug horses and dogs, remember? And not behind the shoulder. Too painful.'

'Terribly sorry. Arthritis, is it?'

'Buckshot. What are you drinking? Tea? Could do with something stronger. Where's the gin?'

'Buckshot?' asked Ratty as he poured her a messy gin and tonic with hands that felt only half attached to his arms. 'You mean some blasted rotter shot you? Who did that to you? Tell me immediately, Mater, and I'll kill them.'

She gave a half smile, loaded with enigma.

'Calm yourself, boy. No point getting angry about it. Sit.'

'But it's not right. No one should be shooting you. Especially in the back. What kind of brigand does that to a lady?'

'No brigand did it.'

'Then who shot you?'

'You did, boy.'

'I did?'

'Can't say I blame you.'

'You mean, I shot you?'

'You shot me.'

'How could I have done that?'

'Been trying to get back to you for days, boy. Bloody nightmare, I've had. When I finally broke away from Mitford's control, I came straight here. I watched you. I trailed you to West Dean while you were trying to piece together my mother-in-law's movements in 1937. I followed you back here again. I tried to bring myself to make contact with you. But I couldn't do it. The guilt was too entrenched. I thought it might be better if I left you to live your life without the upheaval of my return. And then, when I finally gathered the courage to speak to you, you shot me with that damned blunderbuss and two of the old servants dragged me away.'

'I thought you were a poacher, Mater. And I didn't know about the servants.'

'They're out of prison. Grant and Huxtable. They've been watching you, boy. Time is getting short and I had to take a chance to see you whilst we were both still around.'

'I entered the forbidden room, Mater.'

'I know. I'm proud of you. It had to happen to you eventually, as it did for me. And as you've found, once you've entered the forbidden room you embark upon a trail that is long and difficult.'

'I found your Lanvin wrapper. And the message

behind the Dalí books.'

'Took your bloody time, boy.'

'I know. Sorry. Been busy.'

'What rot.'

He looked to see if she had said that with a smile, and reckoned he could just about detect a hint of forgiveness in her face. It wasn't as if he needed forgiving, anyway. She was the one who had walked out. Finally, he would get the opportunity to find out why.

'What did you find in the room in 1975?'

'I didn't want to go in. But the bloody servants were starting to worry me. Never trust a lackey, boy.'

'Well quite. But why?'

'I sensed a conspiracy. I was afraid for us all, but I didn't know why. Down in the cellars I found a box of rusty keys. One night I tried them all until one of them fitted the locked bedroom. Like you, I found the room empty. Well, empty apart from one item.'

'A bar of chocolate?'

'What rot. Of course not. It was a photograph taken by my mother-in-law in 1937. Would you like to see it?'

She reached into her pocket and produced a copy of the wrinkled sepia image. In the foreground was Salvador Dalí, grinning and tweaking his moustache for the camera. He was standing on the ruins of a castle. A wide vista opened out behind him, hills and valleys and something that looked as if it was the sea. But the sky above his shoulder was not empty. The word "Keo" appeared there, in a typeface that resembled that of a digital clock even though such things did not exist in the Thirties.

'Your grandmother wasn't the only person to see it, of course. The locals thought it was skywriting, which was all the rage back then, but Her Ladyship knew differently.

She sensed it had a meaning far deeper than she could ever consciously understand. Would you like to know the full bloody story?'

'Golly, yes.'

At that moment, the kitchen door opened and Ruby and the Patient entered.

'That's not who I think it is, Ratty?' asked Ruby. She stared in disbelief at the mature lady in the kitchen.

'Who is Ratty?'

Ratty held the hand of the old woman and grinned. Lady Ballashiels kissed him on the forehead. The Patient raised his eyebrows and observed, 'Mothers are fonder than fathers of their children because they are more certain they are their own. I think we all can accept the familial bond in this instance.'

'Lady Ballashiels,' the old woman said. 'How do you do?'

'Patient. Pleased to meet you.' The Patient held out his hand.

'I'm sure you are on both counts, but what's your name?'

'He's just called the Patient, Mater. It's a long story.'

'I'm Ruby Towers. Friend of Ratty's.'

Lady Ballashiels looked disapprovingly at her. 'Who's this Ratty character to whom you keep referring, girl?' the old lady asked.

'Sorry. Justin. We were at Cambridge together. You'd have been ever so proud at his graduation. I've always called him "Ratty".'

'What a ghastly name. Please don't use it in the house.'

'Mater, everyone calls me "Ratty" these days. You'll get used to it.'

'What rot.'

'Would the two of you like some private time?' offered the Patient. 'Ruby and I can go for a walk.'

'No. Sit,' said Lady Ballashiels. 'Time is short. There is much I need to say and you might as well all hear it. I expect you're all harbouring a certain curiosity regarding my story.'

'I cannot deny a desire to learn the facts,' said the Patient.

Lady Ballashiels looked at everyone in turn and took a deep breath. 'So Her Ladyship was trotting along with Dalí –' she began.

'On horseback?' asked her son.

'No. It doesn't matter. No more interruptions, boy. What was I saying?'

'Granny. Dalí.'

'Right. 1937. A summer perambulation through France prior to visiting her chum Unity in Germany. Then that damn word appeared from nowhere. "Keo". Hanging in the sky above Périllos. Impossible. Impressive. Impecunious.'

'Do you really mean "impecunious", Mater? Doesn't make sense.'

'Hang the sense of it. I like the sound of it. Shush.'

'Sorry.'

'So, that word in the sky business affected your grandmother deeply,' she continued. 'It was like a religious experience, witnessing the word of God in the sky. Even though it made no sense to her, she nevertheless could think about nothing else. For a day or two she felt she might have imagined it, but when she developed the photograph at Dalí's house in Port Lligat she knew it was all real. And by then it was too late.'

'Too late for what?' asked Ruby.

'To save the world. And don't interrupt, girl.'

'I'm not a girl,' objected Ruby. 'I have a doctorate in Archaeology.'

'Hush. I'm losing my thread. Now, where was I? Yes, the mother-in-law was too late to save the world. She had already failed to take the train from Perpignan. Her original plan was to travel with Dalí to southern France, then take the train from Perpignan station to Paris and then on to Munich.'

'To visit Unity Mitford,' confirmed the Patient.

'Please stop interrupting, children. Yes, Unity Mitford. Alois's mother. Yes. Although the bastard wasn't born yet, of course. Unity and Her Ladyship had been corresponding about Unity's affair with Hitler. It was going badly, and Unity had written of her intention to attempt, you know, a final solution. It was a cry for help, hoping that if she survived it Hitler would fall for her completely. The mother-in-law saw through that naïvety. She couldn't bear to see the effect Hitler was having on her friend. She also didn't care too much for his politics, and was waiting for Unity to grow out of her fascist infatuation. But things got worse. Unity was on the edge of madness, and the mother-in-law grew increasingly resentful of the way Hitler treated her. Total rotter. She intended to take the train to Germany and persuade Unity not to shoot herself. Instead, she had a far more daring plan. She was going to get Unity to shoot Hitler, but of course she couldn't put that in a letter to Unity. It had to be said in person in order to avoid any recriminations coming her way. So she was all set to travel to Germany and change Unity's life for the better.'

'But then along comes Keo and she changes her plan?' asked Ruby.

'Do you, or do you not, wish to hear this story?'

'I don't know what your mother's been doing these past thirty odd years,' whispered Ruby to Ratty, but at a volume sufficient to be sure that Lady Ballashiels could overhear, 'but she's not learned how to be patient.'

'Quiet, girl. There isn't time to be patient. We may have just a few days left on this earth, and I certainly don't want to spend them being interrupted by your kind.'

'My kind? Archaeologists?'

'Lower middle class comprehensive school waifs. And don't deny it. Stands out a mile.'

Before Ruby could get on her high horse about social snobbery, Ratty gently placed a finger across her mouth and calmed her with a wink. 'Let the old matriarch have her say,' he said. 'She's waited a frightfully long time.'

Lady Ballashiels shook her head. 'I don't know. I pop out of the country for a while and everything goes to pot. Once again, where was I? Mother-in-law. Right. So she was set to go to Germany but didn't because of the word Keo in the sky. Unity never learned of your grandmother's plan for killing Hitler. In fact, the poor girl never heard from Her Ladyship again. So, instead of shooting Hitler, she ended up shooting herself in her silly head with a little pearl pistol. Stupid girl. The bullet lodged in her skull and didn't kill her. She was brought back to England on a stretcher and placed in hiding, since her fondness for Nazis had made her rather unpopular, even in these parts. So, you see, it can be argued that it was your grandmother who was responsible for the Second World War.'

'I say, that's a rather strong accusation, Mater,' objected Ratty. 'Granny was into art and photography and wotnot.'

'That, in itself, is no defence,' said the Patient. 'Do not forget Hitler's artistic bent.'

'Well perhaps, but I don't believe Granny ever invaded Poland.'

'History is more subtle and elegant than invading armies and legions of tanks, boy,' said Lady Ballashiels. 'The smallest action or thought can lead to the most horrendous consequences. Your grandmother simply changed her mind. Decided not to visit her friend. She merely changed her travel plans. And that choice, that naïve, tiny decision, was indirectly responsible for starting the most destructive war in history because it allowed Hitler to go off and invade Poland and drag the globe into conflict. She didn't know it at the time, but she blew her one chance to prevent war. So, you see, from the skewed perspective of someone like Alois Mitford, the Ballashiels family has a lot to answer for. My mother-in-law's decision not to go to Germany cost millions of lives and changed the world forever. And all because of one word. Keo. Obviously by the time she realised the impact of that moment on the French hill with Dalí, it was too late. Unity was no longer part of Hitler's life and the mother-in-law had no inroads to stop him. Total bloody mess.'

'And that miserable Mitford chap was born,' added Ratty.

'Born some months after Unity arrived back in England,' his mother replied. 'Born into a world that shouldn't have happened. Born with the inherited guilt of genocide, of ethnic cleansing, of indiscriminate bombing. The truth is, he shouldn't have been born at all. Hitler should have been shot by Unity before she ever became pregnant. Mitford always felt that the mere fact of his birth was inextricably linked to the moment the world took a wrong turning and tumbled headlong into hell. If the word Keo had never appeared in the sky, the world would have been spared all the pain Hitler instigated. Millions of destiny's children never had a chance of being born because their fathers were killed in the fighting.

Thanks to your grandmother, we are living in a post-war world that was never intended to be.'

'Do you think that Hitler fellow had an inkling that Granny may have come close to giving him what for?'

'I suppose we'll never know, boy.'

'It may just be coincidence,' said the Patient, 'but long after the war someone found Hitler's invasion maps of Britain. He had circled the location of his personal headquarters, the place from where he could oversee the administration of his new conquered territories.'

'Where did he choose?' asked Ruby, conscious that if Lady Ballashiels had failed to snap at the Patient for making a comment, she would be able to make a contribution too without fear of retribution.

'Bridgnorth,' replied the Patient.

'Bridgnorth?' echoed Ratty 'That's less than ten miles from here.'

'It was customary to sequester the nearest available stately home in those times,' the Patient continued. 'I have studied the local maps. The most significant house in the area is this one.'

'Hitler planned to base himself here at Stiperstones?' asked Ruby, chilled at the thought. 'How could he have known about it?'

'I'm sure it's nothing sinister, girl,' said Lady Ballashiels. 'Unity was corresponding with Her Ladyship, don't forget. Hitler may have seen letters coming from here. And Unity may have described the house to him in glowing terms from her visits here in the early Thirties.'

'The Mitford guy we met in Spain never met his, er, father,' said Ruby. She was uncomfortable attributing the word 'father' to a genocidal maniac, and swallowed the word self-consciously as she uttered it. 'So how did he find out about what nearly happened with Unity and

Ratty's – sorry, Justin's – grandmother?'

'His mother's papers, of course, girl,' replied Lady Ballashiels. 'His mother died when he was young. Complications from carrying a bullet around in her brain. Mitford found a letter from my mother-in-law saying that she was going to come to Germany after her travels with Dalí and help her solve everything. Obviously, the letter didn't mention the idea of getting Unity to shoot Hitler, as I've already explained, because such a written admission would have been too dangerous if Hitler had found it. But Mitford was intrigued by the concept that Her Ladyship had a way to solve Unity's problematic relationship with the Führer, and in the early Seventies he went to Catalonia to meet with Dalí and ask if he had any insight into the matter.'

'His diaries?' asked Ratty.

'Dalí had reams of unpublished pages from his diaries, and he allowed Mitford access to all of it. The diaries explained in detail what the mother-in-law was planning to do to Hitler, since she spoke of little else on her journey through France. According to the diaries, she said that even if she couldn't persuade Unity to turn her pistol on Hitler then she would bloody well do it herself. There was no way she was going to let Hitler live. And then the bloody Keo thing happened, Her Ladyship's world was turned upside-down, and the rest of the world was plunged into war. In 1973 Mitford managed to persuade Dalí to let him become his personal archivist, a prelude to the Centre for Dalínian Studies that he would later establish, but he was only getting one side of the story from Dalí's diaries. The Ballashiels side of things was unclear to him, and his dissatisfaction with the world into which he had been born was growing stronger by the day. He desperately resented his own birth because to him it symbolised the destruction and the deaths of millions. But he would never contemplate suicide. That was, to him, the easy way out. He wanted a way to fix things. He wanted to undo the damage his father had done. He dedicated his life and his wealth to gaining a better understanding of that moment in time when the face of the world twisted in the wrong direction, to understanding how the word Keo could have caused it all, and to researching whether anything could have been done to prevent it.'

'Where do you enter this story, Lady Ballashiels?' asked the Patient.

'I'm coming to that, boy. In 1974, Mitford attracted a small number of followers. They were misfits, hippies, twisted individuals, probably all from comprehensive schools.' She glanced at Ruby to see if her dig had triggered a reaction, but Ruby refused to give her the satisfaction. 'These were the kind of people who were easy to lure into cultish behaviour. Mitford never really established anything as big as a cult, and he always had the means to pay whoever shared, or pretended to share, his beliefs. I suppose he lacked the confidence to think that ideology alone would suffice for his followers, so he trained them as domestic servants, bribed the staffing agency, and one by one they were all planted as employees here at Stiperstones. I was a young mother, not really paying attention to the type of staff we were being supplied, and at first I had no idea that anything was wrong. But their behaviour became increasingly odd, and I started to sense that the rotters were watching us all far too closely. I felt that we were at the centre of a grand conspiracy.'

'And then you opened the room sealed by your mother-in-law in the Thirties?' asked Ruby, giving in to her urge to be provocative by chipping in to the conversation.

Lady Ballashiels gave her a cold stare before continuing. 'That's when I found the photograph she had taken of Dalí and the word Keo. And, like Mitford, I wanted to know more. But Her Ladyship was long dead by then. I was frightened of the servants. I suspected they were connected to the Keo thing and I didn't want them to know I was looking into it. Their actions had been getting increasingly disturbing, so I needed to leave a message as to my intended journey, but do so in such a way that they would not notice. Hence the Lanvin wrapper and the clues behind the Dalí books. With that little insurance policy in place, I kissed Justin goodnight and slipped away into the darkness, intending to visit Dalí in person and shed some light on the incident my mother-in-law had experienced in France. It was never meant to be a permanent thing. If the servants didn't find me, I expected to be back in a few days.'

She saw Ratty's lips begin to wobble as the memory of the first days of her disappearance returned. He realised he was once more succumbing to emotion and slapped himself on the cheek.

'Sorry, Mother. Grown man now and all that twaddle.'

'Good boy. I know I let you down and that nothing can ever replace those years, but perhaps when I've explained everything you will begin to understand. You see, Dalí was most welcoming. He remembered your grandmother very fondly. He talked about his own interpretation of the writing in the sky, which he considered to be a portal to the future. He showed me a painting he had done inside a cave, where he had tried to express his emotions and fears regarding Keo. But in spending so much time with Dalí I had walked into the centre of the spider's web. Mitford was watching me. Even though I had evaded the eyes of his planted servants, I had simply handed myself to him without realising. I was a fool. He was fascinated by my existence, by my ignorance. I symbolised to him the world that should never have been. I was, like him, the progeny of Keo. He regarded the two of us as the centre of a parallel universe. The wrong bloody universe. He wouldn't let me leave. When his brainwashing attempts failed, he just locked me up. Of course, the mind control attempts continued for years, and sometimes I would pretend to go along with it in the hope that it might trigger my freedom, and there were moments when I even started to believe his rants. But he never had a clear vision of what he could do to right the wrongs of the world. It was vague, a cloudy obsession that never relented for a second. He just couldn't let me go. I missed you so badly, Justin, that I just wanted to go insane. I couldn't handle the loss. One day he came and told me I was legally dead and no one was looking for me any longer. I gave up all hope that day.'

Words were plainly attempting to form upon Ratty's lips, but he lacked sufficient control of his facial muscles to elucidate them.

'Did Dalí know of your imprisonment?' asked the Patient, valiantly stepping in to cover for his fragile friend.

'He had no idea, boy. Even when he came to live in the museum building in his dying years, he never questioned why the turret level was off limits. He was too frail to climb stairs, in any case. When Dalí died in 1989, I thought Mitford might relent and give up his insane quest, but he became ever more controlling, taking over the museum and the archives and studying ceaselessly in an effort to understand the reasons for his birth. Finally, Project Keo was announced by the European Space Agency. A time capsule for the distant future, containing a request to send confirmation of its receipt back in time. That's when he changed. That's when he found a way out.'

'A way out?' asked Ratty, finally able to speak again.

'A way out of this life, boy. A way to make everything as it should have been if your grandmother hadn't seen the word Keo in the sky and had gone to Germany as planned. All Mitford had to do was to stop Keo from ever being launched. If the time capsule doesn't arrive in the future, the request for a message to be sent back in time won't arrive either, and therefore the message won't be sent. And if the message isn't sent, my mother-in-law goes to Germany, persuades Unity to shoot her lover, or bloody well does it herself, and the whole damn war never happens.'

'And Alois Mitford would never have been born?' asked Ruby.

'Precisely, girl. That's what he wants. He doesn't want to kill himself. He wants to erase himself. And in so doing he wants to give millions the chance of life that was denied them by the bloody war.'

'But weren't you born just after the war, Mother?'

'When my father returned, finally demobbed. I don't suppose I would be here at all if it hadn't been for the war. And you, boy, certainly wouldn't be here if your grandmother had been apprehended after bumping off Hitler.'

'I can claim likewise,' said the Patient. 'My grandfather was somewhat involved in the more unpleasant aspects of that time, and the *in vitro* fertilisation experiments he conducted under war conditions and perfected during the following decades led directly to my creation.'

'My parents were first round baby boomers too,' said

Ruby. 'We're all on this planet only because of the war.'

'I don't think your parents have any relevance to this discussion, girl. My point is that we are the ones to whom destiny gave an opportunity of life that was denied to millions of others. My mother-in-law made a decision that changed everything, but that is the reality in which we now live.'

'So if Mitford sabotages the Keo launch, we all suddenly evaporate and get replaced by a different bunch of chaps?' asked Ratty.

'I doubt if evaporation is the mechanism by which such things function,' said the Patient, taking things too literally. 'It is impossible to know the effects of meddling in time in this way, but the sheer degree of uncertainty makes any such alterations unwise.'

'Are you talking parallel universes?' asked Ruby.

'That's not a theory I would want to stake my life upon,' replied the Patient. 'It is a theory that is currently unprovable. All I will say is that the time capsule satellite must be launched, for to remove its arrival in the future from the planet's timeline could have serious consequences for us all right now.'

'Are we going to dissolve like an aspirin if Mitford gets his way?' asked Ratty.

'Worse than that,' replied the Patient. 'I believe that if Keo is not launched, Mitford will achieve his dream of complete erasure from time, and he will drag the rest of us with him. We won't just cease to be. We will never have existed.'

'Keo was originally supposed to be launched ten years ago,' said Lady Ballashiels. 'Mitford has used his influence to create delay after delay, but the launch date is now fixed. That's why he has become increasingly desperate and erratic in recent weeks. He knows that he needs to sabotage the launch in person. He's heading for Guiana, to the launch site. That's why I tried to get back to see you, Justin. Time is running out for us all. I wanted to be with you at the end of time.'

There was a stunned silence amongst the group. The profundity of her words took some moments to sink in.

'There's every chance he won't make it, isn't there?' asked Ruby.

'Mitford is a very wealthy man, girl. Not something you'd know about, I imagine. People are cheap.' She looked Ruby in the eye as she said it. 'If he finds enough corrupt people he will get his way.'

'Then we must stop him ourselves,' declared Ratty.

'You mean go to Guiana?' asked Ruby. 'Do you even know where it is?'

'No need. I understand it's the pilot's job to worry about that kind of thing. We just need to book our flights.'

'I shall come with you, boy,' said his mother.

'I rather fancy you should stay behind. Things might get a little testy out there. And you have so much catching up to do in England. Much has changed since the Seventies. We have more than three channels on the television, now. We have something called the Internet. Oh, and you mustn't be racist anymore.'

'No, boy. I risked everything to find you, and I'm not letting you go again. If he succeeds, I want to be with you for our final moments. Besides, I know Mitford well. I know how he thinks. Maybe I can help.'

'Do you even have a passport, Mater?'

'How do you think I came back to England? Obviously, it's not my passport. For immigration purposes, I am the Spanish lady from whom I stole an identity. Desperate measures for desperate times. I will make it up to her if I get the chance. And you, boy, will find someone to clean up this house. It's a disgrace.'

Ruby wasn't watching, but she sensed that Lady Ballashiels was looking at her when she said that someone needed to clean the house. She sighed. Meeting Ratty's mother had turned out to be less of a pleasure than she had expected. Her sole consolation was the imminent destruction of everything and everyone she knew. If her relationship with Lady Ballashiels was going to test her, at least it wouldn't be a prolonged agony.

Thursday 9th May 2013

Charlie lowered his sunglasses and blinked. He was melting. French Guiana's humidity seemed to suck the moisture from his body. Rocco fanned himself with his passport as they stepped out of the Cessna. He could hardly believe the gruelling journey was over. New York to São Paulo, São Paulo to Belem on Brazil's northern coast, Belem to French Guiana's modest capital, Cayenne, followed by a bone-rattling hop to the airstrip at Kourou in what felt like a small car with wings. All those connections, check-ins, security checks and complimentary nuts made Rocco feel like he had arrived at the end of the world.

Part of the spaceport was visible from the runway, its boxy buildings and full-size mock-up of an Ariane rocket set against a breath-taking background of dense foliage. Futuristic space architecture and primitive jungle clashed like black and white. Somewhere out of sight of the airstrip was the Keo time capsule, installed in a rocket on a launch pad, ready to begin its fifty-thousand-year mission to bring twenty-first-century knowledge and culture to humanity's distant descendants.

Rocco and Charlie were, however, focussed upon a more modest time capsule. Since it had departed New York by sea, they assumed it would arrive by the same means and resolved to check out the fishing docks on Kourou's river.

'Three thousand miles at forty knots,' said Rocco, as they sat in the back of a taxi heading for the docks. 'Even without stopping for fuel, it's going to take that boat three days to get here. And I doubt it has that kind of range, and the sea conditions won't allow him to go flat out all the time anyway, so we're looking at four, maybe five days since he left until he gets here.'

'And it took us two days to make it down here,' said Charlie, 'so we have a day or two to wait. What are we going to do? Hang out at the hotel bar?'

'You're forgetting something, Charlie. I'm a senior employee of the space agency. I have authorisation to access the launch site. The Keo satellite launches in three days. The old man wants me to do something for him.'

'What?'

'He wants me to blow it up on the launch pad.'

'Huh?' Charlie was shocked and impressed in equal measure. 'Why does the dude want you to do that?'

'I still don't know. That's why I'm here. Keo is obviously a major threat for him. I sense this is something far bigger than space technology or money. He was prepared to kill to keep people away from Keo. I'm going to find out why.'

At the fishing dock, an unusual craft was tying up. At its helm was Dick English. He wasn't sure the structure of the wooden dock was strong enough to hold the mass of this flying boat against the flow of the river, but he didn't care. He was certain that he had outwitted Charlie and Rocco by switching from a motor boat to an airplane, and was ready to confront the old man and make his millions. On reflection, he had decided to leave the capsule intact. The drill had damaged the copper alloy skin of the tube, but it hadn't penetrated completely, so the contents were demonstrably original. Offering the old man a complete capsule was worth more to him than satiating his curiosity regarding the contents. It was probably just a weird piece of art that Dalí put into it, anyway, he decided. That, in itself, could be worth millions, and he had a figure in mind that reflected the value of the Dalí contribution, the lost earnings that would result from him never being able to return to his job, the cost of renting a beach house and a boat, and the cost of the flying lessons that had been needed to be confident of making such a long solo flight. It probably wouldn't wipe out Mitford's finances entirely, and since the old man seemed to be preparing for his personal doomsday, money would be of little use to him once he had achieved whatever it was he was planning.

Dick English had plans of his own, involving a tropical island, a private bar and boatloads of beautiful women arriving every week for his pleasure. Life like that didn't come cheap. His blackmail plan had to work perfectly.

Mitford was waiting for him in the bar at Hotel Mercure. For a man on the verge of achieving his ambitions, he was oddly sullen. English thought he had seen death row prisoners with brighter outlooks on life. He almost felt guilty about the blackmail he was about to instigate, but he reminded himself that he had risked his liberty in bringing the capsule out of the United States, and would have to sacrifice the chance of ever returning.

'You have the capsule?' asked Mitford in world-weary tones. The brightening of mood he had experienced on the flight here had been fleeting, soon replaced by resentment that he had been placed by birth into this position in the first place. His duty to change the world was a thankless, anonymous one; he would never be appreciated.

'Of course.'

English showed Mitford a photo of the capsule sitting

in the yacht, before he'd had it transferred to the seaplane.

'You opened it?'

'There's superficial damage from the drill, but the capsule is intact. I haven't cut into it.'

Mitford reached down to pick up a small briefcase. He opened it and showed the contents to English.

'I want to renegotiate our deal,' said English.

'We had a contract. This is a million dollars for you, as we agreed. Take it.'

English pushed it back towards Mitford.

'My costs were more than that,' he said. 'I had to do a lot more. Risk a lot more. Sacrifice a lot more. And if you don't pay what I think it's worth to me, the capsule will end up at the bottom of the sea.'

'How much?'

'Thirty million.' His throat tightened as he said it, almost as if he didn't believe such a sum even existed on the planet.

'Thirty million? Hah! What makes you think I have that kind of money?'

'Forty million, then. Fifty.'

'What?'

'Sixty.'

'You're crazy.'

'I know who you are. I know who your father was, and your mother. That's a pretty substantial inheritance. All that looted gold and artwork, all those countries ransacked, all those people dispossessed. That money didn't disappear, did it? All you needed to inherit everything was a number. Unlock a Swiss bank account and you're set for a life of luxury built on the misery of others.'

'I have never lived a life of luxury.'

'So your Swiss bank account must be full.'

'That is none of your business.'

'Sixty million. It's my final offer.'

Mitford was tempted to play the role of the victim, protesting at being ripped off. He knew precisely how much money sat in his account. The price English was demanding would not even put the slightest dent in it. He earned more than that in interest every month. Sixty million could be transferred to English with no problem whatsoever. He would have no further use for his wealth in a day or two, anyway. In fact, the money itself would cease to exist in that account before the week was out. Every penny would automatically return to the families and institutions from which it was originally stolen. It made no difference how much he had once that redistribution occurred, but the principle irked him. Mitford did not appreciate the hint of blackmail inherent in this deal.

'Sixty million, you say?' asked Mitford, through teeth that seethed and spat.

'That's the price. Take it or leave it.'

'All right. I'll leave it. Thank you and goodbye.' Mitford stood up.

'Wait,' called English, his voice tinged with panic. 'We can talk about this.'

'There is nothing to discuss. You have gone against your word. I refuse to be blackmailed, therefore you will receive nothing.'

'Ten million. That's fair. I did have lots of expenses, and I can give you the capsule intact.'

Mitford stood still, almost savouring the unfamiliar emotion of satisfaction. Ten million was enough of a climb-down. He could live with that. He turned round slowly and looked English in the eye. 'I advise you to make the most of that money. Enjoy it quickly. You will not have long to spend it.'

'This is what Mitford wants me to blow up,' said Rocco, proudly pointing up at the Ariane rocket sitting on its launch pad, one of two rockets being prepared for launch in the next few days from adjacent pads. 'The Keo time capsule is right at the top, and there's a communications satellite beneath it. A GPS unit, I think.'

'I can't wait to see this firework explode,' said Charlie. 'Let's get closer.'

'I could, but you'd have to wait here. You only have a guest pass, so this is your limit, but my staff pass gives me access almost anywhere. That's why I got you in so easily as my personal guest. I think my level of access is what Mitford liked about me. Probably why he didn't assassinate me.'

'How are you going to blow it up?' asked Charlie.

'Why would I do that?'

'You said Mitford hired you to do it.'

'Yes, but I'm not really going to, am I? I'm a conspiracy investigator. I get off on solving mysteries, uncovering dark secrets. This is the greatest trail I've ever followed. Getting close to Mitford is my way of lifting the lid on his plans. Pretending I'll do what he wants is my way of getting his trust. He's planning something big, and the two time capsules are the link, and Dalí is the common thread between them. I just wish I knew why Dalí matters and why Mitford gives a damn. Opening a capsule from the Thirties and destroying one intended for launch this year – what is the point? What's in it for him?'

'We should go find him. Get some answers,' said Charlie.

'No, we need to be ready when that Dalí capsule gets here. I want to know what's in it that's so important to everyone,' said Rocco.

He signed out of the space centre and drove him and Charlie the very short distance into town, through streets largely devoid of traffic, and continued all the way to the river where they pulled up at the fishing dock. Still no sign of the motor boat they had last seen near New York. But the seaplane sitting at the end of the dock looked utterly out of place beside the simple wooden vessels used by the locals. Rocco looked at Charlie.

'You don't think, do you …?' asked Rocco.

'Not often,' replied Charlie.

'… he switched from the boat to the plane,' said Rocco. 'He's already here.'

They walked along the dock to check out the plane at close quarters. The door was locked. Charlie pressed his nose against a window. There were objects inside, but nothing stood out as being the capsule.

'Shall we break the window?' Charlie suggested.

'No. It might be someone else's plane,' said Rocco.

'Like who? No one round here has this kind of toy. And the capsule could be in the back beneath all that junk.'

'We're not going to damage this aircraft,' ordered Rocco, taking one of the mooring lines and untying it.

'What are you doing?' asked Charlie.

'We mustn't damage it, but that doesn't mean we have to leave it here. Come on.'

Charlie twigged, and jumped into a nearby open fishing boat and started the outboard engine. He slipped its moorings and motored inexpertly in front of the sea plane. Rocco threw a tow line to him, and jumped into the fishing boat with him, securing the rope across two cleats.

Rocco steered the boat upriver, with the seaplane dragging lazily behind.

'There are only two ways to prevent Mitford from sabotaging Keo,' said the Patient from his squashed position in the rear of a taxi. 'And neither method is infallible, I am sorry to say.'

His companions were scarcely paying attention, their weary eyes distracted by the humbling sight of the two white Ariane rockets that dominated the otherwise verdant landscape. They were already at the outskirts of Kourou and would shortly reach their hotel. It had taken twenty-two hours of travelling to reach this part of South America, including an interminable stopover in Paris during which Ruby managed to achieve a relatively peaceful equilibrium with Lady Ballashiels by ensuring Ratty and the Patient always sat between them.

'The first method,' continued the Patient, regardless, 'is to capture Mitford and restrict his movements until such time as the rocket is launched successfully. But that presupposes that he hasn't yet made his move. If he has set something in motion already, perhaps by sabotaging a component of the rocket, there is nothing we would be able to do about it.'

'And what's the other option for us?' asked Ruby with a yawn.

'We give him what he has long appeared to wish for. We end his life.'

'I'm not spending the rest of my life with the convicts over there on Devil's Island, thank you very much,' said Ruby.

'I fear that if we do not succeed in arresting Mitford's plans, you will not have a life anyway.'

Everyone stared at the passing scenery for a moment. The taxi continued at a leisurely pace along spacious roads, devoid of heavy traffic or any sense of urgency.

Kourou possessed an innocent charm, an understated elegance that was starkly at odds with its status as a spaceport.

'Children, have you ever considered,' began Lady Ballashiels, 'that the people who were denied the chance of life may have made greater contributions to the planet and to mankind than any of our generations were able to do?'

'That sounds like Mitford's brainwashing talk, Mater.'

'What rot, wiffle and waffle. It'd take more than his scrubbing ability to wash my brain, boy.'

'But presumably it was one of his arguments, Mater? And it does make you wonder, doesn't it?'

'The question is one of moral choice,' said the Patient. 'Where is the balance of morality? If you are presented with the opportunity retrospectively to undo the turmoil and killings of the Second World War, and to permit all of those millions who were killed the opportunity to live out their natural lives and to procreate, then you have to balance that good against the cost of erasing the lives of many more millions who have filled their shoes. What is more valuable: actual life or potential life? If you value potential life so highly, then it surely follows that it is a crime not to utilise a woman's every egg cycle for pregnancy, for each period is a potential human life lost. When you take the argument to that extreme it becomes ludicrous.'

'The problem with Mitford is not one of morality or finding the balance of good and evil,' said Ruby. 'The issue with him is that it's personal. He represents one of the lives given a chance that shouldn't have occurred, but his life came from Hitler and Unity Mitford, and that's always been too much for him to bear. It's driven him insane. And that's going to make him a tricky man to catch.'

272

The taxi arrived at the hotel forecourt and stopped.

'Tricky to catch?' asked Ratty, climbing out of the taxi. 'Perhaps. But I'd say perhaps not. Isn't that the frightful fellow in the lobby?'

Lady Ballashiels looked unsteady as she stood in front of the hotel, watching the man who had ruined her life in retaliation for the fact that her mother-in-law had ruined his by not preventing the circumstances that led to his birth.

'I'll have a word with him,' said Ratty.

'A word? Ratty, we have to corner him,' ordered Ruby. 'Get him to come outside, or into a corridor or something. Just get him away from public view so you and the Patient can tie him up. And when you've done that, Ratty, put some proper clothes on. You look ridiculous in that lumpy jacket.'

'If I may make a suggestion,' said the Patient, 'a more subtle approach is far more likely to achieve our desired result. Ratty, I propose that you buy the man a drink. Keep him drinking. Keep him talking. Find out if he has already done whatever he was planning to do. Give me time to buy the drugs I need. We'll spike his drink and secure him in a hotel room when he is unconscious.'

'Mister Patient, that will never work,' said Lady Ballashiels. 'The man is teetotal. He now eschews all forms of drugs because they mask pain, and he feels it is his duty to experience all of the pain that the world puts his way.'

'How's a fellow to knock a chap out in a hotel without drink or drugs?' asked Ratty.

Mitford started walking towards the door. He was accompanied by a man they didn't recognise. Mitford and English climbed into the same taxi that Ratty and his entourage had just vacated. From behind various parked

273

cars they watched Mitford and the mystery man being driven away. Ratty hailed the next taxi and they all squeezed into it and set off on a snail's pace pursuit that ended at the fishing dock.

'We could have walked here at that speed,' said Ruby. 'Could have saved the cab fare.'

They watched from a distance as Mitford and the younger man walked to the end of the dock and started to appear agitated. They argued and gesticulated. Fists started to pummel each other. Mitford took a step back and pulled a gun. With no warning, he shot the other man and let him fall backwards into the river, his body immediately starting the short journey out to sea.

'Did that really just happen?' asked Ruby.

'Shame it wasn't vice versa,' said Ratty. 'Could have saved us a bit of bother.'

'Be careful, children. He's not normally in the habit of shooting people. His mental state is obviously deteriorating. Always assume he will shoot. Don't take any chances.'

Mitford stomped back along the wooden jetty, past the heaps of fishing nets, to the shore.

Ratty crouched behind a fishing boat and shouted, 'I say, would you care to join us for tiffin, old beanbag?'

Mitford looked around for the source of the voice, but could see no one. His shoulders sagged. He held his gun loosely against his thigh, as if about to drop it.

'It might have a somewhat French flavour, of course. Proper cream teas are something of a rarity in these parts.'

Ratty stood up and waved at Mitford. To the horror of all those watching from secure vantage points, Mitford raised his gun again.

'That's not exactly cricket, old boy, is it?' said Ratty, walking boldly towards him. 'Why don't you put that frightful thing away before someone gets hurt?'

'You have had plenty of warnings, Lord Ballashiels,' said Mitford with a deep sigh.

He straightened his arm and fired at Ratty's chest. The aristocrat fell backwards onto the decking. Mitford broke into a run, but he lacked the energy and the determination to give himself a real chance of escape. The shootings seemed to affect him deeply. Remorse yanked him back to the scene of his crimes and he stopped and crouched into an almost foetal position.

'You are a pathetic and despicable man,' shouted Lady Ballashiels, not caring for her own safety as she rushed to her son's side. She picked up Ratty's head and cradled him. 'Ruby, girl, call an ambulance! I'm so sorry, Justin. This is all my fault. You're going to be fine, I promise.' She patently lacked conviction in her words.

Mitford just watched, unable to cope with the rapidly evolving reality in which he found himself. His gun-toting hand twitched, as if controlled by an entity beyond his own mind.

Ruby dialled for help, consciously hoping that Lady Ballashiels would notice her fluent French when the call was answered, but there was no signal on her phone. She ran in circles trying to find a patch of reception, stopping frequently to check the screen, and finding herself in an increasingly distressed state.

The Patient checked Ratty's pulse, looked at his pupils, and listened to his chest. Without a word, he then strolled over to the stricken Mitford, curious as to his mental state. Mitford was flicking the gun back and forth, but there was no real direction to it, no deliberate aiming. The Patient reached out and put his hands over the weapon. Mitford offered no resistance, nor even any awareness of what was happening. His breakdown appeared total, the Patient thought. He plucked the weapon from the old man's hand and pocketed it. He considered restraining Mitford, but such a course of action appeared unnecessary.

'Justin, can you open your eyes?' whispered his mother. 'We're trying to get an ambulance, boy. Can you hear me at all?'

Ruby rushed over to him and held his hand.

'Ratty? Are you still with us? Hang in there. It's going to be all right.'

'I do wish you'd stop calling him by that repugnant name, girl.'

'Lady Ballashiels?' Ruby asked confidently.

'Yes, girl?'

'Shut your snobby cakehole and give your adorable son a kiss.'

Lady Ballashiels noticed a tear forming in Ruby's eye. She could sense the strong bond that this woman shared with her son.

'Are you two more than just good friends?' the old lady whispered. 'Perhaps a kiss from you might help bring him round?'

'Us? Not really, Lady Ballashiels. We've been friends since university, that's all. Nothing more.' But she couldn't stop herself from leaning forward and kissing Ratty on the lips.

He smiled and opened his eyes. 'Well that little lie down seems to have done the trick,' he groaned. 'Mitford took the wind out of my sails somewhat, but I think I'll be right as rain.'

'Don't talk, boy,' said Lady Ballashiels. 'Wait for the doctors.'

Ratty wriggled out of her arms and sat up.

'Doctors? No, thank you. A gin and tonic might go

down well, though.' He put his hand inside his shirt and unzipped one of the many pockets on the utility jacket he was wearing beneath everything. He pulled out a stubby, square paperback on the subject cf Salvador Dalí's works. Just off-centre was a neat hole from which a steaming bullet was protruding. 'Dalí has always been close to my heart,' he said.

The Patient, distracted by Ratty's apparent miracle recovery and by the unfamiliar sensation of holding a gun in his hands, took his eye off Mitford just as the old man seemed to come to his senses.

'You don't matter. Don't you see? Nothing matters. Alive or dead, it makes no difference!' Mitford shouted as he ran towards the trees. 'My agony is almost at an end. I will not allow any of you to prolong it unduly. My one contribution to the planet will be my own erasure. Oh, how I hate the Ballashiels family. You are a plague on this earth. You are a curse on mankind. Stay away from me or face the consequences.'

He disappeared into the trees.

Half a mile upriver was a second boat dock. This was more substantial than the first, a concrete structure designed to receive the barges that carried sections of rocket by sea to the space centre. Charlie looked back. Thanks to a bend in the river, the point at which they had stolen the seaplane was now out of sight.

'How do we park this thing?' shouted Charlie over the noise of the outboard motor. The towed seaplane was still ploughing through the water behind them.

'We just stop by the dock,' Rocco replied.

'Just stop?'

'Sure. We put our motor in reverse and we stop.'

'And what stops the seaplane?'

Rocco looked at him. He slowed his boat gradually. The aircraft continued towards them on its floats, the tow rope now submerged and useless.

'Forward! Quick!' shouted Charlie, ducking as the shadow of the plane loomed over him.

Rocco pushed the engine to full power. Their boat sped forwards. Charlie looked over his shoulder to see the rope snap out of the water. A sharp cracking noise distracted him. One of the cleats to which the tow rope had been tied had sheered clean off, taking part of the wooden hull with it.

'Er, Rocco, my feet are wet,' complained Charlie.

'Shit. Hull's breached,' said Rocco, throwing the engine into reverse.

'No, don't stop!' shouted Charlie. 'The plane's right behind us!'

'Hang on,' said Rocco. He turned the boat a hundred and eighty degrees, tilting it so far to one side that it scooped up a few more gallons of water, and pulled up adjacent to the seaplane. 'Climb onto the floats.'

With the two of them clinging to the port side float, and the stolen fishing boat now fully submerged, the seaplane began to swing in an ungainly arc across the river, spinning out of control with the breeze. The dock reached out halfway across the river ahead of them. Collision was inevitable.

'Think I've worked out how to stop the plane!' shouted Rocco. 'Hold tight!'

The tail of the seaplane wedged itself above the dock, while the fuselage scraped against the concrete wall and pushed the nose down into the water. The aircraft halted to the sound of stressed aluminium pulsating with the force of the water. The two passengers climbed onto the dock and whooped their expressions of satisfaction.

In a locker on another fishing boat Rocco found some tools and held up a selection of them to show Charlie.

'What do you think is best for getting that door open?' he called. 'Screwdriver, spanner or pliers?'

While Rocco was contemplating the options, Charlie put his foot through the cockpit window. Perspex shards exploded all around him. He put his sleeve over his hand and cleared enough fragments away to be able to reach inside and open the door. Behind the pilot's seat was a sheet. He lifted it up and was relieved to find the Westinghouse time capsule beneath it.

'Come and help me carry this thing,' he shouted.

'Quickly,' said Rocco. 'Pass it out before the plane gets dislodged by the current.'

Charlie squeezed into the rear of the plane and fed the heavy capsule through the pilot's door to Rocco. Once he had a secure grip on the ring at the end of the tube, Charlie joined him on the dock and together they dragged the capsule out of the tilted seaplane and onto dry land.

'Now what?' asked Charlie.

'Get it into one of those huts so we can open this thing up,' said Rocco. 'If we can saw one end off, everything inside it should tip out.'

Charlie ran around the boatyard opening doors, looking for something resembling a workshop, relieved that the place seemed to be deserted. In a country of less than a quarter of a million people, it seemed fitting that parts of it would appear empty. When he found a suitably equipped shed he ran back and helped to carry the capsule inside.

'Close the door,' said Rocco. 'Surgery is about to begin.'

'What if Dalí put poison gas in there?' asked Charlie.

'Keeping the door open won't make a lot of difference if he did,' said Rocco. 'Anyway, I don't think that was really Dalí's style. He never hurt anyone.'

Rocco began to saw through the copper alloy, following a shallow groove that had been created for that purpose and was clearly marked with the words 'cut here'. Despite the implication that there was nothing of value behind the cut line, he rotated the capsule to avoid cutting in too deeply. When the inner seal was pierced, there was a release of gases that made Charlie scramble for the door with his sleeve over his face.

'It's nitrogen,' Rocco explained. 'They filled it with the stuff to stop anything decaying.'

It took ten minutes to decapitate the capsule. Rocco pulled the head off gently and tried to look inside. Everything was tightly packed, with glass wool filling the few spaces that remained.

'How do we know what was meant to be there and what was there anyway?' asked Rocco.

'The old man gave me a book,' said Charlie. 'It lists everything that was officially included in the capsule. Anything else is Dalí's.'

'Great,' said Rocco. 'Where's the book?'

'In my hotel room. New York.'

'This could be a waste of time if we don't know what we're looking for,' said Rocco.

'Google,' said Charlie. 'Find it there. Someone must have scanned it and uploaded it as an eBook by now.'

Charlie took out his cellphone in the hope that perhaps a university library copy had been digitised. But no matter how high he held his phone there was no signal available.

'Let me try,' said Rocco. He pulled out his own phone with equal lack of success. 'What a heap of junk! This is a spaceport and I can't even use a cellphone!'

'Just shake it all out on the table and look for anything that seems to be Dalí's,' said Charlie.

'I guess we have no choice,' agreed Rocco.

Charlie tilted the capsule while Rocco dragged the contents out. Nothing slid easily; everything was jammed in tightly. Soon the remaining items were beyond the reach of his arm.

'Go find a stick or a broom handle, Charlie,' he said. 'Anything I can use to drag these things out. Needs to be six feet long.'

Charlie stepped out of the shed and scouted around the outbuildings and boats. While he was peering into the window of a hut he felt a hand upon his shoulder.

'You did well at Flushing Meadows,' said Mitford.

'How did you find me here?' gasped Charlie, shocked to see the scary face of the old man here on the other side of the world.

'There are just two boat jetties in Kourou,' replied Mitford. 'Once I discovered English's seaplane had been stolen from the first one, I deduced I would find you here. And I am glad to have found you, even though you are not the person you pretended to be.'

'The *Men in Black* disguise?' Charlie asked, looking his boss up and down. Mitford was sweating badly, his clothes drenched as if he was feverish. Charlie realised his lower half was more than sweaty: he was soaking wet up to his waist, as if he'd been wading through water.

'I know you are not a professional art thief.'

'Did I ever say I was?' asked Charlie, confused by the unexpected accusation. 'I'm not lots of things, dude. Not an astronaut. Not an athlete. And I don't give two shits about art.'

'You are not a wealthy man, either, are you?'

'Guess not.'

'I can give you enough riches to last the rest of your days on this planet.'

281

Charlie's eyes lit up with corruptibility. 'I'm listening, dude,' he said.

'You retrieved the time capsule for me. That was excellent work and proves to me that I can rely on you in difficult circumstances. You showed ingenuity and confidence. I like that.'

'You don't look well, dude. You look like you need a cold beer.'

'My health matters not. Listen, I know that when you brought the capsule to the surface it was then taken by the site's security guard. You should know that he was working for me all along. I always employ more people than I need, sometimes working against each other. I find it is a way to breed healthy competition between them.'

'He flew the capsule here. Did me a favour. I was going to drive.'

'He let me down. Got greedy. So guess what? I killed him. He could have been rich, like I am planning to make you, but he was stupid. You're not stupid, are you Charlie?'

'Well, I am kinda dumb sometimes.'

'No you're not. You're resourceful and you're loyal. You'll go far. Here's what I need you to do.'

'Look at that bruise,' said Ruby, as Ratty opened all of his layers to prove that his bulletproofing system had worked. The bruising was almost a perfect square where the book had been imprinted against his chest. It was tender to the touch, but not disabling.

'Mitford may be unarmed, but he still needs to be stopped,' said the Patient. 'And I apologise for letting him go. My judgement as to his physical state was clouded by the shock of Ratty's predicament.'

'Totally understandable, Patient chappy. I appreciate your concerns.'

'There are many ways in which Mitford can sabotage the launch of the Keo rocket,' continued the Patient. 'He can physically tamper with the rocket. He can detonate the on-board explosives if he can hack into the radio frequencies used to control the rocket in flight. He might even be able to hire someone in mission control to detonate it for him on the pretext that it was going off-course.'

'Should we warn the staff at launch control?' suggested Ruby.

'Too bloody risky, girl,' said Lady Ballashiels. 'We don't know how many of them are on Mitford's payroll.'

'So, we should split up,' said Ruby. 'Two of us search for Mitford, and two try to watch the perimeter of the space centre in case he gets in through the fence. Unless anyone has a better idea.'

'I have. Why don't the boys go after Mitford in the woods, while the girls patrol the fence?' suggested Lady Ballashiels.

'That's what I said!' protested Ruby. 'Although not perhaps the pairings I had in mind.'

'And be careful with that gun, Mister Patient,' Lady Ballashiels continued, ignoring her. 'It wouldn't do to shoot Mitford dead, no matter how tempting. We need him to talk in case he's already instigated something that we need to stop.'

Ratty and the Patient ran into the trees on Mitford's trail, but the forested area was vast, and there was no indication as to which direction he had taken.

'I don't suppose you happen to have read a book on tracking people through the old jungle, Patient chappy?'

'I have no need of such a book.'

'Why ever not? Surely it would be jolly handy right now.'

'I fear not, Ratty.'

'Explain?'

'Mitford did not make his escape through here.'

'But we saw him run into the trees, old sniffer dog.'

'Do you not find it difficult to move amongst these trees and bushes? The foliage is dense and challenging.'

'Of course. It's a pain in the old wotnot.'

'And Mitford is almost twice your age and is clearly in a state of distress. It is therefore more than likely that he diverted at the earliest opportunity to the river bank. From there he will be easy to track.'

'Why is that easy?'

'Because the river bank is sandy and the river is tidal. That means footprints are wiped clean twice a day. Given the scarcity of people in this area, any prints we find will probably belong to Mitford.'

'Crikey.'

The Patient turned left and threaded through the trees to the riverbank. The footprints were obvious. One set. Heading upstream, away from the dock where the shootings had occurred.

'Can you run?'

Ratty patted his chest and winced.

'Go on ahead, old chum. I'll see you there.'

The Patient ran through the sandy riverbank, at times sinking up to his knees as the sand became a thin mix of silt and mud. A small tributary that flowed through the trees and into the main river necessitated splashing through warm water up to his waist, but he pressed on, following the footprints that were clearly imprinted ahead. Finally, he reached a jetty and a spread of small huts and buildings, which serviced the boats that were moored there. He noticed a seaplane with a broken window, and could hear banging coming from one of the sheds, but Mitford was nowhere in sight.

He scouted around the area. The footprints disappeared as soon as solid ground replaced the soft river bank. Tracking his prey would be virtually impossible now. His only chance of locating Mitford was if he was still in the vicinity, and for that to be successful he had to keep out of sight. He crouched behind a random hut and listened intently.

Moments later the unsubtle tones of Charlie's voice carried across the breeze. The Patient peeked in the direction of the voice and saw Charlie walking slowly alongside Mitford, deep in conversation.

'Charlie, I recommend that you walk away from Mitford,' shouted the Patient, stepping into full view and confidently aiming the weapon he had earlier confiscated from Mitford.

Charlie stood between Mitford and the gun that was pointing at them.

'And what if I refuse?' Charlie asked.

'Perhaps you don't understand. I am aiming this gun at Mister Mitford. He is a dangerous man who must be contained, and I intend to apprehend him. I have no quarrel with you, Charlie, so please step aside.'

Charlie wobbled left and right, torn between his innate cowardice and the lure of great wealth. The Patient wouldn't shoot him, he decided. He could see this through. He could protect Mitford, earn his briefcase full of cash and come out of this experience on top, for once.

Ratty arrived, sodden and exhausted. Charlie waved a polite hello to the aristocrat as he backed away from the Patient, sheltering Mitford with his body all the while.

'You have cut the capsule open?' Mitford whispered to Charlie.

'Kinda. Lot of junk got stuck in there.'

'I need to see.'

'I thought you wanted me to help you get to the launch site for Keo?'

'I can't bear the thought of erasing myself and the wrongs of the world without seeing what Dalí contributed to the Westinghouse capsule. Please help an old man indulge his curiosity.'

'Sure. What harm can it do?'

Charlie opened the door and showed Mitford inside. Rocco looked horrified to see him, but faked a smile.

'Never mind that,' said Mitford. 'I don't care how you feel about my presence. All I ask is that you permit me five minutes with my time capsule.'

'Of course not,' said Rocco.

'Let him have his time with the capsule,' ordered Charlie, in a tone that carried a degree of authority that surprised even him. It was amazing what the prospect of wealth could do.

'We dug it out,' objected Rocco. 'We're going to see what's in it.'

'I knew you would not be trustworthy,' said Mitford. 'That is why I never relied on you.'

'Rocco, we are going to let the dude help us empty the contents of the capsule. Make room for him.'

Charlie got Rocco to stand behind him while Mitford examined the half-empty tube.

'Please hold it for me,' said Mitford, as he produced a wire from his pocket and reached inside the capsule. 'They packed everything very carefully so that it would last five thousand years. But there is something in here that renders the capsule pointless. Something that was

286

added secretly in order to make the world a better place.'

Charlie heard something sliding within the copper tube. A triangular bundle of leather, secured with a narrow strap. Mitford opened the pouch and extracted a 9mm Luger pistol with a bevelled walnut grip. There was something engraved on the barrel. Mitford held it to the light. A single word.

Mitford ran his finger across the chiselled steel and closed his eyes for a moment, savouring the discovery, allowing its reality to sink in. Dalí had not lied. Its profound symbolism was proof to him that his mission would work. He opened his eyes and pointed the pistol at Charlie.

'Coolsville,' said Charlie. 'So Dalí put a gun in the capsule!'

'Why would he do that?' wondered Rocco.

'The circle of time is more complex than you could ever understand,' Mitford replied. 'But Dalí planned for this day. My needs were fulfilled before I was born in order that I would have the tools required to undo my birth. Stand back.'

'What about my ten million bucks?' protested Charlie, fearing his prospects for sudden and easy wealth were evaporating fast.

'What ten million bucks?' asked Rocco.

'Make way,' ordered Mitford, making it clear that no one would be receiving anything from him. Charlie and Rocco made space for Mitford to leave. Outside, the Patient found himself in a situation where shooting Mitford would be unproductive. Both were armed equally. It would be mutually assured destruction. The Patient lowered his weapon and let the old man leave.

'All that for a gun?' asked Rocco, emerging into the light, followed by a sheepish Charlie. 'That doesn't make sense. He knew there was a gun in that thing, but why go to the trouble of getting it dug up and flown halfway across the world, bribing everyone he comes across, just so he can have a weapon when he gets here?'

'It's his second gun today,' said Ratty. 'The fellow already shot me in the Dalís with the first gun.'

'There's no logic to his actions,' Rocco went on. 'You'd expect Dalí to have put something profound and meaningful into the capsule, not just a gun.'

'When you apply such logic,' said the Patient, 'it appears inevitable that the profundity and meaning must be contained within the gun itself.'

'So it's not a real gun?' asked Ratty.

'In an existential sense it is real,' replied the Patient. 'But its firepower is less relevant than its symbolism. If only we could know what it meant.'

'I know what it meant,' said Charlie.

'With respect,' said the Patient, 'I doubt that you really have the requisite background knowledge to understand the symbolic status of that weapon.'

'I know that it's something to do with Keo,' said Charlie, completely indifferent to the put-down he had just received.

'How?' asked Rocco.

'The gun had the word Keo engraved on its barrel,' said Charlie.

Rocco instinctively grabbed Charlie's shoulders to prevent the source of this profound knowledge from slipping away.

'Not sure what the font was,' Charlie elaborated, wriggling out of Rocco's grip, 'but he held it close enough to my face to see three letters there. In capitals.'

'Well why didn't you say so?' asked Ratty.

'Thought I just did,' replied Charlie.

'If Dalí placed a gun in the time capsule with the word Keo written on the barrel,' said the Patient, 'it is the corroborating evidence needed to prove beyond doubt that in 1937 Dalí witnessed the response from those who will receive the Keo time capsule in the distant future. As such, it gives Mitford a boost in his confidence. It reinforces his belief in his plan.'

'Forget the rest of the contents of the time capsule, then,' said Rocco. 'None of that matters. Mitford's the target now. We have to stop him.'

Lady Ballashiels was astonishingly resilient to the heat and humidity, thought Ruby. The two of them had walked for miles around the perimeter fence, and they now appreciated that two people could not possibly hope to watch every inch of it. Without the need to speak a word to each other, they concluded that they had to find a suitable vantage point to oversee the launch centre. Eventually they found a spot where the view of the rockets was relatively unimpeded.

'Is there anything you'd like to ask me about Ratty – I mean Justin – from the years I've known him?' Ruby asked, breaking the uncomfortable silence.

'Well, one thing's been bothering me, girl.'

'What's that?'

'This "Ratty" thing. How did that ghastliness come about?'

'Not sure. He was always Ratty since I met him at Cambridge. He said it was to do with his nose or something. I know he's no George Clooney, but I think he's sweet and he has the kindest heart on the planet.'

'It means a great deal to me to hear that, girl.'

'It does?'

'I know we didn't quite hit it off at Stiperstones, girl.

Our personalities seem to grate, and I know I snapped at you somewhat, but I'm not really a crocodile.'

'Might help if you stop calling me "girl" and modernise your Seventies prejudices.'

'It's not been easy for me. Incarceration plays havoc with the mind. And I didn't think the world was going to change so much during my lifetime. You'll never comprehend what I went through, knowing that my boy has had to grow up without his mother's guiding hand.'

'That's rough.'

'So don't jump at my throat when I say something that doesn't go down awfully well in a modern society with which I have no familiarity. I'm still learning to be free. I'm learning to be a mother again. Learning to be a woman again. At my age these things don't come naturally.'

'Your son pretty much raised himself,' said Ruby, 'and you know what? I think he's done a fine job of it.'

'That's kind, Ruby.'

In an attempt to disperse the bad air between them, Ruby gave Lady Ballashiels a tentative hug, a literal embrace of their new *entente cordiale*.

'What's happening with the rockets?' Ruby asked as they released each other.

'I don't know. You must have better eyesight than me, girl!.'

Ruby glanced at Lady Ballashiels with a stern eye.

'Sorry. Ruby.'

'Better.'

The elegant Ariane rockets stood next to their utilitarian gantries. Each a coupling of beauty and the beast, enjoying their brief companionships. Ruby tried to see them clearly, but the heat-haze-induced wobble strained her sight. Everything seemed to be moving: the rockets, the gantries, the trees, even the air.

'Is that smoke coming out of one of them?' asked Lady Ballashiels.

'Probably the venting of cryogenic fuels. Super-cooled gases turn to steam in the air. It could mean this one's fuelled and about to launch.'

'How come you know so much about rockets, girl?'

'Comprehensive education.'

The two women continued to watch the distant Ariane turn the air above it white as it snorted and puffed, seemingly alive and eager to launch. And something else seemed alive. A shape, moving in the gantry. A person, wearing white. There were no vehicles around, no co-workers, no signs of any official visits.

'Mitford!' exclaimed Ruby and Lady Ballashiels in unison. Their mutual outburst almost made them smile, but the devastating implication of his presence on the gantry did not merit humour.

An indistinct figure climbed across from a gantry arm to the top of one of the two solid boosters that were mounted either side of the rocket. He seemed to settle comfortably upon the framework that coupled the booster to the body of the Ariane. It was hard for them to be sure with the naked eye, but it appeared that he had strapped himself securely in place.

'It's got to be Mitford,' said Ruby. 'This is the moment he sabotages the launch. But he can't expect to get away with this. He'll be spotted by cameras on the gantry and on the rocket.'

'I'm sure he's thought of that, girl. The bloody camera operator will be on his payroll. There will be no live feed. He'll have arranged for video loops to play, showing the rocket as it was without him.'

'Well then, we've got to report this.'

'I fear not, girl.'

'What do you mean?'

'There's no one we can trust at launch control. We have no contacts in the space agency. Mitford has slipped through our bloody fingers one last time. There's nothing now that we can do.'

'There must be something!' screamed Ruby.

'Perhaps it's time to let go.'

'You're just going to let him win? Let him destroy Keo and erase us all from history?'

'It's too late, girl. He's already on the rocket. The bloody satellite will never make it to orbit. Even if someone believes us, the launch will miss its flight window, there could be years of delay, and the result could be that the time capsule is never found, or found by someone else who doesn't send the confirmation of receipt back in time.'

'I'm sorry, Lady Ballashiels, but I can't accept this.'

Ruby started climbing the mesh and barbed wire fence. The Ariane now began venting white plumes from its base.

'Don't be silly, girl. You'll hurt yourself.'

'At least if I can feel pain I'll know I'm alive. Don't feel all that keen on oblivion, to be honest, even if it would give me a rest from hearing you call me "girl" all the time.'

'But that thing looks like it's about to launch.'

'Then I really have nothing to lose!' called Ruby from the top of the fence.

A car pulled up. Ratty flew out, closely followed by the Patient, Rocco and Charlie.

'It's too late!' shouted Rocco. 'The countdown has started. They changed the launch time in secret. Keo's going now.'

'It can't!' screamed Ruby. 'Mitford's on the rocket. He's strapped to one of the boosters.'

'That will make it too heavy to make it to orbit,' said Rocco. 'It won't follow its planned trajectory and its automated flight termination system will blow it up.'

'Don't you see, that's exactly what Mitford wants?' Ruby's voice was contracted with emotion as she climbed down from the fence. 'He'll die up there but that won't make any difference because he'll have ceased to exist. And so will all of us.'

A spark ignited beneath the Ariane rocket, followed by a fireball, silent at first and then an intense roar as the sound waves reached the witnesses.

'So this is the end of the line for half of the world?' shouted Ratty above the relentless thunder. 'Quite a turn-up. Not something we expected.'

A wide grin appeared on Rocco's face. He made no attempt to hide it, and seemed to relish the effect it was having upon his companions who were having difficulty enough in coming to terms with their erasure from history without having to cope with a rocket scientist who had gone insane under the pressure of the situation. When the smile burst into a full scale laugh, Ruby slapped him on the cheek.

'I've been wanting to do that since I first met you!' she yelled.

'Relax guys,' screamed Rocco amid his own manic, uncontrollable giggles. 'Enjoy the fireworks. Everything will work out just fine.'

The Ariane rocket had now cleared the tower and was accelerating in an arc that took it out over the Atlantic. Ruby, Ratty, Charlie and the Patient clung to hope, figuring that a rocket that still burned still had a chance of success. The powerful engine and its twin solid fuel

293

boosters could surely cope with an unexpected hitchhiker. Computers would counteract the drag and alter the course accordingly. Somehow it would reach its designated orbit.

Lady Ballashiels was silently resigned to her fate, meditating calmly as she watched the spectacle.

Rocco snorted into his hands, attempting feebly to suppress his laughing fit.

A piece fell from the Ariane. Through the heat haze it was indistinct, but the flash that it created in the ribbon of fire beneath the rocket was unmistakeable. An audible gasp erupted from all who witnessed it. Had they just seen the demise of Mitford? Had he been shaken from his shackles and tumbled directly into the intense fire, incinerated in a moment, high above the Atlantic? Those who yearned for a miracle drew strength from that incident. Mitford's mass was no longer affecting the airflow, speed and direction of the rocket. There was a chance it could recover and still make it to orbit.

Ruby found herself hugging Ratty so tight that he could barely breathe. Charlie began yelling,

'Go baby, go!'

But the rocket was off-course. It was too low to reach orbital velocity. Mission control was out of options. With no warning, the trajectory of white smoke ended with a dazzling explosion, and the rocket rained down upon the ocean in a million fragments.

Ruby let go of Ratty and stared at Rocco, as if appalled that he had made it to heaven with her, especially when she had never believed in any kind of afterlife in the first place. Everyone pinched themselves and each other, unsure whether their unexpected conscious reality was a permanent fixture or a temporary blip. Charlie's attempt to pinch Lady Ballashiels was met with a firm slap across his cheek.

'How dare you, boy?' she screeched. 'Keep your gelatinous hands off me. I don't even know who you are. Or you, for that matter,' she added, looking at the guffawing Rocco. 'And if you don't stop laughing, young man, I will –'

'Mater, calm yourself. We're alive. I think that's more important than formal introductions.'

Rocco's laughter slowly faded as he brought himself under control.

'Madam, my name is Doctor Rocco Strauss,' he announced, with only the slightest of giggles.

'Charlie,' said Charlie. 'How's it hangin'?'

'What rot,' the old lady replied. 'I don't need you here. Go back to whatever you were doing.'

When the last of the fragments had fallen from the sky and the smoke began to dissipate in the sea breeze, Rocco cleared his throat and spoke without the distraction of accompanying laughter.

'Sorry about all that,' he said. 'Always been a bit of a practical joker, haven't I?'

Part of the assembled group nodded reluctantly.

'In what way is the explosion we have just witnessed a practical joke?' asked the Patient.

'We are not amused,' said Ruby.

'It wasn't a joke on you. The joke was on Mitford. You see,' explained Rocco, 'Mitford got half of what he wanted. The half in which his life was ended, and all the guilt and crap he was carrying on his shoulders is gone. But he didn't get the other half. He didn't get to stop Keo from launching.'

'What rot. We just saw Keo explode, boy,' said Lady Ballashiels.

'No, we saw a rocket explode. Not Keo. Keo still sits safely on the other launch pad. I couldn't tell the team at launch control about Mitford because I didn't know who might be on his payroll. I couldn't alert anyone to the threat he posed, but I've been at ESA for over ten years, I have contacts, obviously. I got the launch pads swapped on technical grounds. Whoever Mitford had on the inside didn't get to him in time to tell him of the last minute change of plan.'

'That somewhat costly firework we just witnessed was not Keo?' asked Ratty.

'No. Keo is still safe. It's there, on the other pad.'

'Does that really mean the world is safe, then? Nothing bad is going to happen?' asked Ruby.

'Keo will launch,' said Rocco. 'Dalí and Ratty's grandmother will see the message in the sky in1937, at the ruins of Opoul castle near Perpignan in France. It will definitely happen there, and not in our lifetimes.'

'How can you be so sure?' asked Ruby.

'Because I've added my own message to the Keo database asking the recipients to do precisely that.'

'You asked them to send a message to Dalí in 1937?' asked Ruby.

'Just as an insurance policy. We never knew why the message appeared so early in the first place. Now we can be sure that it will happen. I mean, will have happened. Or something.'

'But does that not mean,' began the Patient, 'if I may extrapolate the situation, that you, Rocco, have become the person responsible for ensuring the Second World War went ahead?'

Heads turned to him, accusingly.

'Hey, guys, don't look at me like that. You only exist thanks to me.'

'And you only exist thanks to yourself,' said Ruby. 'Isn't that a paradox?'

'True. Guess I might vanish in a puff of smoke after all. But listen, nothing bad will happen now, because all the bad things have already happened. The war was a terrible wrong for the world, but to undo all of its consequences is an even greater evil. I had to leave history untouched.' The intense stares heading his way caused him to deflect the subject. 'Now this is over, anyone interested in my next project?' He ignored the shaking heads and continued. 'The millionaire priest in France. Saunière. Died a century ago without revealing where he found his money. Or where he left it. It's a huge conspiracy, of course, and I'm going to crack it.'

A Mona Lisa smile inched across the face of Lady Ballashiels.

'You know the story?' asked Rocco.

'The legend is not entirely unfamiliar to me,' she replied.

'Then you'll know there's a fortune waiting to be found.'

Lady Ballashiels looked down, saying nothing further.

'A fortune?' muttered Ratty, his eyes widening, not realising he had said it aloud.

Lady Ballashiels fussed with the reclining chair, trying to adjust it to a more dignified position, and preferably one that would enable her to sip her cocktail safely. She had been the last of the group – with the exception of Charlie who had embarked on a doomed mission to find a donut store in Kourou – to arrive at the poolside bar and the first to shatter the otherwise triumphant mood.

'Call this a gin and tonic?' she whined. 'Tastes almost neat. Bloody waiter chap didn't even measure the units. And he certainly took his time to prepare this atrocity.'

'Relax, Mater. We have all the time in the world,' said

Ratty. 'Stop fussing and sit down properly.'

'Can't get comfortable on this bloody chair, boy.'

'Take your towel thingy away,' Ratty suggested. 'Probably creased.'

'Not my towel,' she snapped.

'If it's not your towel then it's not your seat, Lady Ballashiels,' said Ruby.

'What rot. These chairs all belong to the hotel, girl.'

'Yes, but perhaps some unfortunate fellow was sitting there before we tootled on down here,' said Ratty. 'They may want their seat back.'

Lady Ballashiels stood up and whipped the towel off the chair, throwing it disdainfully upon the ground, and revealing that a paperback book hidden beneath it had been the source of her discomfort.

'Problem solved, Mater. A book always makes for an uncomfortable behind. As I often found at school when I was due for a beating.'

'You were beaten at school, boy?' asked Lady Ballashiels.

'Frequently, Mater.'

'Good. Glad to hear they haven't gone soft.' She picked up the paperback from her chair. 'What a ghastly tome,' she exclaimed, looking at the cover and then holding it at arm's length in disgust. '*Confessions from a Holiday Camp*. Ugh.'

'May I see?' asked the Patient. He put his cocktail down and walked towards Lady Ballashiels. He was still a couple of steps away when she flicked the book at his chest. He caught the spiralling pages and returned to his chair.

'It's that Timothy Lea writer chappy, isn't it?' asked Ratty.

'Part of the same series of books in the gamekeeper's

cottage,' said the Patient. 'This is a copy from the same era. An original.'

'Just put the frightful rag in the bin, boy,' said Lady Ballashiels.

The Patient shook his head. 'I fear that would not be propitious,' he said, flicking through its pages. 'Ratty, we have a problem.'

'Can't decide whether to have a pina colada or a caipirinha, old coconut?'

'No. This volume is not just from the same era as the books in the cottage. It is from the same set. It is a book from the former gamekeeper's collection.'

'What rot,' announced Lady Ballashiels. 'How would that rapscallion's literature make it all the way to South America?'

'It does seem an unlikely coincidence,' said Ruby.

'How can you tell, old raspberry? Did the blighter write his name in them?'

'Each of the books in the collection of the gamekeeper had been read in a particular way. Instead of using a bookmark he would fold the corner of a page as a marker. His books were full of such folds.'

'I hate to inform you, Patient chappy, that such a system of bookmarking is, to my everlasting regret, common practice amongst the relatively small sector of the great unwashed who possess something akin to basic literacy.'

'I am aware of that,' replied the Patient. 'But how many of them fold the bottom corner of the page, rather than the top? And how many do so by creating a perfect right isosceles triangle every time? See?'He showed everyone the neat creases that scarred many of the book's pages. 'Obviously this does not constitute valid evidence to anyone who is unfamiliar with the rest of the collection back at Stiperstones, but I can assure you that this looks to be an indication of the presence of the gamekeeper, here in Kourou.'

'Even so, it seems a little unlikely that out of all the bars in all the hotels in this town, that Lady Ballashiels should sit on this man's book,' said Ruby.

'I conject that the presence of this book could be deliberate,' said Ratty, paying no attention to his mother's shaking head and tut-tutting. 'He is here, and he knows we are here, and he wants us to know that he knows that we are here. It might be his way of warning us to keep away from him. Staking his territory with the towel and wotnot. Psychological doodahs and all that.'

'What's the big deal about some gamekeeper?' asked Rocco.

'The covinous rogue used to be a servant at the manor,' explained Ratty. 'But like all the others he must have been secretly in the payroll of Mitford.'

'You really think he's here?' asked Rocco. 'That's bad. That's very bad. The Keo rocket still hasn't launched. This guy could still stop it. It could be Mitford's last stand from beyond the grave. I might not get to solve the Saunière mystery after all.'

'Looks like this frightful business isn't over, then,' said Ratty. 'Such a pity. I was looking forward to going home and taking Mater to see *Billy Elliot*.'

'I saw *Billy Elliot*,' said a stranger, standing behind Ratty. 'Ten years ago. Prison film club. Loved it. But then, books and films were the only things I had to live for. I see you have been perusing my favourite Timothy Lea novel.'

Ratty looked back at the man's face, but he had already recognised the voice. The last of the old gang of servants. The rugged lines in his skin had always been there, as if his strong jaw were held up by tight strings around his head. Everything about his powerful demeanour seemed to signify that this was a man destined for life outdoors, and yet he had been forced to spend half of his life in sunless incarceration. The final rogue in Ratty's personal gallery of wayward staff. Huxtable.

'You!' screeched Lady Ballashiels.

'Remember me, then, do you? The name's Brian. Brian Huxtable for those of you who haven't made my acquaintance before. Pleased to meet you all. And from Her Ladyship, of course, I hope to receive a special welcome.'

He advanced, arms outstretched, towards Lady Ballashiels.

'Kill him, boy! Get him out of here! Throw his body in the sea!' she shouted, squirming in her seat, agitated and terrified.

Rocco and Ratty sprang out of their seats, each taking one of the gamekeeper's burly arms.

'Don't you think killing him might be construed as a tad excessive, Mater? We have him now. Let's just tie the old green-fingered chap to a tree until the rocket goes up.'

'After what happened today,' began Rocco, 'I am sorry to tell you that the Keo rocket must inevitably face a considerable delay. The Ariane launch system is usually very reliable. There has not been a catastrophic failure in the last fifty-five launches, until this one. They will have to analyse the data and learn lessons from the incident before they can risk another launch. It will take months. And even if we can do our bit to keep the rocket safe from interference in all that time, there is still the possibility of technical failure or of human foul-ups on the day.'

'What are we to do with this scoundrel for all that

time?' asked Ratty.

'Just get him out of my sight!' shouted Lady Ballashiels.

But Huxtable was grinning. 'Lady Ballashiels ... or shall I call you Sarah? Been a long time, hasn't it?'

'You say another word and I'll order them to slit your devious throat,' she growled.

'They won't do that, because if they do they'll never get to hear what I have to say, and I think they're going to be very interested in my story. About the true reason you disappeared in 1975.'

Lady Ballashiels sank back in her chair. The fight was gone from within her. Huxtable was trouble. No one present could realistically be expected to cause the man physical harm and she didn't have the emotional strength to try to stop him.

'You're not here about the rocket, are you?' she sighed. 'Just tell me what you want from me. Let's bloody well get this over.'

Huxtable shuffled out of the loosened grip of his captors and walked to the bar, returning after a short time with a beer. 'French lager. Never could stand this stuff. No good asking for a pint of best bitter round these parts, though.' He pulled up a chair besides Lady Ballashiels and sat down. She refused to look him in the eye when he stared at her. 'Still got that same cute nose,' he said. 'And those curves –'

'I say,' cut in Ratty, 'no need for familiarity and all that how's your father, Huxtable. Most inappropriate.'

'You really don't know, do you?'

'How does a man ever know what he does not know?' asked the Patient.

'Mmm. Justin, your mother and I go way back,' said Huxtable.

'Well, obviously,' replied Ratty. 'You were a servant. You carried out her daily instructions.'

'I suppose you could say that, in a manner of speaking,' the gamekeeper agreed, grinning.

'Oh for God's sake,' burst out Lady Ballashiels, 'just bloody well get on with it and tell them that we had an affair.'

Ratty almost dropped his glass. Huxtable drank deeply from his. He now had the rapt attention of all present. 'Well that seems to have broken the ice,' he announced.

'Now say whatever else is on your mind and bloody well get out,' snarled Lady Ballashiels.

'Well, as Sarah has just mentioned, we had a little something going on between us way back when. A fling. A romance. Some might even call it love.'

'Love? What rot.'

'Whatever,' said Huxtable, 'but it was proper intimate stuff, if you know what I mean. Filling in where His Lordship was lacking.'

'You mean, he's my real Pater?' asked Ratty, tearfully.

'Don't be ridiculous, boy. You were already at boarding school by this time.'

'And I think any boy of mine would have been a little more, how can I put this ... physical,' said Huxtable.

'Physical?' asked Ratty.

'More of a man. A real man. You know the sort.'

Ratty's attempt to adopt a more manly pose failed to have the desired effect.

'Anyway,' Huxtable continued, 'love or not, I paid dearly for our relationship.'

'And you think I didn't, too? Listen, boy,' she turned towards her son, 'I want you to know that this was just a bit of summer madness. Everyone was doing it back then. The concept of free love was finally reaching the shires.

303

But I loved your father and tried to cool Huxtable's ardour. When I told him it was over, he threatened to tell His Lordship.'

'Didn't you see that I was just desperately in love with you, Sarah? And when you disappeared I was as distraught as the rest of them.'

'I thought you vanished because of the conspiring servants,' said Ratty.

'Of course, boy. I did. But the Keo mystery wasn't the only thing they were conspiring about.'

'What do you mean?'

'They all knew. Huxtable here couldn't keep his bloody mouth shut. They all took a frightfully keen interest in our goings on. It wasn't just Huxtable who was threatening to tell all.'

'Oh, Mater!'

'Whether your father used his contacts to have all the servants locked away because of the Keo conspiracy, or because he couldn't be sure if they'd all been sleeping with me – which, I hasten to add, was not the case – I really don't know. Maybe it was a bit of both. Either way it changes nothing now. I suspect he thought that having a clean sweep in the manor would remove any awkwardness on my return.'

'Only you never returned,' said Ruby.

'Well obviously, girl.'

'Enough pleasantries,' declared Huxtable. 'As you will surely have guessed, our meeting today is not by chance. I'm here to ask for your help.'

'Whom are you addressing, Huxtable, old cuckolder?' asked Ratty.

'All of you. Please hear me out. I want to tell you my story. Will you permit me that opportunity?'

'Well at least he's not interfering with the rocket all

the time he's talking to us,' said Ruby.

'You may proceed, old Lothario,' said Ratty.

'Thank you. I was born in India. 1938. Final years of Empire.'

'Not a war baby like Mitford, then?' asked Ruby.

'No. My birth had nothing to do with the war. My parents came to India in the Twenties. Big house. A dozen servants of our own. Oh yes, I wasn't always an underdog, Sarah. I grew up with more staff than Stiperstones has ever seen. That's why I had the confidence to regard you as an equal.'

'What rot.'

'Whatever, Sarah. Anyway, I stayed on after India gained its independence. Easy decision, really, as I'd became rather fixated upon one of the chambermaids. Beautiful girl, but very low caste. Not the done thing, of course. Not that I cared about that snobby stuff, but even her own family would have disapproved. Everyone too set in their ways, sandwiched in their own slice of social class.'

'Quite right, too.'

'Mater!'

'In '58 my family made the decision to return to England. I had no choice but to come with them and leave her behind. When we reached our cold and damp house after weeks on a ship, there was a letter waiting for me. She was pregnant with my child. She faced becoming a social outcast. Destitute. I stole some money and sent it to her, enough for her to buy a ticket on the next ship. We were to start a new life together in England as soon as her ship docked at Southampton. We were to be a family, devoted to bringing up our baby together. I went to Southampton to meet her. I arrived a day early and waited, but the ship never made it to the dock. Rumours began to spread of an explosion. Finally, the news reached the port that the ship had hit a mine in the Atlantic, close to northern France. It had deviated from its planned course by just two degrees, which had taken it through a stretch of water that the Germans had mined heavily during the war. Ships usually avoided that area, even though minesweepers were supposed to have found, and removed, all of the devices by then. But there was just one mine that they missed. The ship went down too fast. No one was saved. My dreams died that day.'

Everyone looked at him. Huxtable savoured the moment, pausing long enough to conjure the strongest sympathies in his companions.

'Doesn't wash with me,' said Lady Ballashiels, finally breaking the atmosphere. 'It sounds just like the type of rot Mitford used to spout at me, day in, day out.'

'I never told you this before, Sarah. Because I never told anyone. I couldn't speak of it. But the truth is that having been born on the other side of the world, entirely unaffected by Hitler's destructive power whilst he was at his height, and having returned to Europe when everything should have been safe, my world was shattered by the legacy of war. Even though long dead, Hitler stole my happiness.'

'Actually, I think you'll find the evidence points to him being alive in the late Fifties,' corrected Rocco. 'He was living on this continent by then, in isolated pockets of expat, Nazi communities. Didn't die until 1962.'

'Rocco is rather partial to conspiracy theories, in case you haven't noticed,' said Ruby.

'And that's why Mitford's philosophy appealed to me,' Huxtable continued. 'Even though his father was responsible for everything that went sour in my life, he had the vision to put things right. He convinced me he could find a way to make amends for his father's wrongs.

It was the only thing I could cling to, however unlikely it seemed. And eventually he found a way. His lifetime of dedicated research into the meaning of Keo finally joined all the dots in history together. He found the solution to the war. He found a way to save millions of lives. And in so doing, he found the way to save the love of my life and my unborn child.'

'So you are the rotter's back-up plan, after all?' asked Ratty.

'Mitford was no rotter. He was the antithesis of his father. He was a saint. If his plan succeeds, he will have been the greatest saviour of mankind that the world has never heard of. For he would have made the ultimate sacrifice for his fellow men. His own erasure from history. No one will ever know the true extent of the debt they owe to that man.'

'Let me get this straight,' said Rocco. 'You want to stop Keo from launching, just like the Mitford guy? But the difference is that you'll still be here in the new timeline. Your birth had nothing to do with the war. You have nothing to lose and everything to gain.'

'Not only me, but millions of people around the world. The slaughtered soldiers, the Holocaust victims, the ordinary folk buried in their homes due to aerial bombardment – all of these people have the chance to have lived full lives, to procreate, to populate the world with the men, women and children who should have been here in the first place. The Middle East would be cured of its problems. Great European cities would retain their architectural gems and avoid the concrete monstrosities that filled the gaps caused by air raids. There wouldn't have been a cold war and so no need for nuclear weapons. We could have had a peaceful, utopian society but for this single moment in 1937 when the word Keo appeared in the sky above southern France. Yes, some who were born as a result of the war won't exist in that timeline, but surely the cost of their lives has been too high? Surely the greater good is the establishment of a peaceful and happy world?'

'Mitford's brainwashing all over again,' sighed Lady Ballashiels. 'Heard it all before.'

'Please help me,' Huxtable continued. 'Help me to save millions of people. Help me to undo the suffering of the Jews. Help me to erase this stain on the planet's history. A single word in the sky, that's all I want to change. It's such a simple thing, but I can't do it alone.'

'All right for you, old buffer, but you'd still be here if Keo hadn't happened,' said Ratty. 'The rest of us would vanish in a puff of wotsit.'

'Yes, and who's to say that out of the millions who would live instead of us there wouldn't be someone ten times worse than Hitler?' suggested Ruby.

'Indeed,' said the Patient. 'If there is, as some philosophers posit, a guiding hand in the universe, something that mitigates against the most extreme excesses of man's free will, it is entirely conceivable that the Hitler episode was the least worst option.'

'And why just undo that war?' added Ruby. 'It seems arbitrary to single out one event. There were plenty of other bad things in history. The 1918 Spanish flu pandemic killed more people than both world wars together. Why not try to fix that? Or Pol Pot?'

'Or why not go back and remove the right to bear arms from the United States constitution?' suggested the Patient. 'More Americans have been murdered by private guns in America than were killed in all the wars in which that country has ever fought.'

'Because we can't,' replied Huxtable. 'We have no influence on what has happened. We can only change the future, but the future trajectory we're currently on will change the past to fit where it all ends up. Do you see? This is a unique opportunity. Nothing like it will ever happen again. Please will you join me and help me to save my child? Please, I beg of you.'

'What, and see ourselves annihilated? Are you crazy?' asked Ruby.

'He's not crazy.' whispered the Patient.

'I say, didn't quite catch that, old boy,' responded Ratty.

'I said he is not crazy. He is planning something.'

'Well quite. I believe he's planning to blow up that rocket contraption and he needs our help to do it.'

'I do not for a moment believe that to be the case,' continued the Patient. 'I sense another agenda. His requests are too unrealistic. He knows none of us would help him. And by making his plan clear to us he has put himself at risk that we could restrain him and prevent his plans being carried out. A man who has had so many years in prison to plan this event would not make such a basic error of judgement.'

'Is this true, Huxtable?' asked Lady Ballashiels.

Huxtable said nothing. He downed the rest of his lager and remained silent.

'I take that to be an admission,' said the Patient. 'Mr Huxtable does indeed have a different plan to his stated aims.'

'Goodness!' shrieked Ratty. 'I think I know what the ne'er-do-well is doing. He's stalling us. He's keeping us here because he needs to, and that must mean –'

'There's someone else!' shouted Ruby.

***

309

The second bakery was as disappointing as the first. Croissants and baguettes. A total cliché of French rural cuisine, thought Charlie, exported to this South American outpost, authentic even to the point of being closed while people were still hungry. The donut hunt through the suburbs of Kourou would have been a pleasant stroll were it not for the fact that he hated walking. The afternoon humidity was making him sweat to an undignified degree. Admitting defeat, Charlie elected to pause the walk back to the hotel to enjoy a moment of relatively cool shade.

A face in a passing taxi glanced at him and gave an uncomfortable nod of recognition. Charlie closed his eyes and tried to recall the face. A shaved head. Chubby. Double chin. Snappy dresser in an undersized suit. Where had he met that person before?

Some kind of butler to Mitford, he recalled, eventually. The sweaty man who had been present at the meeting in the museum when Charlie had been given his spending money and told about his mission. His name was Grant. Stuck-up English asshole. That meant Mitford wasn't here alone and Keo could still be in trouble. He had to get back to the hotel and warn the others, but without a functioning cellphone and without sufficient fitness to waddle there in under half an hour, he figured his best chance lay in finding a cab. Across the street sat a nondescript Peugeot saloon with its engine running. Charlie approached it and banged on the driver's window.

'*Oui*?' asked the frightened woman inside.

'Taxi?' asked Charlie.

'*Non*,' replied the woman. She fumbled with the button that locked all the doors from within, but in her panic she pressed it twice and the doors remained unsecured, allowing Charlie to squeeze into the rear seat.

'I need to get to my hotel. It's called, er, the

310

Something Hotel. Or the Hotel Something. You know the place?'

The woman looked in her rear-view mirror and saw the stranger babbling at her in English. Charlie offered her some American dollars and pointed in the general direction of where he wanted her to go.

'No wait,' decided Charlie, now pointing in a different direction. 'I've wasted too much time. Go straight to the launch site. It's an emergency. Someone is going to sabotage the next launch. Maybe I can stop him.' He mimed a rocket taking off and used the bundle of American dollars to mimic an explosion by throwing them into the air.

'Why do you make a mess in my car?' she asked with a strong French accent. 'I do not need your money. Pick it up.'

'You speak English?' asked Charlie, scrabbling to collect the unwanted notes from the seats and the floor. 'Listen, I think I saw someone who wants to harm the second rocket. The one with the Keo satellite on board. This guy's connected to the man who sabotaged the first rocket. I have to try to stop him. Can you help?'

'I work for the space agency,' she replied. 'I know how tough our security is. There's no way anyone can get close enough to harm an Ariane. So please get out of my car and leave me alone.'

Charlie felt his face redden. His muscles tensed.

'You gotta help me, lady!' He thumped the back of her seat. 'Come on!' He wasn't sure if he sounded aggressive, but there was a passion in his voice, which to an unfamiliar ear might have sounded threatening. It seemed to work, in any case. Charlie felt his back press gently into the seat as the car accelerated. He scrambled for the seat belt and held tight.

311

***

The crumples in the suit and the dust on the shoes betrayed the urgency and energy with which Grant had been working since he had come to the shocking realisation that Mitford had sacrificed himself on the wrong rocket. When the Ariane had launched, he was sure that in a moment he would awake to a new reality, to a mind free of the aching memories of half a lifetime of incarceration and to a planet free of the legacy of the wrongs bestowed on it by Mitford's father. And when the rocket exploded, in plain view of the entire town, he had chinked a champagne glass with Huxtable, watched the wreckage and smoke descend gracefully over the Atlantic, and waited.

And waited.

When Grant's flute had held no more than a bubble and a sweet aroma, he had wanted to say something but the tremble in his lip had rendered him temporarily without speech. Huxtable's dependable frame remained solid, but his eyes projected an inner disquiet. Years of entrenched beliefs were challenged by the obvious reality around them.

Mitford had always filled Grant with confidence. Mitford had been an idol, an inspiration. Mitford could not fail. And this profound faith meant that Grant had never expected that the crude back-up plan of which he was a part would have to be initiated. Deducing the chain of events had taken no more than a phone call to the publicity department at the space agency to confirm that the Keo satellite was still on the ground and about to be rolled back to the vehicle assembly building pending a revision of its launch schedule.

Grant glanced back and saw a distant car apparently driving towards him at considerable speed. If it really was

Charlie that he had just passed, then Huxtable had not succeeded in his plan to keep the blasted Ballashiels entourage in one place. Grant felt the pressure build in his veins. The car was still gaining on him. Pressure turned into a sense of panic. He threw double the amount of the pre-agreed fare onto the front passenger seat and instructed his driver to turn swiftly into a small side road after the next bend and pull up beside the trees. Before the taxi had even halted he leapt out, urgently waved his driver on, and tumbled into the cover of the ferns. The car pursuing him would discover too late that he was no longer on board.

He brushed down his suit and wiped the perspiration from his shaved head. The perimeter of the launch site was still a mile away, but there was somewhere he had to visit first: a cache of weapons, planted two days earlier as insurance against the unlikely event of Mitford being unable to destroy Keo.

As he located the tree beneath which the wooden crate had been buried, his mind filled with memories of Mitford's life and the times they had spent together. He felt no sorrow for Mitford's passing, only a sense of calm, a feeling that a lifetime of mental suffering was at an end. Now he simply wanted to do justice to Mitford's vision, to fulfil the dream of healing the world of the ugly scar that had grown across its wound.

But he was underprepared. He had never used the weapons that awaited him, never honed his aiming technique or familiarised himself with the recoil and the noise. For that reason, he had to get himself to a point from where he could not miss. Point-blank range was essential. It didn't matter if he triggered an explosion of rocket propellants that blew him to pieces. And it didn't matter if ESA security shot at him, provided he got his shots in first. They were welcome to pepper him with bullet holes when his job was done. It also didn't matter who he had to kill to get there. He knew that whatever happened to him at that moment, he would inevitably wake up in another part of the world, unharmed, having lived a different life and utterly unaware of the parallel history he had just erased.

The French woman halted her car abruptly at the security checkpoint on the perimeter of the launch site and opened her window.

'Great idea,' said Charlie. 'Get their security guys on the case. Tell them that asshole Grant is on the loose.'

A gendarme approached the vehicle. The French woman shouted rapidly in French and pointed to the man in her rear seat. Charlie smiled and waved. Remnants of that smile were still in place even as he found himself being dragged from his seat and thrown face-down on the concrete with a semi-automatic weapon aimed at his back. Plastic cable ties were whipped around the wrists and ankles of the suspect and tightened. Charlie's protestations in English were ignored. Someone was telephoning for back-up. Within a minute an armoured personnel carrier arrived. Soldiers from the 3rd Foreign Infantry Regiment of the French Foreign Legion carried Charlie into their vehicle.

The French woman thanked the gendarmes and soldiers profusely. They assured her that her kidnap ordeal was over.

Grant counted at least fifteen technicians coming and going near to the Ariane. He guessed they were overseeing the removal of cryogenic fuel from one of the propellant tanks, either liquid oxygen or liquid hydrogen, prior to moving the rocket back into its assembly building. If he could aim a shot that pierced one of the propellant tanks before it was empty, the effect of his attack would be magnified exponentially. And even if the workers succeeded in draining the rocket before he was ready, there would remain the twin solid boosters – the successful ignition of one of these boosters would create an unstoppable fire. However, the rocket itself was partly obscured by launch site paraphernalia, and he would have to come out into the open in order to begin his attack.

A vehicle came into view, wobbling in the distant heat haze. An army patrol. He had seen several of these. The perimeter had been thick with them, necessitating a frustrating wait in the undergrowth before making his dash for the short tunnel below the fence. Someone on Mitford's payroll had dug the shallow tunnel at the only blind spot in the network of closed circuit television cameras, and Grant was thankful that no one appeared to have followed him into the heavily guarded area.

He eased himself back into the drainage culvert beneath the road. Down here he was invisible. The culvert was part of a system of ditches that ran like a dry moat around the raised fortress of the launch pad, and was designed to evacuate surplus water used in cooling the rocket exhaust during take-off. The water was supplied by a tower as high as the rocket itself. Grant peeked outside and looked up at it. The tower offered an unobstructed view of the rocket and point-blank range, but while the access route to the top was via an internal staircase, the chances of making it to the tower and forcing open the staircase door unseen were zero. A second army patrol vehicle was now approaching.

The level of security seemed far higher than Mitford had told him to expect. Grant retreated again. His mind clouded. A sense of impossibility overwhelmed him. Huxtable's failure to control the Ballashiels clan surely meant that those soldiers were now looking for him. Did he really have the courage to go out in a blaze of glory? Of course not; it wasn't in his nature. Never mind the theoretical knowledge that it didn't matter who he killed or whether his own life were terminated so long as Keo was destroyed, the cold realisation that he was now running low on options and might have to take such a route was terrifying. It wasn't that he wanted to abandon the operation – he still believed in its ultimate purpose – but achieving it in a messy and gory manner wasn't his style.

He closed his eyes and considered the problem. A single-handed attack against dozens of highly trained soldiers would be foolhardy. It would be suicidal. The world deserved better. He had to sabotage the Ariane from a position of safety, but he had limited range with his hand-held weapons, and the further back he positioned himself the more likely it was that he would miss. One shot and he would be discovered. There would be no second chance. If he couldn't take his shot from close-range, was there a way to achieve his goal from a safe distance? He considered the ongoing process of removing fuel from the rocket, which he believed to be taking place at that moment. There were no tankers in the vicinity, so the fuel must be being piped directly from the rocket to a storage facility nearby. If he could follow the pipeline, he would arrive at the end of something akin to a long fuse. With the focus of security around the Ariane itself, the fuel depot might be a soft target. A spark in the holding tank could ignite fuel all the way along the pipe and into the heart of the rocket. The Keo satellite wouldn't stand a chance atop such a bomb.

For a moment, he was convinced he had the answer, but then doubts took over. The designers of the supply pipe might have installed automatic safety valves that would shut off the supply to the launch pad in the event of a fire at the holding tank. And even without such valves in place, would the fuel successfully ignite along such an extended distance, or just burn at one end until it ran dry?

A suicidal charge towards the Ariane seemed the only option after all.

He peeked out from his hiding place once again and discovered that his face was inches from the barrel of a weapon belonging to the French army. Strong hands dragged him from his lair so rapidly that he didn't even have the opportunity to appreciate the scale of his failure.

'Why are they keeping us waiting?'

Ruby had broken the uncomfortable silence and everyone turned to her as if their frustrations could be laid at her feet. After the manic rush to bind and gag Huxtable securely in Ratty's hotel room before piling into a taxi to the spaceport where they reported their concerns to the receptionist at the visitor's centre, the lack of apparent action was deeply concerning. The young lady at the desk had made a couple of brief phone calls and invited the stressed and sweating group to sit calmly and fill out their guest passes, but several minutes later their state of agitation had worsened rather than improved.

'They didn't understand your French, girl,' snapped Lady Ballashiels, forgetting the *entente cordiale* that she had previously shared with her companion. 'Where did you pick up such an appalling accent?'

'France.'

'It's a big spaceport,' said Rocco, defusing the tension. 'More than eight hundred square kilometres. That's as big as Singapore. We've asked them to look for one man. We don't even know who it is or what he looks like. I'll go over to the security building to ask what's happening. You wait here.'

'Come on, Rocco, old boffin, why don't you take us with you?' asked Ratty. 'Flash your wotsit at them and get us all in.'

Rocco stood up. 'Follow me.'

He led the group out through the main doors and across the roasting concrete car park to a smaller building. He flashed his badge at the gendarme guarding the entrance, and the door was opened for them.

'Hey guys, how's it going?' asked Charlie from the steel bench to which he was cuffed just inside the door. 'I was trying to explain to these gooks that I'm on their side, but they've all run off. Besides, they don't seem to speak any language known to man.'

'Your American English is not a language,' said Lady Ballashiels. 'It is an abomination.'

'Where did the police go?' asked Ruby, ignoring the old woman's belligerence.

'No idea,' said Charlie.

'The room through there is where the security systems are monitored,' said Rocco, pointing at a door that was marked 'Private'. 'Let's go in and take a look at what's happening.'

'Are we allowed in there?' asked Ruby.

'You're not. I am. So act like you're on a visitor tour. And behave yourselves.'

'What about me?' asked Charlie.

'I suggest you stay put,' said Ratty, as Rocco opened a door through to the vast control room, where ten banks of monitors filled the wall, watched by a team of nine security experts. The system was connected to cameras around the space centre, but the staff were paying particular attention to a small area displayed on a cluster of monitors.

'This is the hub of the spaceport's security system,' announced Rocco, slipping into the character of a tour guide. 'Six hundred and seventy cameras all link to these ten banks of screens. You can see the launch control room, the visitor centre, the pads, the fuel production facilities, the rocket assembly building – all from this room. This spaceport is one of the most closely monitored patches of ground on the planet.'

'So how come they didn't spot Mitford on the rocket?' asked Ruby.

'Shush,' Rocco replied. 'Look,' he whispered. 'Nine staff. Ten banks of screens. One empty chair. Get it?'

'Gone to spend a Euro, has he?' asked Ratty.

'It was an inside job,' Rocco continued, keeping his group to the back of the room, behind the rope that cordoned off the visitor's viewing area and ensuring that the security employees were out of earshot. 'Either he turned off the cameras that could have shown Mitford on the launch pad, or he played a recording of a previous launch. Either way, he's taken his money and fled. Mitford clearly has no further influence here.'

'What are they all looking at?' asked Lady Ballashiels.

One of the banks of screens displayed images of a man being dragged by soldiers across the ground, close to the launch pad. The incident was shown from several angles. A van pulled up and a dozen gendarmes jumped out. One of the screens showed soldiers plucking weapons from a drainage culvert. Ratty hopped over the cordon and strolled up close to one of the displays. Security staff yelled at him to retreat to the permitted visitors' zone.

'How do you do?' Ratty asked, offering his hand.

'Lord Ballashiels. Eighth Earl and all that how's your father. What are we all watching on the goggle box today? *Blockbusters*? *Countdown*?'

Urgent conversations spun around him in French too rapid for him to comprehend. He allowed the white noise to wash over him and peered even more closely at the screen.

'Grant!' he shouted. 'It's that rotter Grant. And he's still wearing one of his ghastly suits.'

'The butler?' asked Lady Ballashiels.

'The very same,' her son replied, walking back to the others, to the obvious relief of the monitoring team. 'But it appears that they've caught the cad.'

'So this time it really is over,' said Lady Ballashiels, her throat tight with emotion.

'A less demanding process of resolution than we had perhaps anticipated,' said the Patient.

'Now we just have to get Charlie freed,' said Ruby.

'Do we?' asked Ratty. 'I thought he seemed rather content in his situation.'

'Ratty, don't be mean,' whispered Ruby.

'Girl, don't keeping using that distasteful word,' growled Lady Ballashiels.

'And don't keep calling me "girl"!' Ruby retorted.

On some of the screens, Grant could be seen being loaded into the police van. The incident had drawn the attention of the entire security team in the monitoring room, but the Patient was observing a different display. It showed a wide view of the launch control centre: rows of desks and computers, and a huge projector screen at the front. The launch centre was deserted save for a single person, moving quickly amongst the desks as if unfamiliar with the environment, searching for something.

'What is it, Patient chappy?' asked Ratty. 'You look as

320

if you've seen a ghost.'

'An appropriate assumption, I fear. What do you see in that display over there?'

Ratty followed the direction of his finger. Rocco, Ruby and Lady Ballashiels followed likewise, drawn by a sense of dread and disbelief to the image on the wall.

Range Safety Officer: the tidy plaque on the desk belied the true power of the individual tasked with sitting there during the dramatic first minutes of every launch. Alois Mitford ran his fingers over the textured letters of the sign. He sat down and sensed the comfort offered by the Vitra chair. He breathed the cool air blown down from the ventilation system above. These would be among the final sensations he experienced in his long life. A modest prelude to a blissful oblivion. It was all he wanted. It was time to destroy Keo.

Time was short. The emptying of the liquid oxygen tank would soon be completed; the smaller liquid hydrogen tank had already been drained. After that the technicians would disconnect the Ariane from its launch pad umbilicals and commence its journey back to the assembly building. Once disconnected, the computers at launch control would have no influence on the Ariane. The ability to activate the on-board detonation sequence would then be lost.

A wave of loneliness swept across Mitford. He felt detached from humanity. At peace and yet unsettled. Oblivion would not equal death, he reminded himself. He was not going to suffer. He would not die. He hoped his essence would drift to the outer reaches of the cosmos, to a hidden dimension where unborn souls waited for the spark of life to pull them from their eternal slumber. It would be beautiful. Painless.

So why did a knot of fear twist within his stomach? Mitford wondered if he was starting to doubt his beliefs. He looked at the detonation button. It was covered by a plastic safety shield, and required a key to unlock it before it could be pressed. His contact in the video control room had served him well. He took the key from his pocket and inserted it.

His pulse quickened. He withdrew his hand from the key. What if the refuge of the infinite void wasn't there? What if he was immediately born again, to suffer another life of shame and guilt? He closed his eyes and breathed slowly, removing the negativity that powered his panic attack. The world, he reminded himself, deserved what he was about to do. It would be the single greatest thing an individual had ever done. He possessed the omnipotence of a deity. The button to reset the universe was at his fingertips. He was going to heal the planet.

He turned the key and activated the power supply to the switch. He placed his finger on the detonation button and felt its warm, indifferent plastic against his skin. This was the culmination of a life dedicated to making things right. This was the moment he would erase Keo, World War II, and himself, from history.

The lights above him flickered for a millisecond. It distracted him and he looked around. No one else was present. He had secured the door. A new sound was in the air, however. A soft purr from a deep throat beneath his feet. The back-up generators. Someone had cut the power supply to the room and the emergency diesel motors in the basement had cut in smoothly, as they were designed to do. It meant that he had been spotted, but that fact did not concern him as greatly as the hammering sound upon the door.

His anxiety returned. He moved his hand towards the

button once more and was shocked to notice the severity of the shakes to which he had succumbed. He wiped a tide of sweat from his forehead and tried to concentrate.

'I say, Mitford, old foundling, I think we'd all prefer it if you sort of bashed off and went to live on an island somewhere. What do you say?'

Mitford looked up behind him and saw the rodent-like features of Lady Ballashiels' only son staring down from the visitors' gallery, separated by a panel of glass. He had been speaking via the intercom.

'Go, Justin. It's over for you.'

'I must say, we all thought it was curtains for you already. Had us rather fooled for a while, don't you know? Sorry about that confounded banging, old chap. That will be the gendarme fellows trying to reach you.'

'Impossible,' snapped Mitford. 'They are all at the launch site, wasting their time rounding up Grant. They can't reach me in time.'

Ratty knew he was right. Somehow the threat of an elderly woman, a scientist, a philosopher and an archaeologist trying to break down a door didn't seem so intimidating.

'You obviously had an inkling that Rocco had switched the order of the flights,' said Ratty.

'I am not without influence myself, you seem to be forgetting. I knew of the situation. It seemed the perfect opportunity to put you off the scent by making you think I was dead.'

'What was it? Shop mannequin? Guy Fawkes dummy? Inflatable night-time companion?'

'A Dalí original, if you must know. One of the life-size golden figures that he created for the inner courtyard of his museum.'

Mitford moved his hand once again towards the

button. The worsening tremors betrayed an inner conflict that was as yet unresolved. His head filled with memories of Dalí the man, the friend, the confidante. Pressing the button would not erase Dalí from history, since he had already been a successful and famous artist before 1937, but his works after that point would surely be affected: the war had been a powerful influence on his creative process. Perhaps the museum of his works would never be built? Perhaps his fame would diminish in later life instead of growing to the point of him becoming a legend? And that was just one man's life that he was about to change. That change in direction after 1937 would be repeated across millions of lives, each with their own stories that would play out differently without the interference of Keo.

'You don't have to do this, old tyrant,' Ratty continued. 'No one is forcing you to change the world. Bad things do sometimes lead to good things, you know. It happens. What if that meteor hadn't landed on that dinosaur's bonce? Cleared the way for our little monkey ancestor fellows, didn't it? As that chap who was in somewhat dire straits used to warble, there will be sunshine after rain, there will be laughter after pain and all that drivel. Seems to be the way of the world. Good and bad, hot and cold, wet and dry, debt and credit, anger and forgiveness. These things dance around each other, taking turns, keeping the planet spinning, keeping everything pirouetting like they're doing some sort of bloody *pas de deux*. Excuse my French.'

The shaking hand still hovered near the button, and the door sounded ready to split open under the beating to which it was being subjected.

'You are a child, Justin. You were not there. None of this sits on your shoulders.'

'And none of this is on yours either, old fruitloop. Let

it go. You're not your father. You're not responsible. But if you press that button you'll become as big a monster as your pops. You'll wipe out as many people as he did. And you know what? You know why you really shouldn't press that silly button? It's because you simply don't have the right. No one has the right to change the planet like that. I don't know why we're here, and I know it's frustrating that we can't mould the world to suit us, but I know we can all make a difference in a small way. And that's what we have the right to do, to improve our little corner of the world. To try to go through life and leave this planet just a little better than it was when we first crawled onto it. That's a goal that will never require the deaths of millions. It shouldn't hurt anyone. But give it time, and the cumulative effect will be the same as the one you're trying to achieve. Take it slowly. Let's all make a small contribution. Let's look forward, not backwards, and mould the future that we want without changing the past. I forgive what you did to me. I forgive what you did to Mother. Resentment won't make it better. I accept my past and that means I can make the best of my future.'

There were tears on Mitford's cheeks. He wiped them with his unstable hands and snivelled. He felt himself shrinking, a pathetic, dried-up shadow of the man he had once been. Ratty's words had connected with him. They had initiated the emotional response that it was clearly their intention to trigger. Mitford was spiritually broken, but he knew what he had to do.

The door crashed open. Rocco, the Patient, Ruby and Lady Ballashiels ran inside accompanied by the gendarme from the security building. Mitford glanced at them and formed a weak smile.

He steadied his hand and pressed the button.

FRIDAY 10TH MAY 2013

The iron key had remained hanging on a nail in the wall of one of the basement rooms for longer than anyone could remember. The shank was damp, almost as if it were capable of producing its own sweat. She gripped it firmly and climbed the narrow servants' staircase to the attic level. The ceiling was low here, paper hung limply in curls from the walls, windows were small and cracked.

She recalled the passionate entreaties of her family never to do what she was about to do. But that was in the past. She had every right to pay no attention to the ramblings and superstitions of those who went before her. What harm could it possibly do to open a cupboard? Besides, she knew full well what it contained.

She presented the key to the lock. It slid in with difficulty, and turned with a scraping sound that echoed through the roof space. As it clicked open a ridge of dust cascaded to the floorboards, making her cough. She stepped back and allowed the air to settle before pulling the door fully open.

There were three shelves inside. Two of them were stuffed with old books. She picked one up at random and flicked through it. A political work about a relatively unknown German leader and the ways in which he was trying to rebalance the German economy. *Hitler's Economic Miracle*. She put it back and looked at the third shelf. It seemed to contain what she had expected to find.

The film tin was tarnished, but it was intact and its label was still legible. She smiled to herself.

'Mater? That you up here?'

She looked back and saw her son standing in the dim light of the window.

'Just wanted to take a look at something, boy,' she replied, closing the door and turning the key to secure it.

'Come downstairs, old thing. Everyone's waiting for you.'

Lady Ballashiels slipped the weighty key into her pocket and followed Ratty down to the kitchen. Ruby was making tea for everyone. Despite the wrong order in which tea was making contact with milk, Lady Ballashiels bit her lip. She had promised not to criticise her son's best friend for at least a day, especially while everyone was so tired and tetchy after the long flight home, and besides she was too intrigued by her discovery to care about the minutiae of aristocratic behaviour. She looked at Ruby's features – not an unattractive girl, perhaps someone who could be moulded to become the next Lady Ballashiels at a push, although it would be an uphill struggle to iron out those comprehensive school giveaways and that Guildford accent. The Patient had class, despite his peculiarities. She had become rather fond of his calm intelligence, and his inability to say a bad word about anyone.

When the four of them had been served with tea, she dribbled a little gin into her cup and held it up for a toast.

'To the past, the present, and, not forgetting, the future.'

'Hear, hear,' said Ratty.

'And may Mitford rot in a French jail for the rest of his days,' added Ruby.

'Has anyone called Rocco since we landed?' asked the Patient.

'There was an electro-mail thingy from him,' said Ratty. 'There's a bit of paperwork to shuffle, but he thinks Charles will be released to the wild on Monday.'

'Why not tomorrow?' asked Ruby.

'Weekend,' explained Ratty. 'And I think we owe Rocco a remote toasting. If he hadn't arranged for the Ariane to be disconnected from the launch control computers we'd be living in an altogether different world.'

'Or not living at all, boy.'

'Quite, quite.'

'It's hard to imagine a world where someone like Hitler is just a minor footnote in history, a forgotten leader amongst hundreds of others,' said Ruby. 'I can't help feeling sad that it isn't the case, but I know it's the only moral option now.'

'What will you do now, girl?' asked Lady Ballashiels.

'Back to Spain, I suppose. Finish the job I started at Empúries. Still a few goddesses to dig up, I shouldn't wonder. After that, no idea.'

'Why don't you stay?'

Ruby looked at the old woman as if she were potty.

'Where are you going to be?' she blurted out.

'I'm going to live here. With Justin. And mister Patient there. And you know what, girl? I'd like it if you would stay here too.'

Now it was Ratty's turn to look aghast at his mother.

'What is it Rat – er, I mean, Justin? Wouldn't you like that?' Ruby asked.

'On the contrary, it would make me the happiest Earl in the land. Feel rather ashamed that I never asked you myself, that's all.'

She put down her tea and gave Ratty a hug.

'I'd love to hang out here. Just for a while. Might be

fun. Like old days at Cambridge.'

He hugged her back.

'And what will you do?' Ruby asked her host.

'Still somewhat low on readies,' replied Ratty.

'You'll find a job?'

'Good lord, no. Working for a living? Not my cup of Earl Grey at all. Had a more interesting scheme in mind. Mater and I were discussing it on the flight home. Rather an exciting prospect. It's a bit of a treasure hunt, actually.'

'Right,' said Ruby. 'Because your treasure hunts always succeed, don't they?'

'This time it can't fail,' he told her. 'Mater thinks that if I work with you on this, then, with our combined skills, we could find the lost treasure of the legendary millionaire priest, Bérenger Saunière.'

'Saunière?' she echoed. 'As in Rennes-le-Château? As in the latest looney aspirations of Rocco? It's just a wildly inflated conspiracy theory based on greed, lies and optimism. There's no treasure there, Ratty. I've already read up on it.'

'Don't close your mind, Ruby. Rocco got me thinking. There's a frightful amount of historic gold unaccounted for. What about the lost treasure of Jerusalem? The gold of the Merovingian kings? The hidden wealth of the Cathars? What if Rocco's right? What if Saunière is the key to finding it?'

'Right, children,' shouted Lady Ballashiels, as if calling a riotous classroom to order, 'I can see Ruby is going to take some convincing. There's a reason why I believe you have what it takes to succeed in this quest because there is something in this house that will furnish you with a unique advantage.'

'Don't tell me you think Saunière stashed his gold here at Stiperstones?' asked Ruby.

'What rot. I don't suppose anyone here is a fan of Charlie Chaplin?'

All three avoided eye contact with her.

'Many years ago I was told about a tin of old film in the attic. There's something odd in the reel. Some sort of anomaly. And it has a connection to the Saunière story. I'd like you all to take a look at it. Justin, prepare the projector. We are shortly to have our first film evening.'

THE END

Feisty independent publishing

 /AccentPressBooks

@AccentPress

@accentpressbooks

www.accentpress.co.uk

29643696R00197

Printed in Poland
by Amazon Fulfillment
Poland Sp. z o.o., Wrocław